T0147139

THE GABRIEL CHRONICLES

Book 4—Sharkra

Also written by Dennis Flannery:

The GABRIEL CHRONICLES
Book 1—The Beginning

The GABRIEL CHRONICLES
Book 2—New Home

The GABRIEL CHRONICLES
Book 3—The Superiors

The GABRIEL CHRONICLES
Book 4—Sharkra

Lenny

THE GABRIEL CHRONICLES

Book 4—Sharkra

DENNIS FLANNERY

authorHOUSE

AuthorHouse™
1663 Liberty Drive
Bloomington, IN 47403
www.authorhouse.com
Phone: 833-262-8899

Published by AuthorHouse   10/21/2022

ISBN: 978-1-6655-7418-1 (sc)
ISBN: 978-1-6655-7416-7 (hc)
ISBN: 978-1-6655-7417-4 (e)

DEDICATION

I dedicate this novel to my wonderful children, Vance, Jennifer, and Sean, and our grandson Quinn. And our angels, Aidan and Eryn. And a special thanks to my wonderful wife, Zelia, for her undying support, patience, and love over these past forty years. I'm a lucky man.

A special thanks to Audra Gerber the finest editor I've ever worked with.

CONTENTS

AUTHOR'S NOTE

Following is a brief description of the first three novels in the series. I have added this to give some background to those who, such as myself, have a weak memory or those who have not read the first three novels

---

This science-fiction novel is not based on conflict and violence, as most are. Rather, it's based on the lives of human colonists as they progress on their new planet and their interaction with other races. Most of the science depicted in this and my previous novels is based on scientific fact, generally accepted theory, or promising new technology.

The Gabriel Chronicles: Book 4—Sharkra is the continuance of the Gabriel Chronicles series. It tells the story of the extraordinary lives and adventures of exceptional men and women. The following explanatory notes are for the benefit of those who have not read the first three novels or for those, such as myself, whose memories are a bit weak.

SLF (pronounced "self") stands for "synthetic life form." A person meeting a SLF will not be aware they are not human. They are perfect replicas in every way. At the beginning of this novel, there are twelve SLFs living on the planet Gabriel: Vance and his wife, Lara; Alex and Aidan; Teddy and Colleen; Dale and Tomaco; Troy and Clair; and Gary and Pat.

STARSHIPS

There are seven starships portrayed in the Gabriel Chronicles.

The first is the *Norman*, a single sphere one hundred meters in diameter and containing twenty decks. It was designed and built for the sole purpose of traveling to and colonizing another planet. Aboard were twenty humans in stasis and piloted by the first SLF, Vance. The *Norman* left Earth in the year 2030.

The starships *Marian*, *Vance*, and *Alexander* are more than five times the size of the *Norman*. Each was made up of four spheres the size of the *Norman* and one larger center sphere. The four smaller spheres surround the larger center sphere like moons around a planet. They are connected to the center sphere by corridors sixty meters long by six meters wide. These ships look similar to a giant jack in the children's game jacks. These ships were built for the express purpose of transporting as many humans as possible off Earth before it was destroyed by a massive asteroid. Each ship was piloted by two SLFs and contained five hundred humans in stasis. The three ships left Earth in the year 2445.

The *Marian* headed to the planet Gabriel to join the established civilization.

The *Vance* headed to an unknown-but-habitable planet they would name Isley after Dale Isley, whose genius created not only the propulsion system for the starships but also Isleium, the substance of which all SLFs are made.

The *Alexander* headed for a third planet, which was believed to be ideal for human colonization but turned out to be a disaster.

The *Velgot* is a massive alien ship. It is a single orb five kilometers in diameter (three miles). It is a ship of the Arkell. They make their first appearance in *Book 3—The Superiors*. They turn out to be dear friends and saviors of the humans of the planet Gabriel. There are 120,000 Arkell aboard the massive *Velgot*.

The *Geaalo* is also an Arkell ship, more ancient and larger than the *Velgot* but not nearly as technically advanced. These Arkell are not friends of the humans. The Arkell of the *Geaalo* are a scourge of the galaxy. There are 150,000 Arkell aboard the *Geaalo*.

The *Yassi* ships are by far the most beautiful in the known galaxy. The Yassi are friends and trading partners of the humans of Gabriel.

PLANET TIME VERSUS SHIP TIME

The faster a ship travels, the more the time differential widens. The time on a ship traveling near the speed of light slows down relative to stationary objects such as planets. Time on planets advance one hundred years while the time on a ship, traveling near the speed of light, advances just ten years.

Stasis is a state-of-the-art method of putting living beings in a frozen hypersleep. The colonists aboard the Earth's starships were transported while in stasis. The colonists in the *Norman* remained in stasis for eighty-two years while Vance seeded the planet Gabriel. During the eighty-two years ship time, including the thirty-two years on the voyage to find a new home, the planet aged close to five hundred years.

The colonists of the *Marian*, the *Vance*, and the *Alexander* remained in stasis just thirty-two years ship time before arriving at their destinations.

When a SLF wanted to go into stasis, they simply turned themselves off for whatever period of time they wished.

CHARACTERS

Vance Youngblood is a retired SEAL captain of old Earth. He is of average height, powerfully built, and has an olive complexion, menacing dark eyes, and wavy black hair that starts low on his forehead. He is highly intelligent and clearly not a man to be trifled with. Vance provided the planning and security for the WGC decades before becoming a SLF. He volunteered to captain the *Norman* from Earth to Gabriel.

Troy and Gary were Earth's last president and CEO of the WGC (World Guidance Council), Earth's governing body. They became the driving force in the emergency building of the three starships to save as many humans as possible before Earth was destroyed by the asteroid. They became SLFs in order to help build and pilot the three starships.

Troy is of medium height and slender, with short-cropped brown hair and brown eyes. He looks and acts like the CEO of a large corporation.

Gary is a tall, dark man, with black salt-and-pepper curly hair and dark eyes, and possesses an excellent scientific mind. He was second-in-command of the WGC in the years prior to Earth's destruction.

Alexander Gabriel is tall, blond, and handsome, with striking blue eyes and an average build. Alex was the main protagonist in the first novel, *Book 1—The Beginning*. He was the driving force in creating the WGC five hundred years before Troy and Gary were born.

Teddy is as warm, caring, and funny an individual as can be found. He is a born entertainer and a lifelong friend of Alexander Gabriel. He appears in all three previous novels.

Dale Isley is a small, tidy, good-looking man. He has brown hair and a manicured beard and is considered one of the greatest minds in history. Among his many accomplishments, he invented Isleium, the substance of which the SLFs are made. He helped design the weapon that allowed the WGC to take over all of Earth's governments and enforce mankind's conformity to the new laws imposed by the WGC. In addition to the hundreds of designs and inventions of over a lifetime, he also designed the propulsion system for the *Norman*, and its basic design was used over four hundred years later on the *Marian*, the *Vance*, and the *Alexander*.

The planet Gabriel has six continents: the North Pole and the South Pole, which are uninhabited; the Vast Continent, the largest; the North Dumbbell and the South Dumbbell; and the Ring Continent, where the planet's colonization began.

There are five other alien races depicted in the Gabriel Chronicles.

The Vout are an advanced race. They are tall, thin, hairless, friendly, and quite boring. They were the first to befriend the humans.

The Malic are short, hairy, ugly, and vicious. They attacked the humans of Gabriel, which resulted in a short war that killed two dozen humans and all but four of the Malic.

The Yassi are short, cute, hairless, and delightful. They are more technically advanced than the humans and Vout, and became fast friends and allies. Their starships are stunningly beautiful. The Yassi woos when pleased or amused in lieu of clapping or whistling.

Aside from the two main starships on the planet Gabriel, the *Norman* and the *Marian*, there are smaller ships called runabouts, both large and small. There is nothing fancy about these ships. They appear to be little more than stylized boxcars with pontoons. They are the workhorses and are used as transports of supplies and personnel. There is also a beautiful shuttle built by the Yassi and gifted to the humans of Gabriel.

Home Bay is the original colony of Gabriel. It's located on a beautiful bay on the west coast of the Ring Continent.

It was decided early on for those on Gabriel, the days, months, and years had to be adjusted to sync with the actual length of days, months, and years of their new planet. The actual time the planet Gabriel took for one revolution was divided into twenty parts, becoming twenty-hour days. Gabriel orbited its sun every two hundred eighty of these days, so that became the length of their year. Those two hundred eighty days were divided into ten parts, giving ten months containing twenty-eight days each. The months were named Mo-One through Mo-Ten. A date of January 5, 2021, on Earth would read, "Mo-One 5, 2021," on Gabriel.

The first in the trilogy, *Book 1—The Beginning*, follows the life of Alexander Gabriel, a brilliant investment broker who is shot back in time to begin his life over, starting at age eight. It tells of his accumulation of a vast fortune over the ensuing decades. Alex will use his massive wealth and the assistance of three other exceptional men, each with a unique area of expertise, to change the world.

The second in the trilogy, *Book 2—New Home*, continues the story of three of these four men. Dr. Isley creates a substance that allows him to build natural-looking prosthetics, giving amputees around the world functional, lifelike limbs and paralyzed people new functional nerves. Years later, he takes this incredible technology to its ultimate conclusion. He builds a complete synthetic life form, a SLF. The synthetic body and brain are designed to accept the complete intelligence, personality, and abilities of any human. Vance Youngblood becomes the first SLF.

With Alexander Gabriel's money and Dale Isley's brilliance, the WGC builds a colossal starship designed to take a small number of colonists to a distant planet. The SLF Vance Youngblood captains the ship. He alone, over the next fifty years, develops the planet Gabriel, making it suitable for human habitation.

Alexander Gabriel and Dale Isley appear as holograms in *Book 2*, and again in the first half of the third novel. Their intelligence, personalities, and appearance had been stored in the starship *Norman*'s computers. They become SLFs halfway through *Book 3—The Superiors*.

PROLOGUE
YEAR 205

There were now just under four hundred thousand people living on Gabriel. About seventy percent lived on the Ring Continent, the balance scattered around the other three habitable continents. Home Bay continued to be the center of the small-but-growing government. By necessity, over the years, the governing body had to create a water department, power department, agricultural department, transportation department, and global banking system. All were to be housed in a new government building located three kilometers east of Home Bay in a beautiful spot overlooking the Vance River. Functions that had historically been handled first within the *Norman*, outgrowing that, had been switched to the much-larger *Marian*. But the growing number of personnel within each department forced the governing council to build a dedicated government building. The new building not only housed those various departments, but they had included a meeting room that would accommodate up to two hundred people

"Never occurred to me that it would come to this," said Vance after the ribbon-cutting ceremony. "We have a government building."

Governing was not difficult on Gabriel. The planet had just one central government, one language, one monetary system, and one legal system.

The golden rule would always be applied to any changes proposed that would have an effect on people planetwide. That being the case, challenges to the status quo in any form were usually handled without serious disagreements.

Home Bay had already surpassed Vance's wish that the populations of all towns on Gabriel be limited to twenty-five thousand people. Home Bay was now just over thirty thousand. Vance, with the backing of the rest of the planet's leadership, put restrictions on any further population expansion in and around Home Bay. There would be no more homes built within ten kilometers of the town's center.

There were now over a hundred small towns and communities around Gabriel with an average population of under seven thousand. Just six were approaching twenty-five thousand. Following Home Bay's lead, they all agreed to keep their towns small and close-knit.

Other than the Arkell's occasionally providing advanced technology and protection for the humans, two races—Yassi and Vout—had, over the past two hundred years, supplied Gabriel with, in exchange for gold, thousands of needed or wanted items that could not yet be manufactured on Gabriel. Among them were equipment and machines needed for manufacturing steel, lumber, and farm equipment, plus personal items such as viewing screens and audio systems, hydrogen fuel cells, and thousands of other items both large and small. Although manufacturing on Gabriel had, over the decades, grown to a level that fewer products were required to be produced off planet by Yassi or Vout, it was estimated it would be three more decades for Gabriel to be completely self-sufficient.

It had long ago been determined on Earth that hydrogen-powered fuel-cells were the most efficient and pollution-free source of electric power. The Yassi had been incorporating fuel cells as their major power source for centuries. Separating hydrogen from water is a relatively simple process, and hydrogen is the most abundant element in the universe.

Five years ago, the Yassi had begun manufacturing and delivering fuel-cell-powered trucks, buses, and cars to Gabriel. All were of great quality but necessarily expensive. It wasn't that the Yassi were taking advantage of Gabrielites; it was simply expensive to manufacture these vehicles and deliver them, via a Yassi freighter, from two light-years away. Few Gabrielites could afford such an extravagance on their own, but it didn't take long for two or three families to partner up and purchase a car or truck to share. The more enterprising individuals, individuals who had managed to accumulate a larger fortune over the years, were able to buy a vehicle by themselves.

It was the personal automobile that had become most in demand by the Gabrielites. There were three basic models: a four-door with rear hatch similar to old Earth's sports utility vehicle, a small truck similar to Earth's pickups, and a stunning sports model. All were spectacular in appearance, as was the case with anything attached to the Yassi. To fill the growing demand, the Yassi had built a small fleet of freighters to deliver the vehicles to Gabriel. Dozens were delivered every six months or so, but due to the demand, a lottery was set up to give all who wished for a vehicle a fair chance to buy one in the next delivery.

In addition to vehicles, Yassi also produced and delivered huge fuel cells to power manufacturing plants and supply new communities and towns with the power required for living a modern life. The Yassi also had perfected a microwave system that transmitted electricity wherever it was needed without the need for wire.

Gabriel did not yet have the ability to manufacture fuel cells, but they had purchased wind-powered and solar plants from the Yassi that were designed to separate the hydrogen from oxygen in sea water to power the fuel cells.

Just recently, a cement plant had been constructed with most of its parts and machinery supplied by the Vout; the balance could be produced on Gabriel. The primary purpose of the new factory was to start construction of concrete roads in and around the bay to mitigate the dust blown up by the various modern vehicles. In addition, there was a growing demand to pave the road traversing the mountain range between Home Bay and the three large towns located on the shores of the massive inland freshwater sea, a sea that dominated the center and the majority of the continent. The gravel road that existed wasn't used often because few had transports required to make the trip. A single small shuttle had been used, for decades, by those three towns, to deliver fresh seafood and a variety of other produce to the Home Bay restaurants and markets. Due mainly to the growing population and subsequent demand for fresh fish and vegetables, a small shuttle was no longer practical for the job. So one of the two large shuttles replaced the small one. But even that after a few years soon became too small. So it was decided to pave the hundred-and-fifteen-kilometer road. This not only would allow the transport of fish and other produce with newly acquired trucks but also would allow the people living on the shores of the great inland sea to drive to Home Bay in less than two hours. The planet Gabriel was becoming a full-fledged civilization.

CHAPTER 1

A COMMUNICATION
FROM AFAR
MO-5-205

As was the case just about every morning, when on Vance's Island, Vance and Lara were sitting on a comfortable swinging couch on their deck overlooking their tastefully landscaped grounds as it gently sloped toward the Lara River.

"More coffee, sweetie?" asked Lara as she stood.

"I believe I will, thanks," said Vance as he handed her his cup.

"Whoa," said Lara as she was about to turn and head into the kitchen.

Vance turned to see what Lara was looking at. "Whoa is right," he said with a big smile as he leaned forward on the couch.

Across the river, a small group of gorillas were emerging from the thick forest and ambling casually toward the river. In all these decades, Vance and Lara had never seen these mighty apes this far west on the island. There were just ten in this group, one large silverback male, five females, and four young ones ranging in age from about six months to maybe three years. Vance reached over to the end table and retrieved a pair of binoculars.

"Look at that sumbitch," said Vance while getting a close-up view of this beautiful animal.

Lara set their cups back on the end table and sat back down next to her husband. Vance handed the binoculars to Lara.

"He's as big as Kong was at his prime—maybe bigger," said Vance. "Must be near two hundred fifty kilos," he said without taking his eyes off the silverback.

"That is a big boy," Lara said while scrutinizing the huge ape. "He has to be the fifth generation after Kong."

After a couple seconds of calculating, Vance nodded in agreement. "That's right, five generations."

"He would be the great-grandson of Jake, the baby gorilla I was carrying when we first met," said Lara with a hint of nostalgia.

"That was a long time ago." Vance smiled at the memory. "And one of the best days of my long life."

Lara smiled brightly. "Hundred and five years ago, as a matter of fact. And it was my best day."

This Lara had now been a SLF for thirteen years. It had actually been the human Lara who was carrying the small ape when she and Vance met over a century before. It was the human Lara who had transferred all her memories, emotions, and personality to her SLF just a few days before she ended her human life at the age of one hundred and ten.

Vance slowly nodded his head. "Hundred and five years, wow."

"I wonder if they'll stay in this area?" said Lara, getting back to the subject at hand.

"What?" Vance's mind was reminiscing on the number of years they had been together, temporarily forgetting the gorillas.

"Gorillas in the area?"

Vance came back to the present, "Oh yeah . . . time will answer that. I hope they do. We'll be able to keep tabs on them."

Lara nodded in agreement. "That big fella is nearly as handsome as Jake," she said. "Still miss the old guy. He was quite a character and very gentle for a silverback."

Vance smiled. "He was gentle because a certain young lady spent nearly as much time with him as his biological mother."

"That's a bit of an exaggeration," said Lara as she gently elbowed Vance's ribs.

"Vance, are you available?" Alex's voice could be heard coming from Vance's communicator.

Vance retrieved his communicator from his belt. "Yes, sir, what's up?"

"A lot, actually. Just received a communiqué from Henry Hendrick, the captain of the *Vance*."

Vance sat up straight. The gorillas no longer had his attention. "What did he have to say?"

"They are heading to Gabriel."

Vance looked over at Lara. "Really? Did he say when they expect to arrive?"

"As a matter of fact, yes." Alex paused for a moment. "They're only a year out, planet time, but then the message stopped abruptly."

"Stopped?"

"And we don't know why."

"Well that's not good," said Vance.

"No, it isn't."

"And," said Vance, "why would they wait nearly ten years to inform us?"

"Dale and I think that may be considerate."

Vance's brow wrinkled. "How's that?"

"Had they informed us as soon as they left Isley, we would have waited, according to Dale, about thirty-three years planet time for their arrival. That takes into consideration their communiqué would travel at the speed of light, whereas the ship is traveling at .96 of light."

"Good point, Dale."

"Thank you."

All humans knew all about time and space travel. It was part of their history. They knew that while ten years passed on a ship traveling at near the speed of light, the time on a planet would advance a hundred years. So this ship, the *Vance*, had already been heading toward Gabriel for nearly a hundred years planet time.

"We need to contact them and ask for some details. Chief among them would be why they left Isley."

"Agreed," said Alex.

"There are a lot of details we should know," said Dale. "How many people they are bringing, the condition of their ship, the condition of the planet Isley, etcetera."

Vance was pensive for a moment. "Let's send a message to the Arkell. See if they know of anything about this."

"I would think if they knew of any problems, they would have informed us already," said Dale.

"Of course," said Vance. "We'll have to wait for an explanation from Hendrick. I'm assuming there is nothing holding us back from communicating with the *Vance.*"

"Except if they can't send, they may not be able to receive either," said Dale.

"Hopefully that isn't the case," said Vance.

"I've notified Troy and Gary. They both know Henry Hendrick. All became SLFs at about the same time," said Alex. "They're on their way to the *Marian.*"

"Okay, good," said Vance. "We'll head up to Home Bay ASAP and compare thoughts before sending a message to the *Vance.*"

"Agreed," said Alex. "See you soon."

The small shuttle entered the docking bay of the *Norman* in the early afternoon and settled on its designated pad. A minute later, the hatch opened and Vance stepped out, hand in hand with Lara. They walked directly to the open elevator and stepped in.

"Deck 20," said Vance.

A few seconds later, Vance and Lara walked down the *Norman's* ramp and out of the cave. They turned left and headed to the *Marian,* which was located two hundred meters south of the *Norman's* cave. They took their time and stopped to greet and talk to old friends who were enjoying the day in and around Home Bay.

Twenty minutes later, they walked onto the *Marian's* bridge. There to meet them were Troy, Gary, Alex, and Dale.

"Nice to see you two in person," said Troy.

"Same here," said Dale.

Vance and Lara spent little time in Home Bay these days. There had been virtually no problems on the planet that required Vance's attention for over a decade, and he liked it that way. The peace and quiet on his island in the company of his beloved Lara was all he needed. He had spent centuries doing things for the planet that only he could. And now he was enjoying his retirement.

Lara was known to Vance, Alex, Teddy, and Dale for hundreds of years. They had been close friends while they were all human on the now-extinct planet Earth. The human Lara was one of the last people to see and speak to the human Alex the day he died on Earth, year 2043. But this Lara was a SLF of the Lara who had been cloned just one hundred thirty years ago on Gabriel. Her memories did not go back to those of the original Lara of Earth. But her personality, intelligence, and sense of humor were nearly identical to the original. There were volumes of information in the archives of both the *Marian* and the *Norman* covering the past lives of the SLFs now on the bridge, and a considerable amount of information on the human Lara, Colleen, and Aidan of Earth, all of whom were now SLFs. The cloned Lara of Gabriel, when told she was to be Vance's mate, had studied and absorbed all information contained in the archives and, over the past century, had come to know all these remarkable men, of old Earth, every bit as well as her original.

Lara, as always, gave Alex and Dale big loving hugs. "I do miss seeing my old friends." She turned to Troy and Gary. "And my relatively new friends." She gave each a hug in turn.

Vance smiled. "Guess we haven't been to town for a while."

"Three months, twelve days," said Dale.

"Really?" That surprised Vance.

"Yep."

"That tells me that the planet is getting along just fine without my input."

"I'm happy to concede that is, in fact, the case," said Alex.

They spent the next couple of minutes exchanging pleasantries before Vance got down to the reason for this meeting. "Troy, you and Gary knew Henry very well. Do you have any idea or thought as to why he is heading here?"

"If I can interrupt for a sec," said Lara. "While you five have your meeting, for which I can't think of a thing I could add that would be of any use, I'm going to visit with some friends." She turned to Vance. "When and where do you want to meet later?"

"Where else, Carlon's Pub," Vance said with a big smile. "How about fifteen bells?"

Lara smiled. "I'll be there." She looked over at the four men. "Be nice to have you join us. We can catch up a little."

All quickly and cheerfully agreed.

"Great, see you later." With that, she gave Vance a quick kiss, turned, and headed back to the elevator.

"Back to the issue at hand," said Vance.

Troy nodded. "Henry Hendrick is an academic. A very intelligent man. If he's heading here, there has to be a very compelling reason. It would not be on a whim. He's not the explorer type."

"Agreed," said Gary. "Something unbearable had to happen on Isley."

"I don't know why Henry didn't contact us at the beginning of the voyage here. This is out of character for him. He's a thorough man. Detail orientated," said Troy.

"I might have an answer to that," said Dale.

"Let's have it," said Vance.

"After the communiqué from Henry, I ran a test on the relays the Arkell put in place years ago. They are, as far as I can tell, nonfunctional."

"How can that be?" asked Vance.

"Probably a malfunction," said Troy.

"I don't think anything the Arkell built and put in place will malfunction," said Dale.

"Agreed," said Gary. "If the Arkell build something, it is probably designed to last forever . . . maybe a little longer."

"It's possible that one of the relay legs has been struck with some space debris," said Troy.

"Yes, that's a possibility," said Dale "Very slim but possible."

"Well, at the distance the *Vance* is from Gabriel, we don't need a relay. So let's ask Henry what the hell is going on," said Vance.

"Before doing that, let's send the Arkell a message and let them know what's happening," said Troy.

All agreed.

The message was sent to the *Vance* knowing it would take a full month for the ship to receive it and they would wait three weeks for a response. The *Vance* would be in its long deceleration phase. It would take nearly a year to reduce its speed from .96 of light to just a few thousand kilometers per hour before arriving at Gabriel.

Nearly two months had gone by and still no answer from the *Vance*.

"There is clearly a problem," said Dale. "We should have had an answer a week ago at the latest."

"It could be something as simple as their communications system breaking down," suggested Alex.

"That would be the ideal answer, but there are several redundancies on that system. The chances for all of them to break down would be astronomical," said Gary.

Vance nodded in acknowledgment. "All we can do now is wait for the *Vance* to arrive, hopefully at the time Hendrick said they'd be here."

CHAPTER 2

THE *VANCE* ARRIVES

"Vance, have you got your ears on?"

"I do."

"We just picked up the *Vance* on our long-range sensors," said Dale.

"That's great," exclaimed Vance, obviously delighted. "How far out?"

"Just over a week. And all seems normal. Their speed is what it should be, and it's decelerating at a normal rate. But we still can't communicate with it."

Vance was silent for a moment. "Well, I guess we'll have to wait to get a report when they arrive."

Five days later, the *Vance* could be seen by ground-based telescopes as it approached Gabriel. A huge crowd began gathering in and around Home Bay in anticipation of this historic arrival. All knew of the problems. All had opinions as to what happed. All would prove to be wrong.

"I've shut down the shield," said Dale.

Just before the Arkell of the *Velgot* left Gabriel, after their first visit in the year 142, they installed a highly advanced planetary shield. The shield would prevent anything that could be damaging to enter the planet's atmosphere, including uninvited and unwanted alien ships—specifically the rogue Arkell of the ship the *Geaalo*. These Arkell's mission, motives, and attitude were nothing like the Arkell of the *Velgot*. Over the millennia, these ancient Arkell seemed

8

to have lost all compassion and empathy. They had become a scourge of the galaxy. They had become destroyers.

A few hours later, the *Vance* arrived. It came in at a proper speed and altitude but did not go into a geosynchronous orbit, as was normal prior to a landing. It came straight in, lowered the landing gear on all five spheres, and settled a hundred meters south of the *Marian*.

"I've turned the shield back on," said Dale.

Vance nodded. "Good."

After a few minutes of no communication from the *Vance*, feelings of dread began creeping into the minds of the four SLFs.

"What the hell?" said Troy.

"Something's wrong," said Gary.

"Let's get out there," said Vance as he quickly turned and headed toward the elevator.

The three had trouble making their way to the *Vance* through the throng of people also heading toward the new arrival. When they finally arrived, they stood with dozens of Gabrielites just below the center sphere, the controlling sphere, where an exit ramp would normally be lowered.

They waited. Seconds turned into minutes. Minutes were starting to add up before Vance's patience gave way.

"Alright, there's a rat in the crackers here. How do we open this ship up?"

"Codes," said Gary. "We have the operational codes for all three of these ships. The *Marian, Vance,* and *Alexander.*"

"Do you have them in your memory?" asked Vance.

"No, but I'll have them in a second." Gary pushed a button on his communicator. "Sam, can you hear me?"

"Yes, sir."

"Pull up the operational code for the *Vance.*"

"Yes, sir, just a sec."

A few seconds later, Sam's voice came over Gary's phone. "Have the code for the *Vance.*"

"Good, feed that into the *Marian*'s computer and take control of the *Vance*'s mainframe."

A few seconds later, Sam said, "Done."

"Drop the main exit ramp," said Gary.

"WAIT!" said Vance with urgency.

Everybody within ear shot turned their attention to Vance.

"Clear this area all the way back to the gazebo," Vance yelled loudly. "Quickly, please."

There was a loud murmur of disappointment rising among the Gabrielites as they reluctantly began backing away from the *Vance.*

Vance turned to Troy and Gary. "We three are going to get armed before we open up this ship."

"Really? What do you think might be a danger?" asked Troy.

"Have no idea. But something has been wrong or off-kilter with this ship from the get-go. My old instincts are jumping up and down right now. So we'll be armed before we enter this ship."

Twenty-five minutes later, the three SLFs were again standing below the center sphere of the *Vance.* This time, they had on protective armor designed and manufactured by the Arkell on their last visit to Gabriel. The armor included a full helmet that included the face with a clear material over the eyes. All three had sidearms and held long guns. They had not yet put on their helmets.

Gary put a camera on a tripod that would point up into the ship when the ramp came down.

"Let's put the helmets on."

Once that was done, Vance nodded at Gary.

"Sam, lower the ramp halfway and be ready to raise it quickly."

As the ramp started its descent to the ground, Vance moved to the left while Troy and Gary remained on the right. All three had their attention on their small wrist viewers.

When the ramp reached the halfway point, it stopped. The camera was showing a dark interior.

"This is bad," said Gary.

"Very," added Troy.

"Let's get some light in there," ordered Vance.

"Sam," said Gary, "turn on the lights on the ramp deck."

"Yes, sir."

Light came on in seconds, illuminating the deck.

"Did you see that?" asked Vance.

"I saw something," said Troy. "Don't know what. Too quick."

"Replay the last twenty seconds," ordered Vance.

The three were staring intently at their wrist viewers.

"Freeze frame as soon as the lights come on," said Vance.

"That's not a human," said Gary.

There in freeze frame was an Arkell. He was trying to get out of sight but failed. He had on some sort of armor and looked to be armed.

"Shit!"

"What now?" asked Troy.

"Close the ramp," ordered Vance.

An hour later, the three SLFs were again below the center sphere. Vance had ordered the thousands of Gabrielites who had come to welcome the *Vance*'s personnel to Gabriel into the *Norman*'s cave for their protection. He also picked a dozen men to act as backup for the three SLFs.

"Each of you, take one of these rifles," Vance pointed to a small wheeled cart containing the weapons.

When the men had their weapons, he placed them fifty meters out in a semicircle around the *Vance*'s ramp. He took another look at the placement of the backup. "All of you, lay prone facing the ramp. You'll make smaller targets." Vance waited until the last of the men were prone. "I want you to shoot anything that comes down that ramp that isn't human. Do you understand?"

A dozen affirmatives came back.

He turned to Troy and Gary. "You ready?"

"Ready," they said nearly in unison.

"Lower the ramp."

As the ramp lowered, they could see the lights were still on. "Keep five meters apart and head to the elevator," ordered Vance.

As soon as the ramp touched the ground, the three, with Vance in the lead, ran up the ramp and into the interior of the ship.

There was no resistance. They cautiously made their way to the elevator. To Vance's surprise, the elevator was still functioning. *I wouldn't have left the lights on or the elevator in working condition*, he thought. *Makes no sense.*

"Bridge," said Troy.

Up they went, unimpeded.

The elevator doors opened to a pitch-black bridge. Their helmet lights automatically came on. They quickly scanned the interior, but all they saw was a single body sitting in the captain's chair. Vance signaled Troy to head to the right and Gary to the left.

After a minute of checking for any danger, Vance said, "Sam, light up the bridge."

The lights came on and revealed an empty-but-tidy bridge. All eyes immediately went to the captain's chair.

"That's Henry," said Troy.

Henry was destroyed. His body was shredded to the point that his right arm and right leg were being held in place only by his uniform. His chest had been torn open, exposing his power pack and all his internal parts. The only part of Henry that seemed to be undamaged was his head.

"Jesus, Henry," Gary said softly.

"Ah, hell," said Troy, obviously saddened.

Vance took a long look at Henry before nodding. "This is a rage killing."

"Why?" asked Gary.

"Let's find out," said Troy.

"We need to find the Arkell who are responsible," said Vance in a commanding voice. "We'll go from deck to deck and search 'em out."

"Yes, sir," said Troy.

"Might I suggest we start in the cryo decks?" said Gary. "We need to see if any humans have come along on this trip and what condition they're in."

"Roger that," said Vance.

They all turned and headed back to the elevator.

"Deck 10," said Vance.

"Want to split up to speed up the search?" asked Gary.

"No, we'll stay together until we find and eliminate any and all Arkell aboard," answered Vance.

The elevator stopped on deck 10 and its doors slid open. Again, they were met with pitch black.

"Sam, lights on in deck 10's anteroom," said Vance.

"Yes, sir."

The lights came on. Among other ship's facilities located on this deck, it was the location of the four sixty-meter-long corridors that led to the outer spheres.

The four outer spheres were each the size of the *Norman*. And each had a cryo deck containing one hundred and twenty-five cryo beds. The humans hadn't put all their eggs in one basket. If one of the outer spheres was damaged or destroyed, all the human's colonists would not be lost.

Above the hatch of each of the four corridors was its designation, sphere A through sphere D.

"We'll take 'em in order," said Vance.

They walked to hatch A.

"Gary, you stay here and keep alert. Don't want anyone sneaking up behind us."

"Yes, sir."

From this vantage point, Gary could see the other three hatches around the anteroom that surrounded the elevator shaft. These were pressure hatches. If by chance any one of the four spheres were compromised, the pressure hatches on both ends of the corridor would slam shut and seal the sphere from the other spheres and the ship.

"Stand to one side," said Vance as he pushed the hatch A's button. There was a faint hissing sound as the hatch swung open and up. Again, they were met by darkness.

"Sam, light up corridor A."

"Yes, sir."

As soon as the lights came on, both men stuck their heads around the corner and took a quick look down the corridor before pulling their heads back to safety.

"These corridors look a lot longer when a man's life is at stake, particularly if it's mine," said Troy with just a touch of humor.

The two men walked carefully down the sixty-meter-long corridor, keeping their eyes on the closed hatch at the far end. When they arrived, Vance pushed the hatch button and the hatch opened.

The cryo decks in each sphere were a hundred meters in diameter. The helmet lights were bright but not bright enough to adequately penetrate to the far side of the deck.

"Sam, lights on in cryo deck A," said Vance.

The deck flooded with light.

"Wow," said Vance as he quickly scanned the rows of cryo capsules. "I'd forgotten how big these decks are."

Vance continued to scan the huge deck. "Troy, you start on the outside left and I'll go right. Be ready to shoot at all times."

"Yes, sir."

Troy started heading left. When he got to the first capsule, he stopped and looked inside. "Holy shit!"

"Oh my god!" said Vance at nearly the same time. "Dead—yours?"

"The same."

Inside the capsules were Arkell, clearly dead. Some decomposition was evident. Next to each capsule was body armor and weapons, weapons of a sort Vance hadn't seen before. He picked up a long weapon and turned it over in his hands, inspecting its mechanism. "I've never seen anything like this."

Troy bent over and retrieved one of the weapons. "I wouldn't even know how to use it."

After a moment, Vance set the weapon down. "Keep your eyes open for a live one while we check all the capsules."

"They'll be wide open," said Troy, also setting the alien weapon down.

They as quickly as possible checked each capsule as they passed. All Arkell—all dead. It was apparent that all would have, had they lived, been well armed and very lethal.

As they started to exit sphere A, Vance picked up the armor and weapons of the closest capsule. After leaving the sphere, he pushed the button and the hatch dropped and closed. They returned to the anteroom.

"Dead Arkell?" asked Gary.

"Very," answered Vance.

"What do you have there?" asked Gary, gesturing at the equipment in Vance's hands.

"Arkell armor and weapons."

"Oh shit."

They all knew what this revelation meant.

They moved to the cryo deck on sphere B.

Following the same procedure, the results were the same. All the capsules contained dead Arkell, none alive.

When they opened the hatch on sphere C, a high-pitched sound was followed by a burst of green light that hit Gary directly in the chest, throwing him three meters back and into an opposing wall.

"SHIT!" yelled Troy as he dove out of the line of fire coming from the far end of the corridor.

Vance didn't hesitate. He quickly fired a burst from his long gun as he, too, jumped out of the line of fire.

"Gary, are you alright?" asked Vance.

There was no answer.

Gary was still in the line of fire from the corridor. He lay motionless, his head propped up against the wall, his body flat on the deck.

Vance stuck his head around the corner, took a quick look down the corridor, and pulled his head back from the line of fire. "The Arkell is not where he was. He's gone into cryo deck," he said loudly as he reached over and pushed the button, closing the C corridor hatch. "Let's get Gary out of the line of fire."

He signaled Troy and they both quickly walked over to their fallen comrade, took him by the arms, and dragged him around to the elevator entrance. Vance kneeled down and took off Gary's helmet.

"Gary, can you hear me?"

"Ouch," said Gary quietly.

"Are you okay?" asked Troy.

"Felt like I got hit by truck. If I had lungs, it would feel like I had the wind knocked out of me," Gary managed to get out.

"Any other pain?" asked Vance.

Gary lifted his arms one at a time. Then he slowly sat up under his own power. "I think I'm going to live," he said with a small smile.

"The armor works," said Vance. "That burst was strong enough to blow you in half."

"Bless the Arkell," said Troy.

Vance said nothing for a moment. "Okay, you and Gary head to the *Marian* and get checked out. I'm going to go kill that sumbitch in the cryo deck."

"Alone?"

"Yes, sir."

Troy nodded. There was little point in questioning Vance when it came to a fight. The man knew what he was doing.

Vance helped Gary get to his feet. He stood next to him to be sure he was stable. After a couple of off-balance moves, Gary straightened up and smiled. "I'm fine, I think."

"Okay, you two head to the *Marian*. I'll be along shortly."

Troy held on to Gary as they stepped into the elevator.

Vance waited until the elevator door slid shut before turning and heading to the C corridor. He put a fresh clip in his rifle before pushing the corridor button.

A quick look told him that the Arkell was still in the cryo deck. He didn't hesitate before walking quickly down the long corridor, his rifle at ready on his shoulder. When he reached the hatch, he could see the blood on the deck. *Hit him*, he thought. *Hit him good.* There was a lot of blood on the deck and blood on the hatch button. He stepped to one side and pushed the button.

As soon as the hatch opened, a blast from the Arkell weapon shot out. Then another and another. *Firing blind*, thought Vance. *He's panicked.*

"I would suggest you put your weapon down and surrender to me," said Vance in a loud voice. "If you do that, we will not harm you further and will, in fact, provide you medical attention. If you choose to continue this fight, I will personally kill you within the next few minutes—your choice."

A few seconds later, five more blasts from the Arkell weapon shot down the corridor.

"Wrong choice," yelled Vance as he jumped into the room and behind one of the cryo beds. There were no shots from the Arkell. Vance nodded to himself. *He didn't see me come in.* Vance started crawling down the outside row of cryo beds on the right side of the room. That way, he didn't have to be concerned about an attack from the right. He just had to pay attention forward and left.

There was another blast from the Arkell weapon, but it wasn't aimed anywhere near him. He quickly popped his head up and back down in a fraction of a second. It was long enough to spot the Arkell at the rear center of the deck. Vance smiled to himself. *The rogue Arkell of the Geaalo—with all the damage they had inflected on various planets of the galaxy, they apparently didn't encounter any real resistance from those they terrorized. Otherwise, they would have been a whole lot smarter in a gunfight.*

Vance now knew where this Arkell was and proceeded to work his way toward the front and center using the cryo beds as cover. When he was in position, he, with rifle ready, popped up and took aim at where the Arkell would show himself. He didn't have to wait long. The Arkell rose from the same position he had just shot from. The split second he spotted Vance was the same split second that a single bullet tore through his head. Fight over.

A few minutes later, Vance walked down the ramp, into the sunshine. The twelve men on station as backup stood from their prone positions.

As Vance took off his helmet, there was wholehearted applause and wooing.

"Gather around," said Vance.

The twelve men closed the distance and, within a few seconds, were in a tight group around Vance.

"I managed to take out one Arkell, but I believe there is another still alive. But there are five hundred dead Arkell in cryo beds."

The response was immediate. All twelve men started talking at once. Many questions, many filled with colorful expletives.

Fifteen minutes later, Vance joined Alex, Dale, Troy, Gary, and Sam on the bridge of the *Marian.*

Vance looked closely at Gary. "How are you doing?"

"Checked out at one hundred percent—no damage. That Arkell armor is amazing. Apparently, the force of whatever hits it is distributed over the entire suit."

"I'm not surprised," said Dale.

"It was clearly an invasion force," said Vance. "And had they not died in the cryo capsules, we may have been wiped out."

"A Trojan horse," stated Alex with no reservation.

"Exactly what it was," said Vance. "Little doubt that days before they landed, they would have come out of cryogenics and been fully revived. I would bet they would have dropped the ramps of all five spheres the second they landed, swarmed out, and easily overpowered us within an hour."

"Holy shit," said Dale.

"Very smart," said Troy.

"We invited them into our castle." added Gary.

"I want Shem here ASAP," Vance said in a commanding voice.

"Yes, sir," said Dale.

The humans' first and only encounter with the ancient Arkell ship, the *Geaalo,* was frightening. The rogue Arkell of the *Geaalo* made it clear when stopped and questioned by Oruku, the front man of the *Velgot* Arkell, that their only purpose was to take the gold that Gabriel had in abundance. They did not ask permission, and they had no intention of bargaining; it was their intention just to take. The Arkell of the *Velgot* knew these particular Arkell had little if any compassion or empathy for the indigenous species or the planets they plundered. According to Oruku, these planets and moons suffered vast damage from their mining. They stripped away vegetation and damaged or destroyed natural water resources. If any indigenous species tried to intervene, they were simply annihilated. Having greater technology, the Arkell of the *Velgot* drove off the *Geaalo* and admonished them never to enter this sector of the galaxy again under the threat of destruction.

Shem entered the bridge of the *Marian* twenty minutes later. "I have an inkling of what's going on." He smiled. "A lot of talk going on among the population," he continued as he walked toward the five SLFs and Sam gathered in the middle of the bridge, having a conversation.

"You're going to have more than an inkling in a couple of minutes," said Dale.

"Good, I think my inkling isn't going to be much more than an appetizer," said Shem as he shook hands with the other men.

Shem was now eighty-four years old but looked to be no more than a healthy forty. Their Arkell genes assured he and Jarleth a long life.

"You ready for the main course?" asked Alex.

Shem nodded once.

"The floor is yours, Vance," said Alex.

"Rogue Arkell, we assume from the *Geaalo,* have managed to invade the planet Isley and commandeer the *Vance.*"

Shem nodded once in understanding, saying nothing.

"What else might have happened to the citizens of Isley we have no idea, but I have the feeling whatever happened could have been horrible."

Again, Shem nodded.

"We found five hundred dead Arkell in the cryo capsules," said Troy.

Shem's left eyebrow went up.

"Clearly these Arkell's main objective was to gain access to our planet. And subsequently, our gold," said Troy.

"The *Vance* became their Trojan horse," said Shem.

The five SLFs nodded in unison. It didn't take Shem but a second to come to that conclusion.

"Exactly," said Vance.

"I've been told you killed an Arkell."

"I did," said Vance with no joy in his voice. "He wouldn't listen to reason."

Shem nodded.

"I believe the one I dispatched is not the one we saw at the top of the ramp," said Vance. "That one is still somewhere on the ship."

"Any thoughts?" asked Troy.

Shem nodded slowly, clearly still mulling over the situation. "In my opinion, it will be too dangerous and time-consuming to look for an armed Arkell in such an enormous ship with its thousands of hiding places."

"Agreed," said Vance.

"How about me getting on the ship's intercom system and asking the Arkell to give himself up?"

"'That's a good idea." Vance smiled. "Very good."

Shem returned the smile. "Okay, while I'm on a roll, I'll keep going."

"Please do," said Dale, impressed, as usual, with Shem's quick grasp of the situation.

"Okay. If we're successful at getting the Arkell to surrender— how about me performing Waoca with him to find out what the

Arkell's plans were, what happened on Isley, and where the *Geaalo* is presently located?"

Vance smiled again. "Any more thoughts?"

"Not at the moment."

"Good, we are all on the same page," said Vance. "I suggest we see what you can do to get that Arkell off the *Vance*."

"Sam, can you turn on the *Vance*'s inter-ship communication?" asked Shem.

"Yes, sir."

Three seconds later, Sam pointed at Shem and nodded.

"My name is Shem. I would like to communicate with the Arkell who are aboard the *Vance*. You can talk from wherever you are on the ship. I will hear you. We want you to know that no harm will come to you if you wish to communicate in person. No harm will come to you under any circumstances other than your attempting to harm one or more of us. I will wait for your response."

The bridge of the *Marian* was silent. No one said a word. No one made a sound. Five minutes passed before Shem spoke again. "I am partially Arkell. I will not lie to you. We can perform Waoca if you wish."

There was silence on the bridge for a full minute. "Now I am alone," said a clearly conflicted voice.

"Would you like to meet me?" asked Shem in a friendly voice.

A minute went by. "I am alone. I am sad. I don't know what to do."

"Would you be willing to meet me outside the ship?"

"I am afraid you will kill me."

"We will not harm you in any way."

"I don't know what to do."

Sam got Vance's attention and handed him a note: "I know where he is."

Vance nodded he understood and then mouthed, "Turn on the viewer."

Sam nodded. Up on the *Marian*'s main viewer appeared a disheveled Arkell. He was pacing around the large central cafeteria on deck 8.

"Would you be more comfortable communicating over the viewers?" asked Shem.

"I don't know how to do that."

"You can use any viewer you are near. Just tell us where you are so we can activate that viewer." Shem wanted the Arkell to believe he was safe where he was. "You will be able to see me and see that I am telling you the truth."

The Arkell quickly looked around and spotted the viewer at the front of the room. He froze in place while staring at the blank screen of the viewer. After a minute, he began pacing. This was a disturbed individual.

"Do you wish to talk?" asked Shem.

The Arkell again stopped pacing and quickly looked around the cafeteria as if expecting a force to enter the room.

"What is your name?" asked Shem.

The Arkell turned his attention to the viewer for a moment before returning to his pacing.

Shem signaled Sam to cut off the communication.

Sam nodded and gave an okay sign.

"This is one terrified Arkell," said Shem. "And mentally unbalanced."

"Agreed," said Vance. "Where do we go from here?"

"Let's try putting my image on the viewer so he can see that I am Arkell."

"Can't hurt," said Vance.

"Sam, make it happen, please."

The viewer in the cafeteria now displayed Shem from the waist up.

"Look at the viewer," said Shem.

The Arkell quickly looked at the viewer. His troubled expression began to fade. The sight of Shem seemed to be having a calming effect.

"As you can see, I am Arkell. Do you want to stay where you are, or would you rather meet so we can talk in person?"

The Arkell stood, not taking his eyes off the viewer.

"I can now see that you are in the main cafeteria. We can meet there, or I would be happy to meet you at a place of your choosing."

The Arkell continued to stare at the viewer for many long seconds before answering. "Here . . . we can meet here."

"That's good," said Shem in pleasant voice. "But I need to know if you have a weapon with you?"

The Arkell paused for a moment before replying, "I do."

"I would ask you to either dismantle it or, if you wish, put it in the corridor outside the cafeteria. I will not be armed when we meet."

"How do I know that you will not be armed?"

"If we wished you harm, we would have already done so."

That seemed to make sense to this Arkell. "I will put my weapon out of this room." With that, he walked to the far side of the cafeteria and retrieved a long weapon that was lying on the deck. He then walked to the door, opened it cautiously, and threw the weapon out.

Everybody on the bridge of the *Marian* breathed a sigh of relief.

Vance gave an approving nod and smile to Shem.

"What is your name so we can talk as friends?" Shem asked again.

The Arkell looked at the viewer. "Ooat," he said, "Ooat is my name."

"Ooat, it will take me a few minutes to get to your location. I'm looking forward to meeting you."

"I'll wait for you here."

Ten minutes later, Shem walked into the *Vance*'s cafeteria.

Ooat's face quickly displayed considerable fear.

"I greet you, Ooat," said a smiling Shem as he slowly closed the distance between him and the Arkell.

Ooat's face began calming.

Shem continued to smile. "If you wish to perform Waoca on me, please do."

"Yes, I need to do that." Ooat extended his hands toward Shem's face and paused for a moment before making contact with Shem's temples.

His reaction came quickly. His face went from fear to confusion to calm within a few seconds. "You are not my enemy. You wish me no harm." Ooat removed his hands from Shem's temples. "This is not what we have been told. We have been lied to."

Shem smiled again. "May I?"

Ooat nodded. Shem placed his fingers on Ooat's temples but quickly removed them. "Whoa!"

"Why did you do that?" asked Ooat, visibly alarmed.

"Your mind is in turmoil. We need to get your mind stabilized before I can perform Waoca. In its present condition, Waoca might do harm to my mind."

Ooat's facial expression changed to one of confusion.

"Would you be willing to take a medicine that will calm your thoughts?"

Ooat continued to look into Shem's eyes for a few seconds. Then he nodded. "I will do that . . . yes, I will."

"Good, I'll have the medicine brought here. It will take a few minutes."

They spent the next ten minutes in small talk before Dale appeared at the door of the cafeteria holding a vial containing a few small white pills.

Shem walked over and took the pills. "Thanks, Dale."

Dale nodded and left without a word.

Two minutes after taking the tranquilizer, Ooat looked to be somewhat calmer.

"Let me try Waoca again," said Shem.

Ooat nodded.

Shem again placed his fingers on Ooat's temples and again removed them in seconds. "Still a lot of erratic and negative thoughts going on. You need to take another pill."

Ooat quickly agreed.

A few minutes later, Shem put his fingers on Ooat's temples. This time, they remained in place. Shem's face was going through a myriad of expressions as he experienced Ooat's memories and thoughts. After a full minute, Shem removed his fingers from Ooat's temples.

"You have had a horrible life, Ooat, truly horrible."

"I don't understand?"

"I want you to perform Waoca on me again. Take the time to explore my life as best you can. I will try to open my mind to you as much as possible."

Three minutes later, Ooat removed his fingers from Shem's temples. His eyes filled with tears as he sat down on the nearest chair and cried. Shem walked behind him and gently placed his hands on Ooat's shoulders. "You are going to be alright from now on, Ooat. Your life is going to change."

Ooat began to calm down. He looked up at Shem and smiled. "Thank you, Shem. I have feelings. I have peace that I've never had before. Now I can sleep. I need sleep."

"Okay, that's what we'll do first. Get you some sleep. Follow me."

Shem took Ooat to one of the crew apartments of the *Vance*. "You can sleep here uninterrupted for as long as you wish. Just push the button on the intercom when you wake and we'll get you something to eat and begin settling you into a new and wonderful lifestyle."

Ooat had tears in his eyes. "Thank you, Shem. I thank you more than I can say."

Ten minutes later, Shem walked onto the bridge of the *Marian*.

"That was well done," said Vance.

"It was," said Dale.

"You may have just moved a man of misery to one whose life from now on might be something he's not even been capable of imagining," said Alex.

"I couldn't have imagined how horrible a life could be," said Shem. "All I can feel is sadness for all the Arkell of the *Geaalo* who have had the same life as Ooat. It's truly tragic."

"We all here saw what happened with the Waoca," said Vance. "Do you think I should perform Waoca with Ooat?"

"Not for a while. It might cause you harm. Let's let his mind heal for a month or so."

Vance nodded. "Okay."

"But I believe Ooat should do so with Jarleth."

"Why?" asked Vance.

"Ooat received a lot of positive input from me, but until he sees and connects with Jarleth, he will not know what true empathy, compassion, and love really are. She will, in my opinion, add an emotional element I could not impart."

"I yield to your greater knowledge of these things," said Vance.

There was silence on the bridge for a moment.

"So what can you tell us about the Arkell's intentions?" ask Troy.

"Unfortunately, we had it just about right. The *Geaalo* did invade Isley, but did not maim or kill anybody because there was no resistance from the humans. They didn't damage the planet.

There was nothing there they needed. They just wanted the *Vance* for exactly the reason we surmised. They took Henry along because they needed someone who was completely versed on the operation of the ship."

Everybody nodded in understanding.

"The Arkell's plan was to switch two men in and out of cryo sleep once a month to relieve the sentries whose jobs was to oversee the care of those in stasis and keep an eye on Henry. This went well for the first nine years, ship time, until it was Ooat's and the other Arkell's time to be the sentinels. That's apparently when Henry sabotaged the cryo decks by shutting down the refrigeration and turning up the heat. The two Arkell didn't discover the damage until it was too late. All their shipmates were dead."

"I'll bet that was when they started looking for Henry to get some payback," said Troy.

"Without question," said Vance.

"The other Arkell, the one you dispatched, his name was Ttot," said Shem.

"Henry must have known he would be in danger if the Arkell discovered his sabotage," said Troy. "I suspect he kept close tabs on the sentinels. When the time was right, he pulled the plug on the cryo capsules. I assume he knew the exact moment when they made the discovery and that's when he began sending us a message that, had it not been cut short, would have filled us in about the *Vance*'s commandeering and the Arkell's intent."

"That narrative fits well," said Gary.

"Henry had to know his life would be over when his actions were discovered. He must have preprogrammed the *Vance* to approach and land on Gabriel, something he wouldn't have done had he not known five hundred of the invading force were no longer a threat and the two remaining wouldn't be able to carry out their plan," said Vance.

"You have it right," said Shem. "When they discovered what Henry had done, Ttot went crazy. It was he who destroyed Henry, not Ooat."

"Henry saved us," said Alex. "He is a true hero."

"He is in fact a hero," said Troy. "Let's make every effort to save him."

"I'll send a team over to retrieve Henry," said Gary. "I'll have them take him directly to our SLF lab. Hopefully the technicians will be able to connect his brain to their computers and retrieve the knowledge it may contain, and if that works, we'll rebuild his body."

"It should be noted," said Shem, "that Ooat was terrified of Ttot and successfully hid from him for the past year. All his friends were dead and Henry was destroyed. He couldn't sleep. All that wreaked havoc with his mind."

Vance nodded in understanding. "He didn't have company as I did with you two," said Vance as he looked from Alex to Dale. "Without you two for company, my mental state certainly would have suffered."

Troy nodded in understanding. "Where is the *Geaalo* now?"

"Ooat doesn't know other than it would be fairly close to Gabriel," said Shem. "His instructions were to send a signal upon landing. And when the planet's shield was turned off, he was to send another signal."

"Hmm," muttered Vance.

"What are you thinking?" asked Alex.

"I wonder if the Arkell know their elaborate plan has been upset?"

"If they do, they'll be long gone. If not, they'll be waiting for the signals," offered Alex.

"We haven't heard back from the *Velgot*'s Arkell," said Vance. "If they were close, we could coordinate an ambush. But since we haven't heard from them, I'm assuming they are light-years away."

CHAPTER 3

THE CAVALRY HAS ARRIVED

"To the commander of the *Geaalo*," said Oruku, "we wish to communicate with you."

Oruku was standing in the control center of the massive galaxy ship *Velgot*. Alongside of Oruku stood Kilee, the chief sentinel of the *Velgot*.

Several minutes went by before a voice came back over the communication system. "This is Accin, captain of the *Geaalo*. What do you want, Oruku?"

Oruku didn't hesitate. "We want to know your intentions. You have been told not to enter this section of the galaxy under the threat of destruction. Yet here you are again hiding behind the star of the planet Gabriel, the planet of our friends the humans."

Another minute passed before Accin answered. "What gives you the right to question our intent? We are on a peaceful mission."

"You are a liar, Accin," Oruku said evenly.

"It is a great insult to be called a liar."

"It is not an insult if it is the truth. You would have to have a greater respect for yourself and others before you could possibly be insulted by anything said about you."

"Are you trying to provoke us into a confrontation?"

"Here's what is going to happen." Oruku remained calm. "You are going to stay exactly where you are. Using one of your smaller transports, you are going to deliver to us fifty of your finest men. We will take them into temporary custody. We will return them to you at a later date."

"Why would we comply with such an outrageous request?"

"First, it is not a request—it is a demand. And second, we will damage your ship to a point of total failure if you do not comply."

"That is where you are mistaken, Oruku," said Accin icily. "We have made many improvements to our shield and offensive abilities. It is you who are in peril here."

Oruku turned to Kilee. "Are you ready?"

Kilee gave a quick nod.

"Do it, please."

The *Velgot* went into attack posture. Then, within four seconds, it moved in space so fast that it looked like there were a half dozen *Velgot*'s surrounding the *Geaalo*, all firing some sort of plasma burst at the *Geaalo* at the same instant.

Oruku said nothing for a full minute and then hailed the *Geaalo*. "We assumed you would make improvements to your armament and defenses. So we upgraded ours. You are now defenseless, and your weapons have been destroyed."

There was no answer from the *Geaalo*.

"We will give you thirty minutes to deliver the fifty men. After thirty minutes, the *Geaalo* will be destroyed."

"Can you give us a little more time?" came the obviously defeated voice of Accin.

"Fifteen minutes. Take care. If we detect any arms or destructive devises on the shuttle, we will destroy it and you."

"Oruku of the *Velgot*, this is Ridiid, captain of the Yassi ship *Egro*."

"Greetings, Ridiid," said Oruku. "We detected your ship heading this way four days ago."

"Yes, we were aware of the scan and scanned back," said Ridiid. "We also became aware of the other Arkell ship in your proximity. And we are aware of that ship's malicious history." Ridiid paused for a moment. "We will arrive at your location in two days and offer any assistance we can to subdue or destroy those evil beings."

"Ridiid, we thank you," said a smiling Oruku. "Be assured, we have the situation under control.

There was a brief pause before Ridiid answered. "I can't tell you how good that is to hear. We've been very concerned. We have pushed our ship to its limit to get there as fast as possible after hearing the message from the *Vance*. We'll slow down at bit."

"Yes, do that," said Oruku. "There will be no danger from the *Geaalo*."

"That is a relief for us. We were not sure our armaments would be effective against them. Don't know what we could have done to detour them from harming either the humans or Gabriel. Until four days ago, we were not aware of your presence in this sector of the galaxy."

"We are pleased you will be here," said Oruku. "We assume you are here on your periodic visit and trade with our friends on Gabriel."

"Yes, that and more," answered Ridiid.

"We are looking forward to getting together with our friends the Yassi and humans," said Oruku. "Let us complete our mission here, and then we'll join you at Home Bay."

"Until then," said Ridiid.

"Vance, are you around?" Troy's voice came over Vance's communicator.

A few seconds later, Vance's voice came back. "What's up?"

"Got a communiqué from the *Velgot*," said Troy. "They wish the leaders of Gabriel to gather on the *Marian's* bridge ASAP."

Vance jumped up from his couch. "Any hint as to what this is about?"

"Nope, just told that they have important information for us."

"Their wish will always be my command," said Vance seriously.

Twenty minutes later, Vance joined Alex, Dale, Shem, Gary, and Troy on the bridge of the *Marian*. All held expressions of curiosity along with an abundance of concern.

In a few minutes, the main viewing screen on the *Marian* lit up with the image of Oruku. It had been a number of years since humans had seen or heard from their friends, the Arkell of the *Velgot*.

"You are all looking well," said Oruku. "Other than Shem, you haven't aged a bit."

Oruku knew that the other five men on the bridge of the *Marian* were SLFs and did not age.

"And by God," said Vance with a smile, "you're looking fit for a man who is over two hundred years old."

"Two hundred sixty-one, to be exact. And I'm feeling in the pink, to use an old Earth expression."

"I haven't heard that one since I was a kid," said Vance.

"To what do we owe the pleasure of your visit?" asked Alex.

"We have captured the *Geaalo*," said Oruku matter-of-factly.

"Captured?" said Vance, obviously surprised.

Oruku smiled. "We have them held stationary in space under threat of annihilation. That is something we do not wish to do. We have something else in mind."

"Which is?"

"Change their thought process, their mindset," said Oruku. "We believe if Shem and Jarleth perform Waoca with the Arkell of the *Geaalo*, it will have the same effect as it had on Ooat."

"You know about that?"

"We monitor all your communications."

Vance smiled. "Guess you've been doing that for thousands of years."

Oruku smiled. "Yes we have and, with your permission, we will continue to do so."

"Permission granted," said Vance without hesitation.

"We didn't realize you were close enough to come to our aid once again," said Dale.

Oruku smiled. "We received the original message sent from Henry Hendrick of the *Vance* and, like you, suspected something was up. So we headed your way." Oruku paused briefly. "We thought it best not to inform you under the circumstances. Those of the *Geaalo* might pick up our communiqué and alter their plans accordingly. We were puzzled as to why we didn't receive a message from Isley. But a quick check revealed that our relay satellites were not functioning. We assume they were destroyed by the Arkell of the *Geaalo* on their way to Isley."

"That fits the scenario all right," said Vance.

Shem nodded in agreement. "Do you think Waoca will work on all Arkell aboard the *Geaalo* as well as it did Ooat?" asked Shem.

"No reason it wouldn't, and frankly, we are embarrassed that we did not think to try this the last time we came into contact with them."

"If memory serves, you had other things on your mind at the time," said Vance.

"That is kind of you, my friend."

"Not at all."

Oruku nodded once. "The Waoca could not have been put to a better use, Shem. We are extremely pleased with the results."

"I, too, believe all those on the *Geaalo* will have their attitude changed through the Waoca process," said Shem.

"There may be a few exceptions. Their leader, an Arkell named Accin, is an evil person. He, and some like him, may be hardened against the influence of Waoca."

"So maybe not on their leaders," said Vance, "but hopefully with the majority of the ship's complement."

"That's our thinking," said Oruku.

"How do you want to proceed?"

"We would like you, Shem, along with Jarleth and Ooat, to join us aboard the *Velgot*. We have fifty of the *Geaalo*'s crew already on board." Oruku smiled. "They are not happy."

"How did you manage to get fifty on the *Velgot*?" asked Vance.

Oruku smiled. "We threatened them."

"All things considered, that would do it," said Troy.

Shem came into the conversation. "Wouldn't it have the same effect if the *Velgot*'s Arkell performed Waoca on them?"

"We tried that with a few when they came aboard. They have shown some positive improvements but not the complete turnaround that you achieved with Ooat. We think that your being born and raised in a human environment and being ninety percent human made your Waoca somewhat different than ours. Yours is more effective for this scenario."

"That's interesting," said Shem. "Ooat certainly is, at this point, one happy Arkell."

"Exactly. He, we believe, along with you and Jarleth, will have a dramatic effect on balance of the misguided Arkell."

"We'll take the Yassi shuttle up and join you," said Vance. "By the way, where are you?"

"Far side of your sun. And, as you probably know, our friends the Yassi are on their way to Gabriel."

"That we're aware of," said Alex, "They should arrive in about a week."

"Correction, they will be here in two days," said Oruku.

"You've been in contact with them?" asked Vance.

"They contacted us a short time ago. Like you and us, they were concerned with the communiqué from the *Vance*. They have been pushing their ship to the max in order to get here sooner. They didn't know we were here."

Nobody said anything for a moment.

"They were aware of the *Geaalo* being in the area. They were going to engage it."

"They were going to take on the *Geaalo* by themselves?" asked Troy.

"It seems they were," said Oruku.

"We . . . we are blessed by our dear friends," said Alex. "To risk one's life for another is . . ." Alex was choked up with emotion.

Oruku nodded in understanding. "In all likelihood, they would have been destroyed in the effort."

"They will be getting a hero's welcome when they arrive," said Vance.

Three hours later, the beautiful Yassi shuttle, a gift to the humans from the Vout and Yassi, gently settled on the flight deck of the *Velgot* and six people exited. There were Jarleth, Shem, and Ooat. Joining them were Vance, Alex, and Dale.

Ooat's head was on a swivel. The look of wonder as he took in the immaculate interior of this deck was almost funny.

Oruku was all smiles as he greeted and hugged all except Ooat. When he came to Ooat, he stopped. "My name is Oruku," he said to Ooat. "May I perform Waoca on you?"

Ooat was noticeably having trouble making eye contact with Oruku. He nodded his head without looking at Oruku.

Oruku gently placed his fingers on Ooat's temples. A full minute later, he removed his fingers and stepped back. "You have had an unfortunate life, Ooat. But undoubtedly you have rejected the past for a wonderful future."

Ooat nodded as he looked into Oruku's eyes. "May I?"

"Yes, we Arkell of the *Velgot* have nothing to hide from anyone."

With that, Ooat stepped forward and placed his fingers on Oruku's temples. He maintained Waoca for two minutes, a very long time.

When he removed his fingers, he had tears in his eyes. Oruku stepped forward and gave him a hug.

"Thank you, Oruku. I cry for the thousands of years we have shown no compassion, nor empathy, for all other beings, including ourselves."

Oruku nodded in understanding.

"I am anxious to relay my feelings to the Arkell of the *Geaalo*," said Ooat. "When can we start?"

"Soon," answered Oruku. "But we must be cautious. You will let your shipmates perform Waoca on you, but you must not do so with them."

"I fully understand," said Ooat. "We could be reinfected, for lack of a better description."

"Exactly," said Oruku.

"Might I suggest," said Ooat, "that Shem start the process followed by Jarleth and lastly by me?"

"That is our thought too," said Oruku.

Shem and Jarleth quickly agreed.

Oruku turned to the three SLFs, his dear friends. "Dale, if I'm not mistaken, you would like to spend your time on this ship with our scientists."

"Yes, I would . . . as is always the case."

"They are looking forward to seeing you too." Oruku smiled. "As is always the case."

Thirty minutes later, Shem was seated in a small but nicely appointed room. The first Arkell was led into the room, and Shem stood to greet him. "My name is Shem," he said with a small smile.

This Arkell was young and clearly hostile. Judging from his uniform, he held a high rank among the Arkell of the *Geaalo*. He evidently had chosen not to cooperate with anything. He did not return Shem's greeting. He just stood defiantly.

"I am not your enemy, but I am hoping to become your friend."

A small twitch from the Arkell's eyebrow told Shem his words had some effect on this young man.

"I wish you to perform Waoca with me."

The Arkell's head cocked a little. He obviously didn't expect this. "Why?" he asked.

"Because I want you to know that all I tell you and all you will hear from us will be the truth."

The Arkell was seemingly confused, but after a moment, he stepped forward and, without a word, placed his fingers on Shem's temples. His reaction was similar to that of Ooat's. His defiant facial expression morphed to one of surprise and then one of calm. He removed his fingers from Shem's temples and stepped back a pace.

"You are not fully Arkell."

"No, I am about ten percent Arkell and ninety percent human."

The Arkell nodded. "Human minds are different." He paused for a moment. "Don't know, just a different feel."

"Yes, we process thoughts using slightly different paths in most circumstances."

"I don't know what is happening to my mind. My thoughts seem to be slowing down," said the confused Arkell.

Shem smiled. "Your mind isn't slowing down. It's calming down."

"Calming? Yes, that may be right."

"It is our intention to perform Waoca with all the Arkell of the *Geaalo*, starting with the fifty we presently have aboard the *Velgot*.

"Good . . . good."

"You've been made to believe the life of the Arkell is one of mistrust and disrespect of all other species in favor of enriching the population of the *Geaalo*. You have not been exposed to any sort of affection, love, kindness, or respect of others. You have just experienced some of that through me."

The young Arkell started to tear up, something completely out of character for him.

"My name is Ssamp."

"Thank you, Ssamp."

Ssamp nodded with a small smile.

Shem returned the smile. "We now want you to perform Waoca with another. She is in the next room and is my wife. Her name is Jarleth."

"I'll do that," said Ssamp without hesitation.

Shem led him into the next room. As they entered the room, Jarleth stood to greet them. She was dressed in a dark-blue, loose-fitting jumpsuit. Her platinum hair was pulled back in a simple ponytail. But even in plain clothes and a conservative hairstyle, she was still a stunner at age eighty-four. Her Arkell genes, even more than Shem's, kept her looking less than half her actual age. She looked to be in her midthirties.

Ssamp stopped dead in his tracks. The look of wonder was almost comical. Clearly, he had never seen a woman who looked like this. He looked her up and down. "This is . . . your wife?"

Shem smiled. "I am pleased to say it is." He turned his attention to Jarleth. "Jarleth, I would like to introduce you to Ssamp. Ssamp, please meet Jarleth."

Jarleth stepped forward with a big, beautiful smile. "Pleased to meet you, Ssamp." She extended her right hand.

Ssamp had no idea what she wished him to do. His confusion was apparent. He looked from Shem to Jarleth and back to her outstretched hand.

"We have a custom of greeting friends with what is called a handshake," said Shem. He reached over and took Jarleth's hand and gave it a gentle shake. "Like that."

Ssamp nodded and extended his hand. Jarleth took it and gently shook it.

"I have never seen a female like you," said Ssamp.

Shem smiled. "Few have. Jarleth is among the most beautiful women in the galaxy, in my opinion. But most of the women on our world are beautiful."

"I would like it if you would perform Waoca with me," said Jarleth.

"Me?" Ssamp was visibly awestruck. It was all Shem could do to stifle a laugh.

Ssamp stepped forward and slowly placed his fingers on Jarleth's temples. His expression of confusion became one of calm, followed by a look of bliss. He slowly removed his fingers from Jarleth's temples. "I don't know what's happening here," he said quietly. "This is . . . wonderful but . . . very confusing."

"You are beginning to grasp what the rest of the galaxy feels in their minds and hearts," said Jarleth. "Hate and evil have no lasting place in the universe. They are both destructive."

"I'm starting to understand," said Ssamp before pausing for a full minute. "We have been lied to throughout our history. Little we have come to accept as the way of the galaxy is true."

"It is our mission to show all the Arkell aboard the *Geaalo* the truth they have been denied for most of their history."

Ssamp stood straight up with his shoulders back. "How can I help in that endeavor?"

Shem and Jarleth both smiled brightly.

"You will meet a fellow Arkell from the *Geaalo,* who is in the next room, he has joined us as you have. His name is Ooat."

"I know the name Ooat. He was one of the chosen to infiltrate your planet and turn off your shield. He is one of the leaders of our troops."

"That is correct."

"They failed . . . fortunately," said Jarleth.

"Good," said Ssamp.

"Let's go meet Ooat," said Shem.

When they entered the room where Ooat had been waiting, Ooat stood and walked rapidly to embrace Ssamp. This took Ssamp a moment or two to accept. It may have been the first time in his adult life he had been hugged. When Ooat released Ssamp, he stepped back and extended his hand. Ssamp's brow furrowed for a brief moment before he smiled in understanding, took Ooat's hand, and shook it. Then Ssamp performed Waoca with Ooat.

CHAPTER 4

CONVERTS SAVE TWO

One at a time, the fifty Arkell went through this procedure. Just two refused to perform Waoca and were escorted to another room where they would wait until it was time to return to the *Geaalo*.

After the forty-eight Arkell had successfully gone through the Waoca process, they, along with Ooat, were returned to the *Geaalo* with the instructions to perform Waoca with as many of the *Geaalo*'s population as possible. Then these Arkell would perform Waoca with others, etcetera.

Oruku had contacted Accin and told him that under no circumstances were these fifty Arkell to be hindered or intimidated in any way. Any interference would cause the instant demise of those interfering.

The new converts continued the Waoca process until all had been converted. Because of the chain-reaction effect, it would take less than four hours before all one hundred and fifty thousand-plus Arkell, both male and female, to be successfully converted.

Shortly thereafter, Ooat was returned to the *Velgot* and reported to Oruku what had happened.

"After the conversion, we took control of all decks except the main control bridge. I, along with Ssamp and twenty others, armed myself before trying to convince Accin and his lieutenants of the wonderful benefits of conversion. They refused to perform Waoca, and they refused to yield the control bridge to us. We managed to force open the hatch and took them into custody. They were not armed."

"Where are they now?" asked Oruku.

"We placed them, along with the over five hundred Volen, in a secure holding deck near the bottom of the ship. It was and is an agricultural deck that has been modified to be self-supporting. It has everything they will need to survive indefinitely there."

"You will want to be careful. They will do whatever they can to retake your ship."

"Without a doubt. We have told them that they can rejoin the *Geaalo*'s population anytime they wish. All they have to do is perform Waoca."

"Good. I'll assume that within a very short period of time, most will join you."

"We think so too. I wouldn't want to be locked up with those five hundred ill-tempered and stupid beings."

Oruku nodded in understanding. "What we know of the Volen is to stay clear of them."

The Volen were a tall race at over two meters. They had exceptionally long arms and legs but very short torsos. Their heads were small on top of long necks. Their eyes were wide-set, more like prey than predator. Their teeth were short but sharp, much like sharks. They were basically carnivores but had adapted to eating some vegetables, and they were particularly fond of a grain similar to corn.

"We've always been able to control them, but that was when we had no aversion to inflicting pain. Pain is about the only thing Volen respect. But in a fight, they are very effective and created a lot of terror because of their appearance and their viciousness. I can't imagine deploying them now." Ooat paused for a second. "It is to our shame we ever did. How do we atone for that?"

"Do whatever you can to assist those you have damaged."

"So many over so many centuries," said Ooat with sadness.

"What is your plan now?" Oruku asked, changing the subject.

Ooat paused for a moment before displaying a small smile. "We are going to go home."

Oruku's eyebrows lifted before he nodded in understanding. "You know that's a thousand-year trip."

"We do. None of us will be alive by the time the *Geaalo* arrives at Arkell, but our prodigy will. When they arrive, it is our hope that they will be as enlightened and sophisticated as the Arkell of the *Velgot*."

Oruku smiled. "We will provide you with copious amounts of intelligence on our history, culture, experiences, and technology. The study of all that may take a few centuries."

Ooat smiled. "We will have the time."

"Indeed you will." Oruku smiled. "What are you going to do with the Volen?"

"Their home planets are not far off the path to Arkell. We'll drop those still alive back on their planet. We decided not to allow any more breeding among them. The Volen's intellectual level is about on par with the old Malic."

"I wouldn't recommend getting between a Volen and the object of his desires," recommended Oruku with a slight smile.

Ooat laughed. "We talked about that. We decided to put a contraceptive in their water supply. They can fool around all they want without creating more offspring."

"They will be a challenge," said Oruku. "Be careful."

It took three full days to affect repairs on the *Geaalo* with the help of dozens of the *Velgot*'s engineers and craftsmen. These Arkell were instructed not to perform Waoca with the crew of the *Geaalo*. Despite their recent conversion to one of peace and respect, the Arkell of the *Geaalo* were not to have certain technologies.

"I was hoping Ooat would choose to stay with us," said Vance.

"He considered it," said Oruku. "It was a happy coincidence that Ooat deep down was a warm and caring person and, apparently, a respected leader. Quite intelligent, I might add. He will make a fine contribution to whatever civilization he is part of. He just happened to be born into a rogue culture. He wants to help guide the Arkell of the *Geaalo* to a wonderful future."

"I've no doubt he will do just that," said Shem.

CHAPTER 5

A HERO'S WELCOME

Another example of the Yassi's penchant for beauty dropped out of the bottom hatch of the magnificent mother ship. This was a wonderful new design of the now-famous Yassi shuttles. The shuttle, as was a tradition, would land on the same spot that all visiting ships landed.

It was the custom of the Gabrielites to have a large welcoming party at the site. Visitors from other planets arrived every two to five years; they were not an everyday occurrence. Today, the welcoming party was a great deal larger than normal. Once the Gabrielites heard what the Yassi were willing to do to save Gabriel from the *Geaalo*, the normal crowd had at least tripled. Leaders representing every town and hamlet around the planet were there on this special day.

Once the stunning shuttle settled on the landing site, the people moved in and began wooing. Wooing was introduced by the Yassi on their first visit to Gabriel. It was their way of showing pleasure and agreement rather than clapping, as was the humans' expression. Now the population of five planets used both.

The wooing and clapping continued as the hatch opened and the ramp extended.

Down the ramp came the little Yassi—six in all. All were dressed the same in light-green shirts tucked into dark-green blousy pants and wide belts. All bore big good-natured smiles.

"Welcome to our friends the Yassi," said Vance as he Alex, Dale, Troy, Gary, and Shem approached the six.

The large crowd clapped, whistled, and wooed at length.

The Yassi's smiles got bigger as they stepped forward and extended their hands to the six Gabrielites.

"My name is Ridiid of the *Egro*," he said as Vance took his offered hand and shook it firmly. Then Alex did the same.

"The *Egro*?" said Vance.

Ridiid's smile broadened. "You recognize the name?"

"With great fondness. We had the pleasure of his company in our year 52, over a hundred and fifty years ago," answered Vance. "Our first encounter with the wonderful Yassi."

"We have historical records of that meeting," said Ridiid. "That voyage and the meeting of the humans is part of our history, a story that is often told and a story that is taught in our children's schools." Ridiid paused for a moment. "The magnificent gift you gave to the Yassi, at that time, is still a popular centerpiece and attraction in our main museum."

In Vance's mind, he could still see the incredible sculpture of a charging elephant, created by a gifted twelve-year-old girl and then cast in solid gold.

"Egro and his shipmates are not only a delightful part of our history but a delightful part of my personal memories," said Vance with a warm smile.

"Egro is an honored historical figure because of his many contributions to our home planet. The meeting with humans paving the way to our long-standing relationship is certainly among them."

Vance nodded in agreement. "He was a great ambassador for the Yassi."

"Naming our newest and largest ship in honor of Egro was, in all ways, a perfect choice."

"A great honor for a deserving man," said Vance.

Within a few minutes, the six Yassi had met the six Gabrielites.

The crowd were enjoying being witness to this historic event.

"We have heard about and watched many videos of this beautiful planet for centuries. The videos do not do it justice," said Cadsir, Ridiid's second-in-command.

"Thank you. This man"—Alex nodded at Vance—"is responsible for just about every living thing on Gabriel."

"I simply followed the directions given by people a great deal smarter than me," said Vance.

"We have heard the stories, sir," said Cadsir. "Fifty years, by yourself, planting the seeds on a nearly barren planet that has become, due to your efforts, among the most beautiful worlds in the galaxy."

"Thank you for the compliment, but I was not alone," said Vance. "I had these two men with me the entire time." Vance gestured toward Alex and Dale.

Ridiid turned to Alex. "What a great pleasure," said Ridiid. "You and your extensive and remarkable history is well known on our planet."

"I am humbled, Ridiid," said Alex. "When the Yassi have been here in the past, I did not exist in a body. Now, I'm sure you know, I am a SLF."

"We do. You have the wondrous technology to create what you call SLFs and have used it wisely to reproduce your finest leaders."

"Thank you," said Alex.

"You are as close to being biological as can be," said Ridiid. "We have created and used sophisticated automatons for hundreds of years, but they are completely mechanical."

Alex turned toward Dale. "For that incredible technology, we have to thank this man, Dale Isley. Actually, we credit Dale for even being here on this planet."

"One of the great minds of our Galaxy," said Ridiid as he bowed slightly toward Dale.

"I had a lot of help," said Dale. "Many fine minds contributed to our successes."

"You are truly a humble man," said Ridiid.

"Speaking of fine minds," said Dale, taking the subject away from himself, "this man possesses one of the best." Dale took Shem by the arm and turned him toward Ridiid.

"You are Shem?" asked Ridiid.

"I am."

"We are delighted to meet you, Shem. We have seen pictures and videos of you from our past voyages to Gabriel." Ridiid cocked his head a little. "You must be at least eighty of Gabriel's years, yet you don't look half that age."

"Arkell genes." Shem smiled. "Although I'm only about ten percent Arkell, part of that ten percent contains the genetics for long life."

"So you may live to be over three hundred years?"

"It's possible, I suppose."

When the introductions of all dignitaries from both races were complete, Ridiid turned to Vance. "We have Byuse on our ship."

Vance's eyebrow went up. "Are you heading to Byuse?"

"We are. We have thirty Byuse aboard in cryo sleep. We are taking them home."

"Have you determined why the Malic want the Byuse back?" asked Shem. "You believe the Malic's intention is honorable?"

Unexpectedly, after three centuries, the Malic had sent word that they wanted to invite the Byuse back to their planet. That invitation caused a great deal of speculation throughout the galaxy. Why would the Malic wish to have a race who possessed a far-superior intellect back on their planet?

"We do," said Ridiid. "We've had a great number of communiqués over the past few years. We are convinced the Malic want the Byuse back. They admit they do not have the mental capacity to advance their technology for the betterment of their population."

"I find this incredible," said Shem.

The Byuse were a passive race much like the Vout. Because of their historical aversion to violence and aggression, they had been driven off their planet by a far-inferior race, the Malic. The Vout, being kind and compassionate, had accepted millions of Byuse as migrants to their planet. And eventually the Byuse had also, with the approval of the Yassi, migrated and set up colonies on Yassi.

Gabriel also had a colony of Byuse, thus putting them on three different planets in the galaxy. There was also a Yassi colony on Vout and Gabriel—and human colonies on Vout and Yassi, all done to assure the continuation of a race, should anything catastrophic occur on any of their home planets.

It was known that the original Malic had their genes altered by the Arkell, not only making them look different but apparently causing them to change their hostile attitude.

CHAPTER 6

A LITTLE PARTY

Four days after the Arkell had taken control of the *Geaalo*, Oruku invited the leaders of Gabriel and their wives plus Teddy and Colleen to join him, along with a few select Arkell from the *Geaalo*, to a small social gathering aboard the *Velgot*. Also invited were Ridiid of the *Egro*, along with his command staff and their wives. Oruku had included in the invitation the wives of the contingent from the *Geaalo* to join the party but had been informed, by Ooat, that they would not be able to attend. Oruku understood why but said nothing.

On the evening of the festivities, an Arkell shuttle from the *Velgot* dropped down to Home Bay to pick up the invitees. It landed just where the first Arkell shuttle had—with Oruku at the helm—landed sixty-three years in the past. The spot was now a small, meticulously kept, historical park. In the center of the park was a circular concrete slab the exact diameter of the first Arkell shuttle. A bronze plaque had been embedded in the center of this slab, describing the history of the *Velgot*'s first visit. Historically, this park was used for all subsequent visits by the Arkell and as a landing site for all races visiting from another planet.

Now another Arkell shuttle sat on this site. After its hatch opened and the ramp was extended, the waiting Gabrielites, dressed in their finery, walked up the ramp into the interior of the shuttle.

When the fourteen Gabrielites were aboard, the shuttle's ramp retracted and the hatch silently closed. Then, without warning, the shuttle shot up to the *Velgot* and landed on the flight deck, the hatch opened, and the ramp extended, all in less than five seconds.

"Holy shit!" said Vance.

"I didn't feel a thing," added Alex.

"We're here already?" said a shocked Lara. "That was just a few seconds."

"I was just about to ask where we were going to sit when the hatch opened," said Aidan. "Wow!"

Shem was smiling brightly. "Good one."

"Well, I timed that trip at five point two seconds," said Teddy seriously. "Not bad, but I'll bet they can do better."

"Timed? You liar," said a smiling Colleen as she smacked Teddy on the arm.

"Ouch," said Teddy with a big toothy smile.

Vance just shook his head and smiled. "Ladies . . ." Vance gestured toward the open hatch. "After you."

Lara led the other six women down the short ramp. Vance, followed by the men, joined the ladies on the flight deck.

There to greet them was Oruku, smiling brightly. "Couldn't wait to see you."

"Nicely done," said Shem.

"Thank you. We thought you might enjoy a quick trip."

"Five point two seconds by my count," said Teddy as he leaned away from Colleen to avoid being smacked again.

"That was your count, was it?" said Oruku with a smile. "Actually, it was just under five seconds. We had to allow time to slow down. Didn't want to run into the *Velgot*. Would have made a mess."

"That was certainly my concern on our way up." Teddy continued the false scenario.

Everybody laughed except the four Arkell of the *Geaalo*. They had little concept of humor.

Their stoic demeanor wasn't lost on Teddy. He had a challenge ahead of him.

Standing beside Oruku were Nola and Janos, the ancestors of Shem and Jarleth. These were the same three who greeted the humans on their initial contact so many years ago. Also on the flight deck were Ooat, Ssamp, and two other Arkell of the *Geaalo*, Rree and Ppinn, who were, as yet, unknown to the Gabrielites.

Vance nearly laughed out loud when he saw the Arkell staring at the beautiful ladies of Gabriel. *They haven't seen such beauty in their lifetimes*, he realized. Vance had seen videos of the women of the

Geaalo. It wasn't that they were ugly, but they weren't very feminine. Although they could easily be differentiated from the men, the difference was sometimes subtle. They had not been chosen as mates for their beauty or brains but for their strength and ability to fight alongside their men. That was not the case with the human women, nor the women of the *Velgot,* who were favored for intellect, charm, and beauty. They were very feminine.

When Ooat and Ssamp first met Jarleth, she had purposely dressed down to lessen the impact of her beauty. That wasn't the case tonight. Her form-fitting electric-blue jumpsuit, made of cloth supplied by the Yassi, set off her extraordinary blue eyes and perfect figure. Her platinum blonde hair framed her face and flowed across her shoulders and down her back. It would be difficult for anyone to take their eyes off such beauty, but to have never seen it before would make it all but impossible.

It did help that these awestruck Arkell had six other human women to meet. All seven ladies would be considered very attractive to extremely beautiful by any standards. Aside from ogling Jarleth, they seemed to lock onto Colleen and Aidan. The two were biological sisters, and they looked a great deal alike. And they were gorgeous. They both wore tailored jumpsuits of an emerald color. Colleen's was a shade darker, and Aidan's was a lower cut around the chest, exposing more cleavage. These two and Lara were redheads, a hair color these Arkell had never seen. Dale's wife, the diminutive Tomaco, wore a gold jumpsuit of an Asian design, including a mandarin collar. Her straight black hair was cut in a long shag, which framed her delicate oval face perfectly.

Troy's and Gary's wives also wore perfectly tailored jumpsuits. Gary's wife, Pat, had chosen a dove-gray color, which was an ideal complement for her dark skin and hair. Troy's wife, Clair, had chosen a suit of bright red. Each of the ladies was introduced and shook hands with the enchanted Ooat, Ssamp, Rree, and Ppinn.

"Ah," said Oruku. "Our friends the Yassi will be here in moments."

The large hatch on the flight deck reopened, and the magnificent Yassi shuttle silently flew in and hovered for a moment before settling softly on the deck as the hatch closed behind them.

In a few seconds, the shuttle's hatch opened and the ramp extended. A moment later, three Yassi couples walked down the ramp and proceeded toward the small gathering just twenty meters away.

Yassi women wouldn't be described as beautiful but, instead, very, very cute. Their faces were definitely feminine. Their large eyes differed from the males in shape and color. Their noses were straight and petite. Their lips were small and pouty. But it was their clothes that were remarkable.

They each had a different color combination. And the colors were spectacular. They wore billowy pants that were small at the waist and small at the ankles but ballooned toward the outside. The pants had broad vertical stripes in three different colors. One was red, green, and purple. Another was blue, orange, and yellow and the third blue, green, and black. The material seemed to be the same as Jarleth's electric blue. The colors seemed to glow. Their waist jackets were of one of the colors of the pants, the sleeves another. The collars of the jackets were the third color, and the collars fanned out and up behind their heads. These fans extended from their necks and arched to a few millimeters above their heads. The effect was dazzling.

The mouths of the human and Arkell women were agape.

"I feel like a slug," Colleen whispered to Aidan.

"Ditto."

Teddy looked over to the Arkell of the *Geaalo* just in time to catch their reaction to these amazing beings. They were clearly and comically stunned, much to Teddy's amusement. He had to stifle a laugh.

As the three Yassi couples reached the gathered group, Teddy said in a disappointed voice, "Geez, we were hoping you would wear something colorful."

Everybody, with the exception of the Arkell, exploded in laughter. The Yassi laughed the loudest.

"Teddy!" said Ridiid. "Is it really you?"

All Yassi were as familiar with Teddy's history as they were with Vance's or Alex's. His comic routines designed specifically for the Yassi were recorded on videos and were famous on their planet.

"It's me alright," said Teddy as he stepped forward and gave Ridiid a hug. Then, without so much as a "may I," he proceeded to hug the other five Yassi in turn. There were no objections, just lighthearted giggles.

When Teddy finished his hugging, Oruku proceeded to make all the introductions.

The Arkell of the *Geaalo* were completely out of their element. They had never been to a social gathering of any kind. They had meetings, but their meetings were anything but fun. They normally revolved around planning a raid on another moon or planet or how to best extract or steal contraband from another race. Fun and humor did not exist in their world. They had never been in a situation like this. To see all this diversity together with the obvious deep affection displayed for the other races was beyond their ability to comprehend.

Shem could see that these Arkell were actually, if not voluntarily, backing away from the group. They were suffering from sensory overload.

"Excuse me for a second," said Shem as he separated himself from the group and approached the four Arkell. "Follow me, if you will," he said quietly as he turned and headed away from the gathering. The four Arkell followed Shem to the far side of the deck without saying a word. When they were effectively out of earshot of the others, Shem stopped, turned, and addressed the four. "I would like you four to perform Waoca with me right now. I believe you will better understand what is going on here if you feel my emotions."

A moment later, Ooat stepped forward and placed his fingers on Shem's temples. Shem could see his confusion fade as he started to understand how Shem felt about these other races and this gathering. After a minute, he smiled and removed his fingers.

"I . . . I'm starting to understand. This is wonderful. We have never experienced anything like what is happening here." He held his smile as he motioned Ssamp to approach Shem.

When the four Arkell had finished the Waoca with Shem, it was apparent they were ready to join the party. They all had smiles on their faces.

When Oruku saw them return, he nodded at Shem before he gestured toward the two small transports. "Climb aboard and we'll head to the party room."

The evening was going well. Aidan, Colleen, Jarleth, and Lara made an effort to spend some time socializing with the *Geaalo*'s Arkell. With the exception of Jarleth, none of ladies at the gathering were Arkell, nor could they perform Waoca. After an hour or so, and a couple of cocktails, Rree and Ppinn, the two Arkell, who hadn't directly performed Waoca with Jarleth, got up the nerve to ask her permission to do so. She immediately and graciously agreed. With the other ladies looking on, the two young Arkell performed Waoca with Jarleth. The looks on their faces told anybody witnessing the process all they needed to know. They were completely smitten. They were actually speechless for a while. By the end of the night, there were four Arkell visibly infatuated with all seven Gabriel women.

While Alex, Vance, Teddy, and Troy were engaged in light banter with half a dozen Arkell of the *Velgot* and their lovely wives, a short distance away, Shem, Dale, and Gary, along with their wives, were talking to Oruku, Janos, and Nola.

"We have a favor to ask," said Gary.

Oruku nodded and smiled. "Let me guess. You need Isleium to repair Henry Hendrick."

"We do. He was severely damaged, as you are aware."

Oruku nodded. "As you were during the encounter with the Malic."

"Yes." Gary smiled. "And I thank you again for facilitating my extensive repairs."

"It was our pleasure to assist in your rebuilding. You are a tremendous asset for Gabriel."

Shem, Dale, and their wives quickly nodded in agreement.

"Well . . ." Gary was a humble man. He said no more.

Oruku understood and smiled. "We have taken it upon ourselves to produce what you require plus a great deal more. In addition, we have created four more SLF skeletons of various sizes. All this has been delivered to the *Marian*'s SLF lab as of an hour ago."

"How—I was going to ask how you knew what we wanted, but you probably knew what was required before we did," said Shem. "Thank you."

Gary smiled. "Thank you."

"You realize by providing four SLF skeletons we will engage in endless conversations trying to figure out who our new SLFs will be?" said Dale.

"All part of the fun," said Oruku as he turned to face all the other people in the room. "May I have your attention for a moment?"

All turned to look at Oruku.

"We believe it will take your SLF technicians no more than three days to reconstruct Henry Hendrick. So, before we leave your beautiful planet, we propose to load the *Vance,* along with Henry, aboard the *Velgot* and return them to the planet Isley."

There was an instant expression of astonishment coming from all the humans but an expression of confusion from the *Geaalo*'s Arkell.

"You can actually put a ship the size of the *Vance* aboard the *Velgot*?" asked a surprised Dale. "There is a hatch big enough to accommodate the *Vance*?"

"The hull of the *Velgot* is flexible, for lack of a better description. It is not a solid as such."

"Really?" said both Shem and Dale in unison.

Oruku nodded. "Tricky material."

"Tricky?" said Dale. "Can we get a little more info on that tricky part?"

Oruku smiled broadly. "I'll set you, and anyone else who's interested, up with someone who can explain it to you. It's certainly not me."

"Great," said Dale.

Gary's and Shem's hands both shot up. "Us too."

"Where are you going to put the *Vance*?" asked Troy.

"On an agricultural deck. Plenty of room in one of our grain fields. We'll just farm around it for a while."

"Farm around it, of course," said Teddy. "Just set it off to one side of the field . . . no problem . . . geez."

"This is wonderful," said Alex. "The planet Isley will be surprised and ecstatic to get Henry and their ship back. There can be little question they have greatly missed both."

"Why are you taking the time to do this?" asked Dale. "Why not just let Henry pilot the *Vance* back to Isley?"

"Because the trip under the *Vance*'s propulsion system would take a hundred years planet time. We'll get the *Vance* back to Isley ninety years sooner."

"Of course," said Dale. "Traveling at light speed, time doesn't change. Time on the ship and time on a planet remain synchronized."

Oruku nodded.

"I don't know what to say," said Vance. "The Arkell of the *Velgot* are truly humankind's guardian angels."

Ooat, Ssamp, Rree, and Ppinn, for the first time in their lives, were witnessing a truly selfless act, an act that did not benefit those perpetrating the act in any tangible way. The four had felt the compassion and empathy of the other Arkell through Waoca, but this revelation put an actual example in their personal experiences. This act would be done simply because of the Arkell's love for these fellow beings. These four, after a few moments to absorb the emotion behind the motivation, smiled and nodded in understanding. They would have much to communicate with their fellow Arkell aboard the *Geaalo*. This evening would be a wonderful and permanent memory for the rest of their lives.

Dale turned to address the *Geaalo*'s Arkell. "So you know, the refrigeration in the *Vance*'s cryo decks was turned back on as soon as the *Vance* was secured."

Vance's left eyebrow went up, "Why . . . ?" he stopped talking and smiled while nodding.

Dale continued. "We will release these bodies to you to do with as you wish."

This was another example of compassion and empathy requiring no reciprocal action.

Ooat was first to react. "That is kind of you—very kind." Ooat turned to his three companions. "These were our shipmates. I believe we should bring them aboard the *Geaalo* and give them the honor of cremation and burial as we do for all Arkell."

"We will assist in the transfer," said Vance.

The gathering was a success. Everyone was having a great time, particularly the Arkell of the *Geaalo*. They hadn't been part of or had ever heard of such a party. They, in the beginning, were self-conscious, but as the evening progressed, they began getting into the spirt of the thing.

At one point, Shem and Oruku were alone in deep conversation. At the end of their conversation, Oruku nodded and then hugged Shem.

Alex and Vance noticed the two talking privately and saw Oruku nod. "Hmm," said Alex.

CHAPTER 7

CLEANING TIME

Ooat, Ssamp, Rree, Ppinn, and eight other Arkell, four men and four women, of the *Geaalo* were in a meeting with Oruku and three other Arkell of the *Velgot*.

"My recent visits to this magnificent ship have shown me the pristine condition in which you have maintained it," said Ooat. "We who have seen some of the interior of the *Velgot* are ashamed of the *Geaalo*'s condition. Let me alter that statement. We are extremely ashamed of the *Geaalo*'s condition. We are going to change that." Ooat gestured toward his companions. "These men and women represent different functions of our ship, from engineering to maintenance to farming to ranching to power production to medicine and health care to teaching, etcetera. It is our intention, with your permission, to make video records of various aspects of your ship to help us in our mission to renovate the *Geaalo*."

"We thank you for the compliment," said Oruku. "I believe I can speak for us here in this meeting. We will be delighted to accommodate you in your task to renovate the *Geaalo*."

Ooat said nothing for a moment. "This is another example of a kindness and compassion that unfortunately drifted away from us over two millennia in the past. I don't know how we could have let our civilization deteriorate to such an extent or how we became the scourge of the galaxy. It is our intent to right as many of the wrongs we have forced upon other worlds over these millennia as possible. We won't take too long to tour the *Velgot*. With the help of your section managers, we should gain enough intelligence to make a huge difference in our ship's condition and abilities."

"You can take all the time you need. Your goal is commendable. We will aid in your quest as best we can," said Oruku.

"Thank you, sir," said Ooat.

Oruku smiled. "My name is Oruku. We have no 'sirs' on our ship."

All four Arkell nodded in understanding.

Ssamp nudged Ooat while raising one eyebrow.

Ooat nodded once and turned to Oruku. "There is one more thing we are going to ask."

"Which is?"

Ooat was clearly uncomfortable with the question. "Would it be possible to take some eggs or female embryos from your beautiful and intelligent women to . . . upgrade our women?"

Oruku had not anticipated this question, but he understood and he managed not to smile. "That's a request I'm going to turn over to Nola."

Oruku's prediction that the SLF technicians would be able to rebuild Henry in three days was accurate, to no one's surprise.

After being revived and rebuilt, Henry Hendrick gave his account of what had happened during the Arkell's invasion of Isley. It closely followed the accounts of Ooat and Ssamp. No major surprises. Henry confirmed what had been assumed by Vance, Shem, and Gary. He told them when and why he had turned off the refrigeration on the cryo decks, resulting in the deaths of five hundred Arkell troops. He remembered everything about those perilous times, up to the second he was destroyed by Ttot.

"He seemed to be upset with me," said Henry with a big smile.

After being debriefed and having his rebuilt SLF body "tuned to perfection," as Gary put it, Henry spent the next two weeks touring Gabriel with Alex and Vance, meeting hundreds of Gabrielites. The name Henry Hendrick quickly became a household name around the planet. The Gabrielites were anxious to meet this SLF, this hero who had saved Gabriel from a devastating defeat from the Arkell of the *Geaalo*.

Henry didn't consider himself a hero. "Any human or SLF would have done the same thing," he repeated often during his travels. "There was no choice."

On his tours around Gabriel, Henry was in awe of the remarkable and extensive development of Gabriel. Everything was designed beautifully and built to a very high standard. In an effort to duplicate, as closely as possible, the development on Gabriel, Henry had been making videos and taking still photos of dozens of homes, businesses, roads, bridges, and parks. He was accumulating invaluable knowledge concerning dos and don'ts to take back to the citizens of Isley. He knew his efforts would be of immense help to their future. The humans had landed on this planet five hundred years before humans set foot on Isley, and the Isleites had a lot of catching up to do.

After Henry's time touring Gabriel, it was time to board the *Velgot* in preparation for the departure to Isley.

In the grand gazebo in Home Bay were dozens of well-wishers gathered to say farewell to Henry Hendrick.

The semiformal gathering was being broadcast around the planet and to the *Velgot* orbiting above Home Bay.

Included at the two head tables were all twelve SLFs, and among the non-SLFs were Jarleth, Shem, Oruku, Nola, and Janos.

"Henry," said Troy, "I never thought I'd see you again after we left Earth heading in different directions. Then, centuries later, you show up on Gabriel, totally out of commission but, thankfully, repairable."

"I can only imagine your surprise and dismay," said Henry.

"Your condition saddened all of us," said Alex. "But what you did that caused your near destruction will be remembered and celebrated for centuries to come."

Henry smiled. "As I've said a time or two, any human or SLF would have done the same thing."

"Nonetheless," said Vance, "it was you who saved us from Arkell domination. Gabriel, our planet, our Eden, would have been taken from us."

"If I'd failed to stop the Arkell of the *Geaalo*," started Henry, "and they had, in fact, taken over Gabriel, their reign and lives would have been short-lived. These wonderful loving people"—Henry gestured toward Oruku and the other four Arkell—"would have taken it back for you."

All in attendance enthusiastically clapped, wooed, and whistled. Oruku nodded in acknowledgment.

"We certainly won't dispute that," said Alex.

Troy stood. "I raise my glass to you, Henry Hendrick. You will be in our hearts and minds forever."

Anytime he wished, Henry could retire to the *Vance*'s captain's quarters and shut himself off for any length of time. But living on the *Velgot* differed little from living on a planet. It was, in reality, an outside-in world. With its parks, rivers, mountains, wildlife, domestic animals, and towns, it was a complete and vibrant world. Had a person not known he or she was inside a spaceship, they would not be aware. It didn't take but a day before Henry adopted the daily routine of his new Arkell friends—basically, fifteen hours awake and five asleep. It was an exhilarating life aboard this magnificent ship. There was no apparent end of activities one could engage in, like sports such as forms of golf, tennis, basketball, swimming, mountain climbing, or just hiking through the forests. Henry would have the next ten years to become proficient in many activities.

In the evenings, there was a fine variety of restaurants and pubs to pass the time with new friends. It was Henry's favorite time. His interacting with these highly intelligent people was the frosting on the cake of the day.

Henry was never one to sit back and do nothing, so after a few days, he asked what he could do to earn his keep. After some consultation with various department heads, Henry was made a professor of physics and put in charge of teaching those younger than eight the basic physics of the galaxy. But scant time would be taken on that subject. His few pupils were a great deal more interested in the history of old Earth. To have a human who actually lived on that extinct planet was an extraordinary gift to them. It didn't take long before there were more adults than children attending his classes.

CHAPTER 8

NEWBORN

"OUR SON HAS BEEN BORN," announced an ecstatic Shem as he entered the receiving room of the hospital's maternity ward.

Shem and Jarleth's four adult children and a dozen friends stood, applauded, and wooed at the same time. After Shem's children hugged and kissed their father, the rest in the receiving room took turns hugging and congratulating him. All were anxious to hear about the birth. After all, Shem and Jarleth were one of the planet's most famous and beloved couples—and the fact that it had been over forty years since Jarleth had her last child. There was a lot of concern for the mother and baby. How was it possible for an eighty-six-year-old woman to bear a baby?

"Arkell genes," Jarleth had explained at the beginning of her pregnancy. "Not unheard of for Arkell women to bear children after the age of one hundred. But you have to keep in mind that Arkell routinely live to be over three hundred. All things considered, my pregnancy would be akin to a human woman having a child in her midthirties."

Vance, after giving Shem a big hug, asked, "What does the future leader of Gabriel weigh?"

"Three point nine kilos."

"Big boy."

"He has some of your genes—bound to be hefty," said Shem. "I have another announcement to make now."

He had everybody's attention.

"I'm not the only father of this child."

That caused all conversations to freeze.

"What? Why would you say that?" said Vance with a puzzled smile.

"I'm about half a new father. Oruku is the other half."

"What? How?"

"Jarleth and I decided to honor Oruku by using some of his genes along with some of mine to impregnate her."

"Really?"

"Yes, sir, Oruku is as much a father to this boy as I am."

"How is that possible?" asked Vance.

The Arkell have very advanced technology on genetics. Jarleth, you, and I are examples of their capabilities."

"Of course," said Vance bashfully, "what was I thinking?"

"On their last visit, I asked Oruku if he would be interested in becoming a father of a child with Jarleth and me. He agreed. We went through a procedure the following day."

"That's fascinating," said Dale.

"Ya think?" said Teddy.

"Talk about a highbred," said Tomaco.

Everybody began adding their opinions at the same time.

"When do we get to see him?" asked an eager Lara.

"Not sure. They said they'd let us know," said a smiling Shem.

"What are you going to name him?" asked Dale.

Shem smiled and paused for a moment. "Velgot."

"Yes, perfect!" declared Vance.

All agreed, it was the perfect and proper name. Oruku and his shipmates of the *Velgot* were responsible for the birth of Shem and Jarleth. The *Velgot*'s Arkell were the sole reason for the continuing existence of humans and the planet Gabriel. Shem and Jarleth had, indeed, made a great choice.

Five minutes after the initial announcement by Shem, a nurse came into the receiving room.

"We can allow visitors now. The new mom is anxious to present her new son to the world." She looked around the room. "Let's make it just a few at a time."

"Why don't you five go first," Vance said to Shem and his children.

"Thank you. We'll do that," said Shem, anxious to return to his wife and new son.

"Follow me," said the smiling nurse.

After ten minutes or so, Shem and Jarleth's children returned to the receiving room.

"Wait till you see this baby," said the oldest daughter, Terri. "He is something else."

"And then some," her brother Parker added.

After they left the room, Alex turned to Vance and Lara and smiled. "Why don't you two go next? Aidan and I will follow."

"Let's go together," suggested Aidan.

The four followed the nurse into the room that held Jarleth and her son. Jarleth was lying propped up with pillows against the headboard. Her infant son was lying on his back on her chest, and he was fully awake and looking around.

"Holy cow," said Alex.

"Ditto," said Aidan.

This baby was something to behold. He had the head of an Arkell. He had Shem's skin color and Oruku's bronze eyes. To top it off, he had Jarleth's hair. He was a platinum blonde.

"Well, he's certainly going to stand out," said Vance.

"He's beautiful," said a broadly smiling Aidan. She bent over and gave Jarleth a kiss on the forehead, dropped down a few inches, and kissed Velgot on his oversized forehead before looking up at Jarleth. "How are you doing, my friend?"

"Pretty tired, as a matter of fact," Jarleth said with a small smile. "I don't remember being this exhausted with our other four."

"Well, you're just a little out of practice," said Lara. "If you get right at it, the next one will probably be easier."

"Next one!" That made Jarleth laugh.

Teddy and Colleen were the last to visit Jarleth, Shem, and Velgot.

Colleen spoke first. "Holy cow, look at this new person." She took the two steps to where Shem was holding Velgot. "Just look at him. My god, he is an attention-getter."

"That he is," said Jarleth.

"May I hold him for just a minute?"

"Sure," said Shem as he carefully held Velgot out to Colleen's outstretched hands.

She took him gently and brought him to her chest for a few moments, all the while looking down into those bronze and alert eyes. The newborn stared into Colleen's eyes for a moment before smiling.

"Oh my god," said Colleen. "He is aware." With that, Colleen held him out at arm's length. "He has a regal bearing already."

Teddy remained uncharacteristically quiet while never taking his eyes off Velgot.

Shem walked over and sat beside Jarleth on the bed. He reached over and gave her hand a squeeze while watching Colleen fawn over their son.

After a few more moments, Teddy walked over to Colleen. "My turn."

Colleen reluctantly relinquished her hold and passed the infant to her husband.

Teddy carefully placed one hand on Velgot's bottom and the other behind his head before bringing the youngster to his chest. Teddy had not yet looked into the baby's eyes. For a full minute, he slowly twisted right and left. Then he held the baby out at arm's length and looked into his eyes.

"Hi boss," he said softy as he continued the eye contact.

Velgot gave a big smile while managing to get an arm free from the blanket wrapped around him. He reached toward Teddy's face. His arms were too short to bridge the gap, so Teddy brought him closer to where he could reach. And reach he did.

"He loves Teddy," said Jarleth.

Shem smiled. "I could have predicted that."

CHAPTER 9

LONG, INTERESTING TRIP

Henry Hendrick was standing beside Oruku in the expansive control room of the *Velgot*. Henry and Oruku were about the same height, but that's where the similarities ended. Henry had much-darker skin and eyes and coal-black curly hair, whereas Oruku had an olive complexion and bronze-colored eyes, and his hair was white and short-cropped on top of his large Arkell head.

Around them were dozens of Arkell techs manning their stations. This was the nerve center. From this room, located dead center of the ship, the entire ship was controlled, from climate control, gravity, speed, and work assignments to food production, maintenance, weapons, and shields.

"We've just set the last of the relay satellites in place," said Oruku.

"Excellent," said Henry. "Now Isley and Gabriel can communicate again."

"We found the originals in a lab aboard the *Geaalo*," said Oruku. "They didn't destroy them. They just took them aboard their ship to dissect and steal whatever technology they could."

Henry nodded. "Figures."

"I'm assuming you've been told of our arrival approach to Gabriel," said Oruku.

Henry smiled. "About a hundred times on Gabriel and a few times on this ship. Everybody seems to enjoy it. I know the Gabrielites look forward to your visit for many reasons—your spectacular arrival is certainly one of them."

"How do you think the Isleites will react to it?" asked Oruku, displaying some concern.

Henry thought about that for a moment. "Given the invasion by the *Geaalo* more than a century ago, I believe a massive starship, similar in appearance, appearing over their world will really scare them."

"Agreed."

"I will do my best to prepare them for our arrival," said Henry. "I will tell them to expect a surprise, a harmless surprise. I think they will be delighted with the spectacle. At least after they quit screaming in terror." Henry smiled.

Oruku smiled and nodded. "Good."

When the *Velgot* was a month out, planet time, Henry sent a message to Isley.

"This is Henry Hendrick," he started. "Approximately one hundred and ten years ago, planet time, I was taken, along with the *Vance*, by a race known as Arkell." Henry paused for a moment, letting his emotions calm some. "I am now, along with the *Vance*, returning to my beloved home, the planet Isley." Henry paused again.

Oruku understood the emotion here. He silently stood quietly by Henry's side.

After a moment, Henry started again. "At this moment, I am aboard another massive starship, but this magnificent ship is full of dear friends of humankind . . . fear not."

Oruku smiled as he nodded at Henry.

"We are, at this moment, just a month out. In twenty days, we will be straight over Williamsburg, preparing for a landing in the central park. I would strongly suggest that, on that date, you go out in the open and wait for our arrival. Find a comfortable location, lie down, and watch the sky. It will be worth seeing. There is no danger involved."

A few minutes later, an answer was received by the *Velgot*. "Henry, this is Gabriel."

"George?" Henry was delighted. "George, is that really you?"

George was one of the five scientists and one politician who volunteered to became SLFs in order to speed the construction of three starships prior to a rogue asteroid destroying Earth.

Prior to the impending disaster, five of the six, the exception being Troy, had been remotely acquainted through their professions. All were celebrated as the leaders in their fields of astrophysics, engineering, and quantum mechanics. Once the construction of the three new starships was completed, these SLFs would pilot the new starships to three different planets. During this demanding and stressful time, these six extraordinary men became very close friends.

Because of the time required to travel such distances, only SLFs, with their ability to shut themselves down for years or decades at a time, could perform such an undertaking. Humans aboard their ships would remain in stasis for the thirty to forty years it would take to reach their destinations.

Of the six SLFs, Troy and Gary captained the *Marian* to Gabriel, Henry and Daniel captained the *Vance* to Isley, and Gabriel and Posner captained the *Alexander* to the third planet—the planet that, in retrospect, should have been avoided. All humans and the two SLFs who were part of that disastrous landing had, eight years later, been rescued by the *Vance*, taken back, and resettled on Isley.

"It is really me," said George. "I cannot believe I'm hearing your voice again. We assumed you, along with the citizens of Gabriel, were dead or possibly slaves to those monsters who took you and our ship."

"I and the *Vance* managed to survive with no permanent damage done to either and, I assure you, Gabriel remains a wonderland. It's a long story, which I'll go into at a later date."

"Can't wait to see you and hear that story," said George.

A public address system had been set up around the park a few days before the expected arrival. Henry's voice would be piped through this PA system.

"We are now thirty minutes out," said Henry. He and Oruku were sitting at a communications station in the ship's control room. "Now is the time, my fellow Isleites, to go outside and look up. We'll be there soon. And I repeat, there is no danger."

Within minutes, the entire population of Williamsburg and the majority of Isleites living on the continent were lying flat, looking up, wondering what was going to happen. This was going to be a historical day. It had been one hundred and ten years since the Arkell of the *Geaalo* had taken the *Vance* and Henry away, nearly six generations.

The *Velgot* was at light speed before instantly stopping just a thousand kilometers above the capital of Isley. At this distance, the massive ship was just the size of a BB to the naked eye. Tiny in the distance but clearly visible. The midmorning sun was reflecting off the enormous golden globe, giving it a starlike appearance.

"THERE IT IS!" yelled a young woman as she excitedly pointed nearly straight up.

A man with binoculars gave a warning. "That's not the *Vance*. It looks like an Arkell ship."

Those close enough to hear this warning started to become uneasy. Some stood up, looking for a place to hide.

"Please do not be afraid," said George over the PA system. "Our dear friend Henry Hendrick is aboard that ship. He would not let any harm come to us. Remain calm and keep watching. I have the feeling this is going to be spectacular."

A full minute went by while this golden orb remained motionless in space. There was a constant din coming from the huge gathering. This was going to be a historical day.

"Are you ready?" Henry's voice came over the PA system.

The din instantly became silent.

"Here we come."

Then it came in. In three seconds, the *Velgot* closed the thousand kilometers and instantly stopped just above Isley's atmosphere. The screams were quick, loud, and continuous. There, above their heads, was a gigantic golden orb with huge bronze ribs extending from the top axis to the bottom axis. This ship looked to be the size of a moon.

The tumult from the citizens continued. There were those still trying to catch their breath, many laughing joyously, those whose excitement bordered on lunacy, and a few who wet their pants.

There, the *Velgot* would remain motionless for fifteen minutes, its massive ribs turning slowly. The Isleites were starting to calm down but continued staring up in awe and talking excitedly about this spectacular phenomenon in orbit above their heads.

"Oruku," said Henry, "there are no words to express our gratitude for what you and the citizens of the *Velgot* have done, yet again, for the humans of Gabriel and Isley."

"We have always considered the humans our dearest friends in the galaxy," said Oruku. "That friendship includes the SLFs. You are, in our eyes, humans."

"These past ten years aboard the *Velgot* will live in my memory until my end. I am the first to have the honor and privilege of such a long encounter with the finest, most-advanced civilization in the Milky Way galaxy."

"You have made these ten years very enlightening, very interesting for us. Sharing your memories of old Earth have been highly entertaining and informative."

Henry gave Oruku a big hug and then proceeded to hug Kilee, who, under normal circumstances, was not a hugger. But he hugged Henry back. "It's been a pleasure, Henry."

"Are you ready?" asked Oruku.

Henry nodded, turned, and left the control center. Five minutes later, Oruku got a message from Henry: "I'm on the bridge of the *Vance*, ready to go home."

Oruku nodded in the direction of one of the technicians.

A sound, like a gigantic foghorn, blasted from above. All eyes riveted on the *Velgot*. At about halfway between the equator and the bottom of the ship, and just visible to the naked eye, an oblong opening began slowly forming, growing in size as the seconds past.

The crowed began speculating as to what was about to happen. Then from that large opening in the *Velgot* emerged the *Vance*. It stopped as soon as it cleared the opening. Then the opening in the hull slowly closed. There, in space, floated the *Vance* with the *Velgot* sitting mightily above it. Viewed from the planet, the *Vance* looked like a fly speck on a beach ball. A few seconds later, the *Vance* started dropping down toward the planet.

"That's the *Vance*," someone yelled out.

"Oh my god, oh my god," exclaimed another.

Then the thousands joined in with screams, whistles, and shouts of joy.

"We have our ship back."

The *Vance* continued dropping toward a park in the center of Williamsville. When it reached an altitude of one hundred meters, it lowered the landing struts on each orb and very slowly continued downward, giving the crowd time to clear the landing site. Once the area was cleared, it landed gently on the expanse of lawn.

The second it touched down, the crowd swarmed in, most jockeying for position around the center sphere, where the ramp would come down, hopefully followed by Henry. They didn't have to wait long. The ramp started lowering very slowly, giving the population ample time to move out of its way. Two minutes later, a broadly smiling Henry Hendrick walked down the ramp and stepped on his home planet for the first time in a hundred and ten years.

It had been assumed the *Vance* and Henry would be dead or destroyed and would never be heard from again. During this intervening time, the population of Isley had quadrupled and they had managed to tame and safely colonize two other continents. Henry had assumed all humans on Isley were still living on just the one safe continent out of the five. It was the only continent that contained no animals dangerous to humans.

The *Velgot* remained in space above Williamsville until the *Vance* landed in the park. Then it sounded the "foghorn" again.

The huge crowed looked up just in time to see the *Velgot* accelerate out of sight in less than two seconds. It was gone.

Henry was now a hero on two planets, Isley and Gabriel. His tale of the abduction and theft of the *Vance* would be told and retold countless times over the following years and decades on both planets. His decision to end the lives of five hundred Arkell troops was heralded as an extreme act of courage and would become lore on both planets.

"Got a communiqué from our friends the Arkell," said Troy as Vance and Alex walked onto the bridge of the *Marian*.

"You're going to have to be more specific," said Vance. "We have two Arkell friends, ya know?"

Troy smiled. "The *Velgot*."

Vance said nothing for a moment while he continued walking toward Troy. "I'll bet they have successfully dropped the *Vance* and Henry off on Isley. Timing is right. It's been twenty years planet time."

"That's what the message said," said Troy. "Ten years to get there and ten years for the message to get back to us."

"And?" asked Alex.

"Oruku said Henry had contacted Isley when they were still a month out. Told them when and where to expect them."

"They reported nearly the entire population of the planet was there to greet them."

Vance smiled. "Did they happen to approach Isley as they do us?"

"They did and apparently got the same reaction."

"Great!" Vance had witnessed the *Velgot*'s spectacular arrival several times over the decades and always experienced a moment of terror upon their arrival. He loved it.

"That's always a heart-stopper," added Alex.

CHAPTER 10

GEAALO UPDATE

The Arkell of the *Geaalo* were to spend months cleaning and refurbishing their ship as it traveled at nearly light speed toward their home planet of Arkell. Most of the ship's interior had suffered from hundreds of years of neglect; other areas had been neglected for a thousand years. It was filthy. Untold numbers of machines were nonfunctional, living quarters were in disrepair, roads and major infrastructure were in dismal condition, and all this reflected on the Arkell's personalities. The Arkell had, over a millennium, managed to turn their massive ship into what would be considered a slum if it were a city on an occupied planet. The only parts of the ship that were maintained in respectable condition were the propulsion, shield and weapons systems, systems needed to plunder the galaxy with impunity.

There were one hundred and fifty thousand Arkell living on the *Geaalo,* thirty thousand more than occupied the *Velgot.* To facilitate the overhaul of the *Geaalo,* every Arkell would be allocated to a group with a specific area of responsibility. It would be these groups' mandate to bring up their area of responsibility to a very high standard. In addition, plans were being drawn up to add additional features such as parks, lakes, rivers, mountains, and new residential neighborhoods. They were going to duplicate, as much as possible, the incredible interior of the *Velgot.*

It didn't take long for the converted Arkell to get into the spirit of the enormous project. Being converted to a new mindset made this massive undertaking more of a labor of love than a chore.

Ooat, Ssamp, Rree, Ppinn, and the eight other Arkell who had spent days on the *Velgot* studying, making notes, and recording the interior of that incredible ship took charge of the renovation of the *Geaalo*. These twelve would become known as the "Group." There were hundreds of identified areas that needed maintenance, complete rebuilding, or cleaning, and sometimes all three.

Each one of the Group had an area of responsibility. One recruited over ten thousand to tackle the massive chore of trash pickup and disposal on all one hundred and thirty-five decks of the ship. These decks ranged in size from fifty-six thousand square meters at the equator down to six thousand square meters at the top and bottom decks. As each deck was cleared of trash, and the trash was ejected into a gravity field of a star. From there, it would be pulled toward the star and eventually be burned to nothing.

Another even-larger crew began the extensive cleaning process. Two other Arkell, who had been part of the maintenance department, were put in charge of overseeing the repairing or rebuilding of all the defective machines on the ship. This would, in itself, be an enormous and time-consuming project. Another sizable group would head up a road construction and maintenance department. Another was assigned to head up home construction and, in hundreds of cases, the demolition of existing dwellings—structures that had deteriorated to a point where they could not be saved.

Another of the Group headed up a much-smaller group. This group was comprised of those who were the ship's farmers and ranchers. Over the millennia, the production of food aboard the ship had deteriorated to a point that required the Arkell to raid planets and take away as much food in the form of vegetables and meat as their ship's stores could hold. That was not the intent of the ship's architects. The *Geaalo* was designed to be self-sufficient. It would be able to produce its own food for the tens of thousands of years it would take to travel into another universe. To return to the time when food production was sufficient to feed the ship's company, all farmers were required to attended a month-long seminar covering all aspects of farming, from ground prep to seeding to fertilizer to harvesting to packaging. Livestock ranchers attended a separate seminar covering all aspects of livestock production. The Arkell of the *Geaalo*, unlike the Arkell of the *Velgot*, were carnivores.

Within the first six months of their journey toward their home planet, the interior of the *Geaalo* had been improved dramatically. Just the removal of debris and cleaning of all surfaces made a remarkable difference in the Arkell's attitude. The newly found pride in their ship was dramatic. Where the demeanor of the Arkell, in the past, was generally one of malevolence, it was now one of friendliness. Smiles and warm greetings replaced frowns and aloofness.

As predicted, of the Arkell who had originally refused to perform Waoca, all but two gave in within a month and became converts. They were immediately released from the holding area and welcomed to the population. However, they would not be reassigned to their past positions of leadership. Rather, they would be given choices of where they felt they would be of greatest benefit to the Arkell community.

The two who steadfastly refused to convert, Accin and his lieutenant, chose to remain in confinement along with five hundred Volen. That turned out to be a fatal mistake. Just a day after the last of the Arkell had been converted and released from confinement, both Accin and his lieutenant were viciously torn apart by the Volen.

Prior to their conversion, the Arkell would not have grieved much at the loss of two of their own. They were conditioned to shrug off any such loss. But their attitude was now a great deal more compassionate and empathetic. Now they did care. Ooat was incensed.

"How far are we from the Volen home planet?" he asked Llok the navigator.

"Fifty-two light-years."

"Is there an unoccupied planet close to our present trajectory that would be habitable for them?"

A minute later, Llok responded. "There is a planet just four point six light-years ahead that may serve. We have been there in the past." Llok continued reviewing the data on the planet. "Has a nominal atmosphere, heavily vegetated, five continents, and sixty percent of its surface is fresh water, which is why we were there. It has a variety of herbivores, both large and small. And a few carnivores, mostly large and vicious." Llok smiled. "Which is why we left."

"I remember," said Ooat. "They killed and ate four of our shipmates."

"That's the place."

"Can the Volen survive there?"

"They would be on the top of the food chain as far as carnivores are concerned. They will probably be able to hold their own."

Ooat said nothing for a moment. "Head there. Let's drop them off early."

Four point six light-years later, the *Geaalo* was making a slow orbit around the planet, making a survey of each of the continents to determine which would be best suited for the survival of the Volen. Prior to their conversion, they wouldn't have given much thought to the survivability of another species unless it directly affected them. They, more than likely, would have simply ejected the Volen into the void of space. But that was no longer the case.

Over these past five years, the population of the Volen had gone from just over five hundred to just under four hundred. Vicious infighting accounted for the major part of their population reduction, and illness and old age claimed the rest.

They were now in geosynchronous orbit above the smallest continent.

"This looks like the most Volen-friendly continent," said Llok. "They will have competition for food but should be able to survive."

"Let's load them up and get them off this ship," said Ooat.

That proved to be a bigger task than expected. Over the past five years, the Volen had adapted well in their holding area aboard the *Geaalo*. They did not want to be relocated on an inhospitable planet. In order to convince them to board the shuttle, several had to be stunned with a weapon that, before modification, was deadly. Now being shot was just extremely painful. It didn't take long before the Volen understood they had no choice in the matter, so they reluctantly cooperated. To be on the side of caution, two dozen armed Arkell were used to separate thirty Volen at a time and move them to a large shuttle.

It took several hours before the last load of Volen were off-loaded at the landing site. Dozens of cases of supplies, including tents, clothing, seeds of various vegetables, tools, etcetera, and a few rudimentary weapons were left with the Volen to give them as much chance as possible for survival.

"We are finally rid of them," said Ooat. "I hope over time they will evolve into a smarter, kinder race."

"Perhaps, in the future, a ship will drop by and check on them," said Ssamp.

"Let's send a message to the *Velgot* and to the humans of Gabriel and tell them what we have done. Knowing the Arkell of the *Velgot*, I would assume they, in the next hundred years or so, will look in on them."

"Our sensors show a sizable iron mist about a light-week ahead," said Ssamp.

"We'll navigate around it as usual," said Ooat.

"I have another idea," said Ssamp.

"What?"

"The outside of our ship is filthy. It hasn't been cleaned for thousands of years . . . if ever. There has to be several millimeters of space dust along with who knows what stuck to the hull. I suggest we adjust our speed accordingly and fly through the mist."

The iron mist was a massive cloud of microscopic iron sand that had been ejected from a supernova. To hit such a cloud at near light speed would pulverize a ship in a millisecond. But it was theorized that at the proper speed, those microscopic grains not only would blast off the accumulated grime but should put a brilliant shine on the hull.

"Are you thinking about giving the *Geaalo* a polishing?"

"I am. Let's make her pretty on the outside too."

"Can we protect our external sensor arrays, shields, weapons, scopes, etcetera?"

"I believe we can. Most can be retracted into the ship and sealed off. And we can send a team, familiar with the balance of external equipment, to either remove the equipment or protect it from the iron mist."

Ooat nodded and smiled. "Let's get some external pictures and videos before we start the process and again after the completion."

"Good idea."

"How big is this mist cloud?" asked Ooat.

"Just over ten thousand kilometers long and three thousand across. I've checked with our engineers, and they suggest we slow to five hundred kilometers before we enter the mist and slowly revolve the ship around the equator and then around the poles."

"That ought to do it," said Ooat.

When the polishing job was done and outside videos were taken, the entire ship's company were shown the videos of a brilliant sphere named the *Geaalo*. The reaction was one of overwhelming pride. Their ship looked like a bright shining jewel set against the blackness of space. Tears of joy were displayed by a good percentage of the residents of the ship, a pride not displayed for thousands of years. It turned out to be a final turning point for the Arkell. From that point on, the Arkell of the *Geaalo*'s attitude would closely reflect those of the *Velgot*'s.

CHAPTER 11

WHAT'S GOING ON?

"Is it my eyesight or do the days seem to be getting brighter?" asked Alex.

"I've noticed too," said Troy, "but I thought it was just my mind playing tricks."

"Same here," said Vance.

Five SLFs were sitting on the outside patio of Carlon's Pub. It was midsummer on this part of Gabriel, and Home Bay was alive with tourists from all around the planet and hundreds from Yassi and Vout.

There were now just under a million people on Gabriel. Ninety-five percent were human, and the remaining five percent was made up of Yassi, Vout, and Byuse. Most Vout and Byuse preferred to live and remain on their islands, and a few had moved elsewhere around Gabriel. But the Yassi were a great deal more social and adventurous. They were very comfortable among humans, and they were welcome wherever they went. Aside from being congenial and a pleasure to be around, they were great craftsmen, designers, and artists. Wherever they lived, the beauty of the place was sure to be enhanced.

"I'm surprised you've just now thought to say something about this phenomenon. For the past week, I've been checking all my instruments and sensors aboard the *Norman*," said Dale. "They show there is something out of order. But we cannot detect what the problem is. Something's off. Something's not quite right."

"I've checked the instruments on the *Marian*, and they do show a brightness increase, not only during the day but at night too," said Gary. "We don't notice the difference at night, too subtle a change."

"How about checking with the Arkell and Yassi?" said Troy. "See if they are experiencing the same thing."

"Do we know where the Arkell are?" asked Vance.

"I believe they are about five light-years out," said Dale. "I'll send out a communiqué and ask if they have any insight on this." Dale paused for a moment. "Actually, knowing the Arkell, they will send any info they have without our asking."

Vance smiled. "So you're willing to wait five years to get the Arkell's take on this phenomenon?"

Dale shook his head and smiled. "I must be getting old."

"Do you think we may have a problem?" asked Vance.

"At this point, no, not really. But if it continues to get brighter, it will begin to affect all life on the planet," said Dale. "Biological clocks on both plant and animal would become altered."

"An example would be?" asked Alex.

"Off the top of my head, photosynthesis will increase, plants will grow faster—not necessarily a bad thing, but there's no doubt it will cause a problem somewhere," said Dale. "In animals, breeding seasons could be altered, hibernation starting times and duration might change—that could cause a myriad of problems. Birth rates could plummet. Starvation of hibernating animals, etcetera."

"And dozens of other things we can't yet see," added Gary.

It was just about noon when the *Velgot* suddenly appeared over Home Bay. There was no advance notice, no communications of any kind.

Vance and Lara just happened to be outside pruning plants and trees that had grown unexpectedly fast.

"HOLY SHIT!" exclaimed Vance as he dropped his pruning saw.

"WHAT?" was all Lara could say as she involuntarily backed away from the sight before stopping and stood motionless, staring straight up at the *Velgot*.

From their yard, they could hear the startled screams from across the river in Home Bay.

"This is not good," Vance said in a low, slow voice, masking the alarm he was presently experiencing.

"I need to get to the *Marian*," he said as he pulled off his gardening gloves.

"Want company? Never mind, I'm going with you," said Lara as she, too, removed her gloves and brushed away various leaves and twigs from her work jumpsuit.

Vance nodded as he looked across the river and then back up to the *Velgot*. "Let's go."

They were halfway across the bridge when Dale's voice was heard on Vance's communicator. "I'm assuming you are on your way."

"We'll be at the *Marian* in five minutes."

"Everybody will be here," said Dale.

"Any word from the *Velgot*?" asked Vance.

"Nothing."

When Vance and Lara arrived at the *Marian*, they saw that Alex, Troy, Gary, Shem, and their wives were outside looking up. They were not surprised.

"Any activity up there?" he asked as they approached the group.

"Nothing," said Alex. "It's just motionless."

"Where's Dale?"

"Ship's bridge," said Troy as he nodded toward the *Marian*. "He's trying to communicate with the *Velgot*."

"I haven't been this terrified since the gamma-ray threat," said Troy. "The people who saved us then might be the ones in trouble here."

"I may have a heart attack," said Gary without a trace of humor.

"Ditto," said Lara.

The others said nothing but, undoubtedly, all felt the same sense of impending disaster. It may have been that the Arkell of the *Velgot*, the strongest and most benevolent force they were aware of in the galaxy, was in trouble—if not worse.

"Here come Vel and Jupi," said Jarleth.

Velgot, the last child of Jarleth and Shem, was now twenty-nine years old. The confusion in whether the subject was about the ship *Velgot* or the person Velgot quickly became awkward, so it was decided to call the boy Vel.

Vel, for his entire life, had been a standout, a cut above all others on the planet, including his exceptional parents. He was well rounded, a natural leader, an athlete and scholar. He maintained strong bonds with Teddy, Dale, Vance, Alex, Troy, and Gary. He was somewhat reserved with most others.

Vel met Jupi seven years ago when he was aboard the *Velgot* studying advanced astrophysics under the tutelage of the Arkell's renowned physicists, Neron. Neron was Jupi's father, and she was his last child. She had dark hair and dark eyes and stood nearly as tall as Vel. The moment Jupi and Vel met and performed Waoca, their relationship was sealed. To everyone's delight, before the *Velgot* left Gabriel, the two were married. Over the past six years, they had produced four children: two girls and two boys. The boys had white hair; the girls were brunettes. All appeared to be one-hundred-percent Arkell, and all were exceptional in many ways.

"What's the story here?" asked Vel.

"Not known," said Gary.

"Really?" said Vel. "That's not comforting." Vel looked around and realized nobody was comfortable. "Uh-oh."

"Any communication from the ship?" asked Jupi.

"No, and that's our main concern," said Vance.

All eyes remained on the *Velgot*. All minds were praying that this was just a glitch, something mechanically wrong with this massive ship, something that could be readily repaired. The dread was deep and wasn't confined to just these people. All around the planet, the apprehension had become prevalent.

But adding to their concern, this group, these leaders of Gabriel, knew that the *Velgot*, just recently, was five light-years away. And that being the case, how did they cover this distance so quickly? It was impossible.

"Hello," came a shout from a short distance away. All turned to see Teddy and Colleen weaving their way through the gathering crowd, both smiling.

Normally the sight of Teddy brought immediate smiles to faces. Not this time. The expressions of bewilderment and anxiety remained unchanged.

This did not go unnoticed by Teddy. His expressive face went from a smile to a look of alarm. "Who died?"

"No one died," said Lara as she hugged Colleen and then Teddy.

"Then what's going on here?" asked Teddy.

"We don't know," said Alex.

"Then why the long faces?"

"For just that reason. We don't know. We've had no communication with the *Velgot*. We didn't know they would be here. They have never just . . . shown up," said Vance.

"Oh, geez."

"Alex," Dale's voice came over Vance's communicator.

"Yes, Dale."

"Gather everybody and join me on the bridge, please."

"On our way."

A minute later, fourteen people walked onto the *Marian*'s bridge. Dale was sitting in the captain's chair, looking at the large viewer on the opposing wall. Tomaco was standing next to him.

"I believe we are about to hear something from the *Velgot*."

"What makes you think that?" asked Alex.

"The frequency they use opened up a few minutes ago."

"That's a good sign," said Gary, expressing more relief than he felt.

"Let's hope," said Alex.

Two long minutes went by before the viewer lit up, displaying Oruku from the waist up. His features were drawn. He looked tired. He had aged.

He displayed a small smile. "I, first, would say that we know you've been going through a frightening hour or so. Very frightening, if I'm any judge."

"To say the least," said Vance.

Oruku looked at each person on the bridge. He stopped when he saw Vel and Jupi. "Hi, son and daughter," he said while broadening his smile.

"Father," said Vel with a warm smile.

"Wonderful to see you," said Jupi. "But I see you have some great concerns."

"Yes, I'm afraid we do."

"Can you tell us what's happening?" asked Dale.

"I can tell you what we've experienced in the past few hours. An experience that, quite frankly, causes us great concern."

"Well that certainly doesn't make me feel better," said Teddy.

That drew a slightly larger smile from Oruku.

"A few hours ago, we were transported to our home planet of Arkell. The time it took was just shy of a minute."

"You traveled a thousand light-years in less than a minute?" said Dale and Gary at the same time.

"That's all but instantaneous," added Jupi.

"Yes, and we were not the only ship to experience this. The *Geaalo* was there in orbit when we arrived. I will add that the *Geaalo* looked beautiful, looked new."

"Really?" said Vance.

"There's more," Oruku went on. "There were eighty-one other Arkell ships in orbit around Arkell. Ships both larger and smaller than the *Velgot*. Some older, some newer, and some more advanced than our ship."

Everybody on the bridge wanted to talk at once. Vance raised his voice. "People, one at a time, PLEASE."

All stopped talking.

"Dale, why don't you do the asking," suggested Alex.

Oruku nodded in agreement.

"Do you have any idea of what, how, or who is responsible or how it was done?" asked Dale in a calm voice.

"The short answer is no, on all counts. We do know that the eighty-three Arkell ships came from all over the galaxy. Ships that have been traveling and exploring for thousands of years without contact with other Arkell ships. We came to realize we were just one of three who had any contact with other Arkell ships over the millennia. Ours being the *Geaalo*."

"What was the consensus of opinion as to what was happening?" asked Dale.

"All seemed to be stumped. The only thing that was agreed upon was that we were dealing with an entity with far-greater abilities than our own," said Oruku. "Far greater," he repeated.

"That's it?"

"Not quite."

"And?" said Dale.

Oruku seemed confused. He shook his head as if to clear his confusion. "We were . . . made aware that an entity had come from outside our galaxy and would make changes to the galaxy within a short period of time. We believe this entity must possess a great deal more power than anything we can imagine."

"Who told you that?"

"No one, and that's part of the problem." Oruku paused for a moment. "We just knew."

"Knew—how?"

"That I don't know. It just became part of our knowledge, almost like it had always been there but was just unveiled for us to see. We cannot explain it because we simply haven't a clue."

"I can only imagine the amount of speculation aboard the *Velgot*," said Gary.

"No, and there is another enigma. Somehow we knew we would not be able to figure it out. We didn't have the intellect, so we stopped trying. We accepted it."

Not a word was spoken for several moments. This scenario was so deep that not a thread of cohesive thought could be firmly grasped. Nobody was looking at anyone else. All thought and movement seem to have ceased.

"Now you know and feel what we have been experiencing—just nothing," said Oruku.

"I . . . I . . ." Dale was trying to communicate something but failed.

Another minute went by in silence before Vel said loudly, "SHARKRA."

That startled everyone out of their bewildered state.

Everyone's head snapped around to look at Vel.

"Sharkra, the unknown force," said Vel. "Maybe . . . what else could it be?"

"Can you expand on that thought?" ask Shem, clearly intrigued.

"I'll try." Vel paused for a full minute, though it seemed much longer to those on the bridge. Vel began explaining his thoughts. "It has been hypothesized for tens of thousands of years, by the Arkell, that Sharkra, or as humans used to call it, 'dark matter,' might be an intelligence." He paused again. "Maybe even a god or godlike."

There was complete silence on the deck. It seemed no one was even breathing. Oruku also remained mute while maintaining his complete attention on Vel.

"Further, it has been theorized that each galaxy or universe might be an individual god. Maybe the universe has, in fact, billions of gods in the form of galaxies." Vel again stopped for a second. "Maybe some of these gods don't get along. Maybe the invasion you hypothesized is one god trying to destroy or maybe taking over another's territory."

The silence remained. It seemed no one wanted to even breathe in fear of missing a single word.

Alex found a chair and motioned for Aidan to sit. Then he sat down on the deck next to her. Troy followed, and when the available chairs were filled, the rest sat on the deck. Dale rose from the captain's chair and motioned Vel to take it. Then Dale took a spot on the deck close by—Tomaco joined him. Then Jupi moved over and stood by Vel's side.

"Vel," said Oruku, "you may have it right. What else could it be?"

Vel sat silently nodding his head slightly, as his father, Shem, did when in deep thought. "It's possible our galaxy is gearing up for conflict. I don't know, that would be way above my station in life."

"Maybe," started Shem, "maybe the phenomenon of our planet's getting brighter is a result of an invasion or possibly a defense against an invasion."

"That's also an interesting thought," said Gary.

"Agreed," said Dale. "It could be a piece of the incomplete scenario we're in the middle of building."

"Good," said Oruku, "good. Thinking in the abstract may be the path to the truth."

"We have some pretty good thinkers here on Gabriel," said Vance with a smile. "I'm certainly not among them."

"Oh yes you are, my old friend," said Alex. "None of us would be here without your intelligence and energy."

"Agreed," said Dale. "Your approach to a problem comes from a different angle than scientists. And that approach has played a major role in our survival. You have been and are a major asset to the human race," said Dale.

"Everyone on this planet is comforted by the knowledge you are among us," added Alex.

Lara gave Vance a little squeeze on his arm.

"Well . . . thank you," Vance said humbly.

"I haven't told you all that has happened to us in the past few hours," said Oruku, getting back to the subject.

All eyes switched back to the viewer. All assumed this was going to be interesting, possibly terrifying, or both.

Oruku started, "We spent no more than three hours in orbit around Arkell. During that time, we were in contact with all the ships and the planet's representatives. We all, in turn, simply gave our initial thoughts and theories, which, quite frankly, amounted to nothing. Then all the ships left orbit at the same time—actually, just disappeared in an instant. Moments later, we were in orbit over Yassi. Then, after two hours of communication with them, we were in orbit over Vout, then Byuse, then here." Oruku paused for a moment. "By the way, those three planets were also experiencing brighter days and nights."

"My god," said Colleen, before adding, "No pun intended."

"Now we're thinking that all planets bearing life in this galaxy may be experiencing increased brightness," said Oruku.

"That would be a possibility," said Dale.

"But why are the planets with life becoming brighter?" asked Lara.

"What would cause anything to single out something specific among billions of like things?" added Gary. Then he smiled. "Like identifying a needle in a stack of needles."

"That could be it," said Dale. "It's simply to separate out, identify them."

"Agreed," said Vel. "Now all we have to do is figure out why and for who or what."

"I'm thinking that will be the hard part," said Teddy. "Among many," he added quietly.

"The 'why' would be my greatest concern," said Vance.

"Yes, that would be at the top of my list also," said Shem.

"If we could come up with 'who' or 'what,' the 'why' might become obvious," added Vel.

"Actually, if we had an answer to any one of the three, the remaining two might fall into place," said Dale.

Oruku nodded. "It should be noted that it took a while to set up our communication with the other three planets, as it did here. Our systems just went blank and stayed that way for over an hour every time we went into orbit over an occupied planet. We cannot find the reason. Neither we nor the Byuse, Yassi, or Vout came up with any plausible theory, as I believe we now have. This is encouraging."

"I'm just reminding you of theories and lore the Arkell have held for a very long time," said Vel. "I'm surprised it wasn't brought up when you were orbiting Arkell."

All eyes turned back to the viewer, waiting for Oruku's response.

Oruku said nothing for a moment. He was clearly in deep thought. "I cannot imagine why we didn't come to what now seems obvious. It makes no sense."

"I would point out that you had just been transported a thousand light-years in an instant and you may have had your minds occupied with that puzzle," suggested Shem.

"That's kind of you," said Oruku. "And there's probably some truth to it. I know it was foremost in my mind. After all, what just happened to us was impossible." Oruku smiled. "Our minds were blown, as Earthlings used to say."

That got another laugh. The mood was getting lighter the longer this conversation went on. Some intelligent thought was being brought to bear on this seemingly impossible situation.

"Why doesn't this god or gods just tell us what's going on?" asked Teddy.

Vel smiled at Teddy. "Maybe it would be like us trying to explain to an earthworm why we're putting it on a hook."

"Geez," said Teddy, "that's a whack to my ego."

That caused a little laughter among the group, lightening the mood a little more.

Vel paused before continuing. "It has also been hypothesized that time may not exist for the Sharkra. If we were in or part of Sharkra's mind, they might be able to transport a ship or a person instantly from one part of their mind to another. Or wherever the mind was, everything would also be. Time would have nothing to do with it."

"That does it," said Teddy, "I'm definitely an earthworm."

Everybody laughed at length.

Bless you, Teddy, thought Vance.

"The challenge, as I see it," said Jarleth, "is what, if anything, can we do to help our Sharkra?"

"Our Sharkra," said Oruku. "I like that."

"I'm presuming that the other Arkell ships are visiting their known life-bearing planets, as you are, Oruku," said Shem.

"I agree," said Oruku. "It seems to me, or at least it may be possible, our Sharkra may be looking for help. Why else are we, for the first time in tens of thousands of years, starting to put actual credence to the Sharkra?"

"Converting the theory or lore to a fact?" asked Gary.

"Exactly."

"It may not have any bearing on the current situation, but it just occurred to me," said Shem, "that the *Velgot* has been here for several hours now. And I believe you said that you'd only spent two hours at the other three planets."

"That's correct," said Oruku.

Shem smiled a little. "I suggest that this entity may have assumed that if you hadn't figured out or started to figure out what was happening in two hours, it was time to move on, giving the intellectuals on the next planet a crack at it."

"Good, very good," said Vel. "While here at Gabriel, we have come up with a theory, and since the *Velgot* has not been sent elsewhere, our theories might be on the right track."

"That is an excellent thought," said Oruku.

"Outstanding!" added Dale. "I'm starting to get quite excited about this."

Then the normally shy and quiet Tomaco spoke up. "Maybe our Sharkra is not looking for help. Maybe they are simply looking for recognition. Maybe it doesn't want to remain just a theory."

"Great thought," said Shem, followed by all present giving their enthusiastic support for this idea.

Dale smiled brightly. "That's my wife," he said with pride. Dale brought Tomaco's hand up and kissed it.

After a moment or two, Vel spoke. "That's thinking outside the box. Let's see if we can come up with more possibilities."

Vel is taking the leadership role, thought Vance. *Considering the competition, that's no small feat.*

"We know that the three other planets we've visited were also brighter," said Oruku. "We could scan this sector of the galaxy to determine if the brightening is restricted to just life-bearing planets or if other planets are so affected, but that could take hundreds of years for the results of the scan to reach us."

"Time would not be on our side," said Vel.

Oruku nodded in agreement. "We are transmitting, in all directions, what we have been discussing today. But as we know, it will take thousands of years for transmissions to reach most of the galaxy. But maybe someday our conjectures may be of some use to others."

Oruku's face changed expression as he cocked his head a little, presumably to hear what he was being told over his earpiece. "Right now?" he asked.

His expression changed back to one of deep confusion. "We are receiving communiqués from three dozen . . . make that six dozen Arkell ships."

"Which ships?" asked Vel.

Oruku was still gathering intelligence through his earpiece. He held up his hand, palm forward, in an attempt to ward off any questions for a moment. "Understood," he said as he lowered his hand and turned his attention toward those gathered on the *Marian*'s bridge. Then he paused for a moment, gathering his thoughts.

"We have received messages from eighty-two Arkell ships. These messages have come from as far as sixty thousand light-years away."

"Holy shit," said Vance quietly.

"Holy shit is right," said Teddy. "How big is this galaxy?"

"One hundred thousand light-years across," said Dale.

"Geez."

"The same ships that you were in contact with at Arkell?" asked Vel.

Oruku nodded. "Yes."

"What did they say?" asked Dale.

Oruku remained silent for a moment. His expression was one of bewilderment. "They are thanking us for sharing our thoughts on Sharkra. Seems twenty others have come up with a theory that Sharkra is the source of the altered physics. None thought of Sharkra's need to be recognized as an entity. Most liked that theory."

Dale smiled and squeezed Tomaco's hand.

Oruku was again gathering information from his earpiece. "They are all reporting that the life-bearing planets are the only ones that are experiencing increased light."

A silence fell over both the *Velgot* and those on the *Marian*.

Vel was slowly looking around at the people on the bridge, his dear friends and relatives. He was slowly moving his interest from one to another. His brow furrowed a bit before he spoke.

"Two thoughts," he said out of the silence. "One, it occurs to me that we may, individually or collectively, be in the middle of an elaborate dream. None of this is actually happening. Or two, our galaxy may have already been taken over by another Sharkra, one perhaps from a different universe or galaxy, a universe or galaxy with different laws of physics. Those new laws may have already been put in place."

"Geez," said Teddy quietly, "I hope we're dreamin'. I don't know much about our old laws. I'll never learn new ones." Teddy paused for a brief moment. "Earthworm keeps poppin' up in my head."

Uproarious laughter ensued, breaking the tension that had started building again.

"God bless you, Teddy," Jarleth managed to get out as she kept laughing.

Vel was laughing along with everybody on the bridge and Oruku on the viewer. It was a welcome emotional relief.

When the laughter died down, Oruku spoke. "It is, of course, a tremendous benefit to be able to communicate across the galaxy in an instant. Takes most of the trepidation and guesswork out of what's going on."

"I wonder," said Vel, "if we will be able to travel faster than light as you on the *Velgot* have done. If audio transmissions have become instantaneous, maybe the light speed limit has been taken off entirely."

The viewer went blank.

"Uh-oh," said Gary.

"I've never liked surprises," said Vance.

"Shi . . ."

The viewer came back to life. Oruku had a strange look on his face, and his blink rate seemed faster than normal.

"What happened?" asked Alex.

"Well . . . we were just sent to Arkell and back," said Oruku.
Silence.
"They're listening to us," said Vel.
"Whooo?" asked Teddy.
"The new Sharkra," said Vel.

It had been twelve days since the *Velgot* had arrived at Gabriel.
And over the past twelve days hundreds of communiqués had gone
back and forth across the galaxy without the hindrance of time and
space. The entire known intelligent inhabitants of the galaxy were
in agreement that the old Sharkra may have, in fact, been replaced
with a new Sharkra. But, to everybody's relief, nothing seemed to
have been altered in their everyday lives.

That morning, the *Velgot* was preparing to leave Gabriel's orbit
and head for Arkell. The Arkell aboard the *Velgot* were anxious to
visit their home planet. None had ever set foot on it.

"There is a great deal of excitement aboard our ship," said Oruku.
"More than I've ever seen."

"We can only imagine," said Vance. "We're all excited for you."

"If all goes as expected, we should arrive at Arkell in a minute
or so," Oruku said with a big smile.

"Are the citizens of Arkell expecting your visit?" asked Vance.

"They seem to be as excited about it as we are," Oruku said with
a big smile.

"How long do you expect to stay?" asked Shem.

"Have no idea. As long as they'll let us or as long as we want to,
whichever comes first."

"Drop back by when you're in the neighborhood and let us know
how it went," Vance said lightly. "There are more than a few of us
who will be quite interested."

"We'll communicate with you on a regular basis. Let you know
how we're doing and find out how it's going for you."

The *Velgot*, as promised, remained in constant contact with the
leadership of Gabriel, Yassi, Vout, and Byuse. They initially reported

that they had, in fact, traveled to Arkell in under a minute. So the laws of physics had been radically altered. Voice communication between the known life-bearing planets was instantaneous, no different than speaking to a friend living in another town.

Oruku told of the wondrous world of Arkell, a civilization that was near perfect. Oruku tried to describe the beauty of the cities but admitted he was falling short of doing them justice. Many videos were sent from Arkell to the four planets in the *Velgot*'s sphere of influence. Where Gabriel was considered a beautiful planet and Yassi claimed the beautification of just about everything, the planet Arkell was a combination of both.

CHAPTER 12

SPEED TEST

Over the past month, both the *Norman* and the *Marian* took several experimental trips to the planets Yassi and Vout. The trips took just seconds. There were no problems with either the ships or their crews. They did not take shuttles down to the surface during these brief trips but just did a single orbit and returned to Gabriel.

The leadership of Gabriel were about to begin their weekly meeting aboard the *Marian*. These meetings were taking less time as the weeks passed. Nothing new was affecting Gabriel or any of their friends' planets.

Vance opened up that day's meeting as soon as everyone had settled in.

"I would like to suggest we start thinking about ferrying our citizens around the galaxy. The majority of our people have never been off planet."

"That's a terrific idea," said Troy.

"Agreed," said Alex.

"My bag is packed," said Dale with a smile.

"It will be wonderful, and I'm sure educational, to see our friends' planets," said Alex. "Visit Vout, Yassi, and of course Arkell."

"It will take years to take all our citizens to these planets," said Gary.

"They could be just day trips," said Shem. "Leave here in the morning, spend the day on Yassi, and return to Gabriel that evening."

"That's an interesting idea," said Alex.

"Are you assuming all the citizens of Gabriel would want to go into space?" asked Dale.

"I can't think of anyone who wouldn't jump at the opportunity," said Vance.

"You'd be surprised. There will be a few who will reject that offer out of hand," said Dale.

"Really?" said Troy.

"Oh, sure. Not everyone has an explorer personality. But I won't be among that crowd. I'd love to see Yassi and Arkell. Can you imagine?"

"Sign me up too," said Alex.

"Now is the first time we could be able to accomplish such a thing. The trips are now all but instantaneous, no need for going into stasis," said Vance. We could put a thousand people on the *Marian*. Head to Yassi, spend a few days, and return home. It's a quicker trip than from Taupo to Home Bay on a shuttle."

"I would love to visit Arkell," said Vel. "So much to see, so much to learn."

"Okay," said Gary with a smile. "I'll tag along."

"Ditto," said Shem.

"I cannot think of a person who would not want to visit Arkell," said Alex.

"And Yassi," added Gary. "Having been there, I can tell you humans, given a chance, will make it a vacation spot."

"Who gets to go first?" asked Troy.

"I think a lottery would be the fairest," said Vance. "Assign everyone a number and have a weekly drawing."

"There is a record of every person on Gabriel. Simply assign a number to a single individual and one number to a family."

"We could also visit Isley," said Alex.

Dale smiled. "Can you imagine the surprise if the *Norman* were to show up and land in a city park on Isley."

"I think we should make that a priority," said Vance.

CHAPTER 13

A TEMPLE TO SHARKRA

"It was bound to happen," Alex started the meeting. "A group is asking permission to erect a monument to the Sharkra on Terri's Bluff just south of Home Bay.

"I don't know how I feel about that," said Troy. "We haven't had an organized religion on Gabriel. We know, from the history of Earth, that religions caused more hate, pain, death, and destruction on the planet than any other single cause."

"Well first, as far as I know, nobody is suggesting we create a religion . . . yet." Alex smiled. "Second, if memory serves, most of the deadly conflicts came from battles between religions. If a religion were built around Sharkra, it would be the only one."

"Agreed," said Vance. "And never in history has there been more proof of a divine entity."

"The Christians of old Earth would surely disagree with that," said Dale.

"Yes, they would," agreed Alex.

As I recall, when the Arkell, on their first visit here in 142, told us that if the Sharkra could be proved to be a living entity, they would believe the Sharkra were, in fact, a god.

"Well," started Dale, "I personally and strongly believe the Sharkra is a god. No mortal being could alter physics at all, let alone remove the light speed barrier. Transporting galaxy ships a thousand light-years in an instant. I can't think of anything that would cause me to doubt the Sharkra is a god."

"Well to have you, a scientist, believe in God, has gone a long way toward convincing me of the truth of it," said Troy.

"Agreed," said Gary.

"So," said Alex, "all if favor of building a monument, say yea."

All gave an enthusiastic, "YEA."

"Might I suggest we enlist our finest artisans, including Arkell, Byuse, Vout, and Yassi, to submit ideas for the monument?" said Gary.

"And Arkell," added Vance.

"Good, we'll coordinate with the group who brought up the monument and include them in the planning," said Alex.

CHAPTER 14

THE UNVEILING

A huge crowd began gathering midafternoon just south of Home Bay in an area adjoining Terri's Bluff. The beautiful bluff overlooking the Vast Ocean was named after Terri Diggs, the first human expected to have been brought out of stasis on Gabriel. It had been a traumatic, horrifying, and devastating day for Vance —the worst day, by far, in his entire long life. Terri could not be brought out of stasis; she was already dead. To Vance, all the decades of preparing the planet for the human colonists was for naught. He assumed, at that point, all twenty colonists were dead. Fortunately, that was not the case. After being brought out of stasis, the remaining nineteen were alive and well and lived long, productive lives.

A plot of land just south of Terri's Bluff was designated as a special cemetery for the original twenty colonists. The cemetery was just to honor these colonists. Their headstones were made of the gold-bearing quartz that was abundant in most parts of the planet. Each headstone was engraved with the name, the date of birth on Earth, a list of their children, and a brief history of their life on Gabriel.

Artisans, craftsmen, engineers, physicists, and architects from five planets had, for the past eight months, been designing and constructing a monument to Sharkra. During this time, part of the wheat field that surrounded Terri's Bluff had been plowed under and replanted in grass. It had grown nicely over the months and been mowed to a comfortable height, all in an effort to provide room and comfort for those visiting the monument. That evening was to be the unveiling.

The open area around the monument was packed with thousands of Gabrielites, humans, Byuse, Vout, Yassi, and Arkell from the *Velgot*, all anxious to see this edifice, this monument to Sharkra. Most brought some form of lawn chair, and those who didn't just spread a blanket on the grass. Three rows of chairs were set up in front of the monument for the visiting dignitaries from five planets. Audio and visual cameras were in place to hopefully record and transmit the inauguration of the monument to all corners of the galaxy.

The monument, at this moment, was covered by a gold, silk-like material. Whatever was beneath the cover was quite large —twelve meters wide, four deep, and three high. This would not be a small tribute to Sharkra.

As the sun began to set over the horizon, Vance stood up and walked to the temporary podium set up three meters in front of the shrouded monument.

"Ladies and gentlemen, visitors from our five-planet alliance, we are here for the unveiling of our tribute, a monument if you will, to Sharkra. The creation of this monument came into being through a cooperative effort from some of the greatest gifted and artistic minds of our five planets." Vance paused for a moment before addressing those in the chairs in front of him. "If you will, please stand and let the people see you." Twelve men and eight women stood to the enthusiastic applause, whistling and wooing coming from the single-largest gathering Gabriel had ever seen.

When the applause died down to a manageable level, Vance again started to speak.

"I suspect what we are about to see here will be spectacular in many ways. So without further ado, I give you the tribute to Sharkra."

With that, Vance retreated to his chair in the front row as a young woman stepped forward and swiftly pulled off the monument's cover. At that moment, a series of lights came on to illuminate the monument and the ancient music, "2001: A Space Odyssey," began. There, on five separate golden pedestals extending from a massive block of gold-bearing quartz base, sat the five planets of the alliance. They ranged in size from a meter for Byuse to one and a half meters for Arkell. It was a beautiful display. The applause and wooing started immediately. The crowd then emitted surprised sounds as the five planets slowly rose two meters above their pedestals and began revolving on their axis. Then, moments later, the planets began circling around each other on a horizontal plane. These were spectacular renditions of each of the five planets. Each planet was duplicated in living color to perfection. All oceans, rivers, mountains, and continents were there. The rivers seemed to flow; the oceans seemed to create waves on the shores. Even the clouds were in motion around these miniature planets. It was all made possible by projections created from the inside of the miniature planets. The applause and wooing kept getting more intense as the seconds passed and artistic, creative, and technical genius was becoming more apparent.

After a few minutes, the lights began to dim as the planets lowered back down to their pedestals. It became very dark, and the applause and wooing tapered off to silence. Then, with the blast that sounded like a gigantic ship's horn, the sky above the monument became a huge hologram of the Milky Way. It was a hundred meters across and seemingly alive. It was a flat view of this magnificent spiral galaxy as would be seen from space, not from inside the galaxy itself. This was not a model of the Milky Way; it was the Milky Way. A streaming video was being transmitted from a stationary satellite placed in space by the Arkell for just this purpose. The ultra-high-resolution, three-dimensional video was transmitted to Gabriel, converted to a hologram, and projected above the Sharkra's monument. The effect was breathtaking.

The applause and wooing were instant and loud.

After a few moments, Shem's voice came over the audio system. "Here are our stars and planets. We'll start with Gabriel."

A single star in the massive galaxy became brighter and sparkled. Close by, another slightly dimmer light lit Gabriel. The placement in the galaxy was precise.

That brought another round of appreciated applause and wooing.

"Next is Yassi and its star."

Each of the five planets was so depicted as the hologram galaxy continued its slow-motion swirling. Arkell was the last to be lighted and was separated by a great distance from the other four, a thousand light-years. But even at that great distance, it was in the same sector of the galaxy. All the five planets and their stars remained slightly brighter than those in the rest of the galaxy.

"Now we're going to illuminate all planets in our galaxy known to have some form of life."

Pins of light started popping up in their sector of the galaxy. The majority of the galaxy remained unchanged. The crowd continued their applause and wooing during the three minutes spent for them all to illuminate; there were thousands.

The applause and wooing continued unabated.

Vance returned to the platform in front of the monument to address the crowd. "That is it for the—"

Another blast from the massive ship's horn sounded, startling the crowd and Vance.

The hologram of the galaxy began showing more stars and planets lighting up from sectors of the galaxy yet unexplored by the known civilizations. The galaxy continued to become brighter as the minutes went on. Finally, that phenomenon abruptly stopped. There was little sound coming from the spectators. Then the ship's horn sounded again. The black center of the galaxy known by the humans for millennia as a gigantic black hole started to lighten up. It continued for a moment before, in a flash, it became a brilliant, pulsing golden light.

The crowd went wild. Applause and wooing filled the night. All thought this was part of the show.

"What's happening here?" Vance asked Gary loud enough to be heard over the din of the crowd.

"Not part of the programming," Gary yelled back.

"I believe we've just gotten a message from Sharkra," said Dale. "We've just been thanked for honoring them. For me, the pulse we see in the center of the galaxy is simulating its heartbeat."

"Holy shit!" said Shem. "You're right."

"I'm at a loss here," said Vel, as much to himself as to others. This might have been the first time in his life he was caught off guard or confused in any way. He was clearly in shock.

"Ladies and gentlemen," Vance said in a loud voice, nearly yelling. "May I have quiet for a moment?"

The din began to diminish, but slowly.

"Please give me silence," said Vance in a slightly softer voice.

Within a few more seconds, the huge crowd became silent.

"Thank you," said Vance. "What you have witnessed here tonight is a great deal more than was produced by the artisans, technicians, and craftsmen. Their program stopped when the stars and planets of our sector of the galaxy were lighted. After that, the filling in of life-bearing planets in the entire galaxy, and adding the pulsing light at the center of our galaxy, we believe by the Sharkra itself."

The gathered remained dead silent for nearly seven seconds, clearly trying to absorb what Vance had just told them. Then, as if on cue, the applause exploded with screams, wooing, laughing, and some crying. Something extraordinary, something very special, had happened on Gabriel.

"We have a deity," said Dale quietly as he kept his eyes on the magnificent living galaxy.

The galaxy hologram began receding into space, and in a minute, it disappeared. Then the entire sky from horizon to horizon flashed a brilliant gold for a second or two before the sky went dark and the stars and galaxies reappeared.

Again, the crowd went wild.

For the next four weeks, the monument continued to perform its original programming each night just after sunset. The portion added by the Sharkra was not repeated, much to the disappointment of the citizens of Gabriel and the off-planet tourists.

The Sharkra and its now-deified monument became the center of attention throughout the known galaxy and seemed likely to remain so for the foreseeable future. Pilgrims from the five planets began funneling into Home Bay daily, most to pay homage to Sharkra, others simply to see the incredible monument. Some stayed for just a day or two before returning to their home planets, while others stayed weeks. The traffic, in and around Home Bay, had become a major problem. They were not equipped to handle the crowds that were growing daily. There were only two small hotels and a dozen restaurants. Word soon got out that if they wished to be warm and fed, pilgrims needed to come with camping equipment and other necessities. Even with that practice in place, the area in and around Home Bay continued to be overrun.

A meeting was being held by the planet's leadership. All were sitting around a large round table in a room just off the *Marian's* bridge.

"We're simply going to have to limit the number of visitors we allow daily," said Vance. "There's no choice."

"And soon," added Alex.

"Kind of a paradox," said Dale. "The monument was built to honor the Sharkra, who altered the physics of our galaxy, allowing instantaneous travel from planet to planet, clearly and truly a godsend that has now become somewhat of a curse."

"Unexpected consequences have plagued intelligent beings throughout history," said Alex.

"Indeed," said Vance.

"I suggest we calculate how many pilgrims we can comfortably handle daily, divide that number by five, and inform all the planets of the number of citizens they are allowed to visit daily," said Dale.

"Why not just divide by four?" asked Vance.

"To be fair, we need to limit the number of Gabrielites visiting the site from around our planet," said Dale.

"You're right," agreed Vance.

The following day, a message was transmitted to the known galaxy describing the problem and the solution.

It didn't take long for the responses to arrive back at Gabriel. No one was happy with this solution. After all, it was argued, Sharkra was part of the entire galaxy, not just the citizens of Gabriel.

"They have a valid point," said Troy.

"Sharkra is in fact part of the entire galaxy," said Vance, "but it's not their planets that are being overrun. We are being fair about the numbers being allowed per planet."

"Most have acknowledged that," said Alex.

Dale looked around the table. "Any ideas?"

Vel spoke up. "I might suggest we provide the building plans for the monument to our friends, let them build their own monument."

Dale smiled. "A simple solution for a complex problem."

"All in favor?" said Vance.

All were.

CHAPTER 15

ALL IN FAVOR

There were four representatives from each of the five planets assembled in a large meeting room aboard the *Velgot*. At the moment, Oruku held the floor.

"We have all given our opinion on the Sharkra over the past two days. I believe it is time to vote on the three major subjects of our meeting. Can we see a show of hands in favor of proceeding to a vote?"

All but three of the delegates raised their hands. Two of the three were from Vout, the third from Byuse.

"That's a strong majority. We'll get right to it. First, do we agree that Sharkra is responsible for the massive change in the laws of physics?"

All but the same three raised their hands. These three had more or less the same concerns. Simply put, they questioned why it was assumed that Sharkra was responsible for the enormous change in the laws of physics. Could it not have been an entity completely unknown in the galaxy and, they argued, what if in fact Sharkra was declared responsible and wasn't? Might the actual power behind the altered physics get upset with the slight and wreak havoc on the galaxy? That was a weak argument and, most thought, quite a reach. So the three remained in the minority with those beliefs.

Oruku smiled. "Again we have a strong majority. Question two, do you agree that the Sharkra should be elevated to the status of a deity?"

This question was the most contentious by the assembled; there was considerable resistance. Who were they to declare an unknown entity a god? What exactly constitutes a god? Even after the discussion went on for an hour, twenty percent of the delegates were still reluctant to classify the Sharkra as a deity.

During this hour, three remained silent on the subject, Alex, Vance, and Dale. But as soon as all the arguments on both sides tapered off, when no new thoughts were forthcoming, Dale stood up.

"I don't know how anyone can doubt that Sharkra is clearly an all-powerful being," he said. "The ability to alter physics, in any way, is, or was, believed by everyone sitting at this table to be impossible. To alter physics"—Dale raised his voice slightly—"AS HAS BEEN DONE, is an ability that we literally cannot begin to understand, not one bit of it."

Some murmuring began between the elite group around the table.

Dale continued. "I personally have always been an atheist. My rational mind rejected an omnificent being, an all-powerful spirit. How could such a being possibly be?" Dale paused for a moment. "But another part of my mind looked at the magnificent universe. The infinite size, the makeup of elements, the power and energy of stars, the incredible diversity of life. And I would ask myself, can all this be by chance? When did it all begin? How did it all begin?" Dale paused for another moment. "Something or someone altered a major cornerstone of physics. The only thing that could do that would have to be an omnificent being, a true god. And frankly I am greatly comforted by the knowledge that an omnificent being does, in fact, exist."

There was silence in the room for several seconds.

"Well put, Dr. Isley," said Oruku, breaking the silence.

"Very well put, my friend," added Alex.

The gathered burst into clapping and wooing.

When the clapping died down, Oruku stood. "I suggest we now take a vote. Do we believe Sharkra to be a deity?"

Dale's passionate admission of his belief swung the vote to nineteen for, one against.

"We have the majority in favor of declaring Sharkra a deity," said Oruku. "And finally, what should our new deity be called?"

It was Alex's turn to speak up. "Just about every culture throughout Earth's history has called their deity by a different name. I would assume that would hold true throughout the galaxy. So, in my opinion, whatever we here decide to call the deity will not please or be agreed to by every civilization."

"Perhaps, then," said Oruku, "let each call Sharkra what they wish. I can speak for the Arkell. We wish to call the deity Sharkra, as we always have."

Alex smiled. "Despite the fact that 'Sharkra' means 'unknown force'?"

Oruku returned the smile. "We're going to change that definition to 'known force.'"

Vance cleared his throat. "So, Dr. Isley, would your newfound belief in a God include a heaven for the good and a hell for the bad?"

Dale smiled. "I have no idea."

CHAPTER 16

FAR, FAR AWAY

The *Velgot* was in geosynchronous orbit above Home Bay. Dale, Vance, Alex, Gary, Shem, and Vel were sitting in a small viewing room aboard the *Velgot*. All eyes were fixed on the viewer. The looks on their faces varied from amusement to surprise. Oruku was giving a summary of what they were looking at.

"In a nutshell," Oruku continued, "we were transported from Arkell to this planet on the other side of the galaxy. Forty-eight thousand light-years, to be more precise."

"Had you plotted a course to that particular location?" asked Dale.

"Not that exact location but to that sector of the galaxy."

"Travel time?" asked Shem.

"Thirty-two seconds."

No one said anything at this point. Nearly instantaneous travel times had become the norm.

"That's a beautiful planet," said Alex.

"Nearly as beautiful as Gabriel," Oruku said with a smile. "Similar configuration in many ways."

"I assume it is populated with intelligent beings," said Vance.

"It is. And I'll bet you'd like to see them."

"Oh, yes," Dale said with a big smile.

On the viewer came a picture of four inhabitants.

"Oh my god," said Shem.

"I'll be damned," said Vance.

"Who'd a thought?" said Dale.

"We are not alone," said Alex.

There on the screen was a family of what appeared to be humans—a mother, a father, a daughter, and a son—sitting in a nicely appointed room. The room looked to be a living room. The recorder's view moved around the room. On one wall was a stone fireplace. As the recorder continued to move, a kitchen came into view through an arched doorway. Farther along was clearly a dining room complete with a nice table surrounded by six chairs. Then the recorder's view stopped where it started, looking at the family. The family were all smiling, all waving at the recorder.

"What do they call themselves?" asked Alex.

"Namuh."

"What is the name of their planet?"

"Trae," answered Oruku.

"Are they what they appear to be?" asked Alex.

"Not quite," said Oruku. "But nearly—just a few genes off."

"Judging by what they're wearing, it looks like Earth in the early to mid-twentieth century," said Alex.

"That was our assumption also," said Oruku. "And that's close. They use internal combustion engines to power their vehicles and various tools. They have a reliable electricity source in hydroelectric dams, fairly sophisticated appliances, and"—Oruku paused for a moment—"pretty advanced computers, considering their level of technology."

"That's interesting," said Dale.

Oruku nodded. "But, strangely, they have not yet achieved powered flight."

"That doesn't make sense," said Shem.

"Agreed," Oruku responded. "It seems the concept hasn't occurred to them."

There was a momentary pause before Dale spoke up. "All in all, that puts them in Earth's early twentieth century in some ways and mid- to late twentieth century in others."

"That's right," said Shem.

"What led you to this particular family?" asked Vance.

"Sharkra. We simply drove to their home, which was out in the country, secluded from other homes in the area. Very nice."

"Hold on," said Vance. "What did you drive up in?"

Oruku smiled. "Our engineers duplicated a vehicle that was in common use there. It looked a little like an old Earth station wagon. Quite fun to get around in, actually."

"Really? How long did it take them to duplicate that?"

"Two days. Our engineers downloaded the building specs from one of their auto companies' computers and put our multidimensional printer to work. The engineers enjoyed the project immensely. When finished, they drove it all over our ship, giving rides to many. Very entertaining."

"I can imagine," said Alex.

"We took the vehicle down with us in the shuttle, landed in a remote area at night, unloaded it, and sent the shuttle back to the *Velgot*."

"How many went down to the planet?" asked Vance.

"Four, Randa acting as my wife, two children, and me."

"A family," stated Dale.

"Exactly. A family is, universally, a nonthreatening unit." Oruku paused for a moment. "We told them our car was acting up and asked if we might stop there and see if we could fix it."

"They bought that?"

"They did." Oruku smiled. "I'll shorten the story a little. We ended up being houseguests."

"Well," said Alex, "people of goodwill."

"Delightful, just delightful," said Oruku.

"Is their race peace-loving, warlike, or something in between?"

"We didn't detect any signs of hostility, current or past. And we scanned the entire planet."

"Like the Vout or Byuse?" said Alex.

"Except we found these people of good cheer, a sense of humor, and interesting personalities."

"That certainly doesn't fit the Vout or Byuse."

"Not even a little," said Vance with a smile.

"I'm assuming they didn't see the *Velgot*?" asked Shem.

"You're right, Sharkra put us behind one of their six moons."

"And your appearance?" asked Alex.

Oruku smiled. "We also duplicated their clothes, and then we lied to them, told them we were from a family that was stricken by enlarged heads."

"They bought that?"

"A very trusting and open people. We came to the conclusion that they don't lie. Simply isn't done." Oruku smiled. "They offered condolences for our condition."

"Well that's both amusing and refreshing," said Alex.

"Very," said Dale. "I'm sure Sharkra put you there for a reason."

Oruku nodded. "We soon learned through their radio broadcasts that they had a contagious and deadly virus moving quickly though the population of their most populated continent. There was little question it would eventually travel around their entire planet."

"I assume you were able to contain it?" asked Dale.

"It wasn't a problem developing a cure and a preventive vaccine, but determining how to introduce them to this race, without them realizing we were not of their world, was a challenge."

"Why not just tell them the truth?" asked Vance.

"We were not to do that."

"Who told you that?"

"Like many things concerning Sharkra, we just knew they didn't want us to reveal ourselves as aliens."

"That is, of course, why Sharkra hid the *Velgot* behind a moon," said Alex.

Vance nodded in agreement. "How'd you solve their virus problem?"

"They had a number of research labs scattered around the continent. And the mother of this family, Jaspa, was in charge of one of them. Her husband's name is Trebor.

"Probably not a coincidence," said Vance.

"No coincidence, Sharkra led us right to her."

"Actually, her lab was working on a vaccine and, as we ascertained later, they were heading in the right direction. They were further advanced in this technology than in many of their other industries. Quite surprising, actually."

"So you . . . ?"

"We continued our lie, and during one of our many conversations, we told Jaspa that Randa was quite adept at designing vaccines. Suggested that she might take a look at their progress and hopefully make a suggestion or two."

"She bought that?" asked Dale.

"Again, they didn't question anything that they were told. Fascinating, we thought."

"Jaspa graciously invited Randa to visit her lab the next day to take a look at their progress."

"I would think Jaspa would become suspicious if Randa fixed their computer model," said Shem.

"Randa is a clever lady. She soon pinpointed two areas that were, in effect, blocking their path to success. But she didn't correct them. She simply suggested that those two areas of their formula troubled her but did not offer the solution."

"Clever," said Dale.

"Very. Jaspa took her to another area of their research facility where they were working on a cure. Again, they were on the right track but were missing just one chemical process in the sequence. Randa suggested five different chemicals, only one of which would do the job. She left it at that."

"How long after that did it take for them to work it out?" asked Dale.

"Just two days. Jaspa heaped a lot of praise on Randa for pointing out the problem with their formulas."

"Four days later, they announced they had developed a cure for the virus and had an effective vaccine."

"Great story," said Alex.

"How long did you stay on the planet?"

"Seven days."

"How did you frame your departure?" asked Shem.

"Just told them we were continuing our journey, said our farewells, and drove off."

"I'll bet they're still talking about the big-headed strangers."

"I would think so." Oruku smiled. "That was just three days ago."

"Wow," said Shem.

"Anything else worthy of reporting?" asked Dale.

"Oh yes, once back aboard the *Velgot*, we were sent to another planet. Different experience altogether."

"Intelligent life?"

"Oh yes," said Oruku. "Sharkra put the *Velgot* directly over one of their large cities."

"Assuming Sharkra doesn't do anything without reason, I'm thinking they wanted the Arkell to be respected by the indigenous population," said Vel.

"That's our assumption also, son," said Oruku.

Everybody smiled when Oruku called Vel "son." His pride in Vel was obvious. He didn't make a big deal of it, but a person would have to be blind not to see it.

"These were, in fact, a warlike race. We were only there for a matter of minutes before we detected weapons being deployed and pointing in our direction."

"Really?" said Vance. "They decided to take on a race that they should have realized had several thousand years of advanced science on them, brilliant."

"I assume they didn't fire on you?" said Shem.

"No, they didn't. They had to know they had no weapon in their arsenal that could reach us at that altitude. It was just a show of force."

Vance nodded. "What do they call themselves?"

"The planet is called Twis. The two warring factions are called Naissu and Esenic. A third, a neutral continent, is inhabited by the Etiws. All the same species, identical DNA."

So they all started in the same place on the planet," said Dale.

"Yes, and that place was the continent of the Etiws."

"The neutral continent?" said Vance. "That seems odd."

Oruku nodded. "We were able to glean enough of their history to understand there was a great and long conflict between three factions. That finally drove them apart—apart meaning two of the factions managed to build seaworthy ships and simply vacated their home continent. The two sailed to different continents."

"What was your involvement?" asked Shem.

"We tapped into their communications and started to study their languages. As it turned out, each nation continent had a different language. There were naturally a lot of similarities, but most of the vocabularies varied greatly."

"That seems odd, all things considered."

"They'd been separated for thousands of years. Their ships took pilgrims off the Etiws continent and delivered them to the two other continents. We couldn't understand why they didn't maintain communications with their origins on Etiws, as has been the case with many civilizations throughout history. Seems they had no interest in maintaining a relationship with their origins."

"Did you learn them?"

"Thanks to the constant chatter over their airwaves, our translating program had them worked out after a few hours."

"Your translating program is way ahead of ours," said Dale.

Oruku paused for a moment. "We will duplicate ours and give it to you."

"That's great," said Shem. "That is sure to be very useful at some point."

"Thank you," said Dale.

"Happy to do it."

"How did you contact them?" asked Shem.

"We, as you know, have linguists aboard the *Velgot*. Me being one of them. After a day, we had the three languages down pretty well."

"A day?" said Vance. "Incredible."

"And then?" asked Shem.

"Now that we were tapped into their communications and knew their languages, we just listened and gathered information, tried to see which faction seemed to be the most aggressive." Oruku smiled. "Gathering that information proved to be difficult because the speculation about our ship and its intent filled the airwaves, as you might imagine. Very little chatter about aggressions going on two continents. We were able to tap into what served as an archive vault of the most aggressive faction of the planet, Naissu, the one we were in orbit over."

"Sharkra knew exactly where to put you."

"Without question," said Oruku. "The archive provided us with enough detailed intel to come up with a simple plan."

Vance smiled. "Which was to scare the crap on of them?"

Oruku returned the smile. "Basically, yes."

"How did the neutral continent manage to stay out of the conflicts?" asked Alex.

Oruku smiled. "They had managed to remain neutral over the centuries. They were not unlike old Earth's Switzerland."

"That's interesting," remarked Alex. "A place on the planet where one could safely visit or make deposits. Could also be a place to gather opposing factions to talk peace."

"Exactly," said Oruku.

"What did you do next?" asked Shem.

"The following day, we took a shuttle down at midday. Went to what appeared to be a park and"—Oruku smiled—"parked."

"Gather a crowd, did you?"

"We gathered a lot of military types with weapons of all sorts. Quite impressive, actually. Reminded us of old Earth's armament. But we didn't see any civilians at this point."

"Aircraft?"

"Oh yes, all were war planes. Fighters and bombers. Jet propulsion, quite fast."

"Any direct threats from the aircraft?" asked Vance.

"No, it seems they were smarter than that."

"And then?" said Shem with a smile.

"We used more caution with them. We didn't know them like we knew you."

"You spent centuries watching and studying us on EARTH but never made contact. Yet after a day there, you exposed yourselves, why?" asked Alex.

"We had several millennia to study the humans, and we knew you well. We had no prior knowledge of these people. And, importantly, Sharkra put us in plain sight for a reason, clearly wanted us exposed."

"Well I'd be willing to bet you now know why," said Vance.

Oruku nodded slowly. "We do. Since two of the three major factions on the planet had been in conflict and, at times, in all-out war for over two hundred years, destroying everything they could of their enemies' holdings, this destroyed any possibility of evolving into a productive society. This was not only destructive for the warring factions but also hindered neutral Etiws' progress. There were no winners in this conflict, just losers."

"As is generally the case with all wars," said Vance knowingly.

"The story went like this," said Oruku. "As we sat in place there in the middle of the Naisa's largest city, a civilian crowd started to gather behind the military. The military held the civilians back to at least a hundred meters from our shuttle. They then proceeded to surround us with all manner of weapons. Knowing the basic nature of intelligent beings, we just waited for their next move. An hour later, three men cautiously started to approach our shuttle. Two young males were armed. The third was much older and unarmed. The three walked to within twenty meters of our shuttle before stopping."

"Before you go any further with the story, how about letting us see what they look like," said Vance.

"Oh, of course, here you go."

The viewer showed the two, in what must have been full fighting gear. The third, the older man, was not armed and was dressed quite neatly. The two who wore heavy armor had two side weapons and one large weapon that looked like a rocket launcher. These males were under two meters high, quite lean and muscular. Dark straight hair and brown skin. Looked a lot like the Asians of old Earth."

"Okay, thanks," said Vance. "I was afraid they'd look like the old Malic."

"God forbid," said Alex.

"We remained still for a few minutes before we lowered the ramp and opened the hatch. Then I told them, "We mean you no harm. We would like to invite you into our transport for a conversation." They were quite surprised, but after a few seconds of conversation, they stared heading toward the ramp." Oruku smiled. "I informed them that no weapons would be allowed in the transport."

"Did that stop them?" asked Vance.

"No, as a matter of fact, the two young men started walking faster toward our shuttle. We shut the hatch and withdrew the ramp. The two armed men dropped to one knee and pointed their large weapon at the shuttle. The older man barked an order, and they quickly set their weapons on the grass and stood."

"So they had discipline?" said Vance.

"So it would seem. The older man told them to back away, and they did for about ten meters. He told them to retreat back to the hundred-meter line. One balked for a moment before retreating." Oruku paused for a moment. "We took this as a positive sign. We extended the ramp and opened the hatch. I again invited the older man into the shuttle. He hesitated for a second before walking up the ramp and into the shuttle. We left the hatch open and the ramp in place. Didn't want to scare him any more than he was. From here on, I'll let you see for yourself."

The viewer switched to an interior shot of the Arkell shuttle. It showed the man walking up the ramp into the interior. He was a bit startled when he saw Oruku but covered it well.

"Welcome to our shuttle," said Oruku. "My name is Oruku. May I ask yours?"

"Where are you from, and what is your intention?" the man asked without a hint of emotion.

"They speak English?" asked Vance.

Oruku paused the video. "No, our translation program quickly replaces their language with whatever language we choose. For your benefit, we chose English."

"That is remarkable," said Alex. "The movement of his lips even looks like he's speaking English."

"It does," agreed Vance. "Clever."

Oruku nodded and resumed the video.

"I will be happy to tell you everything you want to know, but we consider it polite to introduce oneself before engaging in conversation," Oruku said softly without any malice.

The man stood looking at Oruku for a moment or two before speaking. "My name is Naisa."

"I am pleased to meet you, Naisa. We are not aware of what sort of greeting is custom on your world. Some shake hands, some hug, some bow in respect."

"We bow," said Naisa.

Oruku bowed. Naisa bowed back.

"I will ask again," said Naisa. "Why are you here, and what are your intentions?"

"We are here because the war you have been engaged in for over two hundred years is not and never has been a benefit to anyone on your planet. It is simply destructive for all involved."

"This is your concern—why?"

"Let's just say that a higher power wants it to stop."

Naisa's brow wrinkled. "A higher power?"

"Yes."

"We've assumed you are the higher power."

"We are not even close, Naisa."

Naisa's brows went up slightly.

Oruku continued. "So you are aware, we are going to have a talk with your adversary soon. I can assure you that you both will accept a permanent cease-fire."

"Why would we do that?"

Oruku smiled warmly. "You will have no viable choice, Naisa. You will either accept an armistice or face some unfortunate consequences."

"Are you threatening us?" said Naisa with a defiant tone.

"Not us, we are simply acting as a messenger for a much-greater power."

It didn't take a keen observer to see that statement surprised and alarmed Naisa. "Who is this higher power?" he asked respectfully.

"Not who, but 'what' is the question you should be asking."

"Then what is this vaulted power?"

"Sharkra," answered Oruku.

"Sharkra . . . ?"

"Let's just say that our technology, our intelligence, could be compared to a worm against the abilities of Sharkra."

Naisa thought about that for a couple of seconds. "I don't believe that. That's not possible." He paused for a moment. "We are able to cause you severe damage."

Oruku could see that Naisa made the threat with a great deal more bravado than he felt.

"Naisa, you appear to be an intelligent man. If that is the case, you can clearly see that our technology is thousands of years ahead of yours. Why, then, would you threaten us?"

"We will see who will prevail," said Naisa.

Oruku shook his head in disbelief at the false bravado of this man. "Kilee," Oruku said in a calm voice, "in two minutes, remove all weapons and machines of war that are within striking range of this location."

"Two minutes," answered Kilee.

That quick dialogue got Naisa's attention.

"Naisa, you have just shy of two minutes to have your warriors shed all weapons and evacuate all the war machines in range of this transport."

"Even if I wanted to, I can't do that from here. And there's not enough time for me get out there to comply with your order."

"All you have to do is speak from here. Just give the orders as if you were standing right in front of them."

Oruku could see that Naisa had become tense and confused.

"How about this?" said Oruku as he reached over and touched a button. The walls of the shuttle became transparent. The park, all the crowds, the army and their equipment, and the city beyond were clearly visible.

That seemed to shake Naisa back to the reality of the moment. He could see the hundreds of soldiers manning their weapons as he looked around the park.

He hesitated no longer. "This is Naisa. You are to disarm and vacate all weapons you are in or around, immediately. I repeat, immediately."

There was considerable stirring around by the troops, but none could be seen running from their weapons.

"Twenty-five seconds," Oruku said calmly.

Naisa didn't need any further encouragement. "You will be dead in twenty seconds if you are still with your weapons."

That did it. Hundreds of soldiers flew out of their machines and vehicles. Others dropped their weapons as they fled away from the shuttle.

A few seconds later, hundreds of violet beams emitted from the bottom of the *Velgot* and vaporized all the now-abandoned weapons. It was over in a matter of seconds.

"Holy shit!" said Vance. "I didn't know you had that capability."

Oruku paused the video and smiled. "Neither did Naisa, but as you can see, he has become a believer."

"That was an impressive demonstration," said Shem.

Oruku nodded and started the video again.

Naisa was stunned as he looked around the park, a park that no longer held any weapons. "What is your command?" His defiant tone was replaced with one of great respect.

"We do not command. We ask. We would like you to destroy all tools of war, and I can assure you, your enemy will be doing the same."

Naisa bowed low.

"Then we ask the leadership of both factions to begin meetings on Etiws to settle all differences peacefully. If all this is not accomplished within the next fifty days, we will come back and eliminate both factions' leaderships down twenty places. Then the new leadership will be charged with making a lasting peace."

"Put a little incentive in there, did you?" Vance smiled.

"When did all this occur?" asked Shem.

Oruku smiled. "This morning."

CHAPTER 17

SHARKRA'S BIDDING

The *Velgot* had remained in orbit over Home Bay for the past three days. At the present time, there were thousands of Arkell touring dozens of interesting places around the planet, mostly in the company of human friends—friendships that had matured and grown over the decades.

Some Arkell preferred spending time at the many pristine beaches in tropical locations around the planet. Others went fishing on a human friend's boat or transported boats they had built aboard the *Velgot* to various bodies of water around the planet. Many preferred trout or bass fishing on the many lakes, rivers, and streams on the Ring Continent, while others favored ocean fishing. Oruku himself spent most of his time with Shem, Jarleth, and their extended family. He was like a beloved uncle to them. When time permitted, he, Shem, and Vel would spend hours together talking and hiking the trails surrounding Home Bay. At the present time, they had just reached the rim of the tall hill that made up the south side of the Vance River. They sat down on a bench that overlooked the river and, in the distance, through the trees, could be seen Home Bay.

"This is wonderful," said Oruku.

"One of my favorite spots," said Shem.

Vel nodded in agreement as he took in the view.

The three men looked much alike. Vel's skin color was darker, and he was a great deal younger, but it was clear these three were closely related.

"I could spend—excuse me for a moment," said Oruku. "I have a message coming in."

Oruku listened to his message for a minute before turning toward his two companions. "I have to get back to the *Velgot*."

Thirty minutes later, the three walked across the bridge into Home Bay and on to the shuttle landing site. There, a shuttle hovered while Arkell men, women, and a few children were boarding, while others waited their turn in a fairly long line. All in line were still visiting with their human friends as they approached the shuttle. When the shuttle was full to capacity, the hatch closed and the ramp was withdrawn. Seconds later, it shot toward the *Velgot* as another shuttle dropped down to the landing site. Around the planet, Arkell shuttles were picking up Arkell and returning them to the *Velgot*.

After twenty minutes, the line of Arkell was down to just a few, including Oruku.

Gathered around Oruku was the entire leadership of Gabriel and their wives.

Oruku smiled warmly. "It has become apparent that Sharkra intends to use us Arkell to correct the multitude of conflicts and ills that are prevalent in all sectors of the galaxy."

"That's a lot of territory to cover," said Vance. "Even with the light speed barrier removed, I would think it would take years to solve the galaxy's conflicts and problems."

"It's not just we of the *Velgot* but all the Arkell's space-worthy ships, eighty-three in all."

"Really?" said Alex.

Oruku nodded.

"Still, I'd be willing to bet it will be an enormous and time-consuming task," said Shem.

"That is a possibility, but you must remember we of the *Velgot* and the majority of the other Arkell ships are explorers. Now, thanks to Sharkra, we can explore the entire galaxy. What is being asked of us are not tasks—it is our reason for being."

"Sometimes we look past the big picture," said Vance.

Oruku smiled. "Be back as soon as we've completed whatever undertakings Sharkra puts in front of us," said Oruku as he waved and walked up the ramp into the interior of the shuttle.

CHAPTER 18

LET'S TRAVEL

In the years since the *Velgot* last departed, the citizens of Gabriel, Vout, Byuse, Yassi, and Arkell had been traveling to the other planets on a regular basis. Planet tourism had become more or less an industry in Yassi, Arkell, and Gabriel. Each of these three planets began building more hotels, restaurants, and shops for the aliens to purchase memorabilia to take back to their planets. The planet Arkell welcomed visitors without cost. Arkell had no need for currency. That being the case, everything was complementary to the visitors. In the spirt of reciprocity, there was no cost to the Arkell when they visited the other planets.

Although Arkell welcomed all visitors graciously, it seemed they were particularly fond of humans. Wherever the humans visited on Arkell, they were engaged with Arkell seeking to carry on conversations. The Arkell spoke English with an accent of old Earth, an accent that the Gabrielites recognized from motion pictures they had brought with them from Earth to Gabriel centuries before. That accent had noticeably changed over time on Gabriel.

When Vance, Alex, Dale, and their wives visited Arkell, they were treated as celebrities. They caused great excitement among the normally stoic Arkell. Here, on their planet, were people who had actually lived on old Earth hundreds of years before its destruction—not only lived on Earth but were the planet's beloved and famous leaders, the humans who actually took control of a chaotic civilization and put the planet on a path of lasting peace and prosperity. They were celebrities of the highest order. Wherever they went, Alex, Vance, and Dale were invited to give talks and take questions from groups of Arkell ranging from a few dozen to over a thousand in some venues. They accepted every invitation graciously. After all, without the Arkell, there would be no humans.

Alex's questions normally consisted of how he coped with being sent back thirty-five years in time to start his life over as an eight-year-old child, how he acquired the fortune, the inspiration, and the know-how to take control of all Earth's governments.

Vance's questions consisted of his military background, his meeting Alex, and his role in Earth's government—the WGC. But most questions were of his single-handedly seeding the planet Gabriel with all manner of life over five decades ship time, which amounted to nearly five hundred years planet time.

Dale was questioned about his many inventions and discoveries. Isleium was, in the Arkell's opinion, one of the single-greatest creations of mankind. It was a substance that even the Arkell, in all their advancements in all fields of science, never came up with. The Arkell marveled at the perfection of these SLFs. They were indistinguishable from flesh-and-blood humans.

This interplanetary travel began to include planets that were unknown prior to the Sharkra removing the light speed barrier, planets that would, over the following years and decades, become part of a galaxy-wide allegiance.

It had been seven years since the *Velgot* had been to Gabriel. There was a huge crowd gathered in the gazebo park, and just about every citizen living on that side of Gabriel was outside, most lying prone, looking up, waiting for the *Velgot*'s arrival, an arrival that was always special, always thrilling. The time of arrival was to be ten o'clock. And you could literally set your clocks by the punctuality of the Arkell.

Three, two, one. And in it came. In three seconds, it went from a mere speck in space to a massive orb five kilometers in diameter stopped dead over Home Bay. It never failed to surprise and shock even those who'd seen it many times. Screams could be heard everywhere the population could witness the phenomenon.

"HOLY SHIT!" said Vance. Here was a man who certainly didn't startle easily, but the arrival of the *Velgot*, much to his delight, got him every time.

"This is breathtaking," said Alex.

"I nearly wet my pants," said Teddy.

Nearly three thousand Gabrielites remained lying prone, laughing, and talking excitedly in the park along with all Gabriel's hierarchy. The massive ship had just arrived two minutes before. Everyone's eyes were still riveted on the marvelous *Velgot* when, without warning, a second ship, the *Geaalo*, shot in and took up station alongside the *Velgot*. The screams and laughter were instant and continuous.

"HOLY SHIT!" screamed Vance for the second time in as many minutes.

"I didn't see that coming," said a visibly shaking Dale. "Wow!"

"That is spectacular," said Alex. "Will you look at that? What a sight."

"Get one more ship that size in orbit, and they'll begin to affect the tides," Dale joked.

It was a spectacular sight, the giant golden orb that was the *Velgot* orbiting in tandem with the even larger, bright-silver *Geaalo*.

"Wow, wow, wow," exclaimed Vance as he continued to lie on the grass, cradling his head in his hands. "Just look at that."

"That's a sight one couldn't imagine," said Alex.

"Truly mind-boggling," said Aidan.

"Look what they've done to the *Geaalo*. It's beautiful," said Lara.

"It looked pretty much like a derelict last time we saw it," said Colleen.

"This is what it would have looked like thousands of years ago when it was first built," said Dale. "Can't wait to see the inside."

"And we'll be seeing Ooat, Ssamp, and a few other friends from the *Geaalo*," said Shem.

"I'm looking forward to it," said Jarleth.

"I'm interested in seeing the young women of the *Geaalo*," said Dale.

"Really?" asked Alex.

Dale nodded. "You may recall that we and the Arkell of the *Velgot* agreed to providing the Arkell of the *Geaalo* with DNA of our women in order to 'upgrade' their women."

"I'd forgotten," said Alex.

"My problem is what the *Geaalo*'s women thought of that," said Aidan. "To be told, in effect, that you were ugly and stupid would be insulting at best, heartbreaking to be sure."

"I agree," said Colleen. "They should have demanded they also get DNA from human and *Velgot*'s men."

"Maybe they did." Vance smiled. "And I believe the *Geaalo*'s women not only looked like their men but were just as tough."

"There were probably a few asses kicked when the women heard the plan," added Dale.

"But on the bright side, the mothers of their new beautiful little girls will be delighted," said Aidan.

"Good point," agreed Colleen.

The Gabriel delegation consisted of Vance, Alex, Dale, Shem, Vel, Teddy, and their wives. They had just been transported to the *Velgot* via an Arkell shuttle. Waiting on the shuttle deck were Oruku, Kilee, Nola, Ooat, and Ssamp.

The moment was wonderful for all, old friends getting together after seven years. Hugs and Waoca were in full swing. When all had completed their greetings, they engaged in cheerful banter.

"Tomaco, you had it right," said a smiling Oruku. "Sharkra did want to be recognized as an entity but has not indicated Sharkra needs to be considered a deity."

"We came to more or less the same conclusion," said Shem. "It seems Sharkra is leaving its presence in the galaxy up to the individual to believe as he or she wishes."

"There's been a lot of speculation about this on Gabriel," said Alex.

"Now all over the galaxy," said Oruku. "We, for the past seven years, have inserted ourselves into a multitude of challenges presented in hundreds of civilizations. We have, when appropriate, told them of a power that controls the galaxy. When they ask if this power is to be considered a god, we tell them that designation was to be left up to them—they can believe as they wish. Sharkra has not asked for anything." Oruku paused. "I tried to make it as simple as possible. I told the leaders and, when possible, the entire civilization, that there is but one rule. The rule is that one can believe of Sharkra as he or she wishes. And no matter their belief, it is not to be criticized by those who believe otherwise."

"That is a simple rule," said Vance.

"Do you think all will follow it?" asked Shem.

"Unfortunately, no, but if and when we learn that they are not adhering to this rule, we will pay them another visit and make it clear to them."

Shem nodded and smiled.

"Interestingly enough," said Dale, "throughout history, sometimes when a unique or charismatic individual has been declared a god or prophet, either by themselves or their followers, a new religion is formed. Then the disciples go about demanding that everyone believe their god is the only true deity. Then strict obedience to new tenets is demanded by the high priests or Imams. Death and mayhem always follow . . . always."

"I believe Sharkra is a god," said Alex.

"I, for one, will not criticize your belief," said Teddy while maintaining a solemn expression.

Everybody laughed.

"I believe everybody here has the same belief," said Dale.

Vance nodded. He knew a major contributing factor in Alex's accepting Sharkra as a deity. A day after his parents were killed by Islamic terrorists centuries ago, Alex had a visitation from his parents. Most believed it was just a dream, but Vance knew better. That visitation was just that, a visit from his deceased parents.

"I'll bet you have a few stories to tell," Shem said to Oruku.

Oruku smiled. "We have stories that, if not personally witnessed, would not be believed."

"Even when witnessed, some are still hard to believe," added Ooat.

"I cannot wait to hear them," said Dale.

"We have thousands of hours of video, and we would like to share some highlights with Gabrielites," said Oruku.

"That's a good idea. How do you propose to do that?" asked Alex.

"I suggest we transmit our chronicles around the planet. Let all Gabrielites witness, see, and hear the stories we have to tell," said Oruku.

"Agreed," said Vance and Alex at the same time.

"I'll put out a notice as to when this will occur so everyone can make themselves available," suggested Dale.

"Good," said Oruku. "We think two or three hours in the evening for the next three weeks should give most of the highlights from our interaction with the indigenous populations of hundreds of planets."

"That will make it our first scheduled viewer series," said Alex.

Just about all the viewers around the planet were on. Those who lived on the opposite side of the planet recorded the program while they slept. The vast majority around the planet also recorded the Arkell chronicles. There was little doubt that each episode would be viewed over and over for years to come.

CHAPTER 19

PMUDA

I t was assumed that all viewers around Gabriel were on to watch or record what promised to be some very interesting and entertaining videos. The screen now showed a picture of the planet Gabriel as seen from space. At the designated time, the picture changed to one of Oruku shown from the waist up.

"We thought, while we ran the videos, we would have a few Gabrielites of your acquaintance make comments and ask questions off screen while the videos are running. Hopefully this will enhance the information given by the videos."

The picture changed to a panning shot of Alex, Dale, Vance, Teddy, and their wives sitting on comfortable chairs in front of a large viewer. All were smiling.

"So we begin," said Oruku.

The opening scene from the *Velgot* was spectacular as it approached a planet at a high rate of speed.

"This is the planet Pmuda."

"Wow! That's different," said Alex.

"Eight small continents and a lot of oceans," said Oruku. "As you can see, other than continents at the poles, six of the continents are lined up fairly evenly round the equator. And they are close in size."

"Are those volcanos surrounding all the continents?" asked Shem.

"Yes, there are six to nine small, dormant volcanos around each of the continents," answered Oruku.

"The diversity in the galaxy will never fail to amaze me," said Dale.

Oruku nodded. "We came in from the direction of their sun so as not to be visible from the planet."

The video of the planet grew quickly as the *Velgot* approached before the *Velgot* noticeably began slowing as it drew nearer the planet. Within a few seconds, Pmuda's lone moon came into view from the left as the *Velgot* slowed and took up station behind it.

"We, as you can see, placed the *Velgot* behind Pmuda's one moon. We didn't want the population to be aware of our presence."

The view switched to a view from inside a *Velgot* hangar as an Arkell shuttle exited the ship. The view changed again to one from the shuttle as it approached the planet. The shuttle's approach slowed and stopped as it went into geosynchronous orbit above one of the continents.

The shot became one of a large city. This city was so polluted with smoke that it was difficult to see the infrastructure.

"Our orbiting shuttle could not be seen with the naked eye, and these people didn't have anything like a telescope. Watch this," said Oruku.

The view became a rapidly telescoping shot taken from the shuttle as its camera zoomed into the city and continued until the view displayed an avenue packed with ragged-looking beings.

"Holy shit, that looks like old Earth's Calcutta," said Vance.

"That's just what I was thinking," added Alex.

"We have ancient videos of Calcutta, Bangladesh, and Shanghai at their worst," said Oruku. "And this, you are seeing, is every bit as horrible as those infamous cities. Extreme poverty, crime, and disease was their way of life."

"Geez," Teddy said softly.

"They're certainly not a handsome race," added Aidan.

Oruku smiled. "They look a lot better when clean and fed but they do have some unattractive features."

"Ears and noses would fit into that category," said Teddy. "You'd think their ears would be smaller so as not to pick up all the racket created by that many people stacked together. And smaller noses so as not to smell that may people stacked together."

That caused laughter.

"They have big heads too," added Teddy. "Not that it is a bad thing," he added as he looked at Oruku.

Oruku smiled. "That, as it turns out, was to our advantage."

"There are so many of them crushed together," observed Shem. "How can they live like that?"

"They don't know any better," said Oruku.

"Throughout history on Earth, those who could least afford children had the most," said Alex. "It never made sense."

"They had no way to stop that unfortunate truth. Poor and generally ignorant people had little, if any, access to birth control of any sort. They were either not available or too expensive. And"—Oruku smiled—"sex was one of the few pleasures that cost nothing . . . in most cases," Oruku smiled a little. "Their miserable lives had little else to offer."

"That's it in a nutshell," said Alex.

Oruku nodded. "Pmuda's main problem is fairly simple to state but very difficult to correct. Because of the out-of-control birth rate, they've outstripped the planet's ability to properly feed and shelter the population." Oruku paused for a moment. "People are starving at a horrible rate. Tens of thousands a day die planetwide."

"And tens of thousands are born each day to replace them," said Alex.

"And therein lies the problem," said Oruku.

Nothing was said for a moment or two.

"What is the planetwide development level?" asked Dale.

The video switched from the streets choked with people to what appeared to be large factory buildings, to overhead power lines, to wider streets full of automobiles belching copious amounts of smoke.

"They, as you can see, have factories, automobiles, and power systems. Actually, their technological development is close to what Earth's was in the late 1800s to early 1900s. But we determined it had taken them nearly two centuries longer to arrive at that level of technology than it did humans. They don't yet have television but do have fairly sophisticated newspapers, planetwide, and an exploitable radio system."

"Well that's something to work with," remarked Dale.

"Indeed. Our normal approach of subtle technical assistance or outright intimidation wouldn't work here."

"Was anything being done by the planet's leadership to bring the birth rate down to the level of food production?" asked Vance.

"We could not determine a single strategy toward that goal."

There was a brief pause in the conversation before Alex asked a question "Now for the interesting part, what did you do about it?"

Oruku smiled. "It took some time to pinpoint the leadership of these poor beings. Despite the fact that all six countries were surprisingly democratic and held elections every five years, we found those elected were aggressive, ruthless, and for the most part without compassion or empathy. They maintained their leadership through intimidation and, we strongly suspect, voter fraud."

"Not unlike leaders historically," said Alex. "Psychopaths."

"Unfortunately, that is correct," said Oruku. "Taking lives, torture, imprisonment was all part of their malicious mindset." Oruku smiled. "However, there was one exception."

"Who was?" asked Alex.

"The leader of the continent we orbited over. From what we gathered from their newspapers and radio, this woman, whose name is Ailez, had compassion and empathy."

"Woman?" said Jarleth.

"A woman, yes. We gleaned every bit of information we could about her and her government. Ailez was asking the right questions, prescribing some reasonable cures, and seemed to have a good solid grip on her government. And importantly, she had a high standing with her citizens."

"I'd be willing to bet you included her in your ultimate solution," said a smiling Alex.

"We did, but that took a little doing. Each of the six continents are separate countries. Fortunately, there are no individual countries within the continents. That greatly simplified our task. And thankfully, all countries share a common language and are on par with technology.

"How can that be?" asked Dale. "Are these continents connected?"

"Not now, but our planetwide geological surveys show during the planet's development, four of the six continents were connected via land bridges and the remaining two had a land bridge between them. Then, somewhere between three and four hundred years ago, there was a catastrophic planetwide event. All six continents went through a massive tectonic plate shift that probably took days if not weeks to subside. Those volcanos were created during this time."

"Massive earthquakes and volcanic eruptions that lasted for days or weeks. Oh my god," said Dale.

"I can't imagine the terror those poor people went through," said Colleen.

"We estimate that at least half the animal life on Pmuda perished," said Oruku.

"Horrible," said Alex.

"Geez," said Teddy.

Oruku nodded. "Yes, and it was at this point that the land bridges were destroyed."

"That explains the common language," said Dale. "I'd assume that all continents prior to the tectonic shift had seaworthy ships. And probably had intercontinental commerce."

"Right on all counts, Dale. Their commerce included the two continents who, at that time, had no physical connection to the other four," agreed Oruku.

"And that's why they have a common language. That fact should have made your task much simpler."

"It did indeed."

"How long did it take you to learn their language?" asked Vance.

"Longer than normal. Three weeks with our best working on it." We had the spoken word via their radio broadcasts and printed word via their newspapers but no video of them speaking. We put a team on the ground and recorded dozens of conversations."

"You certainly couldn't approach them in person," said Alex. "How did you present yourselves?"

"We used facial prosthetics to alter our appearance and dressed as successful merchants. Our head size was a benefit here."

The view switched to four Arkell adorned with the facial prosthetics and garments that would fit into this society. All were smiling at the camera.

"Wow!" said Teddy. "That is some impressive makeup."

Oruku smiled. "That's me, second from left."

"I would never have recognized you," said Aidan.

"Incredible," added Shem.

Oruku nodded once. "Once we learned their language, we began to mix with the population, led them into conversations that would give us some idea as to their attitudes on a number of subjects."

"What did you find?" asked Alex.

"Deep down, they were, as a whole, reasonable and compassionate. But on their surface, because of the beliefs instilled in them from childhood on, they held those below their station in life with considerable contemp. Of those above, they were quite envious, some to a point of hate."

"How did they regard their leadership?" asked Alex.

"If they regarded them at all, it was with disdain."

Nothing was said for a few seconds.

Dale broke the silence. "Intellectual and moral attitudes wouldn't be easy to reprogram."

"All but impossible, they certainly weren't susceptible to Waoca," said Oruku. "We knew we had no choice but to replace these despots."

"That would be a huge undertaking," said Vance.

"It proved to be the most complicated and challenging assignment Sharkra asked of us—so far."

"I can't imagine," said Alex.

Oruku nodded and smiled. "We Arkell love a challenge. And this one was a doozy, to use an old Earth expression."

Alex smiled. "I wouldn't know where to start."

"We put our heads together, again, as you would have said on old Earth, and devised a plan to replace the current leadership of all but one country. First, we needed to find those whose IQs, intellects, and moral philosophies would serve our purpose and their individual countries best."

"I wouldn't have a clue as to how to begin finding such people," said Vance.

"So what did you do?" Dale was anxious to learn how the Arkell solved this multi-tiered and complex problem.

"I won't go into details, but using their radio networks and newspapers on all continents, we developed a series of intellectual contests with attractive prizes. It proved to be quite successful. We managed to glean nearly six dozen individuals whose IQs were approaching or above120. Then we factored in their moral test scores. From those, we chose twenty-four 'winners.'"

"Brilliant," said Dale.

Vance smiled. "And?"

"We managed to entice these winners, at our expense, to travel to a luxury resort located on a small island, just off the coast of the continent we were orbiting over. There, they would collect their prizes." Oruku smiled. "One of the contest prizes was a week's stay at this resort."

"Of course it was," said Alex, clearly impressed.

"How did you coordinate that with the owners and managers of the resort?" asked Shem.

Oruku smiled. "We didn't try. We purchased the resort, fired the entire staff, and replaced them with Arkell disguised as Pmudains."

Everybody laughed in appreciation of such a simple solution to what could have been a very difficult challenge.

"How in the hell did you manage to buy a resort?" asked Vance.

"We counterfeited their currency, a lot of it."

"Geez," said Teddy.

Vance smiled and nodded at the simplicity of it. "I love a direct approach."

Alex nodded in agreement. "It always seems to be the most effective."

"Once all twenty-four arrived at the resort, we scheduled them to attend a dinner and talk that evening in the resort's ballroom. We infiltrated these twenty-four with six disguised Arkell as part of their ranks."

"Of course you did," said Vance.

"Just one talk?" asked Dale.

"With that well-designed talk, we managed to create enough interest in our objectives to entice them to attend morning seminars each day for the entire week. The rest of their day was spent enjoying the resort's many facilities. We six, as Pmudains, joined them during these leisure times in order to keep the conversations on our goals foremost on their minds. This proved to be quite successful."

"Wow," said Teddy.

"It should be noted here that we used a great deal of the exceptional media campaign developed by Jason Gould, of your acquaintance. We put a lot of emphasis on the advantages of being childless. Educating them on the problems of overpopulation and the huge benefits to a society with a manageable number of citizens. We gave statistics on the positive effect a less-dense population would have on their starvation and disease death rates."

"That media campaign proved very successful on Earth," said Alex.

"Without the visual aid of television, that would be a great deal more difficult," said Dale.

"It was."

"Then?" asked Dale.

"At the end of the week, we held a vote by the twenty-four plus the six disguised Arkell, to elect six for the top leadership roles. Each of the thirty were to write down six names in order of their preference. They chose well. Three of the six chosen were female, including Ailez as the top vote-getter. We found it refreshing that their votes nearly mirrored what we disguised Arkell wrote down. We then divided the remaining eighteen plus the six Arkell into groups of four and assigned them to the six leaders, creating six teams of five. At this point, all twenty-four were now sold on a planetwide leadership replacement, a coup if you will. They were all now convinced they, in leadership roles, could make a positive change in the lives of the planet's citizens. We invited them to stay at the resort another week at our expense, to devise a plan to replace current leaders in five of the six continents. All were strongly behind keeping Ailez as premier of her country. She, for her part, expressed her intent to instill the four others on her team to specific government roles. The other five teams agreed with this plan and would follow suit after the coups were complete in their countries."

Vance leaned forward a little. "Just how did you manage these coups?"

"We managed, with us disguised Arkell, the twenty-four Pmudains, and a lot of cash, to infiltrate the management of all major newspapers and radio stations planetwide. With the very capable help of the twenty-four, we started calling for national votes on all radio stations and newspapers, again using Jason Gould's propaganda formula."

"How did you handle those in leadership roles who would strongly resist your plan?" asked Vance.

Oruku smiled broadly. "We gathered them up and relocated them to our resort, where they could not make contact the outside world."

"You kidnapped them?"

"We did. But we made them quite comfortable. Actually, we had to collect over a hundred individuals in order to completely remove their influence and resistance."

"How'd they take that?" asked Alex.

"Not well at all. Predictably, they formed an alliance with the intent of overpowering our security and returning to their countries."

It was Vance's turn to smile. "I'll bet they failed in that attempt."

"They did because, again, we had infiltrated their ranks with Arkell."

Vance nodded in appreciation.

"They had a simple plan. Commandeer a small ship and head back to their respective countries."

"Did they try again?"

"Just once more. The results were the same."

"Where are these kidnapped victims now?" asked Alex.

"Still at the resort. We've been reeducating them over the past few months."

"How's that working out?" asked Vance.

"Surprisingly well," said Oruku. "There are just about a dozen who are, as you might say, lost causes. They are true psychopaths."

"What are you going to do with them?"

"There are a lot of prisons on every continent. We transferred these dozens to the respectable prisons on their home continents. All prisons, we discovered, were run horribly. We determined that a large percentage of the inmates shouldn't have been incarcerated at all. So we have added prison reforms to our campaigns."

"Sharkra has indeed given you an enormous task," said Alex.

"Overwhelming, I would think," added Vance.

Oruku smiled. "Again, we love a challenge."

"You had one for sure. How did you proceed?" asked Dale.

"We continued this campaign to remove their current leaders for a full month. The campaign, of course, included our picks to replace the current leaders. Then we called for national votes."

"And?" asked Dale.

"The planetwide election is set for tomorrow."

"How do you think the vote will go?" asked Alex.

"We believe it will go well."

"After the vote, what are the plans?" asked Dale.

"We have continued to use the planet's media to promote birth control. We have put a lot of time into emphasizing there is a simple, painless way to become infertile. We're getting a surprisingly positive response to sterilization planetwide."

"What is that simple, painless path to infertility?" asked Vance.

"We, using similar technology as developed by the scientists in the WGC, designed two birth-control formulas in pill form for male and female."

"How many people on the planet?" asked Alex.

"Just over three billion."

"That would require a lot of pills," said Dale.

Oruku nodded. "We calculated that if thirty percent chose sterilization, their birth rate would decline by close to sixty percent over a generation."

"That's interesting," said Alex.

"That would still require nearly a billion pills," said Dale.

"There are dozens of pharmaceutical companies on Pmuda. They had been producing medicines in various forms, including pills, for decades. Their biggest seller was a form of tranquilizer."

"That, considering the horrible living conditions on their planet, makes complete sense," said Dale.

"Agreed," said Alex.

Oruku nodded. "I won't go into a lot of detail, but we supplied the formula and technical advice for our sterilization pills to most of those companies. They, surprisingly, were able to adapt their machines to the production of the pills in a fairly short period of time."

"And the chemicals required for the pills?"

"The plants and minerals required to produce the chemicals are abundant on the planet."

"Really?" said Dale. "How long will it take them to get into production?"

Oruku paused for a moment and raised his hand to stall further conversation. He was receiving information through his earpiece.

"We have helped these pharmaceutical companies improve the designs of their production equipment. It seems about half the companies are now within two weeks of starting production. We believe together they will be capable of producing a hundred million pills per month. So it will be something over a year before all who wish to be sterile receive the pills."

"It occurs to me," said Shem, "that once the population sees that their fellow citizens are not harmed by the sterilization and see the positive effect it had on those who took it, there will be more wanting to be sterilized."

Oruku smiled. "That is our belief also."

"Is this the last of the challenges on Pmuda?" asked Alex.

"The major ones, yes. We have one hundred eighty-one Arkell still on Pmuda in various advisory roles. As their assignments are completed, we will pick them up."

"Won't they be missed if they suddenly just disappear?"

"They'll have various stories to tell before they leave. Moving to a different country to take care of their elderly parents, that sort of thing."

"I assume you'll drop by Pmuda once in a while to check on their progress."

"For the time being, we are in direct contact with the Arkell stationed on the planet, and we get constant reports on their areas of responsibilities. As we remove the last Arkell from a continent, we will place a satellite in geosynchronous orbit over each continent. We will be able to monitor all radio broadcasts and, as time goes on, television."

"Kind of like you did on Earth," said Dale.

"Exactly."

CHAPTER 20

PREHISTORIC WORLD

"This is an experience we're sure you'll find interesting," said Oruku.

The viewer came on, displaying what appeared to be a dense rainforest. The camera panned around, showing trees and plants of all shapes and sizes along with an impressive array of colors. The panorama slowed and stopped, settling on a wide swampy river slowly meandering through the forest. All was quiet except the calls and cries of a great variety of birds and animals. All in all, a tranquil scene.

"Looks like the Amazon rainforest of old Earth," said Teddy.

"It does," agreed Dale.

"This is a comparatively new planet. Its development is about where Earth was sixty-five million years ago. What you called the Jurassic period."

"That was the time of the dinosaurs," said Alex.

Oruku smiled but said nothing.

Suddenly the viewer exploded with startling sight and terrifying sound. There, charging across the river on two massive legs, was an animal that looked to be more dangerous and deadly than Earth's infamous T-Rex.

"Holy shit!" said Vance.

"Oh my god," added Alex.

The animal was running directly at the recorder.

"This creature was not happy with us being in its territory," said Oruku.

All assumed that was a mild understatement.

There was a quick hum and pop sound, and the animal fell at what had to be the feet of the videographer. Its massive jaws baring long, serrated teeth were opening and closing as if chewing on something, while the rest of its body remained motionless.

"You killed it?" asked Vance.

"Oh no, we wouldn't do that. We just put it to sleep for a while." Oruku smiled. "We needed to give time for our videographer to quit shaking."

"And change his shorts," said Teddy sincerely.

Everybody laughed.

"That would give anyone great cause for concern," said Lara, her eyes glued to the viewer.

"That looks remarkably like a dinosaur," said Dale.

"That's just what it is," said Oruku. "We have named this animal a Traptor."

"That works for me," said Teddy.

"Certainly resembles the Earth's T-Rex," said Dale. "Except for the long, strong-looking arms."

"It's more like a huge Velociraptor," said Vance.

"That's what we thought too," said Oruku. "Thus the name Traptor."

"That is one nasty-looking animal," said Lara.

"The head is nearly two and a half meters long."

"Looks like half of that is teeth," said Teddy.

Oruku nodded in agreement. "We've spent twenty days so far studying this planet. So interesting in so many ways."

"Prehistoric. You, in effect, experienced time travel back millions of years," said Dale.

"That's right. After the encounter you just saw, we set up an observation station here. It's an island in the middle of this river."

"Really?" said Alex. "How big is this island?"

"It's about five hundred meters long and one hundred fifty at its widest point. The river runs the length of it on both sides and comes back together downstream."

"Unmanned, I assume," said Teddy.

"Oh, it's manned. Four Arkell will spend the next few months studying and recording life on this wondrous planet. They have a small transport that will allow them to venture around the entire planet to conduct observations and studies."

"I'm assuming their safety is assured?" asked Vance.

"Oh yes, we've installed a device, similar to the one that stopped the Traptor, on the top of the tallest tree on the island. It will discourage the animals we wish to avoid, from setting foot on the island."

"Just the dangerous ones?" asked Dale.

"We have a technology, similar to your Auratron, to identify the dangerous animals. The second the unwanted touch the island, they will receive a single painful jolt. However, if that fails to turn them around, they will continue to get increasingly powerful jolts until they flee the island."

"Simple but effective," said Vance.

"What about monsters that are already on the island?" asked Teddy.

"Ran the bad ones off using the same device."

"What if that doesn't work?"

"So far, it's worked in every case. However, if the animal somehow can endure the pain and continues to show aggression, that same device can be lethal. Here is a demonstration of its effectiveness."

The view changed back to the downed Traptor as it began to revive. Its huge head lifted off the ground for a moment before dropping back down on the soggy ground. This was repeated several times before it remained up and started looking around. After a few moments, it attempted to get to its feet but failed twice before managing to stand upright. It continued to stand unsteadily in one spot for several moments, looking around.

"How tall is this creature?" asked Dale, not taking his eyes off the viewer.

"Seven meters. About a meter taller than the T-Rex."

After another moment, the Traptor started walking slowly toward the camera. It was coming out of its daze. It let out a terrifying roar and began to rapidly approach the videographer. Another Arkell came into the shot from the right. He held a device in his left hand. He yelled, "Back," at the Traptor and at the same time fired the device at the monster's chest. A soft, *hum pop,* could be heard. The animal screamed in pain and stopped moving for a moment. Then it changed its direction to the Arkell, who just caused him pain and moved forward. The Arkell again yelled, "Back," and shot it again. Again came the scream of pain and rage. The Arkell then advance toward the animal and shouted, "Back," and shot it again. After another terrifying scream, the Traptor stopped moving and stared intently at the offending Arkell. One could almost see the confusion in the beast's eyes. Again, the Arkell advanced, yelled, and shot the animal. This time, the monster started slowly backing up. The Arkell ran toward the animal, yelled, and shot him again. That did it. The Traptor spun and ran back across the river, disappearing into the thick rainforest."

"Holy crap!" said Vance. "That man has a pair on him."

Oruku smiled. "We agree with you. He got a lot of kudos when he returned to the *Velgot*."

"Give him my admiration when you see him," said Vance. "Tell him I want him on my team."

"I will. Such praise coming from Vance Youngblood will be a great honor for him."

"Well . . ." was all Vance said.

"I'd put that outpost way, way away from that monster's territory," said Teddy.

"I'll second that thought," said Colleen.

Oruku smiled. "We'll be careful. That animal is truly a badass, to use an old Earth expression. We determined this particular species was, in fact, the apex of the food chain."

"I can't imagine anything big and tough enough to whip that thing's ass," said Vance, "or even attempt it."

Oruku smiled. "We observed an enormous variety of animal life, none of which would take on this animal. Interesting to note, however, that many of its prey were fleet of foot, and some, we observed, were able to outrun this predator. Those species that couldn't run, mostly huge animals, had developed protections such as extremely thick skin or, in some cases, a strong shell. Many midsized animals had defensive and/or offensive, horns, claws, and spikes. Amazing variety of adaptations."

"I'll bet you have videos of all of them," said Shem.

"Oh yes, and we'll make them available to you."

"Can't wait," said Dale.

"We will start right now," said Oruku. "We're going to take you to a different location on this planet."

The view changed to one from orbit. It clearly showed the continents, oceans, islands, lakes, and rivers.

"That is a beautiful planet from this point of view," said Colleen.

"And an interesting one," said Oruku. "See the large L-shaped island on the upper right?"

"That's a big island. No connection to any of the continents?" said Alex.

"That's correct."

"Like Madagascar on old Earth," added Dale.

"Exactly," said Oruku, "like Madagascar."

Dale looked at Oruku with his head slightly cocked. "I'm thinking the plant and animal life on this island differs from the major continents."

Oruku smiled and slowly nodded. "You will, no doubt, find this interesting."

The viewer switched to a picture of a large town bustling with its inhabitants. Smoke could be seen coming out of the chimneys of at least half of the buildings. There was just a small percentage of buildings taller than one story, and all were similar in design.

There was dead silence from all in the viewing room.

"HOLY SHIT!" said Vance as he leaned forward. "Are those beings dinosaurs?"

"They are."

The picture switched to a close-up of five beings engaged in an animated conversation outside what appeared to be a restaurant.

"Oh my god," said Aidan.

These dinosaurs looked to be just over two meters in height and solidly built. They stood upright with a forward tilt. They didn't have clothes on, but each had a belt around their waist containing what was believed to be personal items and tools. They were hairless but looked to have fine blue-gray feathers over most of their bodies. Their hands, feet, and heads were featherless. Their heads were large, elongated, and sat on a short, strong-looking neck. Their eyes were large, dark, and set wide apart, facing forward like a predator, not on the sides like a prey. The back of their heads came to a rounded point that extended horizontally out about twenty centimeters. They had short human-like arms, and their hands contained three fingers and an opposing thumb. Their nails were more like thick talons than human nails, but they were short and blunt. It wouldn't be hard to imagine these talons being longer, stronger, and sharper. They had a short balancing tail that protruded out less than half a meter. This tail was the reason for their forward-tilting stance, which offset the weight of the tail.

"See those tails?" asked Oruku.

All said they did.

"We believe they will lose that tail completely over time. As it is now, it serves no purpose. At one time, we believe these beings ran and walked on all fours."

"Evolution in progress," said Dale. "Fascinating."

The camera angle kept changing as if the videographer was walking around the group, giving an excellent view of every side of these beings.

"How in the hell did you get close enough to take these videos," asked Vance.

"We developed a tiny drone that we disguised as a common flying insect. It could land on their arm and wouldn't be given a thought."

"Great audio," said Alex. "All that picked up by your 'insects'?"

Oruku nodded.

All watched the video and listened to the conversation for a few moments.

"Their voices and language are very unusual," said Dale. "Have you been able to translate it?"

"It took our audiologists and linguists two weeks before they started working it out. Speech patterns, inflections, grunts, and clicks along with their expressionless faces drove them crazy." Oruku smiled. "But they have it."

Two of the five dinosaurs said something before turning and going into the restaurant.

"Can you tell us what those two said just now?" asked Shem.

"I'll let you listen for yourselves."

The video backed up a few seconds.

"We go in for food," said one.

"See you late day," said the other.

"What the hell, they were speaking English?" said Vance.

Oruku smiled. "No, far from it. The translator is so quick that it looks like they are speaking English or whatever language we wish to listen in."

"That's absolutely fascinating," said Dale. "Language is no longer a major obstacle in communicating with alien races."

"Once we have the translation done, communication is quite easy."

"What do they eat?" asked Alex.

"They're omnivores such as yourselves. Seems they eat a great variety of foods."

"Are you going to interact with them?"

"No, we'll avoid direct contact. There seems to be no problems with their society."

"If it ain't broke, don't fix it," said Teddy.

"Exactly."

The viewer's picture changed again to one from orbit, but this time it revolved around so that they were now at the other side of the planet.

"You can now see a small contingent on the lower side of the planet," said Oruku. "And you can see it is at least two thousand kilometers from the nearest land mass."

"Kinda like Madagascar . . . again," said Teddy with a big grin.

"Exactly, Teddy," said Oruku.

"You're going to shock us again, aren't you?" said Dale.

"Without a doubt," said Oruku.

The picture on the viewer moved as the Arkell shuttle moved to a position over the center of this small continent and then into a fast zoom shot and stopped above a lush, tree-dotted, immense plane. Tens of thousands of animals could be seen from horizon to horizon. It was reminiscent of old Earth's African continent with its vast numbers of herding species.

"Wow," said Alex. "That takes me back to Earth."

"Those animals are not dinosaurs," said Dale. "They look like mammals."

"That's just what they are."

"Mammals and dinosaurs living on the same planet at the same time. Very interesting," said Dale.

Oruku said nothing but smiled as the shot zoomed in to within a hundred meters above the ground. There, walking in single file, were hairy beings dressed in animal skins and carrying long spears.

"Holy shit," said Vance. "Cavemen."

"More or less. These beings are in fact mammals but closer in genetics to old Earth's apes than to humans. Missing links, if you will."

"They clearly are developing intelligence. Weapons and garments," said Vance.

"Their appearance on the planet, as far as we can determine, began about a hundred thousand years after the dinosaurs," said Oruku.

"So they could coexist," said Dale.

"Not necessarily," said Oruku. "We could find no evidence of a dinosaur species that could be a threat to the cavemen. Just two carnivore species that are quite small and have learned to avoid the cavemen. All the other dinosaurs are plant eaters. Some of those are a food source for these 'cavemen.'"

"Someday I would like to visit this planet," said Dale.

"Ditto," said Shem.

"I suspect we all would," said Alex.

"That can and will be arranged," said Oruku. "In the meantime, we've placed half a dozen satellites in orbit over the more interesting areas of the planet. You can monitor them at your leisure."

"I . . ." Dale started to say something but stopped.

"You have a question?" asked Oruku.

Dale's brow furrowed a little. "I wonder why Sharkra took you to this planet. Apparently, there is no action required."

Now Oruku looked slightly puzzled. "That had occurred to us. But we have not figured it out."

"I doubt Sharkra would do anything without a reason," said Dale.

Oruku nodded. "It's one of the subjects talked about in our pubs and various social gatherings. If and when we figure it out, we will let you know." Oruku paused for a brief moment. "We would love to hear any thoughts you come up with on the subject."

"Will do, thanks."

CHAPTER 21

OLD AGE

"Here are a few more examples of the tasks given us by Sharkra," said Oruku.

The viewer again displayed a shot taken from the *Velgot* as it approached another planet. This planet seemed to have a great deal more land mass than the other inhabited worlds. As the *Velgot* approached, the view changed to one of a good-sized city.

"We spent a week studying the inhabitants of this planet. Here is a scene taken in a small town located on a lake on their largest continent," said Oruku.

The viewer displayed a street scene. Everything seemed to be well built with interesting architecture and was quite tidy. The inhabitants were about the size of the Yassi, but they had hair on their heads and fine features. All were dressed neatly in more or less the same clothes, very little variety in style. They were, for the most part, a nice-looking species. Their most notable feature was that the majority of the citizens seemed old.

"It looks like they have a well-ordered society," said Alex.

"Agreed," said Dale. "But I don't see a lot of age difference. They all look like they have some age on them."

"Therein lies the problem. Life expectancy is just shy of forty years."

"Geez," said Teddy.

"They look twice that," said Vance.

Oruku nodded. "This planet's population has grown quite slowly over the centuries. Their technology has also advanced slowly."

"I'd assume their intellect is weak," said Dale.

"No, actually we determined their IQ is quite high. It's their biology that has stood in the way of technical progress."

"I'm not following you," said Alex.

"A short life stifles progress. Those who would have been a great benefit to a society if they had longer lived do not. They die before what would be their most productive years. Intelligence and wisdom don't have a chance to advance or develop as it naturally would over a longer life span."

Nothing was said for a moment while all eyes stayed on the viewer as the old people filed past the camera.

"I'm thinking your task here is to improve their longevity," said Shem.

"You are correct," said Oruku.

"Just how did you go about that?" asked Dale.

"Using a variation of what we have done for the humans on Gabriel," said Oruku.

"You extended our lives through a sophisticated radiation process. But we knew you and knew what you were doing," said Dale. "These beings, I assume, had no idea you were in their midst."

"That's correct. We had to put our heads together again. Ideally, we would alter the genetic code of entire race. But that wasn't possible. One of our scientists, an aged woman at over two hundred years, made a major improvement on the design. The process was cut from thirty minutes to just over five."

"We old folks still have things to offer," said Vance.

"Indeed." Oruku smiled. "We began building dozens of our gene-altering devices."

"And?" asked Dale.

"And, without going into a lot of details, we managed to install them around the planet in what looked to be their equivalent of high schools."

"High schools?" asked Vance.

Dale nodded knowingly. "Breeding age."

"Right," said Oruku.

"How did you get them to subject themselves to using this device."

"That was tricky. We, over several weeks' time, managed to abduct four students, three male and one female, and an administrator from ten high schools on each continent while they slept. We transported them to the *Velgot* and instilled information about the procedure into their subconscious. All while they were sleeping."

Dale nodded in understanding. "Why the administrators?"

"Someone had to be responsible for procuring the devices and placing them in an ideal spot on campus. The administrators were made to believe this was all their doing."

"All the students and faculty were put through the apparatus prior to returning them to the exact spot they were before the abduction. They, as you have experienced, would feel wonderful after they went through the procedure. They only had to entice a few of their fellow students to enter the device before the word spread and lines began forming to go through the process."

"These young people will breed over the generations and the life expectancy will, what, double?" asked Shem.

"That's right," said Oruku. "We thought about tripling their life span. But, in so doing, we would be setting the population up for a different problem."

"Exploding population growth," said Dale.

"Exactly. However, we may, at a future date, revisit this decision."

Dale nodded.

"Satellites?" asked Vance.

"Oh yes."

CHAPTER 22

SEEDING

"We found an astonishing variety of life in the galaxy. But here is a planet that has little plant life and a minuscule variety at that."

The viewer displayed an almost desert-like land mass. Then the screen's images rapidly changed from one continent to another. The only vegetation seen was growing on the banks of lakes, rivers, and oceans.

"That reminds me of Gabriel when we went into orbit the first time," said Vance. "Brings back some old memories."

"Fond memories?" asked Oruku.

"They are now. But at the time, I was a bit overwhelmed. I thought of nothing else for five decades, ship time. It became an obsession."

"You single-handedly took a planet like this one and turned it into a beautiful world with an amazing variety of plants and animals," said Alex. "It's still one of the most remarkable accomplishments of mankind."

"We agree," said Oruku.

"It did keep me busy for a while, and as I've said many times, all I had to do was follow directions. Like my mother used to say, 'If you can read, you can cook.' I could read," said Vance with a smile.

"You cooked for fifty years," added Dale. "All by yourself."

"But I was not alone. I had you two."

Oruku smiled while nodding. "We're not going to spend that much time, but we have begun placing special satellites to disperse seeds at ideal times. Rainy seasons are, of course, ideal. In addition, we've introduced many primitive life forms such as algae in lakes, rivers, and oceans. All this, over time, will raise the oxygen level to a point that will allow animals to survive. In a few years, we'll go back and plant a few animals and fish. In a few centuries, this planet should be a wonderful place for intelligent life."

"That will be very interesting to watch over the decades," said Vance. "Probably be like déjà vu for me."

"We've put a single satellite over one small continent that contains a variety of topography from mountains to deserts. It has a great abundance of rivers and lakes and an ocean."

"A microcosm of the planet," said Vance.

"Exactly. If our seeding works here, we'll know we are on the right track."

"Will we be able to check in on the planet's progress via this satellite?" asked Vance.

"Absolutely."

"We will provide you with all the technology necessary to keep tabs on all the planets we've gotten involved in."

"That's terrific," said Dale. "Terrific, thank you."

CHAPTER 23

JUST TWO CONTINENTS

"Here is another planet that should prove interesting to you." The viewer displayed a planet that looked to be all ocean.

"That looks wet," said Teddy.

"So far, it's the only water-bearing planet we've yet found that has only two continents, one at each pole. And they are both nearly tropical in climate."

"Warm poles? That's a first," said Alex.

"Any life on the poles?" asked Shem.

"Quite a bit, actually—vegetation, trees, vines, bushes."

"Any animals?" asked Teddy.

"Lots of reptiles on the continents and a substantial variety of fish in the ocean. No warm-blooded animals."

The viewer started showing a variety of lizards and snakes.

"Whoa, that looks like one big snake," said Teddy.

The viewer froze on the snake's image.

"About ten meters, I'm told," said Oruku.

"Wow," said Teddy.

"Must weigh at least two hundred kilos," added Vance.

"More than likely," said Dale.

The viewer switched to showing fish. Every few seconds, a different species was shown for a few seconds before another variety was displayed. All watching began commenting on what was being displayed on the viewer.

"Boy, those are beautiful," said Lara.

The picture switched. "Would you look at that ugly sumbitch," said Vance.

"How big is this one?" ask Shem while a massive fish swam across the viewer.

Oruku was getting information via his earpiece. "Twenty-three tons," he said.

"Look at the mouth on that thing. Looks like it could swallow a whale," said Teddy.

"Biggest fish we've ever come across," said Oruku. "It's even bigger than the whale shark of old Earth."

"That would feed—"

"We have to leave now," said Oruku, interrupting Teddy.

The viewer went black.

"What the hell?" said Vance.

"I'm being told the *Velgot* is no longer in orbit," said Dale as he was getting information from his earpiece. "Can't find them anywhere."

"This makes me very uncomfortable," said Teddy.

"Scares the crap out of me," added Vance while not taking his eyes off the now-dark viewer.

"There has to be a major problem for the Arkell to take off like that," said Shem.

CHAPTER 24

ANOTHER GALAXY
ROFINA

The *Velgot* was transported to a section of the galaxy they had not been to. A quick check told them that this was the section the *Geaalo* had been covering.

"What are we doing here?" Oruku asked out loud.

"Not known, we're scanning—wait, we've got something," said Tracc, the chief technician.

"What is it?"

There was no answer for a moment. "The *Geaalo*. It looks to be dead in space."

"Put it on the viewer," said Oruku quickly.

There, shining brightly in the blackness of space, was the *Geaalo*. At first glance, it looked normal, but as it slowly revolved, a jagged hole about nine meters in diameter could be seen just above the equator of this massive ship. In addition, there were many other smaller holes on this side of the *Geaalo*.

"Full shields now," said Kilee.

"Shields engaged," said a tech in a voice louder than necessary.

"Can you make contact with the *Geaalo*?" asked Oruku, concern apparent in his voice.

"Have contact," said Tracc.

"Ooat here. *Velgot*. We are under attack."

Kilee took over the conversation. "We don't see where the attack is coming from?"

"They come and go before we can get off a shot. They are jumping in and out of light speed."

"Were your shields up before the first strike?" asked Kilee.

"No. And they are no longer effective on that side of the *Geaalo*," said Ooat.

"Are they up protecting the rest of the *Geaalo*?"

"We believe so, yes."

"Hmm," said Kilee. "Their weapons must not be effective against the shields. Good."

"Any casualties?" asked Oruku.

"Yes, we are getting reports of many injured and a few dead."

"Is the *Geaalo* functioning normally?"

"No, the first attack disabled us. We cannot leave this sector of the galaxy."

"Does the attack come from the same direction every time?" asked Kilee.

"Yes, always from the damaged side of the *Geaalo*."

"Good, we will know where to aim."

"Can you turn the *Geaalo* on its axis. Point your vulnerable side away from the attack?"

"No, we have no control over the ship's movement."

Kilee said nothing for a few seconds. "Ooat, I believe we can turn the *Geaalo* using the *Velgot*'s shields."

"If you can turn us one hundred and eighty degrees on our axis, our shields should protect us."

Kilee turned to a tech. "How long to spin the *Geaalo*?"

"Two minutes."

"Do it."

"*Geaalo* is turned," said the tech.

"Tactical mode 2," ordered Kilee.

"Mode 2 engaged," said the tech.

The *Velgot* began to alter its position in space twice a second. These were random moves that could not be anticipated by a foe.

"Weapons at the ready," ordered Kilee. "Concentrate on the space in front of *Geaalo*'s damaged side. Don't fire until I give the word."

"Ooat, what's the frequency of the attacks?"

"Five to ten minutes."

"Last attack?"

"Four point five minutes ago."

The attacking ship will not be aware of our presence," said Kilee. "They are in for an unpleasant surprise."

The tension on both ships couldn't be higher. The *Geaalo* was a stationary target—the *Velgot* was anything but.

"Hold on," said Tracc. "A ship just appeared and is heading our way."

"On the viewer," said Kilee.

There on the viewer was a ship that was completely alien and primitive in design.

"I don't recall ever seeing anything like that in our travels," said Oruku.

The ship was just over one hundred meters long and ten meters wide with a vertical "disk" at one end. The disk itself was just shy of thirty meters in diameter and festooned with what looked to be dozens of identical offensive rockets. Along its long body was an array of instruments along with what was assumed to be additional weapons. At the opposite end of the ship was the long ship's propulsion system.

"Primitive propulsion," said Tracc.

Kilee just nodded in agreement. "Consecrate fire on their propulsion systems."

"It has just fired three missiles at the *Geaalo*," said Tracc with a slight smile. "At their protected side."

"Their shields will hold," Kilee replied calmly.

Oruku remailed silent. This was not his area of responsibility. Kilee, as the chief sentinel, was in charge.

The missiles simply disintegrated one by one as they came in contact with the *Geaalo*'s shield.

"Fire on their energy source."

In the next five seconds, the *Velgot* fired its primary weapons from four different locations surrounding the hostile ship.

"All hit the target," said Tracc.

"Damage?"

"Took out a lot of the ship's exterior sensors. None that I—hold on." Tracc was intently manipulating his sensors. "They've fired three more missiles. They're shooting at us, I believe."

"Hoping to get lucky," said Kilee. "They won't."

All five of the missiles missed completely.

"Fire on their ship's end disk—one burst. Let's see if that will slow them down."

The massive *Velgot* again moved with the agility of a hummingbird. Too quick for the eye to follow. The burst hit the intended target.

The huge viewer on the command center's wall showed the alien ship pitch to the left and started slowly tumbling end over end like a gigantic stick.

"That hurt them," said Tracc.

"Let's try and make contact with them," said Oruku.

A tech in the command center began searching the channels. After a minute, he turned to Oruku. "No answer. No indication that our message is getting to them."

"Are there signs of life on board?" asked Oruku.

"Hundreds," said Tracc.

All eyes were on the viewer when retro rockets on both ends of the primitive ship fired in simultaneously and the ship's tumble started to slow. "They're getting control of their ship," said Kilee.

"That's fast. They know what they're doing," said Tracc.

Within a few minutes, the alien ship's tumble completely stopped and the retro rockets shut off.

"Try contacting them again," said Oruku.

"All communication systems are open," said Tracc.

All of a sudden, the alien ship disappeared.

"SHIT!" said Oruku, using Vance's favorite expletive.

"They are able to exceed light speed as we are," said Tracc.

"We may never see them again," added Kilee.

"Let's get a crew over to the *Geaalo*," said Oruku, displaying some disappointment.

"Boarding team is on their way," said Kilee. "Repair team, gather what you need to seal that hull quickly. Doesn't have to be perfect at this time. Just get it sealed."

The small shuttle slowly and carefully entered the *Geaalo* through the large jagged hole in its hull and cautiously set down on a reasonably clear spot.

"A lot of damage to about fifty meters inside the ship," said Krem, the team leader. "No signs of life here."

All in the command center could see what the crew in the shuttle were seeing.

"Can you get to the interior of the ship?" asked Kilee.

"We're just exiting the shuttle. You can follow our progress."

Each team member's pressure helmet held a camera. All were on, and the five views were displayed simultaneously on the command center's central viewer.

"What a mess," said Oruku.

The picture transmitted from Krem's camera showed him moving around burned and twisted metal. The view from his camera stopped moving and fixed on three horribly mangled and burned Arkell bodies lying more or less together in a corner of what looked to be an office. They were two women and one man.

"Oh no," Krem said with great sadness.

"Damn it!" said Kilee.

"Why?" a sad Oruku asked rhetorically.

"Life signs two decks up," said Tracc.

"Heading up," said Krem.

Five minutes later, the rescue team, via emergency stairs, were standing at a pressure hatch. "Hatch is sealed from the inside," said Krem.

"Have one of your team take the shuttle out of the *Geaalo* so the repair team can seal the hole," said Kilee.

"Will do."

"Repair team, seal the hole as soon as the shuttle exits."

"We're ready."

"Rescue team, as soon as the hole is sealed and the pressure is up, get that hatch open," said Kilee.

"Will do."

"Shuttle is out," said Krem.

"Repair team, how much time to seal the hole?"

"Thirty minutes."

"Good."

Twenty-eight minutes later, the repair team's leader reported back. "Hull is sealed. My team is back in our transport and will return to the *Velgot*."

"Rescue team?"

"We're ready to open the hatch."

"Get to it," said Kilee.

Krem pounded on the hatch with gloved fist. "Can you hear me?"

"We can," came a faint voice from within. "The pressure is coming up. Five minutes to full pressure. Then we'll open the hatch."

Five minutes later, a loud hissing sound was heard as the hatch opened. Standing on the other side of the hatch were dozens of Arkell. Standing closest to the hatch was Ooat.

Krem and the rescue team removed their helmets. Krem smiled. "Can't tell you how happy this is going to make your friends on the *Velgot*."

"I would guess we of the *Geaalo* are far happier to see you than you us," Ooat said with a big smile. "Thought we were about to be destroyed."

"How long have you been disabled?"

"Just shy of an hour."

"What?"

"We were attacked just an hour ago. How did you get here so fast?"

"Sharkra."

"Vance, I believe you had better head to the *Marian*. We have company," said Dale.

"Repeat that," said Vance.

"A ship just appeared four thousand kilometers out. It's remaining stationary."

"Any attempt at communication?"

"Not on their part. We are sending greetings on all frequencies. No response."

"I assume Gabriel's shield is up?"

"Yes, sir."

"I'll be there in twenty."

"In the meantime, we'll continue to try to make contact," said Dale.

Just over nineteen minutes later, Vance walked onto the *Marian's* bridge. "Any further intelligence?"

"Some. It looks like this ship has been attacked," said Dale. "Lots of damage."

Vance looked at the viewer. "Holy shit! This is a design we haven't seen before."

"Interesting design," said Dale. "I'd love to know what their propulsion is."

"It looks like a derelict," said Dale.

"What else can you tell me?"

"Ship's just over a hundred meters long," said Dale. "Disk is just under thirty meters in diameter. Can't read the power source. Scanner shows a lot of life signs aboard."

"Someone has shot the shit out of it. There's damage everywhere," observed Vance.

"Indeed."

"Let's err on the side of caution here. Activate all offensive weapons and train them on that ship."

"Really?" asked Dale. "You see something I haven't?"

"No, but in the past hour, the *Velgot* disappeared and this ship appeared. That can't be a coincidence."

"Okay, we have everything but the kitchen sink pointed at them," said Dale with a smile.

Vance nodded without taking his eyes off the alien ship. "That should get their attention."

"The *Velgot* is hailing us," said a bridge tech.

Half the viewer's screen now displayed Oruku while the other half stayed on the strange ship.

"We've been monitoring your communications," said Oruku. "We're relieved to see you're being cautious with the ship in your sector. That ship has attacked the *Geaalo* and the *Velgot*. They damaged the *Geaalo*, resulting in deaths of three Arkell."

"Oh no," said Vance. "Anyone we know?"

"Don't believe so," said Oruku. "We know that Ooat and Ssamp were not harmed."

"That's good to hear, but they lost valued shipmates."

"Ooat is taking this attack personally and is taking full responsibility for the damage to their ship and the loss of friends."

"Why would he blame himself?"

"He did not instruct the crew to raise their shields when the alien ship was first spotted."

"Why not?"

"He didn't perceive the threat. Their scans showed the ship to be quite primitive. It had no shields and an antiquated propulsion system."

"What sort of weapons do they have?"

"Solid fuel rockets."

"Rockets?"

"Had *Geaalo*'s shields been up, they wouldn't have been damaged at all."

"All that considered, why would these aliens attack the *Geaalo*?"

"That is a question we want an answer to. As soon as we help the *Geaalo* affect repairs and whatever else we can help with, we'll be heading your way."

"Good."

"If you and your highly intelligent friends can think of a way to disable that ship until we get there, we'd be grateful."

"Frankly, it looks like it's already disabled. But we'll put our heads together," Vance said with a smile. "Did the *Velgot* have any damage?"

"No, our defenses were more than adequate. We did manage to damage them, however."

"So we see. I'm amazed they managed to get here with that apparent damage."

"Notwithstanding the attack on the *Geaalo*, they seem to have some intelligence," said Oruku. "They made enough repairs to move that ship just minutes after we inflicted that damage. And they moved at more than light speed.

"Really?"

"Yes."

"Hmm, okay, we'll see what we can do to disable them. See you soon."

Vance turned to Dale. "Any ideas on crippling that relic?"

"Do you want the ship completely and permanently disabled?"

Vance thought about that for a moment. "Not permanently if we can help it."

Dale nodded. "Okay, how about using our mining/offensive laser to cut off their navigation array. Without that system, they won't dare move at all. Could run into a planet or star."

"Have you identified the navigation array?"

"I have," said a smiling Dale.

Vance returned the smile. "Disable it."

Two minutes later, a beam shot from the surface of Gabriel to the alien ship.

"That should do it," said Dale. "The damage to the navigation system should be repairable if we allow it."

"Now, how do we contact these folks?" asked Vance.

"How about taking a small runabout up and park it on their end disk?"

"Then?"

"Just knock on their door," said Dale.

"Funny," said Vance.

"Something Teddy might have said," said a smiling Dale.

"I'll pilot the shuttle," said Vance. "Have two men outfitted in pressure suits and armed with long and short weapons."

"Why did that small amount of damage disable the *Geaalo*?" asked Oruku.

"Judging from what we now know about these beings, we believe they just got extremely lucky. They hit a major transference cable. A weakness in our ship's design we were not aware of," said Ooat.

"It shut down just about everything. We have been using axillary power to maintain life support."

"We'll send some engineers over to help with the repairs and help strengthen that weakness."

"We'd be grateful."

Twenty-three hours later, the repairs on that *Geaalo* were complete. The temporary repair to the hull was replaced with plating that matched and was as strong as the rest of the hull. Power was restored throughout the ship, and life therein started to return to normal.

"The Gabrielites have disabled the alien ship and are awaiting our arrival at Gabriel," said Oruku. "Care to join us there?"

"Indeed we would," said Ooat. "We have three dead, and we want some answers."

"Something is happening," said Dale.

All eyes were on the viewer. The video display was taken from the small shuttle that was perched on top of the alien ship's end disk. A hatch was slowly opening. The tension on the *Marian* was peaking.

Vance and two other Gabrielites could be seen standing back ten meters from the hatch with their weapons trained on it.

A helmeted head appeared in the hatch opening. It was a big head and sat atop a large being as he rose weightlessly out of the open hatch. He was tethered so as not to float away in space.

This individual held no weapons, and his arms were held straight out from his body, clearly a sign of surrender.

Vance lowered his weapon, and the two with him followed his lead. Vance signaled his men to stay put as he walked, via his gravity boots, to the alien. When he reached the weightless individual, he took one of the alien's arms and effortlessly spun him 180 degrees, exposing the tether connection. He unhooked the tether and again spun the being 180 degrees. The tether was retracted into the ship, and the hatch slowly closed. Vance nodded as he took the now free-floating alien by the arm and led him to the shuttle. The alien offered no resistance.

"That pressure suit reminds me of old Earth's during the first few years of orbiting space flights," said Dale.

"Agreed," said Vance. "Not exactly state-of-the-art equipment."

As Vance was about to load the alien into the shuttle, the alien said something that sounded provocative and very unfriendly. Vance spun the alien so he could see his face through his visor. The look in Vance's eyes conveyed a "don't screw with me" look. After a few seconds, Vance backed off a little while keeping his eyes on the alien. "We're bringing him to the *Marian*."

"Good," said Dale. "Maybe we can find out why this primitive ship would have the audacity to attack a ship several thousand times their size and clearly far advanced technically."

"We'll see if we can't sweet-talk the answer from him," replied Vance.

Twenty minutes later, the shuttle settled on the flight deck of the *Marian*. A few seconds later, one of Vance's team walked down the ramp and took up a position at the bottom of the ramp, weapon at the ready. He was followed by Vance leading the now-walking alien down the ramp. The third member of the team followed Vance with his short weapon trained on the alien.

"Let's get these helmets off," said Vance.

The three men removed their helmets and handed them to the waiting deck crew.

"Let's get a look at you," said Vance as he made a quick inspection. He reached up, releasing a catch before lifting the helmet off the alien.

The alien was a full head taller than Vance and was humanoid in appearance. He was powerfully built and looked very tough. He looked at Vance defiantly.

His looks did not intimidate Vance. "Let's get you to our translation equipment." Vance took the man by the arm to lead him to one of the ship's labs.

The man quickly jerked his arm away from Vance while saying something that sounded like a threat. Then he displayed a cocky smile.

"Oh, so now you're going to show some balls?" Vance shook his head slowly.

Vance's two team member's posture went to full alert mode.

"Keep an eye on him while I remove my pressure suit," Vance said to his team.

Two minutes later, Vance, now wearing just his jumpsuit, again took the man's arm, and again the fellow jerked it away while repeating what sounded like a threat. A split second later, Vance slapped the man so fast and hard he was knocked back two meters and sprawled on his back. Sounds of pain came from him as he tried to get up.

"Get that pressure suit off of him," Vance said calmly.

Two of the deck crew approached the alien with a little trepidation. His size and demeanor didn't intimidate Vance, but it did them.

The alien barked something at the advancing crew, and it wasn't a friendly tone.

Vance moved quickly. He bent down, grabbed the neck ring of the pressure suit with one hand, and jerked the man to his feet. Then he stepped back a meter.

The surprise on the alien's face was almost comical.

Vance pointed a finger at the man's face and wagged it, at the same time shaking his head.

The alien clearly understood the message being conveyed. His expression changed to one of submission.

Vance signaled the two crew members to continue removing the alien's pressure suit. After the suit was removed, the alien's appearance changed somewhat. He was wearing a sweater and long pants and heavy socks. He looked more human without his pressure suit.

"We're going to have to figure out where in the galaxy you're from," said Vance.

"The *Velgot* and *Geaalo* have just arrived," said Dale.

"Good timing," said Vance. "Ask if they would like to meet here, or we could bring this dipshit up to them."

A minute later, Dale was back on the communicator. "They will be down here in a few minutes."

"We'll wait for their arrival before we start the questioning."

Oruku along with Ooat and Ssamp arrived at the landing site in the same shuttle and walked the hundred meters to the *Marian*.

When the three entered the lab, they had some sort of equipment with them. When the alien saw them, he started to get out of the chair that Vance had put him in. He had a look of surprise mixed with fear.

"Hey!" said Vance as he pointed at the chair with one hand and made a downward motion with the other.

The alien sat back down while not taking his eyes off the three Arkell.

"Looks like he offered resistance at some point," said Oruku while looking at the alien's angry-red and swollen cheek.

"Had to make an attitude adjustment," admitted Vance.

Fifteen minutes later, the alien was sitting with his head fitted with a simple-looking piece of equipment brought by Oruku.

"We'll be able to see images from his brain waves as he speaks. We will have his language translated in about an hour," said Ooat.

Ooat and Ssamp sat a few meters away against the far wall, both staring daggers at this man. Sitting alongside them were Vance and Dale.

A little over an hour later, whatever the alien said was converted to English.

"What is your name?" asked Oruku.

"Neilo."

"What is your ship's name?"

"*Ksidd.*"

"Are you the captain of the *Ksidd*?"

"I am in charge, yes."

"What planet are you from?"

"Rofina."

"In what section of the galaxy is Rofina located?"

Neilo cocked his head a little. "What do you refer to?"

"Dale, would you put an image of the Milky Way on the viewer, please."

A few seconds later, the image of the Milky Way galaxy was on the viewer.

"We are here." Oruku pointed at the location of Gabriel in the galaxy.

Neilo looked very confused. He spent the next few seconds looking at the viewer.

"Where is your planet?" asked Oruku.

"That is not our galaxy. Our galaxy is different. Smaller."

That statement got everyone's attention.

"You appeared here." Oruku pointed at the section of the galaxy where Neilo's ship first appeared.

"That is not possible . . . not possible."

Neilo was becoming agitated, his movements became shaky, and he was looking around like a trapped animal. "This is not real. I am dreaming."

"You are not dreaming," Oruku said in a calm voice and then turned to the four sitting at the far wall.

"He is not lying," said Oruku. "This is a mystery."

"Agreed," said Vance. "Something's askew."

"Neilo, you need to calm down. We mean you no harm," Oruku said softly. "The damage we inflicted on your ship was to stop your attack on us."

Ooat could contain himself no longer. "Why did you attack our ship?"

Neilo looked at Ooat. It was clear he was confused. "Is your ship the giant we fired upon?"

"Yes."

"We thought you were going to attack us."

"Why would you think that?"

"You appeared instantly. And your ship is huge. We wanted you to know we had offensive weapons. We hoped it would scare you off."

"First, we did not appear instantly—you did. We were already there surveying the planet we were orbiting."

"How can that be?"

"Hold a moment," said Oruku. "Do you have images of your galaxy on your ship?"

"Yes, many."

"We would like to see them."

Neilo was calming down. "I would need to contact the *Ksidd*."

"Can you transmit images from the *Ksidd*?" asked Oruku.

"If we knew the frequency maybe."

Oruku said nothing while getting information from the *Velgot*. "We have determined your frequency. Now please ask that your ship's crew transmit the images. We will be able to put them on our viewers."

"How would I contact the *Ksidd*?"

"Anything you say will be relayed to your ship," said Oruku.

"You can do that?"

Oruku nodded once.

"I'll ask them to send an image of our galaxy."

"You are now connected to your ship."

Neilo paused for a moment. "Shard, this is Neilo. I want you to transmit an image of our galaxy to the planet we are close to."

A full minute later, a response came from the *Ksidd*. "Why would do you want us to do that, sir?"

"I'll explain later, but right now I'm ordering you to make that transmission."

"Yes, sir."

Five minutes later, an image of a small galaxy appeared on the viewer. At the same time, Oruku was receiving some information from his earpiece. "Oh my," said Oruku. "This is the Canis Major Dwarf Galaxy." Oruku paused for a few seconds. "It's twenty-five thousand light-years from here."

"What!" said Dale.

"Are you sure?' asked Vance.

Oruku raised one eyebrow.

"Of course you're sure, sorry," said Vance with a sheepish smile.

"Not possible," said Neilo.

"Is this your galaxy?" asked Ooat.

Neilo did not take his eyes off the image on the viewer. "It is."

"Well now we have a quandary," said Oruku. "Are there more than one Sharkra? Or has our Sharkra expanded his influence to other galaxies. Or has our Sharkra taken control of the entire universe?"

Neilo's expression of confusion was increasing by the second. "Who is Sharkra?"

"Not who but what," said Oruku. "We believe Sharkra is the supreme being, a god if you will, who controls everything in what we thought was just our galaxy."

"There is no such thing as a god," said Neilo without reservation.

Vance smiled. "How do you explain the fact that you recently traveled twenty-five thousand light-years in an instant?"

"I don't believe you. It is not possible."

"Believe what you will," said Oruku. "That won't change the facts."

"Tell us about Rofina," said Vance. "What is its population?"

Neilo paused for a moment. "About three and a half billion."

"Gravity?"

Neilo gave a shrugging motion. "About the same as here."

"The *Ksidd* is armed, so we assume you're in a conflict with some other nation?"

"Yes, for a long time."

"What is the conflict over?"

Neilo paused for another moment. "I'm not sure anymore."

"Yet you continue to wage war?"

"Not an all-out war. Just a skirmish once in a while. Don't know how to stop it," said Neilo. "We stopped communicating with our enemies a long time ago."

"Are your enemies the same race as you?"

"I don't know what you mean."

"As you can see, there are differences between humans and Arkell. There are thousands of different races throughout the galaxy. Different genetics."

"No, there are no differences on Rofina. We are all the same."

After two of hours of interrogating Neilo, it was determined that he was telling the truth about the reason for their attack on the *Geaalo*. He believed, in fact, they were acting in self-defense.

"We believe you are telling the truth, Neilo. We are going to repair your ship and allow it to return to Rofina. We would like you to contact your ship and explain what happened and what is going to happen. We expect full cooperation from the crew of the *Ksidd*."

"You are going to repair our ship?" Neilo was clearly surprised at this turn of events.

"Yes, of course," said Oruku. "We bear you no ill will, despite the fact you violently and prematurely attacked one of our ships, resulting in the deaths of three innocent people. We believe you did it out of self-defense."

Neilo was again confused. His expression was that of amazement. "I don't know what to say."

"You could say thank you," said Ooat.

"That seems too little to say considering what you are doing for us."

"I'd agree with that," said Vance. "You're lucky you are dealing with Arkell. It might be a different story if you'd killed three humans."

"I understand and I . . . we are grateful."

"Now that we know what your motives were, I want to apologize for slapping you," said Vance.

Neilo gently touched his cheek. "You hit very hard. You are very strong."

Vance nodded once.

"Please instruct your crew to cooperate with the Arkell and humans," said Oruku.

"Yes, sir."

"My name is Oruku."

Two hours later, two dozen Arkell and humans, in pressure suits, were scattered the length of the *Ksidd*'s hull, removing all the exterior damaged and destroyed equipment. Most of the equipment and sensors would have to be completely remanufactured by the Arkell techs. The *Velgot*'s technicians tapped into the *Ksidd*'s computers and pulled up the design specs for all the sensors, relays, power production, and propulsion.

"Most of the *Ksidd*'s designs are antiquated and inefficient," said Tracc. "Their propulsion is liquid-fueled rockets."

"No surprise," said Oruku.

"We can make significant improvements to most of their systems," said Tracc. "And replenish their fuel."

Kilee entered into the conversation. "I would agree with making a few design changes but not to their weapons."

"Agreed," said Oruku.

Neilo along with Vance, Dale, Ooat, Ssamp, and Oruku were watching the viewer while having a lunch in the *Marian*'s cafeteria. *Ksidd* was in the foreground, while the *Velgot* and *Geaalo* were stationed a thousand meters away in the background. The *Ksidd* appeared tiny in comparison.

"How were you able to build such enormous ships?" asked Neilo.

"Both ships' components were designed and manufactured on our planet and were assembled in space. The *Geaalo* took nearly two hundred fifty years, and the *Velgot* took just under two hundred."

"Hundreds of years, that is amazing," said Neilo.

"If you think that's amazing, your senses would be overwhelmed if you saw the inside of either ship," said Vance.

"This is overwhelming," replied Neilo. "It's huge."

"The Arkell put a duplicate of this ship inside the *Velgot* and transported it ten light-years away to return it to its home planet," said Dale.

"A ship this size inside another ship. I cannot imagine."

"If you find that hard to imagine, you might be interested to know that there are one hundred and twenty thousand people aboard the *Velgot* and one hundred and fifty thousand aboard the *Geaalo*."

That information clearly stunned Neilo. He was speechless for a full minute.

"You have a crew of over a hundred thousand?"

"We have over a hundred thousand citizens. Less than two thousand crew," said Oruku.

"I believe Neilo is finding that hard to believe," said Vance with a smile.

Neilo nodded but remained silent.

Little was said while the six men finished their lunch.

"Hello, gentlemen," said Lara as she and Tomaco walked into the cafeteria and directly to the table.

The expression on Neilo's face was amusing. He, as with most alien races, seemed surprised at the looks of human and Arkell women.

"Neilo, please meet my and Dale's wives," said Vance.

"How long will it take to affect repairs to the *Ksidd*?" asked Neilo.

"Six hours," said Oruku. "It's taking that long because we have to remanufacture most of the equipment."

"You can manufacture our equipment and install it in just six hours?"

"Yes. Our technology is somewhat more advanced than yours."

"Hundreds of years, I would believe," said Neilo.

"Closer to ten thousand years," said Oruku.

"What?"

Oruku nodded his head. "At least that long."

Seven hours later, Neilo was back in his pressure suit, less the helmet, and was being escorted into one of the *Velgot*'s shuttles. After the hatch closed and the ramp was withdrawn, the shuttle shot up to a distance of two hundred kilometers. Neilo would not be aware that the shuttle had moved at all.

"We are going to give you a brief tour around the planet Gabriel before taking you back to the *Ksidd*."

"I would like that," said Neilo. With that, Oruku pushed a button and the hull of the shuttle seemed to become transparent.

That startled Neilo and he involuntarily jumped back from the wall. His gaze jumped from one view to another in rapid sequence. "How . . . what?"

Oruku smiled. "Thousands of miniature cameras installed on the exterior hull of the shuttle that transmit their images to the interior walls of the shuttle. The effect, as you can see, is that the walls seem to disappear."

"How did we get to this elevation?"

"We have a very efficient propulsion and antigravity systems."

During the low pass over the planet, Neilo continually expressed his awe at the beauty of Gabriel.

"This was a lifeless planet before the humans arrived?"

"Just a small amount of vegetation along its waterways. Vance, over a period of fifty years, planted all the vegetation from grasses to trees. He introduced all the animals—fish, mammals, birds, reptiles, and insects."

"How many humans must it have taken to accomplish such a massive undertaking?"

"One . . . Vance was alone."

Neilo's expression was one of incredulity. "Is he a god?"

"No, but he is quite special."

Two hours later, the Arkell shuttle was flying low and slow over the length of the *Ksidd* to show Neilo the repairs and replacement that had been done to his ship.

"This is incredible," said Neilo. "Some of the arrays are not familiar to me."

"We've made a few improvements to some of the *Ksidd*'s technology. Your crew have been instructed on the new systems. You and they will find the changes we've made quite useful."

The Arkell shuttle settled on the disk end of the *Ksidd*. Within seconds, the same hatch that Neilo had exited from nine hours before reopened.

"To return to your planet, all you need to do is set the course we have given to your navigator and fire your rockets. Sharkra will send you home."

"Sharkra willing, we are going to join you at Rofina and will put an end to your conflict."

"How do you expect to end our war?"

"Don't exactly know yet. We'll make an assessment when we get there."

Ten minutes later, the *Ksidd* and the *Velgot* were in a geosynchronous orbit over Rofina.

There was nothing remarkable about Rofina. It had a good balance between land and water masses. It was clear that the Rofinains did not have control of their toxic emissions. Most towns and cities were engulfed in a pollution-permeated blanket of smoke.

"We're home," said Neilo via ship-to-ship communication.

"What is the name of your nation?"

"Nrie."

"And the name of the nation you're at war with?"

"Etah."

"Thank you. And the neutral nation?"

"Neda."

"Thank you." Oruku paused for a moment. "We assume the continent and city we are over is yours?" asked Oruku.

"It is. How did you know where to orbit?"

"We didn't. Sharkra put us where he wanted us to be."

There was no response for a moment before Neilo answered. "I see."

Oruku smiled. "You still doubt Sharkra, despite the fact you and your ship have been transported twenty-five thousand light-years in seconds."

"I've spent my entire life believing there is no such things as gods. Nobody on Rofina will believe it."

"We'll see to it that they do believe in Sharkra before we head back to our galaxy," said Oruku pleasantly.

Neilo smiled. "From what I've witnessed in these past few hours, I believe you will succeed in whatever you set your mind to."

"Incoming rockets," said Kilee calmly.

Oruku smiled. "It seems your country's policy is to shoot before knowing all the circumstances."

"Yes, that had been our practice for decades. Didn't have time to ask questions. Our defenses had to react quickly to avoid as much damage as possible. Are you not concerned with our attack?"

"No, we are in no danger from such weapons."

"I understand. I'll contact them and stop this assault," said Neilo.

"Your citizens can clearly see the *Velgot*," said Oruku, "but they cannot see the *Ksidd*. I can assure you there is a great deal of panic going on down there. Contact them and explain what's happening and who we are. Who is your leader?"

"Our premier's name is Medib," answered Neilo.

"Is he a reasonable man?"

"I can't believe I'm telling you this, but no, Medib is not at all reasonable. Most believe he is an evil man. We all fear him."

"I appreciate your candor," said Oruku. "We would like you to contact Medib and tell him we wish to talk to him."

"He is known to be paranoid. He won't expose himself to any danger."

"As is the case for most despots," said Oruku.

Neilo nodded in understanding.

Oruku paused for a second. "Is there a park close to Medib's office?"

"Yes, adjacent to our capitol building."

"Are there monuments and/or statues there?"

"Yes, many."

"Any of Medib?"

"Yes, again many."

Oruku said nothing for a moment. "Bring up an image of the park. Put it on our and *Ksidd*'s viewers."

Within seconds, the park was displayed on the viewers.

The park wasn't large at about two hundred meters a side.

"Overlay the park with a grid," said Oruku.

The image was overlaid with a box grid, each box four by four meters.

"Neilo, give me the box coordinates for each of Medib's statues."

A minute later, Neilo had identified the location of six statues of Medib.

"Can Medib see the park from his office?"

"Yes, he can. About once a month, he stands on the balcony while addressing the city's citizens."

"Good, now contact Medib, identify yourself, and tell him we wish to meet him in the park in ten minutes."

"I'll try."

Five minutes later, Neilo was back in contact with the *Velgot*. "He will not meet you."

"Yes, we know. We are monitoring your communications."

"Now what should I do?" asked Neilo.

"We'll take it from here," said Oruku. "You can listen in to our conversation with Medib."

"We'll do that."

"Connect me with Medib," Oruku said to Tracc. "Translate our conversations to English."

A few seconds later, Tracc nodded at Oruku.

"Medib, my name is Oruku. I am in the starship orbiting above your capital. We wish to meet with you and your staff to have a conversation."

"We have no interest in talking to you, Oruku," Medib said a few seconds later.

"That is unfortunate, Medib. It shows that you are a weak leader. So we are going to give you a small demonstration as to what you are up against. Go out on your balcony and watch the demonstration."

"Do you think I am stupid? I will not expose myself to your weapons."

"The first demonstration will be in the park. The second will be in your office. I suggest you send someone out to your balcony to watch what happens, and then they can report to you what they have seen."

A moment passed before a response was given.

"I'll do that."

"One minute to the demonstration," said Oruku.

The viewers on the *Velgot* showed an individual walk cautiously out on the balcony. He was looking up at the *Velgot*.

"Tell him to look at your statue closest to your building," Oruku said to Medib.

"Watch my closest statue," Medib yelled out.

A second later, a short burst from the *Velgot* turned the statue into a fine powder.

"IT'S BEEN DISINTEGRATED!" yelled the clearly stressed assistant.

"Now watch the second statue," said Oruku calmly.

"Wait!" said Medib. "What do you want?"

"I want you to meet with me in the park in ten minutes."

"Are you going to harm me?"

"If we wished to harm you, you would be already harmed. There is no cover for you in that or any other building on your planet. Do you understand?"

Half a minute later, he said, "Where in the park?"

"You will know when you get there," said Oruku. "Be there in five minutes."

Four minutes later, the Arkell shuttle set down softly just a few meters from where the destroyed statue once stood.

Less than a minute later, Medib entered the park surrounded by armed guards.

Oruku smiled and shook his head at the stupidity of this man. "Have your guards set all their weapons on the ground and leave the park."

"I will be vulnerable if I do that."

"You will be dead along with your guards if you do not follow my instructions right now."

"A survival instinct must have been strong in Medib." He quickly barked orders at his guard. "Put your weapons on the ground and leave."

All but one did as ordered and started out of the park. The one stood resolutely where he was.

Two seconds later, multiple beams of white light hit the weapons lying on the ground and turned them into a white powder. The remaining guard looked at the remains of the weapons and dropped his quickly. A second later, it, too, was destroyed.

The ramp on the shuttle was extended and the hatch was opened. "Please join me in this transport," said Oruku.

Medib hesitated for a short moment before slowly walking up the ramp into the shuttle. As he walked through the hatch, the first thing he saw was Oruku. His expression was one of surprise mixed with considerable fear.

Oruku was standing three meters back from the hatch. His expression was serious. "I have been looking forward to meeting you. We, as you know, have met Neilo and found him to be a reasonable man. We hope, for your and your country's sake, that you, too, will be reasonable."

"Are you threatening me?"

"Oh, yes."

Medib wasn't used to being the weak hand in any situation. His response was quick. "Who do you think you're talking to?"

"I'm talking to a man whose life is about to change. A man who, if not very careful, will spend the rest of his short life in extreme discomfort."

Medib's survival instinct remained in high gear. As with most despots, there was nothing he wouldn't do to protect himself. There was nothing or no one that he wouldn't sacrifice to remain in power. "What do you want?"

"We want you to destroy all your weapons of war."

"Why would I do such a ridiculous thing? We would be destroyed by our enemies within days."

"No, you won't because your enemies will also be destroying their weapons."

Medib said nothing. He, without a doubt, was trying to figure out how to keep his army and weapons.

"I don't believe we will comply with your demands."

Oruku shook his head. "Tracc, inform the solders in this city that all their weapons will be destroyed in thirty minutes and, if they remain with them, they will die. Tell them to put their weapons outside their homes or the buildings they are in."

"Will do," said Tracc.

Oruku continued. "Put their largest military compound on the viewer please."

A few seconds later, the viewer in the shuttle displayed an area of eight square kilometers. Inside this area were aircraft, tanks, rocket launching pads, ammo dumps, radar arrays, and barracks.

"Medib, inform all personnel in this compound to evacuate all buildings, equipment, and weapons. Instruct them to move on to open spaces in the compound."

"You want me to gather my forces into an open, unprotected area?"

"We are going to destroy all your weapons of war located in that base. Any of your forces still in, on, or around any of them will be killed, and we do not wish to do that."

Medib said nothing.

"You have five minutes to do as I've asked. Then their lives will be on your head and we will point out what you've done to your entire country."

That statement got Medib's attention. "How can I do that from here?"

"Your voice will be transmitted to the compound from here. Just explain to those personnel what is about to happen to their base and tell them, if they wish to live, they must vacate all buildings and equipment in . . . four minutes."

"You said five minutes."

"That was over a minute ago and counting."

"This is Premier Medib. I am ordering you to abandon all building, weapons, and war machines. If you are not out in an open space, as far as you can get from those places, you will be killed in." Medib looked at Oruku for an answer. Oruku held up three fingers. "Three minutes."

A few seconds later, hundreds of personnel could be seen running away from buildings and toward the airfield in the center of the compound.

Three minutes later, the *Velgot*'s weapons began destroying everything on the base. Nothing burned, nothing exploded, nothing survived the attack. In less than four minutes, everything on the base was reduced to a white powder.

"You will now order your entire military, countrywide, to abandon all things related to waging war. In the next few hours, we will destroy all weapons and war-related infrastructure."

"We will be defenseless."

"You will not need to defend your country. We will have a conversation with who you consider your enemies. They have witnessed this demonstration, so we suspect they will abandon their weapons without much resistance."

"Our enemies will not concede defeat," said Medib.

"They will not be defeated, nor will your country. You will simply have to come to understand your new situation and set about making a permanent peace for your planet."

"There can be no peace on Rofina," said Medib. "I hate the Etahoians."

Oruku nodded. "It is clear that you cannot continue to rule over your country. You simply don't qualify for such an important position, either in temperament or intelligence. As of this moment, you are no longer premier."

"You can't dictate who is to run my country."

"We just did. And we are naming Neilo as new premier."

"I'll not give up my leadership."

"This conversation has and is being broadcast to all nations of Rofina. So all on Rofina know you are no longer in charge."

"I'll fight you," said Medib with little conviction.

"You will not only lose the fight, but you, and whoever fights beside you, will regret it."

"We'll see about that," said Medib.

Oruku shook his head while maintaining a slight smile. "Neilo informed us about an island in your North Sea called Zeni. Apparently, you have been using it as a prison for your citizens who disagree with your policies."

You didn't have to be an astute face reader to see that Medib didn't like where this conversation was going.

"Neilo, what do you know about this prison island?"

A few seconds later, Neilo responded. "For twenty-plus years, Medib has sent not only his political rivals there but their families as well."

Oruku turned back to Medib. "Why would you send families there?"

"Smart politics. Why leave a family free to denigrate my government?"

Oruku's expression turned dark as he stared into Medib's eyes.

"How long are the sentences?"

Medib simply shrugged as if it didn't matter. Oruku's expression became even darker.

"Neilo, what can you tell me about the prison sentences?"

"They are all life sentences."

Oruku's eyes were now burning into Medib's. Medib could not maintain eye contact. He looked down at the deck.

Oruku remained silent for a full minute while not taking his eyes off Medib. "Look at me, Medib."

Medib did not look up but instead shook his head.

Oruku nodded in understanding. Medib was a coward.

"We are going to release all those you have imprisoned for political reasons, and we're going to ask Neilo's new administration to review the cases of all whom you have imprisoned."

"Neilo has no administration."

"It amazes us that anyone as dim-witted as you could hold on to power as long as you did, truly astonishing."

Medib said nothing while continuing to keep his eyes averted from Oruku's.

"We are going to transfer you and your henchmen to Zeni. There you will remain until the majority of those you have imprisoned, in the past, ask for your release. Further, all of your and your cohorts' wealth will be confiscated and divided as equitably as possible among those you have imprisoned. Your families will be evicted from their homes but not imprisoned."

"Our families are innocent, so why evict them?"

"It is remarkable to me that you are so self-absorbed you would ask such a question. But I will answer that in saying that your families have had the benefit of your corrupt policies for at least twenty years. They will have to learn to support themselves as I believe most on this planet do."

"Not going anywhere," said Medib without much conviction.

Oruku ignored him. "Neilo, do you know the names of all Medib's associates?"

"I could probably come up with most of them, but those I don't know offhand can be easily identified."

Oruku remained silent for a minute. "We need to separate those who participated in political prosecution and corruption from those bureaucrats who simply work for the government."

"We can do that," said Neilo.

"Excellent. Do you know if the leadership of Etah has the same practice regarding political rivals?"

"Actually, we've come to understand they do not imprison political rivals."

"Thank you." Oruku turned his attention back to Medib. "The leadership of your past nemesis may not, depending on their attitude, be joining you on the island."

The expression on Medib's face was one of total confusion.

"What?"

"You heard me."

"I'm not going anywhere," a clearly defeated Medib repeated.

"You will return to your office and collect your personal belonging and return to your home. We will keep you informed as to when you'll be transferred to Zeni."

A panel opened behind Oruku, and two Arkell stepped into the small control room and walked directly to Medib, and without a word, each grabbed an arm and dragged Medib out of the transport, down the ramp. Then they simply dropped him on the grass.

"Neilo, we would like you to land your ship and proceed to your capitol. We'll see to it you are given the proper respect and safety in the transference of power."

"I don't know what to say," said Neilo. "I'm not sure if I'm capable of running a country."

"We've had a great deal of experience with leadership changes on a multitude of planets," said Oruku. "Over the centuries, we have designed a set of laws, rights, and procedures that will be, if you choose to use them, of great help in governing your nation."

"We will have the documents translated into your language and deliver them to you and the leaders of the other two nations of Rofina."

"I'm looking forward to seeing them."

"Good, you will find these documents useful."

Oruku turned his attention to the camera that had been broadcasting this entire exchange throughout Rofina. "I am now addressing Beitzel, the premier of Etah," Oruku said in a calm voice. "You have seen and been privy to what has happened here on Nrie. We wish to know what your attitude is concerning the new order of your planet?"

A few seconds later, a smiling Tracc spoke. "We have a message coming in from Beitzel, premier of Etah," he said. "He would like to talk to you."

"Excellent, let's talk to him."

Tracc nodded once at Oruku, who returned the nod. Beitzel's image came on the screen.

"Premier Beitzel, I am please you have contacted us. I'm assuming you've been listening and watching what is going on here on Nrie."

"We have . . . I don't know how to address you, sir."

"My name is Oruku, and that is the way all address me."

It took a few seconds for that to sink into Beitzel's brain.

"That being the case, I will address you as Oruku."

Oruku nodded.

"Oruku, we have been watching and listening to your exchanges and directives to the leadership of Nrie. We, the citizens of Etah, are overjoyed. There are celebrations starting all over our nation. The war is over, thanks to you."

It was clear Beitzel was, in fact, overjoyed. His facial expressions and voice inflections were a joy to see and listen to.

"We cannot tell you how happy we are to witness this major turning point in your planet's status. But we, the Arkell, cannot and will not take credit for this. We are simply a hand for Sharkra to do his will."

After a moment's delay, Beitzel spoke up. "Who is Sharkra?"

"Vance, are you there?" asked Dale.

A few seconds later, Vance's voice came over the communication system. "Out at the river doing a little fly fishing. What's up?"

"We just received a message from the *Velgot*," said Dale.

"Are they alright?"

"Yes, they're fine, but Oruku says Sharkra wants them to stay in the Canis Major Dwarf Galaxy for a while."

"A while?"

"They don't know but feel Sharkra wants them to do in the Dwarf Galaxy what they've done in ours."

Vance said nothing for a few seconds. "That could take years." The disappointment in Vance's voice was obvious."

"That's Oruku's belief also."

CHAPTER 25

STRANGERS

"We've been receiving a very strange signal for a few hours now," said Dale as Vance walked on to the *Marian*'s bridge.

"How strange?" asked Vance while briefly scanning the sensor array in front of the captain's chair.

"Unlike anything we've ever received. It's being transmitted by some intelligence. It's repeating itself about every ten minutes. It's certainly not a frequency we're aquatinted with. The only thing we can pick up is a modulating humming sound."

"You're sure it's directed at us?"

"Not sure of anything at this point. We've been trying to route it through the Arkell translator, but so far, no success."

"No strange ships in our solar system?'

"Not in our solar system, but there is something way out, nearly out of range of our sensors, too far to make an identification."

"Is it heading our way?"

"I think so, but if it is, it's moving slowly."

The explosion was incredibly deep, loud, and long in duration, like a massive thunderclap.

"What the hell?" said Vance as he quickly stood up from the table he was sitting at with Lara, Teddy, and Colleen. The three stood quickly, following Vance's lead.

"Don't know what it was, but it scared the crap out of me," said Teddy.

Vance wasn't listening. He was nearly at a run as he headed to the exit of the restaurant. He was followed by the other three and a dozen or so other patrons of the restaurant.

Once he was outside, Vance's eyes were drawn upward. A bright-orange, bordering on red, circular patch, maybe twenty kilometers in diameter, dominated the sky above their heads. Everything within their vision was affected by the sky's color. Rather than shades of green on the trees, bushes, and grass, there were shades of brown. The Vance River color went from sky blue to an off-purple. They could see the *Marian* in the distance; its bronze color had been transformed to a bright gold. As they watched, the orange-colored sky began fading, and within a minute, the sky was back to its normal clear blue.

"What the . . . ?" said Colleen, her eyes moving quickly from one thing to another.

"This is a bit surrealistic," said Teddy while scanning the entire area.

"It is, and I don't like it," replied Vance.

"Hell," was all Lara said.

The sounds of hundreds of alarmed voices were heard coming from all over Home Bay.

Vance grabbed his communicator and quickly called Dale. The communicator displayed nothing but a loud static. Vance continued to look upward as he replaced his communicator back on his belt. "I'm heading to the *Marian*," he said without looking at his wife and friends. He took off at a dead run.

Teddy, Lara, and Colleen looked at the retreating Vance and then at each other.

"Let's go," said Lara, and she turned, heading in the same direction as her husband.

Nine minutes later, Vance was walking onto the *Marian*'s bridge. Except for a single bridge tech, Sam, the bridge was empty.

"Have you heard from Dale?" Vance asked Sam.

"Haven't heard from anyone, sir. There's not an instrument that is working at this time. All went dead just a few minutes ago."

"Shit!"

"Apparently, the elevator is working," said Sam.

"Hadn't thought about that, but you're right. That's good. Not everything is useless."

"Can you tell me, what the hell was that explosion?"

"No idea," answered Vance.

Teddy, Lara, and Colleen walked onto the bridge.

"I'm surprised you left your loving wife behind, Mr. Youngblood," said Lara with half a smile.

"I . . . oops," said Vance.

"Could be the end of the world, ya know," added a wide-eyed Teddy.

"I apologize," said Vance. "Wasn't thinking."

"You were thinking alright," said Lara with a smile. "You were thinking our planet was in danger and you had to act. So, Mr. Youngblood, you have nothing to apologize for. You are being you."

"Thank you, sweetheart," said Vance as he bent over and gave Lara a short kiss. "I'm heading back outside." Vance turned and addressed Sam. "If communications come back online, give me a call."

"Yes, sir."

Vance turned to Lara, Teddy, and Colleen. "You're welcome to come with me or stay aboard the *Marian*."

"We're with you," said Teddy.

Once outside, all four of them scanned the sky. Nothing seemed out of place. Their sky was back to its normal bright blue.

"I like this," said Teddy.

"Oh yeah," added Vance.

At that second, Vance's communicator came to life.

"Vance, are you hearing me?" It was Dale's voice.

"Loud and clear, my friend."

"Been trying to get in touch for a while. Nothing but static."

"I've had the same problem."

"I'll bet you're wondering what the hell happened to our atmosphere."

"I've given it a thought or two," said Vance.

"Looks like the planet's not burning up after all," said Dale.

"What the hell happened?"

"Just guessing here, but I believe we may have been hit with a small asteroid or a large meteorite. Or let me rephrase that. I think something hit the planet's shield."

"Jesus, how big must it have been to cause such an extreme reaction with the shield?"

"Size may not be the important thing, but how fast was it traveling? I'm just thinking off the top of my head, but since we had no warning of an approaching asteroid, which we would have if all else was normal, whatever it was must have been traveling at extreme speed."

"The sensors on some of our satellites would have detected an asteroid, wouldn't they?"

"Yes, they would have and may have, but the object could have been traveling at such speed it hit the shield before the sensors on the satellites had time to sound an alarm," answered Dale.

"Can you retrieve information from our satellites?"

"Should be able to get some data from one or more of them. I'm heading to the *Marian* as we speak."

"Good, we are already here. We'll wait for you."

Twenty-three minutes later, Dale smiled and nodded as he turned away from the computer to address Vance, Teddy, Lara, and Colleen. "Have good data concerning the molecular makeup of what hit the shield. It was an asteroid alright, and I'd guess about thirty kilos."

"That's not very big, was it?" asked Teddy.

"No, I expected something bigger," Dale answered. "But it's the speed that caused the reaction with the shield."

"What was the speed?"

"I estimate one hundred and twenty thousand kilometers."

"Jesus," said Vance. "That's about three times the average speed of a celestial object."

"That's right," agreed Dale. "This wasn't a natural occurrence."

"Can you determine where the asteroid would have hit were it not for the shield?"

"We've done that. It would have hit in the middle of the Vast Ocean."

"Geez, wouldn't that cause a tidal wave?" asked Teddy.

Dale smiled. "That's a good question. That asteroid, that size, traveling at that speed, would have mostly disintegrated when it hit our atmosphere. Whatever was left would have burned up, leaving very little to hit the ocean."

"What the hell?" said Dale in a surprised voice.

Vance's head snapped around. "What?"

"There's a ship stationed directly over Home Bay."

"Where did it come from?"

"No idea."

"Let's take a look," said Vance.

The viewer's image changed to one of a single ship.

"Well that's different," said Vance.

"It may not be from this galaxy," said Dale.

There it was. It was tubular in shape. It was fairly large, and it was gray and had four large "wheels" surrounding it and evenly spaced along its length. The wheels were slowly turning. The two end wheels were turning in the same direction, and the center, considerably larger wheels were turning in the opposite direction.

"What's its dimensions?"

Dale's fingers flew over his keyboard. "One hundred forty meters long and forty wide."

"Pretty big," said Vance. "Those wheels?"

"They are probably their propulsion system."

Vance nodded without taking his eyes off the perceived threat to his planet.

"Doesn't look particularly lethal, does it?" asked Dale.

"No, it doesn't. But you can't judge a book by its cover."

"I haven't heard that old saying for at least a couple of centuries," said Teddy.

Vance nodded. "Agreed, we've had one visitor from another galaxy, no reason to assume there wouldn't be more."

"That's true," said Dale. "Hopefully they'll be friendly."

"Not friendly if they are throwing asteroids at us."

"That remains to be determined," said Dale.

"Really?"

"Something's off here," said Dale. "Something's gnawing at the back of my brain. Can't seem to pull it out."

"Seems obvious to me."

Dale said nothing, just nodded.

"Is there any way to tell if the shield has been damaged or weakened?" asked Vance.

"That, my friend, I can answer," said Dale. "The shields are operating at a perfect level. No damage or weakness that we can detect."

"And there haven't been any more attacks."

Ten minutes later, Troy and Gary walked onto *Marian*'s bridge. Their eyes went to the large viewer.

"Holy crap," said Troy.

"Wow, where is that ship?"

"Right overhead," said Dale.

"How long has it been there?"

"Just a few minutes, actually," answered Dale.

"Just showed up," added Vance.

"Doesn't look lethal, does it?" said Troy.

"Sure doesn't."

Dale began giving a rundown as to what was known and not known.

"We have not been able to ascertain who or what was responsible for the attack on Gabriel. But I have been able to determine the size and speed of the asteroid."

"I'll bet that took a little doing," said Troy.

"As a matter of fact, it did. We had to integrate and program our satellite's computers, *Marian*'s computers, and the shield's computers to act as one. That was a tough program to devise. They were not designed to be compatible. Had the Arkell been available, the job would have been done in minutes rather than the six hours it took us."

"What did you determine?" asked Alex.

"The missile was in fact an asteroid. It was smaller than I first thought might be the case. It was just over thirty kilos in weight and was traveling at one hundred twenty thousand kilometers per hour."

"That eliminates the possibility of a natural occurrence," said Gary.

"It does," said Vance. "I believe that some entity, likely that ship in orbit, did attack us with the goal of inflicting damage on the planet."

"Well," said Dale slowly, "I'm going to disagree. There's more here than what seems obvious."

"Such as?"

"Any entity that can toss an asteroid at that speed would know that the asteroid would be destroyed when it hit the atmosphere. Also, if damaging our planet was their goal, why would they aim for the middle of a huge ocean?"

"They may not have known that Gabriel had a shield," said Troy.

"They do now," said Vance. "And they know what won't work against the shield, but that doesn't stop them from trying something much larger or faster."

"That's certainly a possibility. We could be hit again at any time," said Gary.

"Or," said Dale, "they may have hit us with their best shot. They may not have something bigger and faster."

"Also a possibility," agreed Troy. "If we don't get hit within the next few days, it could mean they've given up and moved on."

Vance had said nothing for the past few moments. "Makes me very uncomfortable not knowing who or what, or their motivation."

"Maybe we need to get up there with a shuttle and take a look," suggested Vance.

"Vance, I will always defer to you in such matters, but any entity who could hurl an asteroid at such speeds is probably a great deal more advanced than we are. I just think that we ought to stay under the cover of our shields until we know who and why."

"You're right." Vance smiled. "I'll hold off for a day or two."

"Good."

"But," said Vance, "let's go on full alert. All offensive weapons manned and ready. If they display any aggression, I'll want to take a shot at them."

"We still have missiles on the moon Faith," said Dale.

Vance smiled. "They are by far our best weapons for this scenario. I'm assuming they are online and ready to use?"

Dale returned the smile. "They will be in about four minutes."

Vance nodded. "Also, let's get the laser ready to fire."

"Will do."

"Vance, do you have your ears on?"

A few seconds later, he said, "Haven't taken them off. What's up?"

"Getting signals from the ship."

"Be there in fifteen," said Vance.

As Vance walked onto the *Marian*'s bridge, his eyes went to the viewer.

The strange ship was still sitting stationary over Home Bay.

Vance smiled. "Have you tried communicating with them?"

"Yes. We're thinking this ship may be the source of the transmissions we've been intercepting for the past month. But we still can't understand the signal."

Shem and Vel walked onto the *Marian*'s bridge. Both had their eyes on the bridge's viewer.

"That's different," said Shem.

Vel said nothing for a moment while keeping his eyes on the unusual ship displayed on the viewer. "How big?"

"About one hundred forty meters long, forty wide," said Vance.

"It doesn't look like a warship at all," said Shem.

"Looks, in this case, may be deceiving. This ship may have been, and probably was, responsible for hurling an asteroid at us," said Vance.

"But now they're stationary in space," said Dale. "The unusual transmissions we've been picking up have intensified greatly. I have no doubt they have, in fact, been coming from that ship."

"We need to find a way to decipher their signal," said Shem.

"Can you duplicate the frequency they're using?" asked Vel.

"We're getting close on that. Their frequency is extremely high."

Vel said nothing for a moment and then looked at Dale. "How about slowing their frequency down to our normal operating frequency?"

Dale rolled his eyes. "Of course, why didn't I think of that?"

Vel smiled. "Too obvious, probably. And, of course, that may not be the answer."

Dale said no more but began quickly typing instructions to the computers. Within a minute, Dale looked up. "On the viewer."

The viewer's display switched from that of the alien ship to black screen with a thin, white, horizonal line dissecting the middle.

"Slowing it down."

In a few seconds, the straight line on the viewer started to show hills and valleys.

"Now we're talking, now we're talking," said an excited Dale. "Thanks, Vel."

Vel nodded once.

"Now I'm going to run this signal through the Arkell translator and see what comes out the other end."

Vance remained silent as he continued to watch the viewer.

"Switch back to the ship, please," said Vance.

"I can't detect any ports, hatches, or instrumentation," observed Vel.

"I don't see any either," said Vance.

Gary walked onto the bridge. "Still just sitting there."

Within seconds of Gary's arrival, Dale said, "It's moving."

"It's heading directly toward us," said Vel.

"It's coming in slowly," said Dale while keeping his eyes on the computer screen in front of him.

"The wheels are turning faster," observed Shem.

The ship held a steady-but-slow speed as it headed to Gabriel. As it approached the shield, it slowed to a crawl.

"This is interesting," said Vel.

The ship was barely moving when it touched the outer reaches of the shield. The contact made the shield glow slightly at the point of contact but didn't seem to inflict any damage to the ship. The ship continued to move forward, but as it did, the shield's glow grew until the ship was at a full stop.

"Did they stop the ship, or did the shield stop them?" asked Gary.

"I believe it was the shield," said Dale. "It looked like they were testing the parameters of the shield's effectiveness. Maybe they thought if they went slowly, the shield would let them pass through without damage."

"That's a reasonable thought," said Vel.

The ship backed away from the shield, and the shield's glow went out.

"Wonder what they'll try next," said Gary.

"Have a signal coming from them," said Dale.

"Anything decipherable?"

"I'll slow it on viewer."

Half the viewer continued to show the alien ship. The other half displayed the signal coming from the ship.

"I'm going to try to send them a message on our frequency and what I hope is theirs. Maybe they have the technology to translate it," said Dale.

"What are you going to say?"

"I'm open to suggestions."

"In the past when we started communicating with aliens, we sent a picture of humans. A picture of a male, female, and child. Be my suggestion to do just that," said Alex.

"Good," said Shem. "Hopefully they'll be able to convert the signal to the picture."

Fifteen minutes went by. "Nothing from the translator yet," said a tech.

All eyes were glued to the viewer. There was silence on the bridge.

"I'm going to send pictures of everything I can think of and include the name of whatever it is and audio saying the name of the object," said Dale.

"That's a good idea," said Vel. "How about sending videos and audios of various actions, such as running, swimming, sleeping, eating, building homes, doctors treating patients, mothers and children, etcetera."

Dale was entering all suggestions being given by all on the bridge. It went on for over an hour.

"I don't know what else . . ."

A single word appeared below the active line on the viewer: "HELP."

"Holy shit!" said Vance.

Another word followed: "SICK."

"They are not trying to attack us," said Dale. "They're needing help with what must be a catastrophic illness they can't control."

Vance remained quiet and pensive for a moment. "Could be a plague ship or a ruse to get them past the shield."

"Suggestions, anyone?" said Shem.

"First we need to establish a dialogue with them," said Vel.

All agreed.

The signal coming from the alien ship stopped. Everybody on the bridge started to hold their breath.

One minute, then two—time seemed suspended to those on the bridge.

At five minutes, Vance's patience gave out. "This is agonizing."

"Patience, my friend," said Alex. "They're probably having as much trouble translating our signal as we've had with theirs."

Vance nodded, not taking his eyes off the viewer.

It was twenty-eight minutes later when a signal finally came in. On the viewer came the words, "We understand."

"YES!" at least five of the men on the bridge yelled nearly at the same time.

A few seconds later, a picture appeared on the viewer. It was assumed that the picture was of an adult male, an adult female, and a child. They looked quite thin, and their heads were triangular in shape, pointed at the chin and broad at the top. Their faces were quite flat with a long, thin nose and large eyes. Their hair was dark and wavy to the point of being curly.

"Geez," Teddy said quietly.

A second picture replaced the first. It was the picture sent to the alien ship of the three humans, but now the picture showed the humans in outline with the alien's picture superimposed over the top of the outline. The aliens were half the height and half the width of the humans.

"They're tiny," said Vance.

"Little over a meter tall," said Dale.

"Kinda cute," added Teddy.

"Their clothes look quite a bit like our jumpsuits," said Vance.

"Jumpsuits are quite practical. Seems advanced civilizations trend toward them in one form or another," added Gary.

Another picture came in from the aliens. It showed another picture, but this time it was one of them lying flat on a cot. This alien looked very sick.

"That doesn't look good," said Vance.

"We need to learn each other's language if we're to be any help to these people," said Shem.

"How long before we have enough translated to be able to help these people?" asked Gary.

"It will be hours if not days," said Dale.

For the next six hours, Dale continued to send pictures along with audio names of each. As the hours went on, the pictures became videos. The videos were accompanied by descriptions. One showed an antelope standing still with the word "antelope." The next video showed the antelope running, with the words "antelope, running." The next had the antelope walking, with the words "antelope, walking. And the back-and-forth went on.

At the beginning of the seventh hour, the viewer's screen went black for a few seconds before the words "Need help" appeared.

"Okay," said Vel, "how about an audio/visual of you, Dale, saying, 'We will help'?"

"Excellent idea," said Gary.

"Good," added Vance.

"Agreed," added Dale. "I'll get right on it."

Five minutes later, another transmission came in from the aliens. It was audio and visual, as was the last transmission to them. The viewer showed the words "We are friendly" and "We need help." Then a curser moved along the bottom of these words while an undulating humming sound was heard.

"Uh-oh," said Dale.

"Uh-oh is right," said Vel. "Their language is in the form of humming. This is going to make dialogue very tricky."

"Need to tell them that we are willing to help but concerned about their intentions," added Vance.

"But they've picked up on everything we've tried. I believe, in time, we can translate their language through the universal translator. It may take a while," said Dale. "I'm going to continue sending pictures of objects while naming them. They, in turn, unless I miss my guess, will send them back in their language."

"I think we're losing track of the main problem here," said Alex. "They need help, and I have to assume, time is critical."

"Agreed," said Vance. "We need to get up there and check things out in person. Send them a note asking them if we can come up and visit their ship."

"Which shuttle are you going to use?" asked Dale.

"One of our small ones. May need the space to bring a few of them down here."

"Why not just turn off the shield and let them come down here?" asked Alex.

"Because we don't know that everything is as it's represented to be. I'm not willing to take that chance. I haven't forgotten about the asteroid."

Alex nodded.

"I'll send a picture of the shuttle along with a picture of Vance, Vel, and Dr. Gonzales. I'll try to make them understand that we want to enter their ship."

"Would that be Lucy?" asked Vance.

Dale smiled. "It would. Jen Aidery's great-granddaughter."

Vance smiled at the thought of Dr. Jen. She was the doctor who, over a hundred years ago, informed the planet's hierarchy that two unusual babies had just been born on Gabriel: Shem and Jarleth.

Lucy was, as far as anyone knew, the shortest human ever to be born on Gabriel. At just over a meter and a half, she was indeed short. But she was also a delightful young lady with an excellent, empathetic mind.

"I'll point out the obvious here," said Alex. "The beings aboard this ship are sick. What their illness is, we don't know. We also don't know what, if any, effect it will have on humans. We SLFs are not in any danger, but we could spread whatever it is to Gabriel's citizens."

"Good point," said Gary. "We'll go through decontamination."

"Agreed."

A few minutes later, Dale said, "Hopefully they will let you into their ship. I've done the best I could."

"While we're waiting for their reply," said Vance, "I'll head over to the *Norman* and get the shuttle equipped with emergency medical supplies and equipment."

"Talk to Lucy and ask what she recommends as far as medicines are concerned."

"Check."

"I'd like to go with you," said Gary.

"Good. I'm sure we'll need all the help we can get."

"I'm going to take a portable translator with us," said Vance.

An hour later, the small shuttle was in orbit beside the alien ship. The four had on their pressure suits, less the helmets.

"Suppose we need to knock?" said Gary.

"They'll know we're here," said Vance. "I still can't see any seams of any kind in this ship's hull. It's smooth as a baby's butt."

"Vance?"

"Yes, Dale."

"Just got a message from the aliens. They want you to move to the front of the ship. They'll open a hatch for you."

"Good, we were getting concerned." Vance paused for a second and then smiled. "Which is the front? There doesn't seem to be any difference in the configuration."

A few seconds later, Dale's voice came back. "The one that's closest to Gabriel."

"We're moving in that direction."

Two minutes later, the small shuttle was ten meters away and was pointed directly at the nose of the alien ship.

Within seconds, a vertical seam began slowly opening in front of the shuttle.

"Ah, here we go," said Vance.

"That's remarkable," said Gary. "So precisely made, it's all but impossible to see until it opens."

A full two minutes later, the hatch opened just big enough to allow the shuttle to enter the interior of the ship.

"Here we go," said Vance.

Without further conversation, Vance eased the shuttle through the narrow hatch and into the ship.

"Well," said Vel, "this is different."

The interior was nearly as stark and featureless as the exterior.

The landing pad was white against the gray overall color of both the exterior and the interior. Standing behind a glass wall a few meters from the back of the pad were four aliens.

"Looks like we have a reception committee," said Gary.

"I don't see any weapons, do you?" asked Vance.

"No, sir," said Vel.

Vance approached the landing pad slowly and carefully, and then gently set the shuttle down in its center.

The ship's outside hatch slowly closed behind them.

An unseen hatch opened a meter from the glass wall, and the four aliens walked through it and stopped two meters in front of the shuttle. They just stood side by side, apparently waiting for the humans to exit their transport.

"Oxygen levels are quite high," said Vel. "The balance is nitrogen and carbon dioxide."

"Good," said Gary.

"Let's put our helmets on anyway," said Lucy. "We don't know what pathogens or viruses are floating around."

Without comment, the four put on their helmets.

"Gravity on this ship is about half that of Gabriel's. Don't go floating off," said Vel.

Vance smiled. "Opening the hatch."

A minute later, the four, with Vance in the lead, walked down the short ramp and onto the deck of the ship. The four had a little trouble walking at first, due to the low gravity, but got the hang of it in a few seconds. Vel was carrying the portable translator. Lucy had a satchel in one hand and was pulling a wheeled cart with the other.

Vance led them to the front of the landing pad, stopping two meters from the tiny aliens.

The jumpsuits on the males were light green and identical in design. The female's was a light yellow. Each, however, had a different-colored stripe on the upper sleeve. One male had a red stripe, another had a white stripe and the third had a blue stripe. The stripe on the female's was brown. The one with the red stripe was holding some sort of instrument.

Close up and in person, these beings looked as if they were quite ill. The four Gabrielites didn't know what the aliens looked like when they were healthy, but one could see these four weren't. Their skin tone looked somewhat gray, their eyes bloodshot, and their demeanor seemed somehow weak.

The one with the translator hummed a few notes. "Greetings and welcome aboard our ship," came the words from the translator.

Vance signaled Vel to hand him the translator and turned it on. "It's working," he said.

"First, we would like to introduce ourselves." The translator gave a short hum. "My name is Vance." The translator hummed again.

The alien with the translator hummed something and the translator said, "My name is Bieirs," he said as he bowed slightly. Then Bieirs handed the translator to the alien on his right.

"My name is Sogee," said the second alien, and he bowed, turned slightly, and handed the translator to the being on his right.

"My name is Aldee," said the third alien. After a short bow, he turned and handed the translator to the fourth alien.

"My name is Dorss," said the fourth. She bowed and handed the translator back to Bieirs.

Vance handed the translator to Gary.

"My name is Gary," he said while bowing. He handed the translator to Lucy.

"My name is Lucy. I am a doctor, and I wish to examine your shipmates to determine whether or not we can be of service. Our race is called human," she added.

The four aliens quickly began a dialogue between them. Bieirs seemed to be in charge. He did most of the humming. After a moment, Bieirs turned toward the humans. "We are pleased you will try to help our sick. We will give you all the assistance we can." Bieirs paused for a moment. "We are called Rootic."

Vance motioned to Lucy that he wanted the translator. She stepped forward and handed it to him.

"We, the humans, welcome you to our planet. Our planet is called Gabriel."

"Tell them, with their permission," said Lucy, "I will start the process of determining what their illness is."

Vance repeated what Lucy had said and got an enthusiastic positive reply from the Rootic.

Lucy smiled and immediately started flipping switches and turning knobs on the portable diagnostic computer. She pulled up a wand-like instrument out of its slot and moved it slowly around and above her head, all the while keeping her eyes on several dials.

After a few moments, she returned the wand to its slot. "Didn't pick up any pathogens. There is nothing registering that would cause any problems for humans."

"Good," said Vance. "Can we remove the pressure suits?

"Yes."

Vance spoke into the translator. "We found no pathogens that would cause us any illness. We are going to remove our pressure suits."

After a moment, Bieirs spoke into his translator. "Excellent. Please remove your outer covering."

The four began removing their pressure suits, beginning with the helmets. The four Rootic started humming rapidly.

"Hold on," said Vance.

The four Gabrielites stopped removing their suits.

Vance spoke into the translator. "Is there a problem?"

Bieirs answered, "No problem. We are surprised at the difference in your appearance. None look alike. Not even the same size or color." Bieirs paused for a moment. "We, as you see, are the same."

Vance smiled. "Yes, there is a great deal of difference in our appearance. Yet we are of the same species. We are friends with different species from several different planets that vary in appearance. None look exactly like us. Now, hopefully, we have another species to call our friends."

This statement seemed to please the Rootic immensely. Their humming took on a melodious and pleasing tone.

"We would like that," said Bieirs. "Please continue to remove your outer covering."

With that, the four set their helmets on the deck and began removing the rest of their pressure suits.

Two minutes later, the four stood in their jumpsuits.

Again, there was pleasant-sounding banter from the Rootic.

"Your bodies are so different," said Bieirs. He looked at Vance. "We've never seen such a powerful-looking intelligent being." He looked at Lucy. "Are all your females shorter than the males?"

Lucy smiled. "Most females are somewhat shorter than the males, but I am unusually short."

Bieirs looked from Lucy to Vel to Gary. "All different, very interesting."

"I'd like to continue to diagnose your illness," said the diminutive Lucy.

"Please continue," said Bieirs.

Lucy nodded and walked over and stopped in front of Bieirs. "May I?" she asked as she took out a cotton swab and visually opened her mouth and pretended she was swabbing and then pointed at Bieirs's mouth.

He understood and opened his mouth wide, bearing an impressive set of molars. It seems that the Rootic had four more molars than did humans.

Lucy didn't hesitate. Even she had to bend down a little to swab the inside of his cheeks and the back of his throat. She then took the swab and inserted it into a receptacle on the face of the diagnostic computer. After a moment, she pushed a button and turned a dial.

Thirty seconds later, Lucy spoke. "Well I see the problem," she said without taking her eyes off the computer's screen.

"What?" asked Vel.

"They have influenza."

"What?" asked Vance. "How would they not know that?"

"And as an advanced species, why couldn't they cure it?"

"Let's see if we can find out," said Lucy.

Lucy turned to address Bieirs. "I have determined your illness. It is what we call the flu. What surprises us is why an advanced civilization, such as yourselves, could not know what was causing their illness?"

This information and question caused the Rootic to hum quickly. After a moment, Bieirs turned toward Lucy. "We, in our distant history, managed to cure and eliminate all illnesses. There has not been any illness among us in several centuries."

This time, it was the Gabrielites' turn to talk excitedly.

"That doesn't seem possible," said Gary.

"Very interesting," added Vel.

"Over the centuries, we have lost our intelligence and ability to diagnose and treat any physical afflictions. There has been no need," said Bieirs.

No one said anything for a few seconds.

Lucy again directed a question at Bieirs. "At what point did you realize you had become ill?"

The four Rootic hummed between themselves for a moment before Bieirs hummed into the translator. "We began noticing illness on our planet a few days after visiting a planet we'd never visited before. This planet was the closest to ours and just a month's travel from our home. The people there were primitive, very dirty, very ignorant."

Lucy nodded. "That sounds like a breeding ground for diseases. How many of your crew have come down with this flu?"

"Almost all have. Three have died."

"We are very sorry for your lost shipmates," said Lucy. "I believe we can help you with a cure so you don't lose any more."

"That would be wonderful," said Bieirs.

The other three Rootic's hums became very melodic, very upbeat.

The humans smiled while listening to the Rootic hum.

Lucy talked into the translator. "I will be sending the data I've collected to one of our facilities. They will start to synthesize an antidote for your flu. How many Rootic are aboard your ship?"

"There are now just fifty-five, counting us."

Lucy nodded. "It may take a day or so to manufacture enough doses to treat all your shipmates."

Lucy was confident that Gabriel labs would have little, if any, problem in creating a vaccine for the Rootic's illness. She typed in a few words on the computer, made attachments, and sent the data down to Gabriel. "They now have the information required to design the cure."

Vance had remained silent during the time Lucy was examining Bieirs and transmitting the data to a Gabriel lab.

Vance spoke into the translator. "I have questions."

The four Rootic turned in unison to face Vance.

"How did you find us, and just where exactly is your home planet?"

A quick conversation ensued between the four Rootic.

Bieirs turned to Vance. "We did not find you. We don't know how we came to be here."

Vance paused for a moment. "Why did you attack us with an asteroid?"

Again, the Rootic had a quick conversation before Bieirs spoke into the translator.

"Asteroid? We did not attack with anything. We are not a violent people. We were sending a help message for weeks but getting no answer. We somehow knew the people of your planet could help us."

"Hmm," said Vel. "When visiting a planet, what is your procedure?"

They started humming for a few seconds. Bieirs hummed into the translator. "Not sure what you are asking, but we simply drop down through the atmosphere and land."

"You don't go into orbit first?"

"No, we know where we want to land and proceed directly to that spot."

"Why didn't you do that here?"

"We detected something exploding above your atmosphere and thought there might be some sort of barrier."

Vel was nodding slowly.

"What are you thinking?" asked Gary.

Vel said nothing for a few seconds. "Sharkra sent that asteroid to warn the Rootic about the shield, not to scare us."

Gary nodded slowly. "That makes sense."

"Yes it does," added Vance.

Bieirs looked from Vance to Gary and back. "We somehow knew your planet was the key to our cure. Don't know how that can be, but it has proven to be accurate."

Vance, Vel, Gary, and Lucy all smiled simultaneously. They knew who or what was responsible.

"Dale thought that might be the case," said Vel.

"He did," agreed Gary.

"And where is the location of your planet in the galaxy?" Vance asked.

The Rootic seemed puzzled.

"We don't understand what you are asking," said Bieirs.

"Well," said Vance, "is this your galaxy?"

The four Rootic began humming among themselves. The tone seemed confused.

"It is interesting," said Gary. "It is easy to tell what their emotion is by their cadence and tone."

"Not unlike us humans," said Vel with a smile.

Gary returned the smile. "Good point."

Vance nodded in agreement as he turned to the Rootic. "I would like one or all of you to accompany us to Gabriel. There are some things we need to clear up."

Again, the Rootic started humming among themselves. After a moment, Bieirs took the translator. "We would be very happy to do that. We all would like to see your civilization and planet."

"Good. How long do you need to get ready?"

"We are ready now."

After stowing the equipment in the shuttle, the eight entered by the rear ramp.

"You'll have to find a place to sit. This shuttle isn't designed to haul passengers. It may be a little uncomfortable on the trip down to the planet." Vance smiled. "However, the trip will only take a short time."

Vance made his way to the cockpit and sat in the pilot's chair. Gary sat in the copilot's.

"The hatch has been reopened," said Bieirs.

Vance didn't pause. He took the shuttle straight up about a meter, spun one hundred eighty degrees, and headed out into space.

"Heading home, Dale. Turn off the shield, please."

Ten minutes later, the shuttle flew into the open hatch of the *Norman* and settled on its pad.

Within seconds, the Rootic's humming went up an octave.

"We are not used to this strong gravitational force," said Bieirs.

"We should have warned you. The gravity on Gabriel is twice what it was on your ship. You may need assistance in moving around. We can provide that," said Vance.

"We, I suspect, are stronger than you may think."

"Good, that will make things easier."

"Should we have brought our pressure suits?" asked Bieirs.

"Not necessary," said Lucy. "Our atmosphere and gases are very similar to yours."

The rear hatch of the shuttle dropped down, becoming a ramp.

Lucy was first to exit, followed by Gary, then Vel. Next, the four Rootic walked down, followed by Vance.

The deck crew smiled when they saw these petite beings. The Rootic saw the smiles and smiled back.

"We are going to keep you a distance from our citizens for a time," said Lucy. "No point in taking a chance of infecting our people."

"Agreed," said Bieirs.

"Lucy," said Vance. "Take them to the lab. We'll be along in a few."

"Yes, sir. If you will, follow me please," said Lucy.

The five headed to the elevator while Vance, Gary, and Vel walked back into the shuttle to retrieve Lucy's medical gear and the pressure suits.

Ten minutes later, the three rejoined Lucy and the Rootic in a lab of the *Norman*.

Lucy requested all who were not working on a vaccine to leave the lab.

Dale walked into the lab a minute or two later. When Dale saw the Rootic, his eyebrows elevated slightly. Then he held out his hand toward Lucy. "Translator please."

The Rootic were taking a good look at Dale. Here was yet another size, shape, and color of a human. Dale's trim beard seemed to be an object of curiosity. The Rootic had no facial hair.

"Dale, please meet Bieirs, Sogee, Aldee, and Dorss," said Vance.

"I'm very pleased to meet each of you." Dale smiled warmly. "I've been monitoring the conversations you've been having on your ship."

"Yes, that is acceptable," said Bieirs.

Lucy smiled. "You can talk while I see how they're progressing on the vaccine."

"Good," said Vance as he reached out to Dale for the translator. "If I may?"

"Certainly," said Dale as he handed the translator over.

"Some questions," he said to Bieirs.

"Yes please."

"Dale, if you would, bring up a picture of the Milky Way."

Dale stepped over to the computer console and typed in a brief instruction. Within seconds, the image of the Milky Way was displayed on the lab's viewer.

The Rootic, after a quick look, began to hum excitedly.

"Is this your galaxy?" asked Vance.

The four Rootic stared intensely at the viewer for several seconds.

Bieirs brought the translator up to his face. "May I ask the location of Gabriel in the galaxy?"

Dale made a few strokes on the keyboard. The location of Gabriel started blinking slowly.

The Rootic seemed shocked. Their humming became louder, quicker, and clearly stressed.

"How is it possible?" Bieirs suddenly stopped humming and walked to the screen. He pointed to the upper left of the galaxy, right to the farthest edge. "Our star is here." He placed his finger on a tiny dot. After a second or two, he turned to Vance. "How is it possible to travel . . . ?" He paused for a moment as he looked back at the viewer and then back at Vance. "How is it possible for us to travel sixty thousand light-years in just a few days?"

Vance smiled. "Sharkra."

The Rootic didn't have many facial expressions, but the look of confusion was quite clear on each of their faces.

"Sharkra?" asked Bieirs.

"I would suggest," said Vance, "we get you all a place to sit. I assume standing in this gravity is hard on you. And the answer to your question will take some time."

The lab techs and Lucy grabbed four chairs and carried them to the Rootic. "Please sit and make yourselves as comfortable as possible," said Lucy.

The four had to jump up a little to sit on the chairs as children that size would have to do.

"Are you aware of a presence in the galaxy that cannot be seen, felt, or identified but, nonetheless, it is there?"

There was humming among the Rootic. "We have been aware of such a phenomenon for as long as we can remember. We don't know what it is."

"We humans called it dark matter because it could not be identified. We have friends, dear friends, called the Arkell. They are an advanced civilization, thousands of years ahead of us in technology, who call the dark matter Sharkra, the unknown force. Some time ago, the physics of this galaxy and maybe the entire universe changed dramatically. The speed of light was no longer a limit. We could travel thousands of light-years in seconds. We later received proof that the Sharkra was, in fact, an all-powerful entity. Most of us now believe Sharkra is a deity."

The Rootic were clearly shocked. Their humming was almost chaotic.

After a full two minutes of very spirited humming, Bieirs hummed what must have been a command. The other three instantly stopped humming.

"We, in our past history, had many different religions on our planet," started Bieirs. "Over the centuries, all but one religion faded and disappeared. The remaining religion is followed by just over half of our citizens."

"What are the core beliefs of that religion?" asked Dale.

"I am one of the believers," said Bieirs. "We simply believe there is a presence in the universe that designed, created, and controls everything in the natural world, a true deity. Our religion, as with the majority of the past religions, believes a person of good character, upon death, is transported to a wonderful new world where the deity itself resides."

Dale nodded. "That is interesting in many ways. It seems most religions we have knowledge of have a similar belief. I noticed that you did not assign a sex to your deity."

"I cannot answer for the beliefs of others," said Bieirs, "but I am buoyed in the knowledge that our beliefs are shared by other civilizations. It never occurred to us that our god would be one sex or the other."

Dale smiled. "You were way ahead of us humans in that respect."

Vance came into the conversation. "When the flu is no longer affecting your crew, we will have them all down here to witness a miracle. Those of you who do not believe in a god or a deity, unless my speculation is wrong, will become believers."

The humming, again, became intense.

"You have a reoccurring miracle?"

"It is not reoccurring, but I believe your presence will trigger a miracle that has manifested itself a few times in the past."

"We don't understand."

"I believe you will after you've witnessed the display."

Three days after the vaccine was administered to the Rootic, they seemed to be well on their way to a complete recovery from the flu. The Gabrielites were pleased to see the remarkable improvement in the Rootic's appearance. Their skin tone became a healthy-looking shade of pink. Their eyes were clear and a gray-green, and their demeanors perked up considerably. And the four, who had remained on Gabriel, seemed to have put on weight.

Vel noticed this weight gain and questioned Bieirs. "You four have gained weight in these past three days."

"Our bodies adjust to the environment quickly. Yours do not?"

"Not quickly, no. Physical stress will cause our muscles to grow, but over weeks or months, not days."

"That must be difficult for you when confronted with greater gravity."

"I guess we have always simply accepted the additional stress as natural and dealt with it as required."

"Interesting."

In these past three days, the humans and Rootic had come to enjoy each other's company as much as the language difference would allow. The Gabrielites could never learn to hum the Rootic's language, and the Rootic could not speak words.

"Bieirs, I believe that today is a good day to witness proof of a deity," said Vance. "My associates think I'm making a mistake in assuming Sharkra will add its special addition to the display you will see and experience. But I know it will."

"Display?" asked Bieirs.

Vance nodded. "We, in our year 236, felt compelled to design and build a monument to Sharkra. It was designed by the finest artisans, engineers, physicists, and programmers from four different planets. It turned out to be a spectacular accomplishment.

"From the first unveiling of the monument in 236, we have, every evening at sunset, activated the monument's mechanics." Vance paused for a brief moment. "I have been in attendance for hundreds of these showings and still get chills watching it."

"We are anxious to witness this display," said Bieirs.

"This evening, we would like your entire crew to join us in that special place."

"I am intrigued," said Bieirs. "We will join you."

"Good."

"We will begin transporting our crew right away. It will take three trips of our shuttle to bring them all down here."

"That will be fine. We will have time to show them our town while we wait for the evening demonstration."

"Excellent. If you will transport me back to our ship, I will get things organized and start bringing the crew down."

"I will show you where to land your shuttle before you return to your ship," said Vance.

"I am very excited."

The fifty-five Rootic were seated on lawn chairs brought for their use. And several thousand Gabrielites were gathered behind them, most on chairs they'd brought, the rest sitting either on the grass or on blankets. The crowd that evening was very large. It seemed the entire population of Home Bay wanted to witness this evening's display. The word had gotten out that Vance felt sure Sharkra would add its miracle tonight, due to the Rootic's attendance. The large field that held the monument could accommodate only five thousand, and there were thirty-five thousand people residing on Home Bay. By early evening, a full hour before the scheduled display, every possible place that would offer any view of the monument or the space above the monument would fill with Home Bay's citizens.

The monument, as usual, was draped with a gold silk cover, and all the Rootic had their eyes fixed upon it. And the humming, from the clearly excited Rootic, was constant and quite melodious.

Just before sunset, Vance stood in front of the gathering and specifically addressed the Rootic. "You will, during the presentation, hear a loud blast from what will sound like a huge horn. Then, if I'm not mistaken, when the programmed show is over, there will be another blast from the horn. This was not part of the program. The second horn and all that follows that is Sharkra's doing."

Vance stepped away from the mic and took a seat with the Rootic in the front row.

Two young men walked to the front. One removed the podium, and the other pulled the silk cover from the monument. Bright lights came on and illuminated the scene. Within the next few seconds, the monument came to life, starting with the music of the film *2001: A Space Odyssey*. Then, after a few moments, the five planets rose two meters from the pedestals and began rotating on their axes and then, within seconds, around each other on a horizonal plane.

The Rootic immediately started humming with excitement. Behind them, thousands of Gabrielites, Yassi, Vout, and Byuse joined with clapping, wooing, and whistling.

Then, as programmed, the lights began to dim as the planets lowered back to their pedestals. All the lights were turned off, and it became very dark. The crowd's noise tapered off to complete silence. For ten seconds, nothing could be seen or heard. Then the blast of the huge horn filled the air. To say that startled the Rootic would be an understatement. Not one of them remained in their chairs. It was all Vance could do not to laugh.

Within seconds, the Rootic returned to their chairs while humming excitedly.

The hologram should have appeared by now, thought Vance just as another blast from the horn filled the air. Then the huge hologram of the Milky Way appeared in the sky above them.

Sharkra delayed this. Vance nodded slowly to himself.

The Rootic again began humming at a high, excited pitch.

The program continued normally to its conclusion, with all the known planets containing life pointed out by brightening their shine, but one more was added to this night's program. The Rootic planet was singled out and became brighter than all the rest.

Again, the Rootic hummed loudly and excitedly.

Vance and all the Gabrielites knew this was an addition made by the Sharkra.

Bieirs, who was sitting next to Vance, hummed into the translator. "Is this the end?"

"It was the end of what was designed and programmed," Vance responded. "But . . ."

Then came an even louder blast from the horn. The Milky Way's stars and planets began lightening up and continued doing so for several minutes, and then the black center of the galaxy started to lighten up and continued for a moment before, in a flash, it became a brilliant, pulsing golden light.

The huge crowd went wild. Vance had it right. Sharkra did add its miracle to tonight's program. All in the gathering had, of course, heard of this phenomenon, but many had never seen it. If there were any atheists in the crowd, they were probably now believers.

The Rootic, en masse, stood up in silence and bowed in the direction of the monument. Then they started humming in an incredible harmony. The sound was unlike anything those in attendance had ever heard. The word "beautiful" would not be adequate to describe it. Fully half of the attendees had tears of joy dripping down their cheeks. It was an astoundingly beautiful tune, and it continued for a full three minutes before stopping. The Rootic remained standing and looking upward at the hologram of the Milky Way. Then the hologram disappeared and, for a moment, the sky was pitch black—no stars, no moons, no light of any kind. Then, after a few seconds, the massive horn sounded again and the sky filled with dozens of meteorites streaking in from every direction. The meteor shower stopped suddenly and was replaced by lightning bolts shooting horizontally across the sky. The sound of thunderclaps was so loud that it became almost terrifying. Then, in and instant, all activity stopped. The sky became pitch black and silent.

The gathered stood speechless. The shock of what they had just witnessed momentarily struck them dumb.

Then, straight overhead, deep in the vastness of space, a soft-white light, the size of a small moon, appeared and began expanding until its light turned the night into day. The light continued to expand until the entire sky from horizon to horizon was lighted. Then, after a brief moment, the light shrank back to the size of a small moon and lingered for another moment before disappearing. The night sky returned to its normal star-filled beauty.

The crowd remained dead silent—no clapping, no wooing, no humming. The unnatural silence remained for a full minute before Vance whispered, "Oh my god."

Then another said something and others joined in. Soon a din of voices filled the night. Still, there was no clapping, wooing, or humming. But thousands of people, who hadn't done so before, were proclaiming their new belief that Sharkra was indeed a deity.

All fifty-five Rootic stayed in Home Bay that evening. The original plan was to return to their ship and prepare to return to their home planet with several thousand doses of the vaccine and the formula and equipment to produce their own. But they asked to stay. They wanted to spend time in this holy place. They wanted to gather more information about this god. They wanted to know what was expected of them in regard to Sharkra.

There were a couple dozen vacant rooms available in Home Bay's hotels, and dozens of offers from citizens to use spare bedrooms in private homes.

It turned out to be a late night for just about the entire population of Home Bay. Nobody, it seemed, wanted the experience of the evening to end. Dozens of groups gathered wherever space could be found. All wanted to relive the evening's experience over and over. It was, for all, the single-most inspiring event of their lives, and they could not bring themselves to leave the company of those who shared the life-altering experience.

The next morning, Vance was up early, and he and Lara joined the other leaders of Gabriel and their wives at the gazebo. They were joined by the fifty-five Rootic. The fifty-five were in a continuous conversation with each other.

Hundreds of Gabrielites were still milling around the town, and hundreds were gathered at the monument's site. Many could be seen heading slowly back to their homes and businesses.

"Looks like even the die-hard citizens are starting to wind down," said Lara.

"They spent the entire night talking and rejoicing," said Dale. "I myself didn't want to stop thinking about the miracle we witnessed."

"What happened here will go down in history," said Gary. "I wish the Velgot would have been here to witness it."

"We will be able to show them the videos," said Vance.

"I don't think so," said Vel. "I replayed the video on my recorder and, much to my surprise, the recording stopped just after the program was taken over by Sharkra."

"Uh-oh," said Dale. "If your recording stopped, I suspect all recordings stopped."

"No physical proof of what happened here," said Vel. "It may be that Sharkra doesn't want the galaxy, or maybe the entire universe, to have proof. Maybe it wants all intelligent life to believe it exists solely on faith."

Alex smiled. "That's certainly a good and possibly correct hypothesis, but I'm going to keep my mind open to what is bound to be dozens of theories."

Bieirs raised the translator to his mouth. "We now believe two things. One, Sharkra is a true deity, and two, this planet, your Gabriel, is special to Sharkra." Bieirs lowered the translator but then brought it back up to his mouth. "We, the Rootic, are now and will remain friends with all races on Gabriel and all the worlds they came from. This experience will become an everlasting and wondrous part of our history."

Vance spoke into the translator. "For the past few hours, I have, as no doubt all who witnessed last night's miracle have, thought about nothing else. What we witnessed last night was a great deal more than what Sharkra has demonstrated in the past . . . a great deal more." Vance paused for a moment. "I personally believe when you Rootic hummed the most beautiful music I have ever heard, Sharkra was deeply moved by your tribute. I believe Sharkra added the spectacular conclusion to the display out of love and gratitude for that incredible tribute."

"That, my friend, is something I will second," said Dale.

All in the gathering quickly agreed. It was the Rootic's tribute that prompted Sharkra to demonstrate its power and gratitude.

Tears filled the eyes of all fifty-five Rootic. Their emotions were on full display. After a few seconds, Bieirs brought the translator up as if he were about to speak but hummed nothing. After a moment, he started to lower the translator but again brought it to his mouth. "We . . . we cannot begin to express our feelings for all that has transpired in these past three days. The deadly disease that infected our world has cured we fifty-five and will cure the rest of our citizens, all on our planet, when we return. The welcoming of the Gabrielites to their world, the love and compassion of all we have met here, will be cherished forevermore. Then we were shown the will and power of God. And now you believe our music moves Sharkra to show its gratitude in such a spectacular fashion."

"It has been our pleasure to welcome a new race as our new friends," said Vance. "At any time in the future that the Rootic need help, of any kind, just let us know. We will always help in any way we can."

That afternoon, after an emotional goodbye with Vance, Vel, Gary, and Lucy, the fifty-five Rootic reluctantly returned to their ship.

"These past few days will be deeply etched in our planet's history," said Dale.

"Without question," agreed Vel. "What a spectacular night."

Lucy smiled. "It was certainly interesting to be around people shorter than me."

Everyone laughed in understanding.

Teddy and Colleen walked into the gazebo.

"Well those little people clearly pleased God," said Teddy with a big smile.

"And all who heard their song," added Dale.

"It's comforting to know that they are already at home and will be immunizing their entire population against the flu," said Lucy.

Vance nodded and smiled. "Sixty thousand light-years in seconds. I can see the smiles on their faces from here."

"Wonderful little people," said Dale.

CHAPTER 26

THE END OF A WONDERFUL LIFE

The *Velgot* was due to arrive over Home Bay in just over five minutes. And, as usual, nearly the entire population of Home Bay and most people who lived within ten kilometers of town were in the gazebo park, lying flat on their backs, waiting for the massive ship to enter a geosynchronous orbit above Home Bay. The Arkell's specular arrival never got old. It had been over five years since their last visit, and the mood was festive.

"*Velgot* will arrive in five minutes." The voice came over the PA system.

"I never get tired of experiencing the *Velgot*'s arrival," said Vance with a big smile.

"Me too," said Alex.

"I don't know a single person who doesn't love this," said Colleen.

"Scares the crap out of me," said Teddy. "But it's sure worth the momentary terror."

Eight SLFs were lying closely together about thirty meters from the landing pad. Troy, Gary, and their wives were on vacation on the Yassi planet.

"Lying here waiting for the *Velgot*," started Alex, "I'm thinking of our lives back on Earth so long ago. At that time, we didn't give much credence to the possibility of aliens. Most thought we were the lone intelligence in the universe. Now here we are, thirty-two light-years from our home planet, waiting for a massive spaceship full of wondrous beings who, themselves, are thousands of years ahead of us in technology—a people who, thank God, have taken

211

the humans into their hearts. The Arkell have saved humanity from extinction on three occasions."

"And I might add," said Dale, "twelve of us are no longer humans."

"That is something that I don't think about very often," said Lara. "Interesting."

"I think about it whenever I see people sick or injured," said Teddy. "I know I'll never be sick and, if I'm damaged in any way, I can get fixed in a jiffy. Makes me feel blessed."

"We are blessed," said Alex. "I can't help but think that Sharkra has had a hand in our development throughout our history."

"Now that we know that Sharkra exists, your particular history makes sense. What else could have sent you back thirty-five years in time?"

"That would tell us that Sharkra has always been part of this galaxy, putting a question mark in our current belief that Sharkra had recently taken control of this galaxy," offered Dale.

"My head is beginning to spin," said Teddy. "I can feel worms starting to crawl around in there."

That statement started laughter.

"You would think us being, in effect, machines would be foremost in our minds," said Colleen. "But it's not."

"It's incredible how the mind adapts," added Dale.

"Five, four, three, two, one," came over the PA.

In those five seconds, the *Velgot* came from a tiny dot in space to a dead stop directly over Home Bay. The park's crowed screamed in unison, including the twelve SLFs.

Vance didn't yell his usual, "Holy shit!" He just quietly said, "Wow."

The other SLFs quickly looked at him with surprised expressions on their faces.

"Damn," said Vance. "Didn't scare me."

"An end to a tradition," said Teddy.

The huge crowd continued their laughing, clapping, whistling, and wooing for a full five minutes before settling down to a near-normal volume.

"Shuttle is on its way," said Dale.

All could see the Arkell shuttle descending through the atmosphere, heading to the park's landing pad.

Vance was the first to get to his feet. Lara and the other SLFs followed, along with Shem, Jarleth, and Vel. They, among what seemed like the entire population of Home Bay, waited happily for the Arkell shuttle to touch down.

A few seconds later, the *Velgot* shuttle settled on the landing pad, the same spot where it first landed many decades ago.

The SLFs slowly moved through the tightly packed crowd until they reached the point where the shuttle's ramp would extend.

Within moments, the ramp extended and the hatch opened. Then a familiar voice said, "Please come aboard, my friends."

Vance took Lara's hand, and they walked up the ramp followed by the six other SLFs plus Shem, Jarleth, and Vel.

There, waiting in the interior, was Oruku and Nola. Both displayed broad smiles of welcome.

All the SLFs could see that Oruku had noticeably changed. He looked much older than he did the last time they had seen him. His features were drawn, his hair was thinning, and his skin tone had taken on an unhealthy tint.

"By the looks on your faces, I can see my appearance has surprised you."

Vance was the first to speak. "You're starting to look your age, my old and dear friend."

Oruku smiled slightly. "Starting to feel my age, I'm afraid."

Nola smiled and stepped forward. "I would love to hug all of you and perform Waoca with the Arkell among you. We understand you've had some interesting experiences since we last saw you."

Again, Vance took the lead and stepped forward and gave Nola a warm hug. As he stepped back, Nola put her hands on his temples. All in the room could see her expressions change from second to second while she visited Vance's memories. The final expression was a big smile as she removed her hands.

"What a delightful race, the Rootic, very warm and caring, wonderful new friends for the Gabrielites."

"May it?" asked Vance before he put his fingers on Nola's temples.

"Certainly. We've had experiences I'm sure all here will be interested in knowing about."

Vance nodded and stepped in front of Oruku and gave him a hug. When he went to perform Waoca, Oruku took half a step back. "Let's wait for a while before we perform Waoca," he said. "I want all of you to hear what I need to tell you at the same time."

The Gabrielites were surprised. This was far from normal greeting. All the happy expressions on their faces changed to concerned.

"However," said Oruku, "I would love to perform Waoca on each of you. I'd love to see what the Rootic are like." With that, he took half a step toward Vance. "May I?"

"Of course," Vance responded with a slight smile.

Each Arkell, in turn, performed Waoca with Nola, and she with them. All followed Vance's lead and let Oruku perform Waoca on them.

"What a wonderful experience you've had with the Rootic," said Oruku. "It is surprising Sharkra did not see fit to make us aware of these intriguing people."

"Surprised us too. At first, we thought they must be from another galaxy. Actually, they couldn't be much farther away than they are and still reside in the Milky Way," said Dale.

"I suspect Sharkra had a good reason," said Shem as he stepped in front of Oruku and gave him a big hug. "It is wonderful to see you, my old friend."

Oruku placed his fingers on Shem's temples and smiled warmly. "I see all is well with you and your family."

Jarleth followed Shem and went through the same procedure.

Vel stepped up to Oruku and gave him a big, warm hug. "It is wonderful to see you, Father."

Oruku smiled brightly as his eyes filled with tears. "I've been looking forward to seeing you, son. This is wonderful." He put his finger's on Vel's temples.

All in the shuttle could see Oruku's loving expression as he performed Waoca with Vel.

"You've had many marvelous experiences in these past five years. Your mind has grown greatly in wisdom. This pleases me beyond telling."

"Thank you, Father."

Oruku backed a pace away from Vel and the other Gabrielites. "Now I will share what I'm sure you all have been waiting for and concerned about."

No one said anything, but their attention was completely on Oruku.

"I have just a year to live," said Oruku.

All eleven Gabrielites became instantly vocal. Oruku held up his hand, palm forward, to stop whatever was going to be said. The eleven went silent and waited for their dear friend to continue.

Oruku smiled. "This will be my three-hundred-twenty-first year, quite a long life by almost any standards. In my lifetime, I have witnessed and participated in thousands of marvelous occurrences, not the least of which is the human story, a remarkable saga of a people who, in a relatively short period of time, went from cave dwellers to space explores, a race of remarkable beings who have held the Arkell's attention for thousands of years."

"Much to our benefit," said Alex.

"And ours," Oruku said softly.

"There is nothing to do that would extend your life, Father?" asked a saddened Vel.

"No, son. My old genes have been renewed all they can."

"We could make you a SLF," said Dale.

"We considered that," said Oruku, "but we decided not to. After over three hundred years, I have seen just about everything and participated in thousands of noteworthy actions. In short, I've seen and done just about everything. Time to leave this life."

"But you could simply lead a life of leisure. No concerns, just doing what you wish," said a conflicted Vel.

Oruku smiled at his son. "I could and have given that a lot of thought. But I believe you are forgetting something, son."

Vel's expression changed to one of confusion, an expression that was seldom seen on this man's face.

"I can't think of—"

Oruku cut him off. "Sharkra."

Vel's look of confusion suddenly evaporated, and he smiled and nodded. "Of course."

It took a few seconds before the rest of those on the shuttle understood what Oruku was alluding to. They all believed that

Sharkra was a deity, a god. That being the case, they also would believe a person of compassionate character and loving heart, upon their death, would join the deity in a magnificent afterlife.

There was a moment of silence before Vance spoke, his voice breaking slightly. "What are your plans . . . for this, your last year?"

"On our way back to Arkell, we are going to try to visit as many, as time allows, of the civilizations and cultures we have interacted with throughout the centuries. I wish to observe their progress and say goodbye to some of them."

There was a sad silence in the shuttle before Vel spoke. "Your plan is to return to Arkell to complete a most productive and wonderful life."

"That is correct. Until Sharkra changed the physics in our galaxy and quite possibly the universe, I could not have considered spending my last days on my home planet. I was not born on Arkell, but I am a proud citizen of Arkell."

Everyone on the shuttle was at the point of tears. This man, and all Arkell aboard the *Velgot*, were the most love and respected people in Gabriel's history.

"Father," said a visibly saddened Vel, "we would like to accompany you on your return to Arkell."

Oruku looked from Vel to Jupi, who smiled and nodded in agreement. Now it was Oruku's eyes glistening with tears as he stepped forward and embraced his son and daughter-in-law. "I would like that very much . . . very much indeed."

Those in attendance remained quiet. But there wasn't a dry eye in the group.

Shem and Jarleth stepped forward and hugged Vel and Jupi.

CHAPTER 27

THE JOURNEY HOME

The final preparations had been made for the last voyage of the *Velgot* under the leadership of Oruku. Oruku, Vel, and Jupi had spent the last two weeks saying goodbye to hundreds of Gabrielites, including those islands occupied by the Vout, Yassi, and Byuse.

The *Velgot*'s departure was a week away. Oruku had asked if his and the *Velgot*'s departure could be kept low-profile.

"I don't want too big a thing made of our departure. I know you Gabrielites will want to give me a big sendoff, and I assume it would be quite similar to a wake." Oruku smiled. "I would rather it be a small, short, and happy bon voyage."

No one said anything for a moment.

"Your wish will be granted," said Vance with all the joy he could muster.

"Thank you."

Vel and Jupi's home, located several kilometers up the Vance River, would be cared for by neighbors during the time they were off planet. A day prior to the voyage, their personal belongs were transferred to the *Velgot* and placed in the home provided for them. Their new home was located in a hilly oak and maple forest located on the sixteenth deck of this massive ship. The home itself sat on top of a shallow bank overlooking a small creek. Although the home was only about half the size of their Gabriel home, it was of a beautiful and functional design. Their view from the front deck was at once relaxing and interesting. The creek made a peaceful sound as it tumbled over rocks and a small waterfall. It was nearly impossible to accept the fact that all this was on the inside of a spaceship.

The day had arrived. The Arkell shuttle sat on its landing pad surrounded by thousands of Gabrielites. The mood was somewhere between sad and festive.

At the prescribed time, the delegation of the Gabriel hierarchy walked out of the *Norman's* cave. In the lead was Oruku, with Vel on his right and Jupi on the left. The three were holding hands. They were followed by Vance and Lara, Alex and Aidan, Dale and Tomaco, Shem and Jarleth, Teddy and Colleen, Troy and Clair, and Gary and Pat.

Oruku looked over at the *Marian* and stopped for a moment, turning toward the *Marian*. "The *Marian*," he said quietly. "Part of my delightful memories." He stood for another moment, looking at the *Marian*, before turning and starting back toward the shuttle.

As they walked toward the shuttle, the throng of people respectfully parted to leave the path unobstructed. Along their path, Oruku spotted dozens of Gabrielites he knew personally. He would stop every few meters and shake hands and say a few words with a friend. At one point, Oruku spotted a young family standing just off the path. The mother was holding her three-year-old daughter. The little girl had long, dark, curly hair and beautiful large blue eyes rimmed with long, dark lashes. Oruku released the hands of Vel and Jupi and stepped over to the brightly smiling family.

"May I?" he said as he reached toward the little girl.

"Oh, please do," said the mother as she held her daughter out for Oruku to take.

The little girl smiled brightly as she held out her arms toward Oruku. Oruku, after taking her, held her out for a moment while looking into her beautiful eyes. Then he pulled her into his chest and gave her a gentle hug. The girl responded by wrapping her little arms around Oruku's neck and squeezing as hard as she could.

After a moment, Oruku pulled her away and again held her at arm's length. There were tears in Oruku's eyes.

"Why are you crying?" asked the girl, a look of concern on her face.

"I'm not crying. My tears are because of the great joy you put in my heart."

That seemed to please the little girl immensely. She reached forward again and gave Oruku another big hug.

After the hug, Oruku handed the beautiful child back to her mother. "You have a treasure here," he said as he gently patted the girl's head.

"Oh, thank you, sir. This will be an honor we will never forget."

"I will never forget either. And"—Oruku smiled—"my name is Oruku."

The group was greeted with claps, woos, and whistles as they proceeded to the shuttle. Dozens of handmade signs displayed the love for Oruku that all Gabrielites felt.

Oruku, for his part, was having a tough time maintaining his composure. It took all his will to hold back the tears. Vel sensed what Oruku was going through, and he gently squeezed his hand.

When they arrived at the shuttle, the leaders all gave Oruku a long, warm hug. The three, who were part Arkell, performed Waoca for the last time with Oruku. Vance, Shem, and Jarleth's deep emotions were understood by all. This was as heartrending a moment as anything they had felt in their lifetime.

Oruku, Vel, and Jupi walked about halfway up the ramp before stopping and turning to address the crowed.

Oruku continued to hold both Vel's and Jupi's hands.

"Citizens of Gabriel and our beautiful galaxy, I wish to thank you, from deep in my heart, for the unwavering love and wonderful companionship you have given me and all Arkell over the decades and centuries."

There was a spontaneous round of clapping and wooing that only tapered off when Oruku raised his hand.

"This will be my last time on this beautiful planet, a planet that was transformed, designed, and created by the minds and muscle of our dear friends the humans."

The leadership of Gabriel stood at the base of the shuttle ramp, looking up with tear-filled eyes but smiles on their faces.

Oruku looked at them through his own tears while maintaining a smile. "Thank you for being my friends."

With that, he turned, along with Vel and Jupi, and entered the shuttle.

"We are going to depart Gabriel fairly slowly," said Oruku. "I want to watch Gabriel as long as possible so I can take in its beauty."

On the bridge of the *Velgot* was an enormous three-dimensional viewer. As the *Velgot* ascended directly away from Gabriel, it appeared as if the *Velgot* had a window in its hull.

"Wonderful, just wonderful," said Oruku as the image of Gabriel shrank until it could not be seen.

CHAPTER 28

VOLEN

The *Velgot*'s first stop was to the planet where the *Geaalo* had marooned the Volen. The *Velgot* took up a geosynchronous orbit above a small continent known to be where the Volen had been deposited. The orbit was high enough to make the *Velgot* all but impossible to see with a naked eye.

"Are we going down to the surface, or do we plan on observing from orbit?" asked Vel.

"I'm thinking orbit at this time. However, if we see anything that warrants a closer or hands-on approach, we may have to drop down to the surface."

"Have them spotted," said a technician.

"On screen," said Oruku.

The viewer switched pictures of the entire continent to what appeared to be a small primitive village. Huts made of mud and palm fronds formed a rough circle around many cooking pits and benches. The Volen could be seen performing various chores.

"Looks like they've settled in quite well," said Vel.

Oruku nodded. "I'm a bit surprised they have survived at all. Let's scan more of the continent to see what else they may be up to."

It didn't take long before spotting another Volen village about eight kilometers north of the first village. This village was about twice the size of the first. And the activity was a great deal more intense.

"Bring the view closer," said Oruku.

"Oh my," said Vel.

The viewer displayed a group of Volen attaching a dead Volen to a horizonal spit, a meter above a large firepit.

"Cannibals," said Oruku with obvious revulsion. "I've seen enough of these beings. Maybe in another millennium, they will become civilized."

"We are going to visit our friends the Namuh, on Trae," said Oruku. "It promises to be a pleasant experience compared to what we saw with the Volen."

"I remember the Namuh," said Jupi, "wonderful people."

Oruku nodded. "The delightful race who look like humans."

"Oh yes, I remember seeing the videos. Fine people," added Vel.

Oruku smiled. "Indeed they are. We're looking forward to seeing them again. It's been sixty-two years their time."

"Do you know what their life expectancy is?"

"Just over one hundred years."

"Chances are, your friends are no longer alive."

"Yes, unfortunately that may be the case. And we'll soon find out."

"I assume you have their aura recorded," said Vel.

"We do."

"Do you still have the vehicle you used when you first visited them?"

"We do, but it would be considered an antique now. We will see what the new personal vehicles are and duplicate one."

As had been done on their first visit to Trae, the *Velgot* took up station behind one of Trae's moons. Under the cover of darkness, ten probes were sent down to the planet's surface and began transmitting images and data on a range of subjects. The probes were no larger than a man's fist, but their technology allowed them to transmit all data necessary to determine what stage of development their civilization was currently in. One probe was dedicated to gathering all data necessary to duplicate the most common conveyance presently in use on Trae.

While they waited for the *Velgot*'s engineers to build the vehicle, the remaining nine probes were gathering and transmitting all the changes and developments the Namuh had made in the intervening sixty-two years.

The civilization had changed dramatically. As the data came in, Oruku, Vel, and Jupi watched the viewer with rapt attention.

"They have learned to fly," said a pleased Oruku.

"Prop planes," said Vel. "They look a lot like earth's aircraft in the middle of the twentieth century."

"It amazes me how the two civilizations, humans and Namuh, have developed in near-identical tracks," said Oruku. "The times of developments vary considerably, but the technology is nearly mirrored."

"That's right," said Vel. "The Namuh had functional computers a couple of decades before the humans, but the humans were ahead of them in developing aircraft."

"We have located Jaspa and Trebor," said a jubilant Oruku. "They are still alive."

"Do we know their circumstances?" asked Vel.

"They are in an assisted-living complex six kilometers from their old home. It looks like Jaspa is in fairly good health, but Trebor's life signs are quite weak."

"Anything we can do to improve Trebor's condition?" asked Jupi.

"We hope so." It was apparent that Oruku was concerned over Trebor's ill health. "We'll make a visit to that assisted-living complex our first priority."

"Agreed," said Randa. "I'm going to have to brush up on their language. I know you won't. You never forget."

Oruku nodded. "Need to give Vel and Jupi a crash course for the basics."

"Vel learns languages quite quickly, gets that ability from you, I suspect," said Jupi. "I, on the other hand, am a bit slow."

Randa smiled. "You'll do fine. Oruku and I will be doing most of the talking."

Two days later, the landing party waited until just before dawn to drop down to the planet's surface. They dropped down as fast as possible; the trip took just three seconds. The Namuh's technology was advanced enough to detect an aircraft of any kind. If the shuttle was spotted at all, it would only be a brief blip on their viewers.

Oruku and Randa, through amazing makeup, were made to look quite old to match the intervening sixty-two years. The modern vehicle, built by the *Velgot*'s engineers, was a far cry from what they produced six decades in the past. Vehicles were no longer powered by internal combustion engines. Now, it seemed, all vehicles were powered by hydrogen fuel cells, a major evolution that was several decades ahead of what humans had developed in the same period of time. The appearance of the automobiles was similar to Earth's at the beginning of the twenty-first century. These vehicles were now equipped with all manner of technology, one being they were self-driving. One had to simply state, verbally, where one wanted to go and the sophisticated computer system would deliver them safely to that location.

Vel, Jupi, Oruku, and Randa got into the new Trae automobile and drove down the shuttle's ramp to the planet's surface. The shuttle withdrew the ramp and closed the hatch and shot back to the *Velgot*.

Once on the ground, Oruku gave the address of the assisted-living home and sat back to enjoy the trip.

"Just look at the progress they have made in such a short period of time," said Randa.

Everything they could see was tidy, well organized, and attractive. The road they were on was as smooth as glass. Tasteful landscaping covered all open surfaces.

"What they have accomplished in these past decades reminds me of the Yassi," said Oruku. "They have been beautifying everything."

"Not yet the scale of the Yassi, but they're certainly heading that way," added Vel.

Twenty-three minutes later, their vehicle pulled up to the entrance of the tastefully designed retirement facility.

"Park in the most convenient spot," said Oruku.

The vehicle turned toward the large parking lot, drove down past several other autos, and smoothly pulled into a vacant space.

The four exited the vehicle. Vel carried what appeared to be a briefcase. Oruku, Jupi, and Randa were empty-handed.

As they entered the facility, they spotted what was assumed to be a receptionist's desk, on the far side of a tastefully decorated lobby. There were a dozen or so older Namuh sitting on comfortable-looking chairs and sofas, most chatting with friends, others watching a large viewer on a far wall.

The four Arkell headed directly to the receptionist's desk.

All conversations and activity in the lobby stopped as these four unusual-looking beings walked the few meters across the lobby. All eyes were on these big-headed people. None said a word.

"Good morning," said Oruku with a warm smile. "We would like to visit Jaspa and Trebor."

The look of shock and surprise on this attractive middle-aged woman's face was quite comical.

It was all the four Arkell could do not to laugh. All managed to maintain a friendly smile.

In a few seconds, the receptionist gathered her wits. "Certainly," she responded with a slight break in her voice. "May I tell them who is here to see them?"

"Yes, my name is Oruku. This is my wife, Randa. And these two young people are our great-grandchildren, Vel and Jupi."

The woman nodded while punching in a three-digit number on her console. "You have visitors."

A few seconds later, Jaspa's voice came back. "Who would that be?"

"Oruku, Randa, and their two great-grandchildren."

There was a brief pause before Jaspa responded in a jubilant voice. "Please send them up."

The receptionist managed a weak smile. "Just take the elevator"— she nodded across the lobby—"to the fourth floor and head left to 406, which will be on the right."

"Thank you."

The four turned and walked across the dead-silent lobby to the elevator. Jaspa pushed the button and the elevator door opened immediately. The four stepped in. As soon as the elevator doors closed, the Namuh in the lobby became animated, all talking at once. This would be something exciting to tell their children and grandchildren.

As the Arkell exited the elevator and turned left, they immediately spotted Jaspa waiting down the hall, outside their suite. Her face displayed how happy she was to see these people.

When the four covered the distance between them, Randa stepped forward and gave Jaspa a big hug.

"It is so nice to see you again," said Randa.

"This is the finest of surprises," said a jubilant Jaspa.

It was Oruku's turn to give Jaspa a hug. "We are so happy to see you again after all these years."

Oruku stepped aside to expose Jaspa to Vel and Jupi. "I would like you to meet two of our great-grandchildren, Vel and Jupi."

Vel stepped forward and gave Jaspa hug. "Very nice to meet you."

"I feel the same," said Jaspa with a big smile. "Is this your sister?" she said as she turned toward Jupi.

"No, Jupi is my wife."

"Oh?"

"It is our practice, with married children, to assume their spouses are also our children," explained Oruku.

Jaspa paused for a moment before saying, "That is quite nice. I like that." With that, Jaspa stepped over and gave Jupi—and then Vel—a big hug. "Very nice to meet you two youngsters."

Jaspa motioned toward the open door. "Please go in, Trebor is excited to see you."

Upon entering the suite, all spotted Trebor lying in a reclining chair. He didn't look at all well. His features were drawn, his skin had an unhealthy tone, and he had lost a great deal of weight.

"Look who's here," said Jaspa.

Trebor looked confused for a moment before his face brightened up and he smiled brightly. "Oh my, this is a big, delightful surprise."

"Please have a seat." Jaspa indicated a long sofa that faced an attractive fireplace.

The four sat, with Oruku closest to Trebor. Jaspa took a seat next to her husband.

There was a momentary silence while Jaspa looked from one Arkell to another before speaking. "You are not from this planet, are you?"

This question took the four by surprise. All eyes in the room went to Oruku.

Oruku looked directly at Jaspa and smiled slightly. "No, we are not."

Jaspa's expression went to surprise and understanding. She nodded slowly. "After you left, something over sixty years ago, we fully expected to see you again, and soon. But time passed and you never came back. We, after the first two years, started making inquiries locally and then, with no results, expanded our inquiries to the entire planet. No one had seen or heard anything about you."

"The deception, at the time, was necessary. Your civilization had not yet achieved flight, so we assumed the concept of space travel would be generations into the future. We did not want to frighten you, but we wanted to help you find a cure for the virus that was killing your people."

Jaspa's facial expression softened. "Your advice and help did save an untold number of Namuh, and for that we will always hold you in high regard." Jaspa's expression hardened a little. "However, deceit is something not practiced in our civilization."

"We are aware of that fact. We were and are delighted with your civilization's candor and honesty. It's a trait that normally takes a civilization thousands of generations to adapt to."

Trebor came into the conversation. "Has your civilization stopped deceiving each other?"

"Oh yes, thousands of years ago. We do not lie or deceive the civilized worlds, most of which are our friends and allies. But we, on many occasions, need to keep our true identities from those beings we want to help. They would not understand and reject, maybe violently, any help we may offer."

"Other civilizations?" said Jaspa.

"There are thousands of inhabited planets in this galaxy alone."

"Thousands?" Jaspa was shocked.

"Yes, and some are highly advanced. Most are not."

"What are you . . . ?

"We are Arkell," Oruku interjected.

"Arkell," repeated Jaspa as to imprint the name in her memory. "Where are the Arkell ranked among the highly advanced civilizations?"

"We are, as far as we know, the most advanced technically in the galaxy."

"The most advanced," said Trebor. "How advanced are you?"

Oruku paused for a moment. "Our civilization and technology are approximately ten thousand years ahead of yours."

"Ten thousand years!" said Jaspa and Trebor nearly in unison. Oruku nodded.

"I don't know what to say," said Jaspa. "It is too big a thought."

"How far away is your planet?" asked Trebor.

"About a thousand light-years."

"Light-years?"

"A light-year is a measurement of distance, not of time. A light-year is the distance light travels in one year."

"And just how far is that?"

"Nine point five trillion kilometers. Your planet, Trae, is forty-eight thousand light-years from our planet."

Jaspa's expression turned dark. "I've never said this to anyone before, but . . . I don't believe you."

"That is quite understandable," said Oruku pleasantly. "Given your experience with us, you have every right to be skeptical."

"How is it possible for you to travel a thousand light-years from your home? That would take . . . forever," said Jaspa.

"Our ship—"

"Ship? Like a boat?" Trebor interrupted.

"No, our ship can be referred to as a spaceship, starship, or possibly a galaxy ship."

No one said anything, so Oruku continued. "We Arkell, presently living on the *Velgot,* hadn't been to our home planet, until recently. The *Velgot* was capable of light speed before Sharkra altered the physics of this galaxy. Now we can travel anywhere in the galaxy in seconds."

"Sharkra?" said Trebor.

"We'll get to that in a little while," said Oruku.

There was silence for a moment.

"Are you saying your ship is over a thousand years old?" asked Jaspa.

"No, the *Velgot* is over three thousand years old. Thousands of generations have been born and died aboard our ship. The *Velgot* is our home."

"Where is this ship?" asked Trebor.

"We left it behind one of your moons."

"It's all nonsense," said Jaspa without hesitation. "Nothing lasts for three thousand years."

Oruku smiled. "Is there anything we can do to convince you that we will never deceive you again?"

"I doubt it," said Jaspa with considerable sadness in her voice.

"Why did you visit us the first time?" asked Trebor.

"Sharkra sent us."

"Sharkra? Who is Sharkra?" asked Jaspa.

"This is going to be hard to understand," started Oruku.

"Your technology has not advanced, in certain areas, to a point that you would be aware of a phenomenon in space we call Sharkra, which translated meant 'unknown force.' Most advanced civilizations became aware of and call the phenomenon by different names. One race called it dark matter."

"Do the Sharkra have a spaceship?"

"Sharkra would have no use for a spaceship."

"We don't understand," said Jaspa.

"Sharkra was just a force, a presence in the galaxy that could not be seen or felt or communicated with. But most advanced civilizations eventually became aware of its existence. It's been a puzzlement since our ancestors first realized something existed that they could not identify. But, very recently, something changed in the galaxy. We and our ship were transported a thousand light-years to our home planet in just seconds. And we were not alone. Eighty-two other Arkell ships were also transported to our home planet. These ships, prior to that time, were scattered all around the galaxy. Of all these ships, we were only acquainted with one other. Since that time, all those ships, including our *Velgot*, have been sent to locations around the galaxy to intervene in various civilizations' problems. We were sent to Trae, specifically to you two, to help you find the cure for the virus infecting your civilization."

"Is this true?" asked Jaspa in a soft voice.

Oruku nodded. "Oh yes. We have been sent to planets that have a myriad of problems. We have been charged with stopping wars, pestilence, pollution, overpopulation, premature aging, and dozens of others."

"We believe Sharkra has chosen the Arkell to be its instrument for these interventions."

"How does Sharkra know when a civilization needs help?"

"We believe Sharkra knows everything. We, along with just about every advanced civilization, were atheists. But only a god, a deity, could alter the laws of physics."

"Really, a god?" said a skeptical Jaspa. "In our distant past, there were those who believed in a god. It's been over a hundred years since the last believers passed on and took their beliefs with them."

"We understand. A few of the civilizations we've encountered have had similar histories. That would include us. Most of the people, of all branches of science, scoffed at the thought of a deity. All of those who have been exposed to the power of Sharkra do now believe there is, in fact, a deity."

It was clear that Oruku's explanation of Sharkra caused both Namuh to reconsider their beliefs.

Oruku nodded his head slowly while in thought before smiling brightly. "How about taking a trip with us to visit our ship?"

Randa's, Vel's, and Jupi's heads snapped around to look at Oruku. This offer was not expected.

"It seems your family doesn't agree with that," said Trebor.

"If they are your family," added Jaspa.

"Vel and Jupi are my family. Vel is my son, which makes Jupi my daughter by their marriage. Randa is a shipmate with great skills and knowledge, as you found out on our first visit."

"So another lie is exposed," said Jaspa without rancor.

"Again, our deception was necessary to give you the help you needed with the virus your civilization was suffering. How would you have reacted if an alien spaceship were to land on your planet and we, with our large heads, got out in full view of your people?"

Jaspa stared at Oruku for a long moment before responding. "We would have been terrified. We probably wouldn't have any positive thoughts as to why you were here. We would be too frightened."

Oruku raised one eyebrow while displaying a slight smile.

Jaspa looked at Trebor and then back at Oruku. Her skepticism seemed to fade away. "We understand. We are sorry that we accused you of deceit. You did what was necessary."

"You were not wrong about our deceit, so there is no need to apologize."

"That's kind of you," said Jaspa.

After a moment of silence, Trebor spoke up. "Can we still visit your ship?"

"Yes, of course. It is an offer that we've never made to a civilization who, themselves, had not begun exploring space. But you, Namuh, are an exceptional people, far advanced in many technologies. On top of that, you are very closely related genetically to another race whom we are very fond of, the humans of the planet Gabriel." Oruku paused for a moment. "At our first encounter, we were delighted and impressed with your openness, intelligence, caring nature, and honesty. It, unfortunately, is not found everywhere in the galaxy."

Jaspa's and Trebor's expressions displayed a newfound trust.

"We came back to your planet to hopefully visit with you two and to see how your technology has advanced. We discovered that you, Trebor, were in ill health."

"How would you know that?" asked Trebor.

"We have the technology to diagnose bio-signs of any living being from a great distance. We, in searching for your and Jaspa's bio-signatures, detected some abnormalities in your physiology. To that end, we brought a device that hopefully will make you feel somewhat better." Oruku nodded toward the case sitting on the floor at Vel's feet.

Trebor's eyes went to the case. "Is it in that?

"Yes."

Trebor smiled. "I am feeling poorly, so anything you can do to improve my condition would be appreciated."

Oruku turned his attention toward Vel. "You're on."

Without another word, Vel opened the case and retrieved a small but sophisticated-looking piece of equipment and set it on the coffee table. Then he retrieved two handheld paddles out of the case and turned a knob on the equipment on the coffee table. A low humming sound could be heard.

"Trebor, I will assist you in getting up and standing," said Oruku.

"What are you going to do to me?"

"Hopefully take away some of your pain."

Oruku stepped over to where Trebor was lying in his reclining chair and held out his hands. "Let me help you up."

Trebor took Oruku's hands and, with considerable assistance from Oruku, managed to get to his feet. He was wearing his pajamas. His back was bowed from advanced arthritis. His hands were crippled with the same affliction. Arthritis had spread throughout Trebor's old body.

"Can you stand by yourself?" asked Oruku.

Trebor nodded. "I'm ready."

Oruku smiled. "Vel will move those paddles over and around your body. His device will reduce, as much as possible, the pain caused from your arthritis. It should make you feel considerably better."

"That will be nice," said Trebor with a small smile. "How long will it take?"

"About twenty minutes. The time varies a little depending on the condition of your cells."

"I don't think I can remain standing for twenty minutes," said a concerned Trebor. "Can I hold on to something?"

"I'm afraid not," said Oruku. "But after the first few minutes, your strength and stamina should improve. I don't think you'll have any problem standing for twenty minutes." Jaspa walked over and stood next to Oruku while not taking her eyes off her husband.

Jupi took up station by the small device on the coffee table.

Oruku nodded at Vel, who bent over and picked up the two paddles.

"Starting now," said Vel.

Trebor flinched but remained standing.

Vel started at Trebor's head by moving the paddles a few millimeters away from Trebor and slowly and methodically worked his way down to Trebor's feet.

"Okay," said Jupi, "I have the initial data. Let's start back at the top."

Vel stood and held the paddles on either side of Trebor's head and moved them slowly up, down, and around Trebor's head, down to his neck.

"Hold there for a moment," said Jupi, not taking her eyes off the console. "Move the paddles a little lower."

Vel moved the paddles.

"Hold again."

A minute went by before Jupi said, "Good, now move from the neck out to the shoulders, one at a time."

Trebor slowly moved his head back and forth and up and down. "This is wonderful. I haven't been able to move my neck like that for years."

"Start down the spine," said Jupi.

All eyes were on Trebor. After four minutes of the paddles moving slowly up and down his spine, he seemed to straighten slightly and his facial features began losing the stress caused by the pain he had been suffering. He managed a slight smile.

Jaspa took Oruku's left hand in her right and squeezed, not taking her eyes off her husband.

After another three minutes, the bow in his back was less than half of what it was and his complexion had improved dramatically.

Eleven minutes later, Jupi turned off the device. "That's it."

Trebor stood for a moment before stepping over to the waiting arms of Jaspa.

"I feel wonderful," he said as tears flowed from both his and Jaspa's eyes.

The two held each other tightly as their tears continued to flow.

"Why don't you two walk around a little while we put this equipment away?" said Oruku.

Jaspa broke her embrace of Trebor, turned to Oruku, and gave him a big hug. "I don't know how to thank you."

"You are doing a fine job right now."

"I feel embarrassed that we called you deceivers. You are wonderful people."

"You are an honest, straightforward person, Jaspa. We do not feel maligned in any way. You spoke the truth."

There was silence for a moment.

"I suggest we wait until nightfall to visit the *Velgot*," said Vel.

"Agreed," said Oruku. "In the meantime, we can catch up on this planet's advances in technology."

Eight hours later, as the six exited the elevator into the lobby, they were instantly spotted by the Namuh, who were, at that moment, engaged in lively conversation. All conversations quickly stopped. Oruku smiled to himself as he realized the number of Namuh sitting in the lobby had at least doubled from that morning. The six walked across the lobby, out the entrance door, and headed to the parking lot. When it was assumed the big-headed strangers were out of earshot, the excited Namuh all started talking at once.

When the six arrived at their auto in the parking lot, Jaspa asked, "Where did you get this vehicle?"

"Our engineers made it."

"Really," said Trebor, "how long did it take them?"

"This one took twice as long as the one we had during our first visit. A lot more technology involved. It took them four days."

"Four days from raw material?"

"Well, that is more or less accurate. We have very sophisticated equipment. We'll peek into a lab or two so you can see for yourself."

Vel and Jupi helped the two Namuh into the back seat and then walked around to the back of the vehicle and pushed a button in the center of the rear hatch. The hatch rose up, exposing a bench seat facing backward. They got in and the hatch closed.

"Everybody ready?" asked Oruku.

Five affirmative answers came back.

Oruku pushed a button and said, "Take us back to where we started."

The vehicle backed out of the spot and headed out of the parking lot.

Thirty minutes later, they sat in the vehicle in a small clearing surrounded by a small forest of deciduous trees. It was a brightly lighted night because Trae's three moons were in a near-perfect alignment for picking up the light from their sun and casting it on the planet.

"I suggest we exit this vehicle and wait for the shuttle to drop down. I think you'll enjoy the sight," said Oruku.

"Agreed," said Vel as he opened the rear hatch. The other four doors opened, and everybody got out and stood together within a few feet of the vehicle.

"I feel great," said Trebor as he moved his arms and legs. "I believe I could actually run."

"Better hold that activity until you get your muscle tone back," said Jupi.

"I'll wait."

"Would you two like to have this transport?" asked Oruku as he put his hand on the fender of the vehicle.

"We don't have much use for a personal vehicle, but we would be happy to find a deserving person or institution who would love to have it."

Oruku smiled. "It is yours to dispose of as you wish."

"That's wonderful, thank you."

"Ah, here comes the shuttle," said Jupi.

The six looked up in time to see the shuttle rapidly descending through the planet's atmosphere.

"Oh my," said Jaspa.

"I didn't know what to expect, but it certainly wasn't this," added Trebor.

The light from the moons was enough to see the size, configuration, and color of the shuttle. The gold color of the shuttle's hull was somewhat dimmed because of the moonlight, but it and the ribs were quite visible.

"I expected your ship to be a great deal bigger," said Trebor as he looked at the shuttle from top to bottom.

"Oh, this isn't our ship. This is a shuttle to take us to the *Velgot*."

"It's somewhat larger," said Vel.

The shuttle silently stopped and hovered about half a meter above the ground. The ramp extended, and the hatch slid open.

"Let me walk you up," said Oruku as he took Jaspa's hand.

"Trebor, I'll take your hand," said Jupi.

With Oruku and Jaspa in the lead, the six walked up the ramp and into the interior of the shuttle.

The hatched closed, and the ramp withdrew into the shuttle.

Trebor and Jaspa looked around the shuttle's interior, their mouths agape.

"Do we sit on the floor?" asked Jaspa.

Oruku smiled. "Shuttle, bring up six chairs facing outside."

Six chairs rose from the deck as if by magic.

"Oh my goodness," said Jaspa. "How in the world?"

"As you can see, the deck has an intricate design. It's not decoration. It has many useful functions."

"Amazing," said Trebor.

Oruku smiled again. "Please take a seat."

The two took a seat and were joined by the four Arkell.

Jaspa's face displayed some confusion. "Why are we facing a wall?"

"That question will be answered shorty," said Vel.

"Are you ready to go into space?" asked Oruku.

"Yes, nervous for sure, but very excited," said Jaspa.

Trebor turned in his chair and looked around the interior of the shuttle. "Not much instrumentation in this ship."

"Not really necessary," said Oruku. "Most commands are given orally, very much like the transport we used today."

Trebor nodded in understanding.

"Take us slowly to ten thousand meters, and hold position," said Oruku.

As the shuttle began to rise, Vel said, "Open projection."

The walls of the shuttle disappeared, giving an incredible view of the planet Trae.

Both the Namuh's heads snapped back. "Oh my goodness," said Jaspa.

"What the . . . ?" said Trebor.

Oruku explained the apparent invisibility of the shuttle's walls to the satisfaction of both Namuh.

A minute later, the shuttle took up position on the opposite side of the moon the *Velgot* was behind.

"Our ship is behind this moon," said Oruku. "Hope you will find its size astonishing rather than intimidating."

"I can't believe, after the day we've had, that a big ship would intimidate us."

"Slowly bring us to within one thousand meters of the *Velgot*," said Oruku.

The shuttle instantly accelerated to a thousand kilometers per hour. But again, the passengers felt no acceleration.

In a few seconds, the shuttle was just behind the moon's horizon.

"Here it comes," said Oruku.

All eyes were facing forward in the shuttle as the *Velgot* began rising above the moon.

"Oh my," said Jaspa.

"I . . ." Trebor couldn't finish what he was going to say as more of the *Velgot* came into their view.

"It's as big as a moon," whispered Jaspa.

Oruku smiled. "To be exact, the *Velgot* is five kilometers in diameter at the equator."

"Hard to comprehend that," said Trebor.

The *Velgot* was now in full view of the shuttle.

"Hold here," said Oruku.

The shuttle stopped.

"Would you look at that?" said Trebor. "Big does not describe it."

"It's beautiful," said Jaspa, her voice displaying a great deal of wonderment.

"Thank you. We think so too," said Randa.

"I'm going to give you a few statistics about our ship, our home, before we go in," started Oruku. "The *Velgot* has one hundred and ten decks varying from five meters high to thirty meters depending on its designed use. There are one hundred twenty thousand citizens living aboard."

"How could that many . . . ?" Jaspa couldn't finish the question.

"The *Velgot* is, in effect, a complete world. We grow all our food on our agricultural decks. There are a dozen towns scattered around the interior."

"Towns, on a spaceship?" asked Trebor.

"You'll see," said Oruku.

"Towns," Trebor repeated in wonder.

All the Arkell smiled. "We, as you now know, can manufacture anything. The *Velgot* is three thousand two hundred three years old."

"Wait just a minute here," said Jaspa. "How can anything last that long?

Oruku smiled. The *Velgot*'s engineers are constantly remanufacturing and reinstalling parts of the ship that are wearing out. There are just over two hundred engineers working full time to keep the *Velgot* in pristine condition. It will never grow old."

"Astonishing," said Trebor.

"Let's enter the *Velgot*," said Oruku.

As the shuttle quickly closed the distance to the *Velgot*, an opening appeared about halfway between the equator and the top of the ship. The shuttle slowed as it approached, entered, and settled gently on the hangar deck as the hatch on the ship's hull closed.

The ramp extended and the hatch opened. Oruku, hand in hand with Jaspa, led the others out of the shuttle and into the hangar deck. There was a six-person transport waiting for them.

"I'm going to leave you here," said Randa. "Have some duties to perform."

Trebor and Jaspa both gave Randa long, warm hugs and said their goodbyes.

The next two hours were spent touring various decks of the *Velgot*. The two Namuh were in a state of constant astonishment. When they entered the forest deck and saw mountains, rivers, and wild animals of an amazing variety, they were nearly speechless.

"I can't tell the difference between this forest and those on our planet. I cannot see any walls or ceiling. How can that be?"

"A lot of sophisticated technology," said Oruku as he turned toward Trebor. "Trebor, we think you will find our manufacturing decks interesting."

Trebor was, in fact, very impressed with the manufacturing decks and, in particular, the massive power deck.

"The scale of everything is so large. I never could have imagined."

They drove through four small towns, each with a distinct style. One seemed to be inhabited by younger Arkell, two with mixed ages and another with an older population. It was here that Oruku pulled over and parked.

"We will be stopping for lunch here," said Oruku.

"One of my favorites," said Jupi.

"I have an appetite that I haven't had in years," said Trebor. "I could eat an Esroh."

"I don't know what an Esroh is," said Jupi with a smile.

"It's a big beast of burden," said Trebor. "And not on any menus I'm aware of."

The restaurant was quite busy, but an elderly woman, after working her way around the tables and diners with surprising agility, greeted them with a big smile. "We are so happy you've come to our restaurant for a meal. Not often we get visitors from outside our ship. My name is Clair."

"Clair, we are pleased to introduce Jaspa and Trebor to you," said Oruku.

Clair held her hand out first to Jaspa and then to Trebor. "Pleased to meet you both."

"Our pleasure, Clair," said Jaspa. "This looks to be a fine establishment."

"Thank you, Jaspa. We take pride in our restaurant."

"It shows," said Trebor.

Clair smiled broadly. "Please follow me."

There was a table open and waiting for them next to a beautifully designed fountain.

After the six had settled into their chairs, Oruku spoke.

"After lunch, we will put you two through a device similar to the one we used in your home, but a great deal more sophisticated. It will renew your genes as much as possible."

"Jaspa too?"

"Oh yes," said Oruku.

After their lunch, they returned to their transport and headed toward one of the hundreds of elevators on the *Velgot*. Ten minutes later, the five arrived at one of the dozens of labs the *Velgot* contained.

After the introductions to Randd, the attending technician, Vel reported what procedure they had performed on Trebor in his home. Randd recorded the information on a console and turned to Trebor. "Trebor, let's start with you."

"Okay. I'd be surprised if you can make me feel any better than I already do, but I wouldn't bet against it."

Randd smiled and motioned for Trebor to enter what looked like a stainless-steel tube about a meter in diameter and two and a half meters high. There was a single small, round window at head height in the door. Randd pushed a button on a console and the door swung open. "If you will, please step into this device."

"Happy to," said Trebor.

A full thirty minutes later, the door opened and Trebor stepped out with a huge smile on his face. "I am new," he proclaimed.

Jaspa stepped over and gave her husband a big hug and then held him at arm's length. "You look ten years younger," she said, tears forming in her eyes.

"I feel thirty years younger."

"You had a few maladies that took some time to clear up. We extracted nearly a kilo of calcium, among other unwanted disorders," said Randd. "Your arthritis has been removed."

"I know, I can feel the deletion," said Trebor, "or more accurately, I no longer feel the pain."

"Then we accomplished what we set out to do," said Oruku with a smile.

"Can you put Jaspa through this procedure?" asked Trebor.

Randd looked over at Oruku and got an affirmative nod.

"Jaspa, if you will, step into this device," said Randd. "We'll see if we can't perk you up a bit."

As the five headed back to the hangar deck, Jaspa reached over and squeezed Oruku's arm. "You have told us the truth about everything. I'm completely overwhelmed."

"Actually, I believe you are holding up quite well considering what you've been exposed to."

As they stepped out of the transport and walked to the shuttle, there was a bit of sadness on Jaspa's face. "We are going to miss our new alien friends," she said. "It's going to be difficult to explain to our Namuh friends what happened to us."

"I would suggest you tell the truth," said Oruku with a slight smile. "We've found that the Namuh get quite upset when deceived."

Everybody laughed.

"We will, of course, do that," said Trebor.

"I would suggest you address your entire planet via your viewer system. Set a time and date and give the entire story, from our first visit on. In doing this, you will eliminate days, months, and years of questions. The downside to our visits will be, you two will become celebrities—and will remain so for the rest of your lives."

Two minutes later, Trebor and Jaspa jauntily walked hand in hand down the ramp of the shuttle and back onto their planet.

"Next we headed for Twis," said Oruku. "We told them we'd return in fifty days. We missed that mark by forty-two years. Hopefully we'll see a planet free of conflict."

"Well," said Vel, "I would think that Sharkra would have made you aware if they remained at war after you left."

"That would seem likely," said Oruku.

A few seconds later, the *Velgot* was in geosynchronous orbit over the same capital city they had orbited over four decades earlier.

After an hour of observing all activity in the city, tapping into their communication network and seeing and hearing, nothing resembling a state of war still existed.

"I am pleased," said Oruku. "They have turned their planet into one of peace and prosperity."

"Everything in this city looks new and far advanced compared to our last visit," said Randa.

"It does," agreed Oruku. "Let's orbit the planet and record the physical changes made to their cities in the past forty years."

Six hours later, the *Velgot* left Twis.

"This next stop on the way to Arkell should prove very interesting. The biggest chore Sharkra has ever given us. Pmuda."

"I've viewed the recordings made during your first visit," said Vel. "What a challenge you had. According to the data we're getting from the satellites, their population seems to be about half what it was."

"I am a bit surprised they have their population under control. It was truly out of control twenty-six years ago," said Oruku.

"As I recall, you put a lot of resources into making that work," said Vel.

Within seconds, the *Velgot* was in geosynchronous orbit behind Pmuda's one moon.

"Care to join me in a shuttle tour of this planet?" asked Oruku.

An hour and thirty minutes later, the shuttle returned to the *Velgot*.

"I can't tell you how impressed I am with what they've accomplished here," said Jupi. "It's like a completely different world."

"Far better than I expected," said a pleased Oruku.

"Their cities are immaculate. The people are clean and apparently quite healthy. The air pollution is about eighty percent lower."

"Even their architecture has completely changed. A whole different look and an open feel to everything," said Vel.

"According to our data collected on Ailez, she is still alive. The data shows that from the time we left until eight years ago, she led her nation out of extreme poverty, and all the misery that went with that, to the most progressive continent on the planet. She's set the example of leadership and was closely mimicked by the other five national leaders. Apparently, she is living very comfortably in a country home designed for retirees."

"She deserves all the comfort and enjoyment this planet has to offer," said Oruku.

"I'm going to credit her with a great deal of the positive changes to this planet," said Vel.

"I agree," said Jupi.

"Next on our schedule is the Jurassic planet," said Oruku. "Let's go see how our researchers are doing?"

"Teddy asked me to get some more pictures of dinosaurs, particularly the Traptor," said Vel.

"We're all enthralled with that creature."

The *Velgot* went into orbit directly over the island in the river that was the main camp for the Arkell researchers. Four research scientists had remained on the planet to do some deep research on plant and animal life on this most unusual planet. This planet had eight different and distinct continents. The indigenous, intelligent natives, on two of its eight continents, were tens of thousands of years ahead of others. One continent was inhabited and dominated by intellectually advanced dinosaurs. There were two very large islands that seemed to be from another planet. One of these islands held beings who looked like cavemen of old Earth. They had developed roughly on the same timeline as the advanced dinosaurs. This highly unusual development was unheard of in the galaxy. There were many examples of one continent being slightly more advanced than others on the same planet, but the difference would be maybe a few thousand years, but no other planets in the galaxy were known to have such a huge divergence.

The shuttle settled on a clear area just ten meters from where the research station was set up. The research facility was, in and of itself, a technical marvel. Its walls, roof, and floor were all made of an extremely robust, inflatable material. The structure itself covered a hundred and fifty square meters of this small island. Aside from the laboratory, it contained two bedrooms, a very serviceable kitchen, and a bathroom equipped with a hot shower.

Four Arkell were waiting just outside the entrance to their station. All had broad smiles as the ramp extended and the hatch slid open.

"Greetings and welcome to our humble complex," said Cirtap, the lead scientist.

Oruku headed directly to Cirtap and gave him a big hug. "We're damn pleased to see you haven't been consumed by a Traptor."

"It's not that they haven't tried," said Cirtap while maintaining a smile.

"You all know Randa and Jupi, but you haven't met my son, Vel," said Oruku.

"No, we haven't, but we've certainly heard of him." Cirtap stepped over and gave Vel a hug.

"I'll bet you four would like to perform Waoca with us," said Cirtap.

"Can't speak for the others," said Vel, "but I would like that very much."

"Then we'll start with you."

Vel placed his fingers gently on Cirtap's temples. After three minutes, he removed his fingers. "Holy shit," he said. "You weren't kidding about the Traptors. They have tried to make you a snack on many occasions."

"Several times for sure. They are true thinkers, quite clever. We need to be watchful at all times when we are off this little island."

"Clearly the deterrent installed here has been quite successful," said Randa.

"Again, these Traptors are very smart. Only one has tried to get to us on this island since the first encounter. He suffered, as did the first one. There have been no further attempts here. There's no question, in our minds, that they spread the word among themselves."

"That's impressive," said Vel.

"They tried to get to us a few times when we were off the island, but fortunately Agroe here is a master of our deterrent system."

Oruku smiled. "We all have seen the videos of your incredible bravery the first time you encountered these monsters. As a matter of fact, I believe just about all the civilized planets have seen what you did to that unfortunate Traptor."

Agroe smiled broadly. "I had confidence in our equipment."

"Yes, clearly you did. I don't remember Vance Youngblood being so impressed. He said, 'I want that man on my team.'"

"That's great praise indeed. To have that man say that is very humbling."

"Those are the scariest animals I've ever seen, maybe the scariest animal in the galaxy," said Vel.

"I would suggest we all perform Waoca with each other," said Oruku.

"Agreed," said Cirtap as he turned toward Vel. "May I?"

Twelve minutes later, the eight Arkell had performed Waoca with each other and now were up-to-date with the others' experiences.

"We've been given the word that the Arkell on this planet are to join us on our return to our home."

"We are certainly pleased with that," said Cirtap. "We have just about covered everything on this planet. Over the past months, we witnessed and recorded hundreds of animals of all shapes, sizes, and ferocity. Been an experience of a lifetime. But living in temporary shelters, as comfortable as they are, are still temporary shelters. We are ready to get back inside our homes."

Oruku smiled. "I'm sure you are, and when you're ready, we can start ferrying up your equipment to the *Velgot*." Oruku paused for a moment. "How would you like to have lunch on the *Velgot*?"

"I think I speak for all of us when I say lunch on the *Velgot* will be delightful. And we have been ready for a few days, knowing you were coming and hopefully taking us back aboard the *Velgot*."

Once all the equipment in the research facility was removed, the air in the facility was released and the whole structure shrank to a cube two and a half meters on a side. Then it and all it contained was placed in the shuttle. Two hours later, there was nothing left on Jurassic that wasn't there prior to the Arkell's arrival.

Once aboard the *Velgot*, the eight went to one of the favored pubs on the *Velgot* and had a terrific lunch.

"I can't tell you how long I've been salivating over a meal such as this," said Agroe.

"I can imagine," said Jupi.

"Before we leave this world, we'd like you four to guide to us, in a shuttle, to the most interesting places on the planet," said Oruku with a big smile.

"That will be our pleasure," said Cirtap. "As you know, Jurassic has more than a few interesting places."

Four hours later, the shuttle entered the *Velgot*'s flight deck.

"Great idea in videoing our tour of this planet. All our friends, throughout the galaxy, will surely be glued to their viewers," said Jupi.

"Teddy is going to be thrilled with the videos we took of the Traptors. Hovering just above where they could reach was an experience of a lifetime. They certainly wanted to get the claws and teeth into the shuttle. Those creatures are ferocious, and they can jump," said Vel.

"Scared the hell out me," said Jupi. "They were clearing the ground by at least three meters."

"Not bad for an animal who weighs five to six thousand kilos."

"You would think the size of the shuttle would intimidate them, but it certainly didn't," said Cirtap.

"Probably in their genes. They have, over the millennia, learned they needn't fear anything," said Vel.

"That's an apt assumption," said Agroe.

"Then to see the advanced dinosaurs right after the Traptors was startling," said Randa.

"Amazing is right," said Jupi. "I would not be surprised, in the not-too-distant future, if the advanced dinos started thinking about traveling off their island."

"If and when they venture off their safe world, I'm sure they will find the Traptors as horrifying as we do," said Cirtap.

"Maybe more so," said Agroe. "They will have no high-tech protection."

"We've made extensive studies of these dinos. It seems their transition to a greatly advanced animal was accomplished over a very short period of time," said Agroe.

"How short?"

"Just four generations."

"How can that be?" asked Jupi.

"Mutation," answered Agroe.

"We were able to trace their astounding gain in intelligence to two females," said Cirtap.

"How did you manage that?"

"With a great deal of time and work. We managed to get blood samples from over a hundred of them."

"Really? Just how did you manage that?" asked Jupi.

"You may recall how we used artificial flying insects to record their language, allowing us to translate and listen in to their conversations."

"I saw the reports," said Vel. "Amazing."

"We modified the insects and gave them stingers, something like a mosquito. From there we were able to procure the blood samples."

"Clever," said Vel.

"It might amuse you to know that we lost three of our insects to strong and quick slaps."

Everyone laughed.

"We learned to sting and move quickly."

"This is fascinating," said Randa.

There was a brief pause before Agroe spoke. "To get back to the origins of their rapid advancement in intelligence, the female of this species lay up to a dozen eggs and sit on them to incubate, as do most birds. A female either was impregnated by a super-intelligent male or, more likely, had some sort of occurrence that caused a mutation in her eggs."

"Occurrence?"

"Could have been several things. She, after becoming pregnant, may have been affected by a very close lighting strike, which, theoretically, the radiation could alter the DNA of the eggs. Or maybe she ate or drank something that contained a chemical or chemicals that altered the eggs' DNA. We think this possibility to be the most likely."

"I would think the lightning would be more probable," said Oruku.

"And that was our conclusion also."

"But?" smiled Oruku.

"There was a second female who mimicked the first. The females were not from the same tribe, if you will, but lived close by. For lightning to cause a DNA alteration on just one female over millions of years is, of course, possible. But for it to happen to two pregnant females within a year or two of each other is all but statistically impossible."

"But for two pregnant females who live in the same area to eat or drink the same thing, in a short period of time, is certainly possible," offered Vel.

"That was our conclusion," said Agroe.

"So now we have, say, two dozen young dinos with mutated DNA, growing, learning, and"— Jupi smiled—"breeding with each other."

"How would they know to breed with other genetically enhanced dinos?" asked Randa.

"Could be several factors contributing to that. An old earth saying, 'Birds of a feather flock together,' may be apt here. These two special dino families lived in close proximity and probably had interactions, of one kind or another, all their lives. These dinos should be drawn to those who have many things in common, as do all intelligent beings."

"Birds of a feather."

"Exactly."

"Have you determined an approximate time all this started?" asked Oruku.

"As a matter of fact, yes, within twenty years anyway. It all began about three hundred and twenty-five years ago. We know that the intelligent dinos started grouping together, away from the non-enhanced dinos, just about two hundred ten years ago."

"So we're looking at a dozen generations, more or less, of selective breeding," said Vel.

Agroe nodded. "Our research found that when the enhanced dinos reached maturity and began having babies, they moved far away from their non-enhanced forebears and started their own colony. We couldn't find any evidence of them having any further contact with their predecessors."

"That would make sense. They are now, in fact, a different species," said Vel.

"Exactly."

"Time to visit another continent," said Cirtap.

"I have a feeling this is also going to be interesting," Vel said with a smile.

"It is indeed," said Agroe. "Here's where we are heading."

On the viewer, a small continent was displayed. It was in the Southern Hemisphere, between the equator and South Pole.

The shuttle had the same speed capabilities as the Velgot. So, within seconds the shuttle was at a standstill at an altitude of five thousand meters above a vast plane.

"We are searching for the present location of the cavemen. They are nomadic and seem to be on the move constantly."

Jupi smiled. "They have no permanent cave?"

Agroe returned the smile. "Actually, they have caves or shelters scattered over hundreds of kilometers."

"They are true hunter-gatherers," said Cirtap.

"I have them," said Agroe.

The shuttle left its station above the vast plain and shot to an area that had scattered and diverse foliage. Again, it took up station about two thousand kilometers above the area.

"There they are," said Agroe, not taking his eyes off the viewer. "Looks like they are hunting the aforementioned dinos."

"Indeed," said Vel. "I've counted just over two dozen cavemen. They have the dinos surrounded."

"The dinos are clearly afraid of the 'men,'" said Randa.

"Those animals are big," said Vel.

"About five times the size of the cavemen but don't possess any offensive weapons, and their defenses were not designed to defeat those spears."

"I'd like to see a close-up of these men," said Vel.

"Can do," said Agroe. "I'm going to drop us down to three thousand kilometers and put us between the cavemen and the sun. Unless they have really effective sunglasses, they won't be looking in our direction. If they do look in our direction, I'll move us so fast that they will think their eyes were playing tricks on them."

A few seconds later, the viewer was showing the cavemen from a much lower angle.

"There are women with them," said Randa.

"They always travel together," said Cirtap. "You will note the females are not carrying spears. They carry baskets and digging tools."

"Give us a close-up of the females and their baskets?"

The camera zoomed into a group of four cavewomen.

"I didn't expect to find them this good-looking," said Randa. "They don't look like the prehistoric women we've seen pictures of all our lives. These are blondes with very dark skin, interesting contrast."

"They remind me of the aboriginals of Earth's Australia," said Jupi.

"Very lean bodies. Not much fat," added Jupi.

CHAPTER 29

EGADLO

"It's been nearly thirty years their time since we dropped by and altered their genes," said Oruku.

"I remember seeing the videos of this planet," said Vel. "Everybody seemed to be old."

"Actually, they were old based on their biological makeup. Old to them was midthirties."

All eyes in the *Velgot* were on viewers located throughout the ship. All were anxious to see if their technology had lengthened their lives.

The *Velgot* was placed in orbit behind a moon, and a dozen small recorders were sent down to the planet to record and broadcast images throughout the galaxy.

The images came in, and the viewer's screen was divided into twelve squares, displaying the scenes of all twelve recorders at once.

"Zoom in on recorder three," requested Oruku.

The panel for the number-three video now took up half the viewer's space.

It was a street scene in a large town. Dozens of Egadlo's citizens were milling about as was normal for any advanced society at this stage of evolution.

"Well it looks like our intervention has worked," said Oruku.

The crowd's age was clearly mixed. At least a third of the population looked to be young, while a good percentage appeared to be middle-aged. The balance looked quite old. Their mode of dress was dramatically changed. Whereas thirty years ago, all pretty much dressed in drab clothing, now the variety of dress was astounding.

"Now, this is how a civilization should look," said Jupi.

Oruku had a big smile on his face. "Makes an old man's head swell."

"Look at what they're doing," said Randa.

Most of the recorders were showing an amazing amount of construction occurring all over the planet. Much of the construction was of designs not previously seen.

"Isn't it interesting the lengthening of their lives causes all sorts of positive changes?"

"Excellent," said Vel. "It will be interesting to drop by in another fifty years to see what they've accomplished."

"Thought next we'd visit a planet that looked to all the world like Gabriel when the *Norman* first arrived there," said Oruku.

"I'm sure Vance will be very interested in seeing the progress," said Vel.

A few minutes later, the *Velgot* was in orbit over the planet. Although there was considerable growth in vegetation, it was far short of what Oruku had hoped for. The vegetation had spread out a few kilometers from their water source, but the planet still looked mostly barren.

"Well, I have to admit, I'm disappointed," said Oruku. "I guess, in my mind, I thought we'd have more growth."

"You weren't exactly able to stay on top of this project as Vance was developing Gabriel. You and the *Velgot* have had a few priority projects over the decades," said Vel.

Oruku smiled. "Thanks, son."

CHAPTER 30

A DIFFERENT GALAXY

"Next stop, Rofina," announced Vel.

"How many years has it been?" asked Jupi.

"Ten years, nearly to the day," said Oruku. "It was the first and last time we visited this galaxy."

"Twenty-five thousand light-years away," offered Vel.

"I'm expecting and hoping that Rofina has remained peaceful in our absence."

A few seconds later, the *Velgot* arrived over Nrie.

"Any sign of military equipment?" asked Vel.

"Nothing we can spot," answered Tracc.

"We need to talk to Neilo," said Oruku with a smile.

"Apparently the feeling is mutual. Neilo is calling us."

Oruku smiled. "On the viewer, please."

A second later, Neilo's image appeared on the viewer.

"Hello, Neilo, how is everything on Nrie?"

"Thanks to the Arkell, everything on Nrie is wonderful or is rapidly heading in that direction."

"We are pleased to hear that. Your relationship with Beitzel on Etah is good?"

"As a matter of fact, we have become friends."

"Good to hear."

"We, along with the leadership of Neda, have been working through a myriad of challenges on all three continents. The decades-long war dictated all sorts of infrastructures, both physical and emotional, that no longer apply. We've had to reeducate millions who were employed in offensive and defensive weapons production?"

"You are pleasing me very much," said Oruku.

"I am pleased to tell you how much the governing-guidance documents you left us have been a most valuable gift. We would have been overwhelmed without them."

"I'm delighted to hear that. Anything else we should know?"

"Yes, I believe you'll be pleased to know the documents on Sharkra you left us have been read and studied by just about every person on the planet."

"That surprises me. How do the citizens of Rofina regard Sharkra?"

"We believe Sharkra is a god."

"Everybody believes this?"

"There are a few, here and there, who don't believe Sharkra exists at all. Others believe Sharkra exists but is not a deity."

"Is the one rule applied?"

Neilo smiled. "It is. Nobody criticizes those who do not believe as they do. Quite frankly, the compliance with the one rule has surprised me."

"The attitudes of our people have changed so much it is hard to understand how that can happen."

"Until recently, your citizens have been at war all their lives. Now Sharkra has eliminated wars and, in so doing, put hope and joy into their lives. Now, knowing they have a supreme being looking out for them is an immeasurable comfort."

"This is all true," said Neilo.

"How is your past leadership handling life in prison?" asked Oruku with a slight smile.

"Not well. Medib didn't survive two weeks before those who blamed him for their being in Zeni prison managed to hang him from the bars in his cell window."

"Well that's unfortunate."

Neilo nodded. "I agree. I would have rather seen him spend years suffering a fate that he imposed on thousands of others, innocent people."

"Going to take you to a disgusting planet," said Oruku.

Vel got a quizzical expression on his face. "Disgusting?"

A few seconds later, the *Velgot* was in orbit over a large planet located a great distance from its star. This was an extremely cold region of space. But the planet itself was festooned with thousands of active volcanos.

"Well, this isn't a very hospitable planet," said Vel as they stood on the *Velgot*'s bridge. "Is there life here?"

"In a manner of speaking," answered Oruku. "Let's get in a shuttle and head down to the surface."

"Surface?" said Jupi. "Got to be awfully chilly down there."

Oruku smiled. "You would think."

Eighteen minutes later, the shuttle was hovering about thirty meters above the surface. The shuttle's cameras were pointing straight down, and the scene displayed on the viewer was nightmarish.

"Holy shit!" said Vel. "What are those things?"

The viewer centered on one of the five most disgusting-looking life forms in the galaxy. They were just shy of two meters in height, a filthy green color, two stump-like legs, no arms, and a long worm-like neck connected to a small elongated head. No eyes or ears could be seen on their slime-covered heads. All these monstrosities were slowly sticking their heads into what looked to be pockets of muck. Whatever they were sucking up could be seen in the form of small bulges making their way up the worm-like neck into the interior of these beasts.

"Those are the indigenous life forms. They are, in fact, mold."

"Mold? It's moving," said Jupi with a look of disdain on her face.

"The only planet in the galaxy, that we are aware of, to have advanced mold."

"Interesting," said Vel.

"They're in an eating cycle."

"What are they eating?"

"Mold. There is, in fact, no other form of life on this planet."

"What's the surface temperature?" asked Vel while not taking his eyes off the viewer.

"Eighty-two degrees."

"Hot core as demonstrated by the multitude of volcanos."

"Very," said Oruku. "It doesn't need heat from a star. It has its own."

"Speaking for myself," said Jupi, "I don't ever have to see this again. It's disgusting."

Oruku smiled as the shuttle dropped down to just above one of the creatures, and then the hatch opened.

The odor seemed to jump into the shuttle. And it was horrific.

"Oh my god," Jupi choked out. "Please close the hatch, before I lose my breakfast."

The hatched closed, and the smell dissipated within seconds.

Oruku smiled broadly. "Just wanted you to experience the total repugnancy of this planet."

"That was the most abhorrent smell I've ever encountered," said Vel.

CHAPTER 31

ROOTIC

"We haven't been to this planet. But I've been looking forward to seeing it and getting to know its people," said Oruku.

"Rootic?" asked Vel.

"That's the one."

"These are the hummers," said Jupi with a smile.

"And their humming clearly pleased Sharkra," said Oruku.

"That was a display, according to the witnesses, that far exceeded what Sharkra had done in the past."

"I'm looking forward to hearing them sing," said Jupi.

"We have their humming translation installed in our translator," said Vel.

"This is going to be interesting."

"We've notified the Rootic of our intention to visit them," said Jupi.

"Did you tell them when and where we would go into orbit and to be outside lying flat and watching straight up?" asked Oruku.

"We did." Vel smiled.

The *Velgot* took up a station a thousand kilometers above the Rootic's largest city. At this distance, the *Velgot* would be barely visible to the naked eye.

Oruku signaled to a tech to turn on the translator.

"Citizens of Rootic, my name is Oruku, and we are Arkell. As you can see, we have put our ship, the *Velgot*, in a high orbit above your largest city, which we believe is your capital city. We do this in order for all, in this city, to see what has become our signature arrival."

Oruku paused for a moment before continuing. "In ten seconds, we will drop down to a much-tighter orbit."

"Three, two, one."

It wasn't known immediately the effect the *Velgot*'s terrifying arrival would have on Rootic's citizens. They knew there would be no screaming or crying.

After ten minutes, Oruku addressed the leadership of Rootic. "We are going to drop down to your planet in one of our shuttles. We wish to introduce ourselves to a people who pleased the Sharkra more than any other. Please know that you are in no danger from us."

A few seconds later, a message came up from the planet. "We are aware of the Arkell. The Arkell are responsible for our continued existence. You put us in contact with the humans of Gabriel. The Arkell are our friends."

"We are pleased you feel that way toward us. We'll head down to your planet in a few minutes," said Oruku.

"We have just sent the coordinates of a place to land your shuttle. It will give you adequate space to land and allow many of our citizens to see you in person."

A few minutes later, the Arkell shuttle settled down in a clear area in what was a heavily wooded park located a kilometer from the Rootic's central city.

CHAPTER 32

PLANET ARKELL

The *Norman* took up station in a geosynchronous orbit over Arkell's capital city of Nevaeh, joining the dozens of ships already in orbit. The *Norman*, once considered a huge ship while being built on Earth, certainly wasn't here. The *Norman*, orbiting among the galaxy's most advanced ships, was tiny. Even the *Marian*, at five times the size of the *Norman*, would be considered smallish among these colossal ships.

Witnessing this largest-known gathering of starships would certainly be a lifelong memory for most. To see it was a spectacular display of orbital coordination. The spacing of the ships, directed by Arkell engineers, kept the ships at ideal orbital positions. There would be no chance of collisions.

"Holy crap," said Vance, not taking his eyes off the large viewer on the bridge of the *Norman*.

"I've never seen this many ships together," said Alex.

"I suspect nobody has seen this many ships . . . ever," said Teddy.

None could keep their eyes off the bridge's viewer.

"There's the Yassi ship," said Dale.

"Wow," said Colleen, "is there no end to their creativity?"

"Spectacular," said Alex.

"It looks like it's traveling at the speed of light while stationary," added Dale.

"Ha," said Vance. "There's the Rootic ship."

"If a person wanted a contrast between two ships, the Rootic next to the Yassi ship would give that contrast."

"Two extremes for sure," said Lara. "I'd feel a little backward if I were the Rootic."

Tomaco smiled. "Put any ship next to that Yassi ship and it's going to look like a lump of clay in comparison."

"Good point," said Dale.

"Arkell shuttles are ferrying occupants of some of these ships down to the monument," observed Alex.

"Strange they don't have shuttles themselves," said Troy.

"I have to assume that most do have shuttles or they land their home ships on planets as we do with the *Norman* and *Marian*," said Dale.

There were a half dozen distinctly Arkell-designed shuttles shooting up to the ships, loading passengers, and rapidly dropping back down to the surface.

"I'll bet the new passengers will be surprised they feel no acceleration when traveling in an Arkell vehicle," said Vance.

Vance switched the view from one of the orbiting ships to the surface of Arkell. They not only could see where the shuttles were unloading the passengers, but on the left side of the viewer, a bit of the monument came into view. Vance adjusted the direction of the camera to take in the whole tribute to Sharkra.

"Will you look at the size of Sharkra's monument?"

"My god," said Dale. "And the beauty of it."

The *Norman* was in orbit directly above the new monument. And they could clearly see the expanse of the new homage to Sharkra.

"How much ground is it covering?" asked Gary.

Dale's fingers flew over the keyboard. "It's four hundred meters long and two hundred wide."

"Wow!"

"Look at those water features," said Teddy.

"Can't wait to see this entire creation from the ground," said Alex.

"Zoom in," requested Vance.

The viewer displayed the monument in a zoom shot and more details came into focus. All on the bridge gave sounds of astonishment at the size and beauty of this tribute to Sharkra.

"That's indescribable, wow," said Teddy. "I'm starting to feel like a worm again."

"Me too," added Troy.

"Message coming in from the planet," said Dale.

The viewer's image switched from the monument to a single male Arkell of an indeterminant age. This particular Arkell looked every bit as distinguished as Oruku.

"Greetings and welcome to our dear friends of the planet Gabriel."

All stood to greet Redael.

"We are honored to be here and visit your wonderful world again, Redael." Vance paused for a second. "And we are very anxious to see what you have created to honor Sharkra."

"Thank you not only for allowing us to extract a massive amount of quartz from your beautiful planet but for your citizens' help in quarrying."

Vance smiled. "There is nothing that the Arkell wishes of us that will not be graciously given."

"Thank you, Vance." Redael looked around the bridge while smiling broadly as he looked at the others. "And to have our dear friends here again. Delightful, just delightful."

All on the bridge greeted Redael with big smiles. All had met Redael and the other prominent Arkell within six months of Sharkra removing the light speed barrier.

"We would like to make a request of you," said Redael.

"Name it," said Vance with a big smile.

Redael returned the smile. "We've had many queries regarding the *Norman*. Many of our guests would love to see the *Norman* up close and personal." Redael smiled again. "An old Earth expression."

"With all that is to be seen and experienced here, in this magical place, I can't imagine the *Norman* being much of a draw," said Vance.

Redael smiled. "You are going to be surprised, my friend. There are many civilizations who are aware of the *Norman* and its crew. Other than the monument itself, we feel the *Norman* will receive the most interest. Your ship has a permanent and wonderful place in our history, and because of our interaction with many civilizations, the tales of your deeds and adventures have spread around the Milky Way galaxy. The dozens of civilizations who are aware of the humans' exploits will surely enjoy seeing your historic ship in person.

Vance looked a little doubtful. "I still suspect the *Norman* won't draw many visitors away from Sharkra's monument."

Redael nodded. "The only practical way to see the *Norman* would be if it were on the surface, close to the monument."

"We can do that," said Dale.

"We have designated a special place for it."

"Well this is all quite humbling," said Vance with a smile. "You just direct us to where you wish us to be and we'll put the *Norman* right there."

"The coordinates are now in your computer."

"We'll be at that place in a few minutes," said Dale.

"Thank you. We are also asking the Yassi to bring their magnificent ship down to the surface."

"That will certainly draw a crowd," said Troy.

Redael smiled. "The Yassi's creativity seems to be limitless."

"My sentiments exactly," said Colleen.

"I would love to just walk around that ship and look at it," said Aidan.

"Maybe they will let us go aboard to see the inner workings," said Dale.

"I have little doubt that will be the case," said Redael. "The Yassi are very fond of the humans."

Alex smiled. "It's a mutual admiration."

Redael nodded knowingly. "We would like to invite our friends of the *Norman* to my quarters for a relaxed gathering before what is bound to be a chaotic couple of days here."

"That sounds delightful. We're all looking froward to seeing you," replied Vance.

"Wonderful," said Redael. "A team will meet you at the *Norman* and will escort you to my quarters. I'm looking forward to seeing you all again."

A few minutes later, the *Norman* began slowly dropping down to the Arkell surface. Alex suggested they drop slowly so as to give all who were interested a chance to see the *Norman* in flight. Fortunately, Vance had insisted that they fly the *Norman* through a thunderstorm to "put a little shine on our dandy little ship." So the now-ancient and apparently legendary ship, which looked to all the world like a huge, bronze soccer ball, was nearly as clean and distinctive as it was when new.

The citizens of various planets, already on the ground, started pointing and talking excitedly as the *Norman* was dropping through the atmosphere. Many began heading toward the *Norman*'s landing spot.

Six minutes later, the *Norman* lowered its landing gear and gently set down on the designated spot. All eyes were on the viewer as they landed.

"Holy cow," said Teddy, "there are a lot of beings starting to head this way."

"Beings?" asked Colleen.

"Well I don't know how else to describe what's closing in on us. There is quite a variety of shapes and sizes. As an example, there's one being with three legs and two of what must be arms. There are two really big beings with green skin and little heads. Look at the muscles on them, geez."

Colleen smiled. "Beings it is."

The spot designated for the *Norman* was just under seventy meters from the entrance to the new monument. Apparently the Arkell wanted to make visiting the *Norman* as convenient as possible.

Within minutes, there was a small-but-growing crowd gathering at the base of the ship. Apparently Redael had it right. The fascinating story and exploits of the humans of Gabriel were known throughout a great deal of the galaxy. The humans had, as a consequence, become unwitting celebrities.

The humans had been special to the Arkell for thousands of years before the humans gave a single thought to space travel. The Arkell had been watching, monitoring, and studying them throughout their history. No one, including the humans, knew more about humans than the Arkell.

As soon as the ramp started slowly dropping down, the small-but-growing crowd started cheering, wooing, and clapping enthusiastically. Within a minute of the ramp's deployment, the humans started down, with Vance and Lara in the lead. The cheering and wooing got even louder. Here were the famous humans: Vance, Alex, Dale, and Teddy, the men of Earth's remarkable history, along with the brilliant and beautiful women who were nearly as famous as their husbands. In addition, Troy and Clair, Gary and Pat, and Shem and Jarleth joined them at the base of the ramp.

The Gabrielites maintained big smiles as they acknowledged the many beings gathered to see them. Many species were not known to them. Some were very strange in appearance. Some were quite small, others very large. And all held their hands out to be shaken. The Yassi, Vout, Byuse, and Arkell were quite surprised when the custom of shaking hands took hold in many civilizations.

"This is a bit spooky," said Teddy after shaking hands with the big, green-skinned powerful-looking being and what was assumed to be its wife, a particularly large and homely being.

Alex smiled. "I'm sure we're in no danger here."

"Here comes our ride," observed Lara.

Within seconds, two young Arkell drove up in a large transport.

The youngest of the two men instantly became awestruck. He couldn't take his eyes off Vance and Lara. And he, apparently, was going to remain sitting, motionless, in the transport for an indeterminate period of time.

The older Arkell quickly saw the problem and tapped his companion on the shoulder, which brought him out of his trance.

"If you will, please step in and be seated, and we will take you to Redael's quarters."

Vance returned the smile as he looked around. He was surprised at the number of aliens already gathering around and under the *Norman*. "Give us a moment."

"Certainly."

"Looks like we should start giving tours right away," said Dale as he looked over what was already a large-and-growing crowd.

Troy nodded as he looked over the expanding crowd. "Clair and I will volunteer to take the first shift."

Gary stepped forward. "Pat and I will join you. It looks like there is going to be a constant wave of people wanting to see the inside of the *Norman*."

Vance looked around at the gathering. "You're right, guess we are a sight to see." Vance smiled. "Thanks for taking the first shift. We'll relieve you as soon as possible."

This parking lot seemed to stretch a thousand meters in three directions. The fourth direction was the monument itself. Already there were hundreds of small shuttles, of every description, parked at the Sharkra temple.

Dale took another look at the spontaneous gathering. "Looks like most visitors are packing a personal translator. That will make your chore easier."

"It sure will," agreed Gary.

"But it's still going to be a fearsome task," said Clair. "We're going to need to set up a manageable system to facilitate these tours."

"Maybe too late," said Troy. "For the time being, we'll just set up a line." Troy paused for a second. "How many do you think we can handle at one time?"

"First," said Pat, "judging from the gathering crowd, we'll need to split up and take four separate groups or we'll never get done."

"I'd agree with that." Dale paused for a second. "Maybe we can enlist some of our Arkell friends to be tour guides."

Tomaco smiled. "I'm sure all we would have to do is ask."

"No doubt," agreed Dale.

"But, for the moment, let's see if we four can handle a dozen tourists each," said Troy.

Gary smiled. "Never thought I'd be a tour guide."

Not only were the growing crowd anxious to meet Vance and Alex, but just about the same number were surrounding Dale and Tomaco.

What neither Dale nor Tomaco had taken into consideration was the fact that they themselves were celebrities. The tens of thousands of scientists throughout the galaxy all knew and had great respect for Dr. Dale Isley. Tomaco's celebrity came from a different direction. Aside from being the wife of the galaxy's most famous scientist, she rightfully was credited with the theory that Sharkra wanted to be accepted as a true entity, not just a theory.

For the rest of the day, ships from the over-a-hundred highly advanced civilizations continued to arrive at Arkell, many from thousands of light-years away. Ships of every size, color, and design were appearing in orbit by the hour. Most ships had shuttles of their own and transported their citizens to the surface. Some stayed in their designated parking spots, while others returned to their ships. Most of these ships and their occupants had never been to Arkell, and most of them hadn't been aware the Arkell even existed until Sharkra removed the light speed barrier.

The crew of the *Norman*, less Gary, Pat, Troy, and Clair, were sitting in very comfortable seats in the expansive sitting room of Redael's quarters. All had a beverage of their choice while enjoying the ambiance of the room.

"We have gotten word that the *Velgot* and the *Geaalo* will be arriving together an hour before sunset tomorrow," said Redael.

"We're looking forward to seeing our friends from those two ships. It's been a while," said Vance.

"We've been informed that Oruku's health is going downhill quite quickly," said Lara.

"Yes, unfortunately that is the case. A very fine man." His words seemed detached, but his voice gave away his sorrow. "A finer representative for the Arkell will be very difficult, if not impossible, to find." Redael paused for a moment. "He has been the face of the Arkell for many civilizations over these past three hundred years. All who came into contact with this dear man are going to be quite sad to hear that this brilliant fellow will not be among us for very much longer."

"I'm hoping to maintain my composure when he passes," said Vance, with grief apparent in his voice.

As did the *Velgot*, dozens of Arkell ships had been doing the bidding of Sharkra. The front men of all the Arkell ships were highly skilled at diplomacy and bargaining; it was part of their DNA. It is what they were born to do. Oruku was the acknowledged master of these skills. Throughout their history, the Arkell had replaced their lost crew with clones of themselves. The replacement embryos were embedded in a surrogate woman at least twenty years prior to their need to replace the shipmate. This provided time for the aging shipmate to teach all that he or she knew about their duties. But Oruku did not do that. There was no one waiting in the wings to take over his highly specialized duties.

CHAPTER 33

MONUMENT

The monument's location was breathtaking. It was laid out in a relatively flat-bottomed, small valley between three small hills located just a few kilometers south of the Arkell capital. The valley itself was approximately three hundred twenty meters wide and eight hundred eighty meters long before narrowing to a long, thin canyon no wider than seven meters.

There were just over two thousand chairs cleverly dispersed in and around the beautiful landscaping and picturesque canal located within the monument's grounds. The outside border of this magical garden was encircled by a hundred and two quartz pedestals, which held the miniature planets representing the technically advanced civilizations. The chairs were reserved for the aliens representing those planets. The surrounding hills provided a natural amphitheater and would hold the additional thousands, the vast majority of those being Arkell. The balance would be made up of the aliens who managed to hitch a ride on their planet's ship but had no reservations.

The hills, and the valley between them, had been groomed to perfection. The grass lawn covered the valley and the hills, providing a comfortable place for chairs or blankets.

After the meeting with Redael, the transport took the Gabrielites to the entrance to the monument.

All had their eyes on the *Norman* as soon as it came into view. All noticed the crowd size had lessened considerably.

"The *Norman* looks different here," said Teddy. "Looks smaller."

"Not in the confines of the cave it dominated," said Dale. "Lot of space around it now."

Alex nodded. "Let's head into the monument."

The ten turned and headed to the monument's entrance.

The spectacular flower gardens in the center of the monument's grounds were designed and planted by the Yassi. Both Alex and Vance commented on the appearance being somewhat like the famous gardens of Versailles on old Earth. Weaving in and out of the fantastic garden was a beautiful canal with breathtaking interspersed waterfalls and fountain displays. This canal wandered throughout the small valley. On both ends of the breathtaking garden, the canal formed islands. These round islands were ten meters in diameter and planted with the most exotic plants and flowers that could be found in the galaxy. This stunning effect was sure to have thousands of pictures and videos taken of them.

At the front of these incredible gardens, right where the valley ended and the narrow canyon began, was an exact duplicate of the original monument on Gabriel, including the original five planets. Arching out from both sides of this now-famous monument were a hundred and two pedestals, placed every twenty meters, surrounding the valley. The pedestals themselves were one and a half meters tall, half a meter wide, and shaped like fluted Roman columns. They, too, were made of the gold-bearing quartz found in abundance on Gabriel. Attached to the front of each pedestal was a bronze plaque beautifully engraved with the name of the planet, its size, the name and number of its population, and the distance from Arkell, measured in light-years. The re-creations of these planets of advanced civilizations were designed and constructed as perfect miniatures. All oceans, rivers, lakes, mountain ranges, forest, grassy plains, deserts, and cloud cover were not just painted on a sphere, but rather the mountains were to exact size, shape, and vegetation. The rivers, lakes, and oceans were projections from inside the miniature planets that made the water appear to be moving in the rivers and created tiny waves on the shores of the oceans. To top it off, the projections also displayed clouds forming, dissipating, and re-forming. If one wasn't aware, one would believe these were the actual planets, as viewed from space, not miniatures.

The placement of the planets on the pedestals was decided by a simple lottery. All the planets' names were placed in a vessel from which an Arkell drew a planet's name and attached a number to it, starting with number one. The planets Arkell, Gabriel, Yassi, Vout, and Byuse were on the duplicate of the original monument and didn't require a pedestal. Most of the hundred additional planets had been discovered within the past three years since the light speed limit was removed. Most of them had received help, in some way, from one of the Arkell ships. All, during the Arkell's visit, had been made aware of Sharkra. Many, it was assumed, did not, at this time, believe Sharkra to be a deity. They had not yet seen the power displayed by Sharkra. It was hoped that this inaugural presentation of the monument would include a display by Sharkra itself.

By the late afternoon, the permanent chairs in the monument's grounds were nearly filled. They were occupied by an astounding variety of intelligent life forms. Most of the visitors had never seen or heard of the other attendees. Fortunately, most had arrived a day or two early and had a chance to meet and mix with beings from other worlds. Many of the attendees were from planets that were known to be in one conflict or another throughout most of their history. That being the case, it surprised many that there hadn't been a single incident of aggressive behavior. It seems that virtually all attendees knew, or possibly felt, there was something happening here that was to be respected. It was hoped that many aliens who had been in conflicts with other worlds would become friends and allies as time went on.

The two hills that sided the small valley were rapidly filling with the overflow of those, mainly Arkell, who did not have a seat assignment in the center of the monument. Fifty of the fifty-five Rootic attending were among the thousands picking a spot on one of the hills. These Rootic all assembled on an area low on the hill and close to the monument. These were the same fifty-five Rootic who hummed a song to Sharkra on Gabriel. The five Rootic that Vance, Lucy, and Gary had met in their ship were assigned seats close to the center monument.

At the exact moment the program was scheduled to start, Redael walked onto the large stage in front of the center monument.

"My name is Redael. I have been given the honor of guiding tonight's proceedings."

The sound system in the monument was incredible. Each attendee had been given an earbud that instantly translated Arkell into their language. To them, it sounded like Redael was standing right in front of them, talking in a conversational tone.

"First, I would suggest you to look straight up," said Redael.

All followed the suggestion.

Within seconds, the *Velgot* instantly appeared in orbit above the monument, followed two seconds later by the *Geaalo*. The thousands assembled had the normal and now-predictable reaction. They screamed loud and long, followed by very enthusiastic clapping, wooing, and cheering.

The sight of these two massive ships set the crowd on an extended, Earth-felt display of love and respect. Most had not had the good fortune of personally meeting Oruku. But all had been made aware of Oruku's history, his thousands of major accomplishments, and his loving personality. All also knew of his ill health, and all were aware this beloved man was going to pass away in the very near future.

After the crowd settled down, a shuttle emerged from each of the two Arkell ships. They united with each other and started down to the planet's surface, a trip that would take a full two minutes at a fairly slow speed.

The thousands observing these two shuttles started clapping, wooing, and cheering. They knew Oruku was coming down to his home planet for the last time. Thousands had tears forming as the shuttles continued their descent to the surface.

At the far end of the monument were two elevated landing sites, designed and designated for these two shuttles.

All the attendees now stood and turned to watch the shuttles as they dropped down.

The gathered became respectfully silent as the shuttles touched down on their designated pads. A minute later, the *Velgot*'s shuttle's ramp extended and the hatch opened. A few seconds later, Oruku appeared at the hatch opening dressed in an all-white traditional suit.

All of the approximately six thousand attendees began heartfelt clapping, wooing, and cheering. Oruku smiled broadly and raised his hands to waist level, palms up, as to gather in the love being displayed. A few seconds later, he was joined by Vel and Jupi. With Vel on his right and Jupi on his left, the three held hands and started slowly down the ramp.

A person would have to be blind not to see Oruku's health had deteriorated significantly. He could barely walk. Within a few meters, he released Vel's and Jupi's hands and took hold of their arms just above the elbow. His weakness was causing him to rely heavily on the support of Vel and Jupi. But his warm smile never left his face.

As they entered the rear of the monument's garden, they took a route that would take them through the monument's gardens via the path that bordered the canal.

As the three walked slowly through the garden, those along the path made eye contact and displayed a sign of respect as dictated by their culture's traditions. Some bowed, some clasped their hands as in prayer, and some held their hands as if they were giving alms or maybe a life force to the recipient and dozens of other acts of respect.

As the three were about halfway through the garden, Oruku stumbled and would have fallen had it not been for the support of Vel and Jupi. The crowd instantly reacted with sounds of alarm. Vel and Jupi's support saved him from falling. But still, Oruku's warm smile remained on his face. After a moment, they continued their walk to the front of the garden without further incident.

There was a special place reserved for these three, the center of the front row. The front four rows were reserved for the front men and women for the many civilizations in attendance.

Oruku was seated in the center of row one. On his right was Vel, on his left Jupi. Shem and Jarleth were seated on the right of Vel. Vance and Lara were on Shem's right. Kilee and his wife, Enna, sat on Jupi's left.

Redael had remained standing throughout Oruku's long, slow walk. As the light of day began to fade, Redael spoke. "We will soon begin tonight's presentation of our monument, our homage to Sharkra. Most of you here this evening have spent these past two days visiting our shrine to Sharkra. During this time, you have met many other races, the majority of which, heretofore, had been unknown to you. It has been reported that there are twenty-one civilizations here who are currently, or have been in the past, in conflict, if not all-out war with each other. The reports stated that all, save two civilizations, have made a true peace. This is wonderful news. Our fervent wish is that these remaining two civilizations will find a path to lasting peace and possibly even a friendship over time. Bringing tranquility to our galaxy has been and will remain a major driving force for us Arkell."

There was an enthusiastic round of wooing, clapping, and cheering.

Redael paused for a moment. "We know and understand that many, if not the majority, of you do not believe Sharkra to be a deity. We feel that, after this evening's display, many of those beliefs will be ended." Redael smiled. "Now I'm going to take a seat and enjoy the inauguration of our monument to Sharkra."

A few seconds after Redael took his seat, an exciting, new, and dynamic musical composition began playing, quietly at first but building in volume and intensity as the seconds passed. The five planets on the center monument began rising from their pedestals and revolving on their axes. A low murmur came from the crowd. The five planets formed a slowly moving circle while rising a few meters. Then they dropped down and moved to be about a meter in front of Oruku at eye level. The planets' circling slowed, and as each passed Oruku, it tilted on its axis toward Oruku as if saying goodbye.

As the sun was setting, the five planets rose to twenty meters while continuing to circle. The music became more dramatic as the hundred and two other planets rose from their pedestals and joined the five. The circle's diameter spread to thirty meters. Then the miniature planets, led by the planet Arkell, broke out of the circle and formed into a single file and headed to the surrounding hills. From a distance, the long line of miniature planets reminded one of a huge snake as it dipped and turned in and around the hillsides. All attendees were cheering and wooing as the planets whizzed close to them. There was no doubt that the crowd was enjoying this incredible display.

As the sun set, the planets returned to hover just a moment above their pedestals before settling down on them. The music hit a dramatic chord, and the Milky Way galaxy appeared directly overhead. Most of the gathered had never seen anything like it, and wooing and clapping again exploded in the crowd.

The volume of the music dropped several octaves before a strong voice started calling out the names of the planets. As each planet's name was called, its place in the galaxy lighted up. This was repeated for each planet. When all the named miniature planets were in place, they became even brighter, making them clearly identifiable within the vastness of the galaxy. All this was part of the planned program.

Redael stood and returned to the stage in front of the center monument. "That was wonderful. To see our new friend's home planets and their location in our beautiful galaxy is not only interesting and informative but heartwarming for us because we, with Sharkra's help, have been introduced to many new civilizations, with new friends, new technology and"—Redael smiled—"new challenges, our reason and passion for being." Redael paused before continuing. "Now I would like to invite all fifty-five Rootic to join me here on this stage."

The little Rootic wasted no time in gathering behind Redael.

"I would now ask the Oruku and Vel to join us up here," said Redael softly in a loving voice.

Vel and Jupi stood and assisted Oruku in standing. The three walked slowly the three meters to the stage and up the three steps. When they reached Redael, Jupi released Oruku's hand, gently hugged him, and kissed him on the cheek and returned to her seat, tears flowing freely down her cheeks.

Now Redael was on Oruku's left, and Vel remained on his right.

Oruku stepped forward, looked over the large crowd, and smiled. "I love you all," he said in a weak voice.

The response was immediate and loud. The wooing, cheering, and clapping displayed a deep-seated love and respect for this man. It went on for a full minute before Oruku raised his hand. "This will be my last opportunity to address the people and civilizations of our marvelous galaxy."

The sound of sadness permeated the monument.

Vel wasn't touching Oruku, but he was within arm's reach and was on alert for any signs of Oruku's further weakening. He knew this wonderful man, his father, had little time left. Vel was having trouble holding back his emotions. He looked to the front row of seats and saw that all his loved ones were in the same condition.

Oruku was clearly getting weaker. He began to sway a little. Vel instantly grabbed his right arm to steady him.

"Thank you, son." His voice was just above a whisper, but his loving smile never left his face.

"I love you, Father."

Oruku smiled and stood a little straighter as he continued to address the throngs with a slightly stronger voice.

"There are no words that can adequately describe my wonderful life. My life, along with all the *Velgot*'s citizens, has been filled with amazing discoveries, incredible civilizations, beautiful planets, a fantastic variety of plants and animals, and . . . extraordinary challenges. These welcome challenges were multiplied, many times, after Sharkra entered our galaxy."

Entered our galaxy? thought Vance. He looked and could see Vel had a slightly puzzled expression on his face.

"Most of you here today," Oruku continued, "are here as a direct result of Sharkra's intervention. We, of the *Velgot*, along with eighty-two other Arkell ships were chosen by Sharkra and dispatched to planets with need, throughout this vast galaxy. It was our directive to aid those who needed help, no matter what their need was. These trips, and the help we were able to give to these diverse worlds, would not have been possible without the blessing and assistance of Sharkra."

There was dead silence in the crowd. No one wanted to miss a single word coming from this man.

Oruku stood straighter, and his voice became stronger. "I now know there is but one lord of the cosmos. A benevolent god who truly loves all beings with good hearts and loving character. He, being the only god, has been engaged, over billions of years, observing the development of all planets in the universe and the incredible life that has sprung from them. Our beautiful galaxy is just one among trillions. But a short time ago, my lord came to monitor our galaxy. The first thing we noticed was the brightening of planets that contained intelligent life. Then, a short time later, the light speed barrier was removed. Then my lord gathered eighty-three Arkell ships, assigning them the task of helping the needy no matter what was required. Sharkra enlisted us Arkell because we, as a species, have developed a great deal of advanced technology and have the compassionate personalities, intelligence, and wherewithal required to do His bidding. We have, as of this moment, completed all that Sharkra has asked of us. We have cured the ill, uplifted the destitute, and put an end to the evils in our galaxy."

The crowd remained silent. All were, no doubt, deep in their own thoughts, trying to grasp the enormity of what Oruku had just told them. There was no doubt that all who were in attendance and all, throughout the galaxy, who were watching and listening to Oruku were in deep thought.

Again, Oruku's knees started to buckle. Again, Vel took him by the arm.

Oruku turned to Vel. "I believe it's time to go, son,"

Vel could only nod.

"Lastly, with the breath left in me, I would like to announce that I, along with all the citizens of the *Velgot*, have chosen my son, Vel, to take my place on the *Velgot*."

After a brief silence, the crowd displayed their approval with a gentle wooing, no cheering or clapping. This was too solemn a moment for that sort of display.

Redael walked over to the edge of the stage and whispered something to a young man. Then he returned to the side of Oruku.

Within seconds, two young men walked onto the platform, bearing between them a beautifully padded chair. They quietly set the chair just behind Oruku before exiting the stage.

"Please sit, my dear friend," said Redael.

Oruku smiled and nodded. Both Vel and Redael assisted Oruku as he sat.

At this point, Sharkra had not changed or added anything to the program. The galaxy's hologram remained overhead.

Redael spoke. "We are now going to ask the Rootic to sing to Sharkra. Very few here this evening were witness to the song they hummed in respect for Sharkra on the planet Gabriel. But it was clear to all who were there that Sharkra loved their song. It is our deep hope and wish that Sharkra will be pleased to hear these wonderful people sing again."

Vel leaned over and gave his father a kiss on the forehead before choking out, "Goodbye, Father."

"Live your wonderful life to its fullest, my son."

Vel couldn't speak further. He nodded, turned, and walked off the platform and took his seat next to Jupi and Vance.

Oruku looked at Vance and mouthed, "Goodbye, my old friend."

Vance nodded once, barely able to maintain his composure. Tears were flowing freely down his cheeks.

The evening became dead still as the Rootic began their song.

It was the most beautiful sound anyone had ever heard. Within a minute, the majority of the attendees had a look of wonder, and many jaws dropped in surprise by the magnificent sound created by the Rootic's harmony. Four minutes later, the humming stopped and the applause, wooing, and cheers began. The Rootic quietly and quickly left the stage and returned to their seats.

Then, in an instant, the galaxy's hologram disappeared. Now, not only was it dead silent, but it was also pitch black. One would be hard-pressed to see his hand in front of his face. Not a single star or galaxy remained visible. Only a single soft light illuminated Oruku as he remained sitting in the center of the stage.

After a full minute, the silence was shattered by the sound of a massive horn, just as it had sounded on Gabriel on two occasions. Over six thousand people were startled, and the sounds of alarm permeated the small valley.

And then it began. Sheet lightning came in waves across the entire sky, followed instantly by massive, planet-shaking thunderclaps. The sound of thousands of startled people could not be heard over the din of thunder. Then the lightning and thunder stopped suddenly. Then came tens of thousands of meteors flashing in from every direction. The crowd became hyperactive with the visual and audio display assaulting their very core. Then it all stopped. It became pitch black once again. The assembled began calming down. Within a minute, there was quiet.

Again, a blast from the massive horn shattered the silence. Then a small light appeared from deep in space and started dropping down rapidly toward the planet. As it approached, it appeared to be a tiny moon. It stopped a few thousand meters above the monument before emitting a beam of warm light, luminating the single man sitting alone on a chair in front of the monument. The eerie silence continued as all eyes were now on Oruku.

Oruku tilted his head up and looked directly into the light. After a moment, his smile brightened and he stood up, not taking his eyes off the light.

Then his appearance began changing. He seemed to become younger as the seconds passed and his body started to regain its youthful tone. He now stood straight, as a handsome young man. His soft smile continued as he brought his arms to waist high with his palms facing upward, as if offering his soul to Sharkra. All six thousand-plus attendees stood in unison, none taking their eyes off Oruku.

Gasps went throughout the crowd as Oruku started to rise off the platform. As he rose, he stretched his arms out wide, his palms still pointing up. The light that had been illuminating Oruku created a soft glow that surrounded him like an orb. The orb's ascent began speeding up, and within seconds, it shot up and became one with the tiny moon.

The crowd gasped again.

The moon turned a brilliant pulsing gold as the massive horn sounded again. The hologram of the galaxy reappeared above the tiny moon, again startling the attendees. The golden moon, now containing Oruku, shot into the center of the galaxy, into the black hole. The black hole became a brilliant, pulsing golden light for half a moment before disappearing completely, leaving the night sky full of the light from billions of stars and galaxies.

The vast majority who were standing dropped to their knees and began paying homage to Sharkra in dozens of different languages.

There would be no atheists left on Arkell, and quite possibly the entire galaxy, after that evening.

The next morning, Redael had requested that all attendees return to the monument for a brief announcement. The mood following Sharkra's manifestation was, without exception, a spiritual uplifting for all who had attended and all who had watched their viewers throughout the planet and galaxy.

"I would first like to thank all who joined us here from around our unified galaxy," started Redael. "I believe all Arkell, and probably the vast majority of our new friends who traveled vast distances to be here, have witnessed miracles such as have never been seen or imagined. I personally take great comfort in knowing that our beloved Oruku is now residing with and as part of Sharkra. There can be no greater honor than this."

"Sharkra has given us but one rule," Redael said as he looked around at the thousands of bright, happy faces. "All are allowed to believe as they wish about Sharkra. All can believe Sharkra is a deity or not. It is up to the individual. Keep in mind that Oruku referred to Sharkra as my lord, not our lord or the lord. It is forbidden to chastise or criticize any, no matter what their beliefs regarding Sharkra's status." Redael paused for a moment before displaying a small smile. "I suspect, but do not know, that my lord may move on to other galaxies in this vast universe. But my lord will always be in my heart—and, I believe, in your hearts as well."

Six thousand individuals responded with a loud wooing.

Redael smiled brightly. "You may remain on Arkell for three more days." Redael's brow furrowed. "After that, I feel you should return home and share your experiences with your citizens." Redael smiled. "May my lord be with you always."

The majority of the planets represented there were able to watch the transmitted program on their viewers and in their languages.

The majority of the assembled on Arkell remained on the planet for those three days following the miracles at the Sharkra monument. Seems they wanted to interact and spend time with all who also bore witness to Sharkra's miracle. Just a few wanted to return to their respective planets to carry the recognition of the god Sharkra. The Gabrielites planned to return home two days following the miracles of Sharkra. All were anxious to relay their personal experiences to their friends and loved ones.

Among the dozens of diverse species of the vast galaxy, the exploits of the humans of Gabriel, their remarkable history, and their building of the first shrine to Sharkra were the subject of many ongoing conversations. Humans were credited with recognizing Sharkra as a deity and now were regarded in very high esteem.

The remarkable accomplishments of Alexander Gabriel on the now-extinct planet Earth was a story told and repeated many times in the past few days by the representatives of dozens of planets. The story of Vance's voyage in search of a new home for just twenty colonists was of great interest to a surprising number of intelligent species, hearing his trip took thirty-two years in a primitive ship, a ship that took seven months of constant acceleration to reach just ninety-six percent of light speed. All heard that, after that long trip, he spent the next fifty years alone, seeding the nearly barren planet with an amazing variety of vegetation. Having completed that chore, he set himself to the incubating, nurturing, and introducing thousands of animal species to what had become a beautiful, vibrant planet. This story was a wonderment to all who heard it.

The *Norman* was still parked close to the entrance of Sharkra's monument. Those who had previously had little interest in this small ship now wanted to know all about its construction, its propulsion system, the cryo beds that held those twenty human colonists, and the bridge from which Vance Youngblood captained the ship. Thousands of pictures and videos were taken of this now-famous ship. Long lines of those waiting for a tour of the *Norman* became a challenge that was shared by the Arkell. Redael assigned twenty young Arkell, both male and female, to be tour guides. Dale and Tomaco gave these twenty Arkell a detailed training tour of the Norman. Being Arkell, they forgot nothing and made wonderful tour guides.

It was decided by the Gabrielites to extend their stay another day to accommodate all those who wished to visit the *Norman*.

Vance, Alex, Dale, and Tomaco were constantly besieged with a great variety of beings wanting their pictures taken with these now-famous humans. Vance, to everyone's surprise, remained cordial and even friendly.

"I would have thought Vance would have made himself scarce," remarked Alex. "He's always avoided the limelight."

"He's surprising us all. My husband's become a diplomat," added Lara with a smile.

"Maybe the Arkell's personalities are rubbing off on him," said Teddy. "The man is smiling most of the time." Teddy's face expressed concern. "I kinda miss his scowl."

It was a big surprise to the humans with the amount of interest they garnered. They came to realize that during the time the Arkell ships were in contact with other species, they relayed stories of the humans of Gabriel. It was well known that the Arkell had, throughout Earth's history, taken a deep interest in humans. Over the millennia, Arkell historians and researchers had written hundreds of books on the development of humans, from the earliest humanoids to the modern human.

Even the diminutive and quiet Tomaco had become a celebrity of sorts for being credited with the notion that Sharkra wished to be recognized as a reality, rather than just a theory. Her husband, Dale Isley, was known as one of the galaxy's foremost inventors and scientists. The story of the *Marian*'s attack by the Malic and their subsequent defeat at the hands of Troy and Gary made them two heroes of some stature.

Now the brilliant Vel, born on Gabriel to parents who were a human/Arkell mix, was named the leader of the *Velgot*—a first in Arkell's long history.

By the end of the third day after the monument's miraculous display, all the starships had returned home. The trip for all, no matter where their home planets were in the galaxy, would take only seconds.

The contingency of Gabrielites from both the *Norman* and the *Marian* had just finished their last walk around the spectacular Sharkra monument. They were accompanied by Redael, Vel, Jupi, and Ooat and Ssamp of the *Geaalo*.

"This was an experience of a lifetime," said Lara as they exited the monument's grounds. "Not only were we privileged to witness Sharkra's power and compassion as never seen before, but we met the intelligent beings from around the galaxy."

"It took a while for me to keep the shocked look off my face when meeting some of the more, should we say, unusual species," added Colleen.

"Imagine my problem keeping a straight face," said Teddy. "Geez."

All within earshot laughed at that.

Vance smiled. "I believe it's time to return home."

"Agreed," said Alex. "I believe all is well in the galaxy."

It had been a month since the *Norman* and the *Marian* had returned to Gabriel, and Vance and Lara had settled comfortably back into their home on Vance's Island. At the moment, Vance was enjoying the view from his favorite location. He was seated on the swinging couch on their deck overlooking the beautifully landscaped grounds and the Lara River beyond. He was hoping to see the band of gorillas that had made this part of the island their new home. He'd seen the signs they were still in the area but, so far, no visual sightings.

Vance's communicator buzzed. He pulled it off his belt and saw the call was from Shem and smiled. "Hello, my friend."

Vance listened for a few seconds. "Oh my, that's . . . interesting."

"What's up?" asked Lara as she set a tray of rolls and coffee down on the end table.

Vance listened for a couple of minutes before saying, "I'll tell her. Give our best to Jarleth. We'll get together soon." Vance sat for a moment before turning to Lara. "That was Shem."

Lara smiled. "I gathered that when you told him to give our regards to Jarleth. What's new with them?"

"He just received a message from Vel. Said the message was sent three weeks ago."

Lara's brow wrinkled. "And he just received it?"

Vance nodded slowly. "It seems, once it was established that all species who attended the dedication of the Arkell's monument had arrived back at their respective planets, the light speed limit was altered by Sharkra to be just ten times the speed of light."

"Really?"

"That's what the man told me."

"Well that ought to get a bunch of attention for a while," said Lara.

Vance nodded in agreement. "There is no doubt, in my mind, that Sharkra has a reason for this action."

"I agree," said Lara. "But this will certainly be a topic of conversation and speculation throughout the galaxy for a while."

Vance smiled. "On the brighter side, Shem said the *Velgot* is heading this way and, other than the altered speed limit, all else was going quite well for Vel in his new position."

"Good to hear," said Lara. "Not that there would be any doubt that young man was fully capable and qualified for such a position."

"I can't think of another who could do as well," added Vance.

"So," said Lara, "if the only change we're aware of is the altered speed limit, it won't take much time to get used to that."

"That's true," said Vance. "Offhand, I can see, what was a ten-year trip prior to the light speed being removed will only take one year."

"However, it also means that we won't see Vel, or our friends on the *Velgot,* more than once a year, at best," added Lara.

Vance nodded. "I'll get ahold of Dale and ask him to inform the citizens of Gabriel right away. Any plans they may have to see other worlds have just been canceled."

Vance reached over and took a cup of coffee in one hand and a roll in the other. Lara followed suit before sitting down on the couch. "Haven't seen our gorillas yet?"

"Nope."

"Okay, my friend," said Dale, "I'll put out a message to the entire planet, and I'll send a note to our close friends and allies on Yassi, Vout, and Byuse to see if they've received the news."

"Good."

"It certainly isn't the worst news we ever had," said Dale, "but a lot of people on this planet and the hundred-plus other planets we're aware of will be disappointed." Dale paused for a moment. "I'm thankful that we were able to see other worlds, other civilizations, and an astounding number of truly different life forms before Sharkra slowed things down."

"We live in a very interesting galaxy," said Vance.

As predicted, the change in light speed was quickly absorbed by the intelligent life in the galaxy. It was now thought that Sharkra had made the change in speed to keep deep space travel to a minimum. The constant planet-hopping throughout the galaxy was creating new challenges and problems. Most planets were not equipped to host ever-growing visits from dozens of alien civilizations. Many aliens' requirements for food, shelter, and medical needs were unique, expensive, and difficult to provide.

A year after the speed change, the *Velgot* was scheduled to arrive at Gabriel. As was normal for decades, all who lived in or around Home Bay were out, lying on their blankets, waiting for the enormous ship's arrival.

Vance and Lara were lying beside Shem and Jarleth, who were a little more than anxious to see their son and daughter-in-law.

Vance was in a good mood as he looked around the park and recognized just about everybody. In his mind, they were all family.

Dale, as usual, was giving the countdown. "Five, four, three, two, one."

And in it came, the beautiful *Velgot*.

"Oh, damn," said Vance, "it didn't startle me this time."

"Sorry, sweetheart, I know how much you love the jolt."

Vance just nodded.

After a few minutes, an Arkell shuttle exited the *Velgot* and started its descent to Gabriel.

Two minutes later, the shuttle settled on the designated landing pad.

Shem and Jarleth, along with dozens of other friends and relatives, were already at the pad.

A few seconds later, the shuttle's ramp extended and the hatch opened. And there stood Vel and Jupi with big smiles on their faces.

They immediately started down the short ramp. As soon as their feet hit the grass, they were engulfed in the arms of Shem and Jarleth.

"It is so good to see you, my boy," said Jarleth as she released him to Shem while taking Jupi into her hug.

Once everyone had completed their warm and heartfelt greetings, Vel and Jupi took each other's hand and both smiled brightly.

"We have a wonderful surprise for you all," said Vel, "particularly for my wonderful parents."

That caused all close by to stop talking and turn their attention to the new front man of the *Velgot*.

"The old Earth expression," said Vel, "'A picture is worth a thousand words' will work well here."

With that, both Vel and Jupi turned and looked to the top of the ramp. There stood an Arkell woman. In her arms was a blue bundle.

Jarleth let out a scream of delight as the woman started down the ramp.

"Oh my god," said Shem. "We have a grandchild."

The woman smiled as she handed the small bundle to the open arms of Jarleth.

"Oh my, oh my," she said, with great emotion, as she lifted the soft blanket off the face of her new grandson. "He's beautiful."

Shem was clearly as delighted as his wife. But he let Jarleth hold the baby while he continued to look at his grandchild. "A very handsome boy." Shem smiled and turned toward Vel. "When was he born, and what is his name?"

"May I, Mother?" Vel said as he held his hands out.

"Okay, but I want him back shortly."

Vel carefully took his son from Jarleth, took the small blue blanket off, and with one hand on the baby's bottom and the other supporting his head, lifted his son over his head so all around could see him. "He was born six weeks ago, and his name is . . . Oruku."

CHAPTER 34

JASON GOULD

Dale was on the bridge of the *Norman*, copying tech files on a compact drive for a new-and-improved digital telescope he was in the middle of designing. After he completed the task and put the files in a carrying case, he began absently looking around the bridge to see what else might aid him in his endeavor. His eyes came to rest on the bulkhead behind the captain's chair. He smiled when a distant memory jumped into his mind. This unobtrusive wall contained a door that was not at all obvious. It looked to be just a section of the bulkhead. But in fact, it was the entrance to a small room that, for hundreds of years, contained Alex's inanimate SLF body. This room was unknown to all but three people, Dale being one of them. It was completely ignored and mostly forgotten for centuries. Dale walked over and, remembering how it was opened, gave a slight push on the right-hand side of the panel. The door opened enough for Dale to get ahold of the edge on the door and open it fully. A light came on, illuminating the small space.

"Wow," said Dale out loud. *I forgot how dusty this room was, and apparently everyone else has too. It's not been cleaned.* Dale made a mental note to have the room tidy up. After all, this room, at one time, contained a very important item: his friend Alex's SLF.

Dale stepped into the room and took a brief look around. It seemed to be just a dirty little room. He was about to step out when his eye caught a slight outline about two meters up the left wall. With the heavy accumulation of dust, it was nearly invisible.

Hmm, thought Dale. He reached up to brush off the dust and found he had to stand on his tiptoes to reach the spot. Having brushed away the dust, it now looked like a small drawer inset in the wall. Dale tried to find a place to get ahold of, but the clearances were too tight. Then he gave it a slight push, and a small door popped open. Dale, stretching as high as he could get, reached up and put his hand in. He felt something inside. With a considerable effort, he managed to get hold of it and pull it out. It was a metal box about thirty centimeters on a side and fifteen centimeters high. It had a lid similar to a safe deposit box in a bank on old Earth.

"What have we here?" he said aloud.

Dale turned and walked back into the bridge, carrying the metal box with both hands. He walked directly to a workstation and set the box down. He stared at the top of the box for nearly a minute before lifting the lid.

"Vance, Alex, do you have your ears on?"

A few seconds later, Alex responded. "What's up, my friend?"

Dale was about to respond when Vance answered the call. "I'm here."

"Good, do you two have the time to meet me in the *Norman*'s conference room?"

"Now?" asked Vance.

"If you can."

"I can be there in thirty minutes," said Vance, knowing Dale wouldn't ask for a meeting unless it was important.

"It will take me a little longer, but I'll be there ASAP," said Alex.

Twenty-seven minutes later, Vance walked into the conference room. His eyes went immediately to the box on the table.

"What's in the box?" he said as he walked over and gave Dale a hug.

"We need to wait until Alex gets here."

"Ah, a mystery. Okay, I'll wait."

Vance and Dale were talking about the planet in general when Alex walked into the room. They stood to greet him.

Alex walked straight over and hugged Dale and then Vance. "So what's up?"

"Sit and I'll show you," said Dale as he indicated a chair to his right.

Alex was about to sit when he spotted the box. "I'll bet that has something to do with this impromptu meeting. He finished sitting.

Vance sat to Dale's left and turned his attention back to the mysterious box.

Dale reached over and pulled the box toward him. "I found this box in the little room that held your SLF body for several centuries."

"Found it today?"

"Yes, sir," said Dale with a smile.

"Why wasn't it seen when we removed the SLF?" asked Vance.

"It was in a small cabinet with a door that blended with the wall. I'm assuming that in all the excitement in bringing out Alex's SLF, nobody spent any time looking around in that very dusty room."

Dale opened the lid. "There are only two things in here." He reached in a pulled out an unusual-looking small, black box.

"What the hell is that?" asked Vance.

"This, my friend, is an antique hard drive."

"It must be of some importance," said Alex.

"That's probably true," said Dale. "Here is the other item in the box." Dale retrieved an envelope and handed it to Alex.

Alex's expression was one of surprise. "This is Jason's handwriting," he said, not taking his eyes off the envelope.

"Agreed," said Dale.

Alex turned the face of the envelope toward Vance.

"No doubt about it," said Vance. "I'm having an ancient memory flash. I'd forgotten how much Jason meant to us."

Alex gently opened the envelope and retrieved the letter inside. After a brief moment, Alex's eyes glistened a little. "I'll read this to you."

August 5, 2030

My dear Alex,

> *I have placed this hard drive in your "crypt" in hopes that someday you will decide to use your SLF body and join the population of your new home.*

The hard drive contains ME. If sometime, in the distant future, you have the technology to build more SLFs, maybe you will build one for Dale and me.

I cannot imagine where you are in the galaxy but, being an optimist, I believe Vance managed to find a perfect planet to settle and continue the human race.

My hope is, someday I will be awakened as a SLF and rejoin my old friends in a new world.

Your loving friend,
Jason

The three sat in silence for a moment, all no doubt remembering their dear friend.

"The old expression 'a blast from the past' is certainly apt right now," said Vance, breaking the silence.

"That letter was written nearly a thousand years ago, Earth time," said Dale.

Alex nodded slowly. "I have to admit, I'm a little choked up here. Until this moment, I'd forgotten what a dear friend we had in this remarkable man."

"Same here," said Vance.

Dale smiled. "The really good news is, we can build him a SLF. We can have this dear man back in our midst."

"YES!" said Alex loudly as he slapped the tabletop.

"Perfect," added Vance with a big smile.

"As memory serves," said Dale, "the Arkell left us with several SLF skeletons and a great deal of Isleium. One skeleton, as I recall, is just under two meters."

Alex nodded. "I don't know how, but the Arkell's incredible intuition and foresight predicted this. I wouldn't be a bit surprised to find the tall skeleton is exactly the height of Jason."

It didn't take a keen observer to see that Dale was motivated. "I'll get things started for the building of Jason's SLF. First, I'll need to adapt this old hard drive into something our modern computers can read. Second, we'll need to pull up tapes, film, and still pictures of Jason. The people in the SLF lab won't have a live body to copy."

"How long will it take?" asked Alex.

"Based on the time it took to build me, I would say a month, maybe a little more," said Dale.

Six and a half weeks after the discovery of Jason's hard drive and letter, his SLF was completed. It was decided to build his SLF as a young man in his late twenties, when human men were at their physical best. Alex was sure this would please his old friend.

When Dale called Alex to tell him Jason's SLF was completed, Alex yelled, "YES . . . I'll be there in fifteen minutes."

Alex was practically running when he entered the SLF lab. Vance was already there, along with six SLF techs and Dale.

Alex didn't stop to greet anyone. He headed directly to the table where the inert SLF was lying.

"Oh my god." Tears of joy rimmed Alex's eyes. "He looks perfect, just the way I remember him." Alex turned toward the techs. "You are miracle workers. He looks perfect. Thank you, thank you."

"Time to bring him to life," said Dale with a big grin.

It was time to transfer Jason's essence, his everything, into the SLF. This process was always the most critical and nerve-racking.

The SLF lab in the *Marian* was abuzz with activity. The six techs were manning their stations while Dale, Alex, and Vance were sitting in chairs stationed in front of a prone SLF. The SLF, at the moment, was lying on a high-tech table, unclothed except for a pair of briefs covering his private parts. There was a high-tech helmet of sorts on his head, and dozens of sensors stuck to just about every part of his body.

"Starting now," said a tech.

A soft humming could be heard, and after a few seconds, twitches started in Jason's arms and legs. This process lasted for just over two minutes before the twitching stopped.

"Phase one complete," said the same tech.

"Starting the final transfer," said another.

"You," said Vance to Dale, "should be proud of what's happening here."

"Agreed," said Alex. "It occurs to me that you, in effect, built yourself."

"That has occurred to me," responded Dale, not taking his eyes off Jason.

"Actually, you built all of us," added Vance.

"Transfer complete," reported the tech.

Two techs walked over to the table and started removing the sensors from Jason's body. The helmet was the last thing to be removed. There was no movement from the new SLF.

"What's wrong?" asked an anxious Alex.

"Nothing," said Dale with a smile. "At this moment, Jason's brain in synchronizing with the rest of his body. It's connecting with his arms, legs, eyes, ears, etcetera. This will take a few minutes. We should see some twitching of his limbs."

As if on cue, Jason's legs began twitching, and a few seconds later, his arms, hands, fingers, toes, and eyelids.

"Holy shit," said Vance, "we're about to get our friend back."

Alex, Dale, and Vance stood up in anticipation of a full awakening of Jason.

Two techs, one on either side of the table, moved to help Jason sit up.

Just shy of a minute later, Jason's eyes opened. But he did not move. His eyes started darting from side to side before slowing and then fixed on the tech to his right.

"Are you ready to sit up?" asked the tech.

Jason's brow furrowed. "Who are you? What . . . where . . . ?" He was understandably confused. His voice was abnormally low-pitched, but that would be corrected or tuned, as Dale had said in the past.

Alex stepped to the other side of the table. "Jason, it's me," he said.

Jason's eyes shot over to see Alex. His expression became puzzled. "Who . . . is that you, Alex?"

"It's me, my old friend. It's me."

"Something isn't right." Jason was looking hard at Alex. "You look different."

"I am younger than the last time you saw me."

"Younger?"

"Would you like to sit up?" asked the tech.

Jason turned his head to see who asked the question. After a moment, he said, "Yes I would."

One tech took hold of Jason's legs right at the knees. The second tech moved to the other side of the table, reached across Jason's chest, and took his shoulders.

"One, two, three." In one smooth motion, they spun Jason and the tech lifted Jason's shoulders, placing him in a sitting position. Jason was swaying slightly, and the tech did not release him until he stabilized.

Jason sat, as if in a daze, for a minute. Then he started looking around the lab. His eyes settled on Alex. "I am very confused right now, Alex."

"I'm sure you are, but I can tell you from personal experience that confusion will pass."

Jason looked past Alex and spotted Dale and Vance. "Oh my god."

"Welcome to your new home," said Vance.

"Ditto," said Dale.

Jason's head cocked a little as if he was trying to remember something. All of a sudden, his eyes got wider as reality grabbed him.

"Am I a SLF?"

Alex smiled. "Indeed you are."

"Oh my god," Jason's expression was one of wonder. He said nothing for a full minute. Everyone assumed he was in the process of absorbing this extraordinary information.

"Am I on a new planet?"

"You are. You're on our new home, the planet Gabriel."

Jason smiled broadly. "Oh my god, you got my letter."

"About six weeks ago," said Dale.

"How long has it been?"

"Time is a little tricky here," said Dale. "Because of distance and speed, time gets warped. But to put it as simply as possible, based on time as counted on Earth, you wrote the letter just shy of a thousand years ago."

"What? How can that be?" Jason was clearly shocked.

"I wouldn't concern yourself with that at the moment," said Dale. "Believe me when I tell you, those past centuries soon will be meaningless to you. The years just won't matter. We need to get you fully functional and get you acquainted with your new environment. You have a lot to absorb."

"You, my dear friend," said Alex, "are going to love your new home. There is so much to see and learn. Dale and I had an advantage you won't. We were privy to all that has transpired over the past few centuries while we lived as holograms. You will spend months seeing, learning, and absorbing the history of Gabriel. We can't wait to show you around."

"I'm overwhelmed," said Jason. Just so much . . . so much."

"It will take some time, but you'll get used to being a SLF," said Vance. "You will be, unless I miss my guess, damn pleased about it."

"This is overwhelming." Jason looked again at Dale and Vance. "Two more of my dear friends." Jason looked from one to the other and then back at Alex. "You three look great."

"We're sure you will be pleased with your appearance also," said Dale.

"Where is a mirror?" Jason asked while unconsciously running his fingers through his hair.

"We'll get you a mirror in a little while. But we need to get you up walking, sitting, running, etcetera," said Dale. "Need to check your eyesight, hearing, and tune your voice."

Jason nodded. "My voice is different. I can hear it."

"We'll tune everything up."

Jason looked around. "Can I stand up?"

"Let's find out," said Dale as he signaled to the two techs to assist Jason off the table and onto his new legs.

The techs each took an arm just above Jason's elbow and slowly helped him slide off the table. His knees buckled, but he quickly straightened them. There he stood for a moment before attempting to take his first step.

"You gentlemen ready?" he asked the techs.

"Yes, sir," they both replied.

"Let's give it a go," said Jason. With that, he stepped forward with his right leg. The techs maintained a firm grip on his arms. Jason took a step with his left foot and then smiled. "I got this." He started walking slowly and a bit unsteadily, but with each step, it improved. A couple of minutes later, he was walking by himself. Jason said nothing for moment. "Let's get the show on the road."

"Okay," said Dale. "Let's start with just basics. Raise your arms, one at a time, and move your fingers."

Without another word, Jason raised his right hand to eye level, opened and closed his fist a few times, and moved his fingers one at a time. Then he duplicated the movement with the other arm and hand. "I'm a SLF," he said with a big smile.

"Well," said Vance, "you're going to do great. You're a quick study."

"We've made some solid improvements to the transfer process," said Jack, one of the SLF techs. "And we're damn pleased with the results." All the techs had big smiles on their faces.

"As well you should be," said Dale.

"Do I get to put clothes on?"

Alex smiled. "Right here." Alex opened a zipped clothes bag and retrieved a pair of slacks.

The techs steadied Jason as he clumsily lifted one foot and slipped it into the pant leg. Then, a little steadier, he put in the second and pulled the pants up by the waistband and over his butt.

"Hey, nothing to it." He buttoned the pants and pulled the zipper up.

"I've never seen anyone adapt quicker," said a mildly surprised Dale.

"Here is a shirt," said Alex.

"A pullover." Jason smiled. "My favorite style." He quickly put it on.

Jason continued improving his movements for hours. Now being a SLF, he did not tire, nor did he require sleep—nor did his long, longtime friends. The four of them were up all night, all of them talking, filling Jason in on the basic history of Gabriel. All the while, Jason continued to train his SLF in everything. He even got to reading and writing.

"My handwriting is slightly different," said Jason. "It's a little neater."

"Interesting," remarked Dale.

The three didn't tell Jason about aliens yet. That would come after he got settled into a new, and no doubt interesting, world.

They also didn't tell him that he was to see other old friends, Teddy, Colleen, Lara, and Aidan.

The following morning, the four men walked down the *Marian's* ramp and onto a recently completed concrete path that led, through the manicured lawn, to a fork. The right fork headed north to the *Norman's* cave and continued to the town, and the left fork took one west toward the beach and the Sharkra monument. Jason looked around with an expression of wonder on his face. He took a deep breath. He could smell the ocean mixed with fresh-cut grass and a hint of wood smoke.

"I don't know what I was expecting, but it wasn't this. This is wonderful."

Vance smiled. "Just wait till you see just how beautiful our planet is."

The view from this spot was somewhat limited, as they stood at the bottom on the ramp, and therefore under the center sphere of the *Marian* itself.

"Look at the size of this thing."

"This ship was built four hundred years after you passed away. It's just a little over five times the size of the *Norman*," said Dale.

"Five times, wow," said Jason. "I remember when the *Norman* was built. We thought it was huge." Jason turned to his right and spotted the town of Home Bay just three hundred meters north of where they stood. "Oh my god, that looks like a nice town."

"It's a great town," said Alex. "We'll be heading over there next."

"What's the population?"

"Home Bay, just about thirty thousand," answered Vance.

"The population is already thirty thousand? Incredible."

"If you think that's incredible, you'll be shocked to hear the population of Gabriel is over a million."

"Nooo," exclaimed Jason, stunned. "How is that possible?"

"It's been over three hundred years since we settled here," said Vance. "People propagate."

"Yes, they do." Alex smiled.

"And that's not counting the five hundred years Vance took to seed the entire planet's vegetation, incubate thousands of fish, fowl, and mammals, and place them in streams, rivers, lakes, and oceans and on land."

Jason was stunned. "How can that be? I don't understand."

"We'll get into the specifics later," said Dale. "As a matter of fact, there is an excellent documentary that describes the five hundred years after Vance's first landing on Gabriel, which, by the way, was over there about a hundred and fifty meters." Dale pointed northwest of where they stood. "You can watch that when you have time. But right now, we would like to take you around to get a feel for your new home."

"Let's walk to town and introduce you to some of your fellow citizens," suggested Alex.

"You will no doubt be surprised to find that the entire population of Gabriel knows who you are," said Vance.

"What?" Jason was again surprised. "Why and how would a million people know who I am?"

"We four, of the old WGC, are credited with saving Earth from destroying itself from within. You were very instrumental in that success. We could not have accomplished what we did without your genius in communication. Our personal histories are completely intertwined. Earth's history is taught at length in our schools. You will be the last of us to be introduced to the Gabrielites," said a smiling Alex. "I can't wait to see the facial expressions of our citizens when we introduce you."

Vance smiled. "That was sure the case when we introduced Alex and Dale to the Gabrielites. And you were more or less already part of the citizenry."

"When we get into town, you're going to draw a lot of attention," added Alex.

"That might be mentally exhausting for you," said Dale. "Maybe we should give you another day or two to get all your faculties brought up to speed."

"Oh no, I want to drink it all in as fast as possible. This is, by far, the most exciting thing to ever happen to me. I don't want to miss a minute of it. And I'm not at all tired."

Alex nodded in understanding. "Why don't we take a walk along the beach to Home Bay and point out some flora and fauna along the way?"

"Agreed," said Vance. "Then to town for a look around. Then we'll head to my place for lunch. There is someone there who is dying to see you."

"Someone?"

"It will be a pleasant surprise."

The walk to Home Bay was fun for all four of these SLFs. The sandy beach ran for ten kilometers, from the mouth of the Vance River, south to the farming community. Vance, Alex, and Dale ran a continuous dialogue, each pointing out different species of the plant and animal life on Gabriel.

"You spent five hundred years seeding the planet by yourself?" Jason asked Vance while his head was on a swivel, taking in everything around him.

"It wasn't as bad a time as you would think. The actual time I was awake and seeding the planet was about five years, following the process and timing written on Earth by some very gifted men and women. Once I seeded, planted, and incubated various animals, normally taking from four to six months, I would take the *Norman* for a ten-year flight at full speed. During these ten years, I would turn myself off. While the ten years passed on the *Norman*, a hundred years passed on the planet."

Jason said nothing for a few moments. "But to be alone during that time would be terrible."

"I was never alone. I had our two friends here. They were and are great company."

"Of course, their holograms would be nearly the same as being SLFs."

Vance nodded. "And I would point out that at the end of the ten-year trips, I got to see the fruits of my labor. I could see grasses', trees', and animals' growth that occurred over the century I was away. And I'll tell you, that was rewarding beyond description."

"You created a living planet."

"Just followed well-written instructions."

The four men walked onto Home Bay's Main Street from the west and immediately ran into four Gabrielites who were exiting a restaurant. At first, they didn't realize who the tall stranger with Vance, Alex, and Dale was. Most didn't spend much time looking at Jason. The three most famous on the planet drew their attention. Then one older woman's eyes got wide when she recognized Jason.

"Are you Jason Gould?"

"I am," he answered with a mild surprised look.

"Told you," Vance said quietly.

Instantly, the other three took a closer look.

"Oh my god," two said in unison while the fourth's jaw dropped.

Jason instantly became the center of attention. Within minutes, the four were surrounded by a dozen Gabrielites. All who had cameras began taking pictures and videos of the four, mainly of Jason. Jason graciously shook everybody's hand with a smile and a "Nice to meet you."

The word spread of Jason's appearance at the speed of light. It took over an hour and a half to walk the length of Main Street, a walk that would normally take fifteen minutes.

When they reached the bridge crossing the Vance River, they stopped. Vance held up a hand and addressed the half dozen that had been following them. "We know you have a lot of questions about how Jason suddenly appeared on our planet but, if you will, give us a little time. Within the next couple of days, be on your viewers and we will explain everything. In the meantime"—Vance smiled—"we are heading to my home for lunch."

The crowd understood and pleasantly said goodbye and dispersed.

The four men crossed the bridge and walked to their left, toward Vance's home. Jason's head remained on a swivel, all the while not missing a word spoken by his three best friends. "Look at these beautiful homes."

A minute later, Vance gestured to his left. "Here we are."

All followed Vance down a paved path to the front door.

As Vance opened the door, he said loudly, "Honey, we're home."

The four had just entered the spacious living room when Lara walked in from the kitchen.

At first glance, Jason's expression went from big surprise to a big smile. "Oh my," he said as he quickly walked over and took Lara in a big hug. "Oh my," he repeated.

Lara wrapped her arms around Jason's neck. "And how are you doing, Mr. Gould? It's been a while."

As the two separated, both had tears of joy rimming their eyes.

Jason continued holding Lara by the shoulders. "You look wonderful. As beautiful as you've ever been."

Lara smiled. "Thank you, my old friend. You're looking as handsome as you've ever been."

Jason's brow furrowed. "I haven't seen myself yet."

Lara looked over at Vance. He nodded once.

"Come with me, my friend," said Lara as she turned and headed for the master bedroom.

Jason followed Lara, and Vance, Dale, and Alex were close behind.

On the far side on the room, in the corner, was a large vanity mirror.

Lara stepped aside to let Jason get to the mirror. Jason quickly walked over and stood in front of the mirror. The four could see some of his reflection from where they stood. He looked shocked.

"This can't be," he said quietly. "This isn't me."

"It's you in your late twenties," said Dale.

"I . . ." Jason was speechless as he continued looking at his reflection. He turned to get a side view and then back. He reached up and ran his fingers through his hair and flexed his bicep before dropping it back down.

"I was old, overweight, gray, and losing my hair," he said while continuing to study his image.

"Not anymore," said Alex.

Jason remained silent for a minute before turning to face his friends. "Thank you. I think I like the new me." He turned and looked back at his image. His head started nodding. "I really like what you've done for me. Thank you so much."

"Hungry?" asked Lara.

She quickly got affirmatives from three.

"I can eat?"

You can, but as with everything, your taste buds may need some tuning," said Dale.

"Taste buds? As I recall, Vance's SLF didn't have taste buds. He didn't need to eat."

"Your old memory is working well," said Alex. When the *Marian* arrived here, they brought with them a great deal of advanced technology for SLFs."

"And," said Vance, "not only can we enjoy eating, but we can enjoy sex as well."

Jason displayed a big smile. "Just when I thought this day couldn't get any better . . . wow."

Lara smiled brightly while nodding her head. "It's true."

"Let's see how your taste buds are working," said Dale.

"We're having lunch on the deck, so I suggest we take advantage of this wonderful day and head out there."

After a very nice lunch, the five were sitting outside on the deck.

"What a terrific view you have here. My god, you can see everything. The beautiful river, the town and ocean. This is fabulous."

The five sat there for over an hour, answering Jason's questions. The answers to many questions created new questions, and so on.

A question came up concerning Earth. It was bound to come up. The first thing Jason wanted to know was if there was continuing contact with Earth.

The four exchanged glances.

"We need to tell you something, some tragic news," said Vance.

Jason's expression changed to one of concern. Vance wasn't given to exaggeration. It wasn't part of his personality.

"What?" he asked cautiously.

The *Marian* and two others like it were built over three hundred years ago to take a total of fifteen hundred humas off Earth." Vance paused for a second. "Before Earth was destroyed by a massive asteroid."

Jason rocked back in his chair. His expression was now one of shock and grief. He put his face in his hands and began slowly rocking back and forth.

His four friends remained silent. They waited until Jason was ready for more information. They waited quietly for a minute.

"Okay," said Jason as he took his hands from his face and leaned forward. "Give me the rest of it."

Vance nodded and continued. "The *Marian* came here to join us, knowing we had a stable planet and civilization. The other two ships settled on planets approximately ten light-years from here."

After another two hours of telling Jason all they knew about the tragic events, including the fact that both Venus and Mercury were also destroyed in what was assumed to be a gigantic chain reaction, they told him that the Earth's sun now had rings around it, made up of the debris from those three planets.

"Like Saturn's?"

"Not nearly as large but similar," said Dale. "Actually, the debris in that ring, I believe, in time, will form another planet, maybe more than one."

Jason nodded in understanding.

"The five hundred who were on the *Marian* are now ancestors to a large percentage of Gabrielites," said Alex. "You will find it interesting that those five hundred were all about the same size and color. The average height for men was close to what you are. The ladies are shorter but still taller than they were on Earth. The blending of races went on for hundreds of years."

Jason smiled. "Just about a thousand years ago, I thought that had to happen. It makes perfect sense."

"It might also interest you to know that the population of Earth at the time of its destruction was just about three billion."

Jason smiled again. "So our efforts to reduce the population worked."

"Thanks in large part to you," said Alex.

"Something else you need to know," said Alex.

"I'm not sure I want to receive any more information."

"This is interesting info," said Vance. "No problems."

Jason paused for a second. "Okay, hit me with it."

Alex had a big smile. "We are not alone."

Jason's brow furrowed. He said nothing for a few seconds. Then his eye's opened wide. "NO WAY!"

"Way," said Alex, maintaining his smile.

"Really?"

His four friends all nodded at once.

"Have you had contact with them?"

The four friends nodded again. All were smiling.

"Really?"

"We have become close friends with several alien races," said Dale.

Jason's smile grew even brighter. "I'm going to love my new life."

In the late afternoon, Jason and Alex bid their friends goodbye and walked to Alex's home located a kilometer up the river from town.

The two very old friends remained in constant conversation. Alex loved giving Jason information, and Jason wanted to know everything. His Isleium brain was a colossal sponge.

"There is so much remarkable history surrounding this planet that you'll be months gathering it all in."

Jason's smile rarely left his face. "This is the best day of my life."

"Here we are," said Alex as they reached his home.

The homes along the Vance River were located between the river and the road that led from Home Bay to the massive freshwater lake in the center of the continent.

Alex led Jason down a landscaped path to the front entrance of his home and then opened the front door and stepped aside while motioning Jason to enter.

"Wow! This is beautiful," he said while his head remained on a swivel. "You Earthlings don't build anything boring." Jason walked across the great room to its wall of windows. From there, he could see the deck that was about four meters wide and ran the length of the home. Off to the right of the deck was a stairway that led from the deck down the rather-steep bank to another deck right on the river. To his right, he could see steep white-water rapids that flattened out and calmed as they passed Alex's home.

"There's some great fishing from that deck," said Alex.

"That's great." Jason nodded in approval. "Are all the homes on this planet as nice as yours and Vance's?"

"Pretty much. The homes here are not large, but they are well designed. As you have seen, we use a lot of river rock and logs in construction."

"I have noticed. Beautiful look."

"There are nearly a hundred different house plans available to Gabrielites."

"Can everyone afford to build something like this?"

"Yes is the short answer. We have a unique monetary system that I'll explain some other time."

"Okay." Jason looked around. "Beautiful."

"I'm glad you like it because this will be your home until we build you your own in a place of your choosing."

Jason looked around. "If I stay in this fabulous home for long, you'll have to evict me to get me out."

"Hello, gentlemen," came a voice from behind them.

Jason turned around and again was floored to see who greeted them. There, walking toward them, was one of the most beautiful women in the universe.

"AIDAN?" Jason practically yelled in his excitement.

"It's me alright. You have a good memory, sir," she said with a big smile.

Jason didn't pause for a second. He stepped over and wrapped his long arms around this beautiful redhead. "Oh my god," he said in her ear.

"You're looking pretty good for an old man."

Jason held Aidan at arm's length. "You're a SLF too?"

"I am, and I'm damn pleased about it." She continued to smile. "Never get old, never get sick, never get hungry, never forget anything."

Jason released Aidan's shoulders and hugged her again.

There was a knock on the door.

"I'll get it," said Alex.

Jason's attention was now on Alex. He knew whoever was knocking was going to be of interest to him.

Alex opened the door, stepped aside, and let Teddy and Colleen walk into his home.

"Oh, Jesus." Jason was again stunned. He didn't move, but Teddy did. He quickly crossed the distance between the two.

"Hiya, Jason," Teddy said with his famous toothy smile before putting the much-taller Jason in a bear hug.

The following day, Alex, Jason, Dale, Vance, and Teddy and the four wives were all sitting at a large table on the patio at Carlon's Pub. When Tomaco was introduced to Jason, she seemed a little starstruck but quickly became a friend to this famous man. The mood of the nine couldn't have been more upbeat. They were having a great time. Jason was introduced to the now-famous Carlon hamburger.

"My taste buds are working great. This is one fine burger." Jason took a swig of his draft beer. "As fine a beer as I've ever had."

"We have a couple of very dear friends who will be joining us in a little while," said Vance.

"I'll bet I'm in for another surprise."

"Wouldn't bet against it," said Alex.

Jason nodded.

The cheerful banter between the nine was in full swing when Shem and Jarleth walked onto the patio. Jason's back was to them, and he didn't see them approach the group.

Vance and Alex stood as the two approached the table.

Jason turned in his chair in time to see these two unusual-looking people close the distance between them. His eyes gave notice of his surprise.

"Hello, all," said Shem.

Then the hugs started. When everyone except Jason had finished hugging, Alex introduced the two extraordinary people to Jason.

"Jason, please meet Shem and Jarleth, two very special people." Alex turned toward Shem and Jarleth. "It's my pleasure to introduce Jason Gould, our friend for nearly a thousand years."

"This is a great honor," said Jarleth.

"A great honor indeed," added Shem.

They all shook hands.

Jason smiled. "I'm assuming you are not from this planet."

"Actually, we are," said Shem. "We are about ninety-percent human and ten-percent Arkell."

"Arkell?"

"Jason has not been told about our alien friends," said Alex.

"So this is kind of a show-and-tell meeting," Shem said with a smile.

"I guess you could say that," said Vance.

For the next two hours, Jason was schooled on the Arkell and their importance, not only to the Gabrielites but to the entire galaxy.

"Without the Arkell, there would be no humans," said Dale.

"Ten thousand years ahead of us in technology—that's hard to get my new head around," Jason said.

"If you think that's remarkable, wait until you see their ship," said Teddy.

"Love to. Where is it?"

"At this moment, it's about three light-years away," said Shem.

Two days passed while Jason continued to be exposed to his new environment. It was like there was no end to new sights, sounds, and facts about the relatively short history of Gabriel.

At this time, Alex, Vance, Dale, and Jason were sitting alone midmorning at Carlon's Pub, enjoying a cup of coffee. These men had a great deal of history together, and they were fully enjoying reliving of some of their centuries-past exploits.

Alex smiled. "Have some friends joining us here shortly."

Jason nodded with a small smile. "I'm onto you now. I'm going to be surprised . . . again."

"More than likely."

Less than a minute later, a Yassi couple, Ergo and Pasre, walked onto the patio and, after a brief look around, spotted their four friends. Both were smiling as they headed across the patio.

This time, Jason was in a position to see these aliens enter the patio.

"Oh my . . . your friends are here."

Alex turned around, smiled, and stood to greet these Yassi. When two Yassi were within reach, Alex stepped over and gave Pasre a warm hug and then hugged Ergo.

Jason's expression was, once again, displaying some surprise, but he was obviously becoming accustomed to being shocked and surprised in this new and fascinating world. He smiled as he stood to meet these two new people. He was surprised at their size. They looked to be just about half his height.

"Jason, it's my pleasure to introduce you to Pasre and Ergo. They are Yassi, and they are very dear friends."

He extended his hand out and down to Pasre. She, with a big smile, took it and shook it vigorously. "Mr. Jason Gould, I presume."

"You presume correctly," said Jason. "I'm very pleased to meet you, Pasre." He released Pasre's hand and turned toward Ergo.

Ergo didn't wait for Jason to extend his hand. He stepped over and gave Jason a big hug before backing off a meter.

"We are so excited to meet you, after all these years of hearing of your history on old Earth," said Ergo. "You are highly respected throughout the galaxy. One of the four brilliant men from old Earth," said Ergo. "A great honor, sir."

Jason smiled broadly. "I have been told of the Yassi since I was 'reborn.' You are certainly a beloved people among the humans. They have great affection for the Yassi. And I can see why that is the case."

"Other than being a truly wonderful species, they are the most creative people in the galaxy," added Alex.

"I've seen one of your shuttles," said Jason. "I've never seen anything that could compare to it. Just beautiful."

"You are very kind, sir," said Pasre.

"Please call me Jason. I already consider you two my friends."

Dale held up his hand. Everyone looked in his direction. They could see he was getting a communication from his earpiece.

Dale smiled. "We just got word that the *Velgot* will be here in three days."

"Yes!" said Vance. "This is going to be fun."

Three days later, the park was packed with people waiting excitingly for the *Velgot* to make its customary dramatic entrance.

The day before, Jason was introduced to Troy, Clair, Gary, and Pat. Troy and Gary were born on Earth nearly four hundred years after Jason had passed away. To Troy and Gary, Jason was another historical figure. His name was always linked to Alex, Vance, and Dale. He was famous.

- - -

All SLFs were gathered together quite close to the landing pad that was always used for visiting alien shuttles.

At this point in time, most people were standing and talking to friends while waiting for the announcement as to when the *Velgot* would be arriving.

It didn't take long for Jason to realize there was something more afoot than just the anticipation of the *Velgot*'s arrival.

The voice over the PA system came on. "The *Velgot* is now visible at its station."

All eyes immediately looked straight up. Jason followed suit.

Within seconds, someone pointed and called out, "There it is!"

Jason spotted the *Velgot* way off in space. Just a speck but clearly a ship.

"Time to get comfortable," said Alex as he spread a large blanket on the grass, sat with Aidan, and gestured for Jason to join them.

Jason looked around and saw that everyone was now lying flat either on blankets or just on the grass. He joined Alex and Aidan.

"Keep your eye on that ship," said Vance.

"Ten seconds . . . five, four, three, two, one."

In came the *Velgot*.

"HOLY SHIT!" screamed Jason.

EPILOGUE

Over the past two centuries, Sharkra had guided the Arkell through the vast galaxy. Their chores were many and varied. The eighty-three Arkell ships had been sent to the far reaches of the galaxy and, on one occasion, to a different galaxy. It had become clear that Sharkra's intentions were benevolent and, quite simply, intended to help hundreds of planets bearing intelligent life through a myriad of problems. The problems and solutions varied tremendously. Sharkra simply sent the Arkell to a planet that required help and left it up to the Arkell as to how to treat the ill, impoverished, overpopulated, despotic governments and to stop conflicts both large and small.

Hostilities among the indigenous people living on a planet were, by far, the most numerous. Hostilities between planets were quite rare but were the most destructive. The multitude of rare and exotic diseases, never before encountered, had to be researched and cures developed and, once manufactured, administered to the population.

The Arkell ships, while solving thousands of problems large and small, had also spread the word of Sharkra to hundreds of civilizations. Their efforts were effective, as the vast majority of the galaxy's populations considered Sharkra a deity, while those who remained skeptical chose to simply obey the one rule they had been given.

The entire Milky Way galaxy, through the direction and guidance from Sharkra, and the Arkell's efforts, had become a united alliance.

After Sharkra's demonstration at the planet Arkell's presentation of their monument, there were few, if any, atheists left in the galaxy.

After the Arkell had completed the tasks given by Sharkra and all the intelligent life had returned to their respective planets, Sharkra installed a new speed limit. The new speed limit was ten times faster than the original but no longer instant.

The population of Gabriel continued to increase at a sound rate. Most towns' populations remained under twenty-five thousand. Jason, the last of the famous four humans, was now part of Gabriel's leadership. The administration of Gabriel was not complicated, nor time-consuming. Once a month, the four SLFs, which now included Jason, gathered at the new government building and discussed what Gabriel and its citizens needed.

Much to the Gabrielites' delight, they could monitor dozens of planets via the thousands of satellites the Arkell had placed in orbit around them.

Jason had his home built just half a kilometer east of Alex's and was enjoying the companionship of a very attractive young lady. Several times a week, the four old friends would meet at Carlon's Pub and enjoy lively banter and a great lunch.

Finished

Printed in the United States
by Baker & Taylor Publisher Services